THE SAFE LANDS

MT. CRESTED BUTTE

CRESTED BUTTE

CLEAN CREEK

Slate River

JACK'S PEAK

Abandoned Cabin

Levi & Jemma's Picnic Spot

GLENROCK

East River

THE TUBE

LOWLANDS

MIDLANDS

HIGHLANDS

Books by Jill Williamson

Replication

The Safe Lands series

Captives

Outcasts

The Blood of Kings series

By Darkness Hid

To Darkness Fled

From Darkness Won

The Mission League series

The New Recruit

Chokepoint

Project Gemini

Nonfiction

Go Teen Writers: How to Turn Your First Draft
into a Published Book

REBELS

BOOK THREE OF THE
SAFE LANDS SERIES

JILL WILLIAMSON

BLINK

BLINK

Rebels
Copyright © 2014 by Jill Williamson

This title is also available as a Blink ebook. Visit www.zondervan.com/ebooks.

Requests for information should be addressed to:

Blink, 3900 *Sparks Drive SE, Grand Rapids, Michigan 49546*

Library of Congress Cataloging-in-Publication Data

Williamson, Jill.
    Rebels / Jill Williamson.
       p. cm. — (Safe lands series ; book 3)
      Summary: "In the final novel in the Safe Lands series by Jill Williamson, Mason
and Omar find themselves trapped in Liberation, while Levi must find a way to lead
the rebellion on his own. At the same time, Jemma has become a pawn in the Safe
Lands' game"—Publisher's website.
      ISBN 978-0-310-73577-9 (softcover)—ISBN 978-0-310-73578-6 (epub)
    [1. Government, Resistance to—Fiction. 2. Science fiction.] I. Title.
PZ7.W67195Rd 2014
[Fic]—dc23   2014016812

The author is represented by MacGregor Literary, Inc. of Manzanita, OR.

Cover designer: Brand Navigation
Cover photo credits: iStockphoto/Shutterstock/Steve Gardner, PixelWorks Studios
Interior design: Ben Fetterley and Greg Johnson/Textbook Perfect

Printed in the United States of America

14 15 16 17 18 19 20 21 /DCI/ 20 19 18 17 16 15 14 13 12 11 10 9 8 7 6 5 4 3 2 1

"The purpose of life is not to be happy. It is to be useful, to be honorable, to be compassionate, to have it make some difference that you have lived and lived well."
— Ralph Waldo Emerson

To Larry Nielsen and Michael Vernor
for your brainstorming genius.

CHAPTER
1

Levi woke to the sounds of chaos. Footsteps thumping through the house. Giggling children. Screeching children. Women shushing.

Not that the children seemed to be listening. The noise came through the closed door of the bedroom Zane had given to him and Jemma for the night. He rolled over. No sign of his wife. She must be up already and keeping the children out of the room.

It all came back then: Mason and Omar had been captured. Mason had been shot in the leg. Omar had been beat up by General Otley.

At least Otley was dead now.

What would become of his brothers?

Outside the room, someone banged against his bedroom door, followed by a screeching giggle.

Levi wondered what time it was, but this room had no clock. This was no way to remain inconspicuous to neighbors. Not in a place where children live only at the boarding school.

When he'd finally laid down that morning — after having seen his brothers captured and after Nash had brought Shaylinn, the medic named Ciddah, and Kendall's baby boy to Zane's house — there had been over fifty bodies crammed into the small dwelling in the

Midlands. They'd covered the floor, sleeping side by side and head to toe.

Now all of them seemed to be wide awake and filled with energy.

Levi slid out of bed and opened the door. Three little girls ran past, nearly knocking him over, filled with the shrieking giggles of pure joy. They all met at the end of the hallway, colliding like cornered chicks.

Then, "Give it back!" one yelled. "I found it!"

They ran back toward him.

He reached out and caught the first. It was Eliza's Kaylee, pinching a rhinestone butterfly between her fingers. The other two stopped behind her, and she stretched out her arm to keep her treasure away from her pursuers. "No running in the house, Kaylee," Levi said. "And you must keep your voices down."

One of the other girls pushed up against Kaylee, snatched the butterfly, and ran off.

Kaylee's eyes flashed wide and she tried to pull away from Levi. "It's mine!" she yelled. "Give it back!"

"Shh!" Levi turned Kaylee to face him. "We have to be quiet. Do you want the enforcers to come here and take you away?"

"No!" Kaylee jerked away from Levi's grasp, and he barely kept hold of her. "Don't send me back there, Uncle Levi, please!" Her bottom lip trembled.

Maggots. He was no good with children. Where was Jemma? He scanned the house and caught sight of her brown hair in the kitchen. He looked back to the little girl. "No one will take you away, Kaylee, but you must try and be quiet. Quieter, at least." He released her, and she ran after the other two girls — silently, for now.

Levi closed the bedroom door and walked into the kitchen where Jemma and Shaylinn were putting together sandwiches. Peanut butter and jam, by the looks of things.

"Hi, Levi," Shaylinn said.

Jemma spun around, a smile on her face. "Levi! Sleep well, my love?" She set down a knife and embraced him.

He held her close, breathing her in, suddenly overwhelmed by the stress of their situation. He wished the first few months of their marriage had gone differently, that they might have lived in the cabin he'd built in Glenrock. "What time is it?"

"Five thirty."

"At night?"

"You slept all day." She kissed his cheek and pulled away from him.

He released her reluctantly. "You should have wakened me." He couldn't believe he'd lost an entire day. There was much to be done.

"It was a stressful night for all of us. You needed rest." She picked the knife up and kept cutting.

Other things came to his mind then. The move from the cabin. The birth of Jordan's son. "How is Naomi?"

"Doing fine. The baby too. 'Harvey,' Jordan called him this morning."

After Jordan's father. "Nice. Where is Ruston?" He scanned the house. "Where are the other ladies?"

"Ruston tried waiting for you, but there were just so many people in here that he had to start taking them below. The other women, plus Jordan and the Jack's Peak men, went down with him to see the new homes. He also took two of the little Safe Lands boys to his wife."

"How long have they been gone?"

"They left after lunch. Ruston said that when they got back, the adults would know the way to the new homes and could guide the rest of us. Said it was better than all of us going down at once and frightening the people who live there."

"The Kindred."

"I think it's romantic. Just hearing about it makes me think of the Amish."

"Who?"

"People of Old who chose to live apart from society and didn't use modern conveniences like electricity or motor vehicles."

"Why?"

"They felt it weakened the family structure and got between them and God. And they preferred to live lives of hard work the way people did for thousands of years before the Industrial Revolution. I heard Ruston explaining the Kindred to Eliza and, I don't know, I just thought of all my Amish books." She set down the knife and sighed. "I miss my books. I miss reading."

He rubbed her shoulders. He wanted to promise that they'd get out soon and that she could read all the books she wanted, but he was tired of showering his wife with empty promises. They were going into hiding. That almost seemed further away from freedom.

Another shriek turned his head to the living room. "These kids are being too loud."

"We've been doing the best we can. Lunch kept them quiet, so hopefully dinner will too." She handed Levi two plates, then took two herself.

Levi helped Jemma pass out plates with sandwiches. The kids sat cross-legged on the floor, which left room for Levi, Jemma, and Shaylinn to eat at the table.

"Did Zane go with Ruston?" Levi asked.

"I believe he's down in the nest, monitoring enforcer radios or something," Jemma said. "I'll have Shaylinn take him a plate when we're done."

"No need."

Levi turned in his chair at the sound of Zane's voice. His friend wasn't alone. Ruston, Nash, Jordan — everyone had returned.

"Is there enough for us too?" Jordan asked.

"Yes, of course," Jemma said. "You can help yourself in the kitchen or wait until I finish."

Jordan wandered into the kitchen. "Where is Naomi?"

"Lying down with the baby in the other bedroom," Jemma said. "Ciddah was in there with her for a while."

"Elyot and Kimi finally fell asleep," Jemma said. "So hopefully Naomi is sleeping too."

Jordan pulled out the chair on Levi's left and sat down. "Harvey didn't sleep very well."

"New babies rarely do," Aunt Chipeta said.

"Tell me about the new living arrangements," Levi asked, just as Jordan took a huge bite of sandwich.

Jordan chewed a few times, then spoke over a full mouth. "It's weird. A bunch of tunnels hook everything together. And there's a park with real grass."

A park? "How do you have grass underground?"

"We have special lights that enable plants to grow," Ruston said. "There are ten empty homes below. The list you and Beshup created only utilizes eight of them. Are you sure you don't want to spread the people out a little more? The houses are quite small."

"There aren't enough adults," Levi said. "As it is we had to divide up three families of Jack's Peak's children."

"We will try it this way," Beshup said. "Once we are down there for a few days, we will discover what works and what does not."

Levi didn't like how vulnerable he felt with everyone inside this little house. Once the women and children were settled in the basements, he could focus on other things, like finding Mason and Omar and helping Beshup free the Jack's Peak women from the harem, the Safe Lands' compulsory in vitro program.

"When can we go?" he asked.

"Right away," Ruston said.

"Once everyone has eaten," Jemma added.

And so Levi ate, finishing long before most of the children, who were too busy giggling to finish in a timely manner. Finally they divided into groups and, one group at a time, descended into the basement. Levi's group waited until last so that Ruston could take his time showing Levi the way.

Levi's new household consisted of Jemma and Shaylinn, plus Nell, Trevon, Jake, Joey, and Carrie, who were Levi's nieces and nephews, and Grayn and Weiss, two Safe Lands refugees who were friends with Trevon and Joey. When they finally went down the stairs and into the basement, Zane was waiting.

"I'm going to come too," Zane told his father. "I'd like to see Tym and the girls."

"Are you sure?" Ruston asked.

"I'll be fine. You worry too much."

Ruston gave his son a silent nod.

The basement was a small, cement room with a ratty old couch, a combination washer/dryer, and a long bookshelf that hid the entrance tunnel to the nest, where Zane worked.

But rather than moving the shelves that led to the nest, Ruston rolled the washer/dryer combo out from the wall, which revealed an airlock door similar to the one that led to the bunker. He opened it, revealing a different passage. It appeared to be a storm drain at first, but it wasn't round and the floor wasn't wet. Ruston led the way with a flashlight. Shaylinn went next with Joey and Weiss, holding a boy's hand in each of hers. Then Nell and Jake, followed by Trevon and Grayn. Then Jemma, holding little Carrie. Levi followed his wife, and at the end of the line, Zane pulled the washer/dryer back into place, then closed the gateway door behind them.

"Where light go?" Carrie said.

"Ruston has the light," Jemma said.

"It won't be dark for long," Ruston called back. "Maybe twenty yards."

"What is this place?" Levi asked, inching along at the back of the line.

"One of seven gateway tunnels the Kindred built over the years," Zane said from behind him. "Entrances to tunnels that weave above the storm drains and remain separate from them, which keeps our homes safe from curious enforcers and from flooding."

"The door to the bunker?" Levi asked. "Is that a gateway?"

"Used to be," Zane said. "It's been closed off from the basements for years. There used to be ten gateways, but we no longer use the three under the downtown Midlands area."

"So I'll come back out through this door when I need to go above?" Levi asked.

At the front of the line, Ruston stopped and shined the light back to Levi. "No one leaves without my permission. Even you."

That stopped Levi in this tracks. "You can't be serious."

"This isn't like the bunker," Ruston said. "The basements are my people's home. They allow us to live a somewhat normal life. You should know that there are some Kindred who don't want you to live with us. They fear I'm bringing corruption to our doorsteps. I explained that you are not Safe Landers but Outsiders. And, like us, you are descendants of Seth McShane."

"But we're trying to get out of here," Levi said. "We've been prisoners above. Now we're going to be prisoners below? That seems worse."

"You're not prisoners," Ruston said. "You simply cannot go to and from the basements into the Safe Lands whenever you choose. You must take care and let me know when you want to use the gateway. This is for all of our safety. Plus, this particular gateway empties into my house, and my wife wouldn't like people passing through our home at all hours of the day or night."

Ruston turned back toward the path and the line began to move again.

"She doesn't like much," Zane said. "My mother."

Wonderful. Levi didn't like it but had no right to argue. He was tired of being totally dependent on others, though, and he wanted more than anything to get out of this place and back to Glenrock.

They reached the end of the tunnel at what looked like a regular wooden door. Up ahead, Ruston opened it, and dim light seeped into the corridor. The line started to move again as they passed through the door.

"You have electricity?" Levi asked Zane. "How?"

"We have our own powerhouse," Zane said. "It's underground, built right underneath the Highland-Midland wall on the wall side of Lake Joie. It is actually connected to the biofiltration system for Lake Joie, though the Safe Lands Guild doesn't know it."

"So, it's a dam?"

"A little simpler than that, actually. It's a series of waterwheels. Some are connected to the fountains and waterfalls in Lake Joie Park, some are hidden throughout the storm drains, and we've engineered the drains to send the water through them. It works quite well."

Levi followed Jemma through the door and into a living room with carpet and furniture. No windows. Zane followed and closed the door.

"But what about in the winter?" Levi asked. "When the water freezes?"

"LPG-powered generators," Zane said. "Dayle gets us most of the gas through the Highland DPT office, or I work out the credits for emergency purchases. But we try to keep power use to a minimum." Zane slipped past him then and approached a boy who looked to be in his early teens. "Hay-o, Tym."

"Hay-o." The boy embraced Zane.

"As I told the others," Ruston said, "enjoy your new homes, but take short showers or they'll get cold fast. All our light bulbs are compact fluorescents. Turn off lights you aren't using. The houses don't have central heat. There are space heaters for when it gets cold and lots of blankets. And we use ceiling fans or portable fans for when it's hot. We wash laundry in cold water and don't use dryers. Hang out clothing to dry it and —"

"To your room, Tym. Now!" a woman yelled.

The volume of her voice put a hush over the crowd of people. Levi looked over the heads of the others. A woman stood in the doorway that led out of the room, clutching two girls, one to each leg. The girls looked to be five and ten. The woman was glaring at Zane and the young teen.

"Obey your mother, Tym," Ruston said.

"Yes, sir." And the young boy smiled at Zane then passed through an open door on the left wall, closing it softly behind him.

"You must be Ruston's wife," Jemma said, hefting Carrie up her hip.

Ruston squeezed through the crowd until he stood beside the woman and girls. "Yes, this is my wife, Tova, and my daughters, Resi and Luz. That was my son, Tym, who's now in his room. And the new boys from the boarding school should be around here somewhere."

"They went to the park with Nash," Tova said. But that's all she said. No polite greeting or kind words. She simply stared at all of them like she wanted them to leave her house as soon as possible. She did eye baby Carrie though.

Her youngest girl reached out and took hold of Carrie's chubby fingers. "Hi, baby."

"Kids," Carrie said, waving her other hand. "Hi, kids."

"This is Carrie," Jemma said. "Her mommy is away right now, so I'm taking care of her. These are some of her brothers and sisters and their friends."

"None of them are yours?" Tova asked, frowning.

"No, Levi and I have only been married a few months. No kids yet." Jemma blushed, and Levi thought she was the most beautiful creature in the world.

"Let's get you to your new home, then," Ruston said. "Dathan? Are you coming?"

Dathan — Zane's given name. Those who went into the Safe Lands all had aliases to protect themselves.

Zane was still standing beside his mother, who was glaring at him as if she had just discovered that he had betrayed his people in the same way Omar had betrayed theirs. "Yep, I'm coming. Bye, Mom. Bye, Resi. Bye, Luz." And he walked past them to where his father stood by another door.

"Bye, Dathan," the younger girl said.

Tova took the girls by the arms and led them into the kitchen without a word to Zane.

Odd.

Ruston led Levi and his household out the door and into a narrow corridor that was similar to the one that led from the basement of Zane's Safe Lands house to Ruston's underground home, though this one had light bulbs hanging from the ceiling every five yards.

They walked to the end of the corridor where it met a crossroads. Straight ahead was a little alcove and another door, but to the left and right, the corridor stretched out until it curved out of sight.

They followed the left corridor for maybe two hundred yards, passing by two alcoves with doors before Ruston stopped and turned into another alcove. There was a number on the door: 16 – 1.

"That one on the right we just passed leads to the library," Ruston said.

"Can we use the library?" Jemma asked, her voice so hopeful that Levi chuckled.

"It's always open, so feel free to go in and read books. If you take them to your home, try not to keep them too long. Straight through the library is the school. If you decide to send the kids, that's the path they'd take. We have good teachers — all volunteers, of course. We all do our part down here. If any of you ladies see a place where you'd like to serve, speak up. I'm sure we'd all appreciate your help."

Levi wasn't convinced. If the way Ruston's wife had acted was any indication of how other Kindred might respond, Levi doubted anyone here would appreciate their help.

Ruston opened the door and walked inside. It was a house similar to Ruston's. It opened into a living room that was furnished with two cream-and-blue-plaid couches. The floor was worn brown carpet. Around a short wall, Levi found a tiny kitchen. There were four other rooms. Two doors behind the couches each led to a bedroom. And the two doors off the back of the kitchen led to another bedroom and a bathroom.

"The front doors only lock from the inside," Ruston said. "As you can tell, this place will be a tight squeeze."

"It's wonderful," Jemma said, setting Carrie on her feet. "Thank you."

Carrie toddled to the sofa at a near run and threw her face into the cushions, then looked up, smiling, and did it again.

"It might be best if you ladies get everyone settled and I walk Levi around. He can take you all out later."

"That sounds great," Jemma said.

"I'll be back later." Levi kissed Jemma good-bye and left with Ruston and Zane, back out into the corridor. "I don't understand these tunnels. They're higher than the storm drains?"

"Yes," Ruston said.

"So, these houses are actual basements of houses in the Safe Lands?"

"That's right. But we've closed them off. Not us, really, but our ancestors. My grandfather. Back then, things weren't what they are now. They lived in the houses above ground. But when the government threatened to take their children away, this was how my grandfather and his friends fought back. It took time, granted, to build all this …"

"But once the houses above were abandoned, no one found the secret doors to the basements?" Levi asked.

"There are no secret doors, not in most houses. They built walls, closed off the basements entirely. The seven gateways are all in safe aboveground locations."

"Some got caught, though," Zane said. "There was one story of a basement home that was found when the property was demolished to build an apartment building. Thankfully, the Kindred who lived there at the time were able to destroy the tunnel leading off from the basement house."

"And that's another reason we've expanded under the warehouse district, away from downtown where they're always digging deep and building more apartment buildings," Ruston said. "Someday they'll likely stumble upon one of our houses again, but it's my hope we won't be here then."

"You want to leave too?" Levi asked.

"Of course. Most of us — the women, especially — have gotten used to life as is. But your being here is forcing everyone to remember our long-term goal of getting out. It's a good thing, even if everyone doesn't understand that yet."

The corridors were mostly in a grid that followed the city streets above — there were even graffitied street names on the wall, marking the routes overhead. Occasionally a corridor took a sharp curve, cutting across the middles of city blocks above. Every few yards, alcoves jutted off to one side or the other, leading to doors of houses or other locations.

"There are sixty-three basement houses down here that are habitable," Ruston said. "The basements exist under seventeen square city blocks. Besides the houses, library, and school, we also have a park, a gymnasium, a public square, a meeting hall, greenhouses, the power-house, and the trash dumpster area."

"What do you do with the trash?" Levi asked.

"Ever been to Bender's old warehouse on Fifth and Sopris? We have a freight elevator that goes up into there. We raise dumpsters to the surface, inside the warehouse, of course, and trade them with empty dumpsters."

Levi saw no other person until they reached what he was told was Kindred Park. It was as if someone had built a park in a cave. The way the lampposts lit the area with bright white light reminded Levi of the Safe Lands' Champion Park at night. The grass was green and bright, and it filled the space of a whole city block. Dirt paths weaved around the park, connecting to corridors on all four walls. There were bushes and flowers around the perimeter and a playground with two slides, a swing set, and various bars and steps for children to climb.

Some children were climbing them now. A man and woman stood watching them, but their heads turned when Ruston, Levi, and Zane entered.

The woman walked forward and to the side until she stood between her children and Levi's view. She crossed her arms, eyes wary and sharp.

"Hello, Ruston," the man said, lifting a hand in a wave.

"Kirkland, Olivia," Ruston said.

"Dathan." The man nodded at Zane. "How are you?"

"Still alive, much to my mother's dismay," Zane said.

The woman rolled her eyes and turned her back to them. The man chuckled nervously, as if he wasn't sure if he should laugh at the joke.

"This is Levi of the tribe Elias," Ruston said. "He's Elias McShane's great-grandson."

"That so?" Kirkland said, casting his gaze on Levi. "Pleased to know you."

Levi nodded at the man. "You've got quite a place down here."

"Yes, it suits our needs," Kirkland said.

"Kirkland." The woman had gathered her children and held them by the hand, a boy and a girl. "We should go."

"When I'm finished," Kirkland said, as if trying to prove who was boss. Yet he said to Ruston, "I should go. I'm sorry the women are, well ..." He gestured to Zane. "I'm sorry."

"Keep working on them," Ruston said.

And the man left, walking away with his children and his wife, who glared over her shoulder twice before they vanished into a corridor.

"You have some enemies down here or what?" Levi said to Zane.

"I've been exiled. That's what the women's council does to flakers like me."

"Your own mother?" Levi asked.

"When I turned sixteen, I left the Kindred against the will of my parents and the councils. When that happened, the councils declared me a deserter and I was exiled."

"But you can still come down here?"

"I can now. The men's council voted to end my exile when I made peace with my father."

"The men's council is more lenient," Ruston said. "I vouched for his change of heart, and the men accepted that. But his mother still refuses him, and because of that, he has no one to appeal to the women's council on his behalf. So he's still officially exiled, though I can grant him asylum as long as he is in my presence."

Levi had taken Omar back despite his many transgressions. "Will she ever relent?"

"I doubt it," Zane said. "Even if she wanted to, doing so would make her look weak to the other women. So she'll continue to deny me to please them."

"Why do they insist on denying you at all?"

"Fear. You saw my mother yell at my brother for speaking to me. She's afraid I'll corrupt him. That when he turns sixteen he'll leave the Kindred too and fall into sin like I did. You saw that woman glare at me just now. I'm a bad influence to the people here."

"Then why do you come back?" Levi asked.

"Because this is home. My family is here. And I love my mother even though she will not admit that she loves me too."

When Levi returned to his home at number 16 – 1, Jordan was waiting inside. And from the scowl on his friend's face, Levi knew something had happened.

"What's wrong?"

"I told the medic and her parents that they weren't allowed to leave, and the parents freaked out. Yelled so loud they woke Harvey and the other baby. Then the medic said she wanted to speak to the man in charge, as if I were nothing more than a maggot that she could step on."

"Where are they now?" Levi asked.

"At my place, probably driving Naomi nuts."

"Lead the way."

Jordan's house was in the next block, around a big corner and right before one of the entrances to Kindred Park. 15 – 2. Levi found Ciddah and her parents inside, all sitting on the couch. Ciddah was holding baby Elyot with his head above her shoulder, bouncing him and patting his back. Her mother, Losira, sat beside her, arms crossed. Her posture and the glare on her face reminded Levi of the wary Kindred mother he'd seen in the park. Droe, the father, was asleep in an armchair.

"What seems to be the problem?" Levi asked Ciddah.

"He said we can't leave this house!" Losira said. "Ever."

"No, I said until you hear differently," Jordan said. "That's doesn't mean forever."

"The Kindred don't allow just anyone to live down here," Levi said. "My people were approved by both councils, but you three … Ruston had to fight to get you down here at all."

"What have we done to deserve this?" Losira asked.

"It's not what you've done or not done," Levi said. "It's just —"

"It's me," Ciddah said. "They don't trust me. And that's fair."

"Oh, it most certainly is *not* fair," Losira said.

"I've done some things I'm not proud of," Ciddah said. "I'll explain later."

"That's my concern, I have to admit," Levi said. "That you're still working for Renzor and that you're only here to be his spy."

"I'm not. I swear it on Elyot's life. On Mason's life."

The desperation in her tone gave Levi pause. He stared into those cold, blue eyes. His brother claimed to love this woman, had even mentioned marrying her. Levi didn't get it. Not only was she a flaker, she was a flaker who'd been in a relationship with Lawten Renzor, a man who had approved the destruction of Glenrock. Why did Mason trust her?

"It's not only that, though," Levi said. "It's also you two." He nodded to Losira and Droe. "Non-Kindred are rarely given access to the basements. Only when the rebels see someone's loyalty and it's necessary to hide them, then the Kindred vote to extend asylum. And sometimes that vote is a no."

"But they said yes?" Ciddah asked.

"On the condition that you stay in this house. Unless accompanied by someone. One of us, one of them. And that has to be approved by me or Ruston."

"I understand," Ciddah said. "What are you doing to find Mason?"

"I haven't had time to think about Mason," Levi said, "but there's nothing I can do. Zane can still see through their contact lenses, however. They're in the Rehabilitation Center. But we don't have the connections Omar had when he got Jemma and me out of there. His old enforcer friends have been assigned new tasks in the Midlands. And Zane doesn't know anyone who works in Surveillance."

"You can't just let him be liberated," Ciddah said. "He did everything you asked him to."

"Except rescue you. I asked him *not* to do that. And had he listened, he'd be here right now."

"Levi, that's not fair," Naomi said, walking out of a door in the back of the house. "Shaylinn wouldn't be free either if it wasn't for Mason and Omar."

He had no response to that. "I'm sorry that you're stuck here. We all are. And you can take my word that I'm doing everything I can to get us out of here soon." And he turned to leave.

Jordan followed him into the corridor. "I don't like those maggots in my house, Levi."

"It was the only way. And she is a medic. If anything goes wrong with Naomi or the baby ..."

"Well, you don't have to live with her. Or her weird parents. I swear, if that woman doesn't stop oohing and ahhing over everything ... And Droe. All he talks about is teeth. It's mad weird."

Levi slapped Jordan on the shoulder. "Do what you can to survive, brother. Rest tonight. Tomorrow we'll meet with Ruston to talk about what to do next."

"We need to get out of here. What else is there to talk about?"

"The Jack's Peak women are still in the harem. Mason and Omar are in the RC. And we need to decide if we're going to help Ruston and Zane with their rebel plot."

"I thought that was Bender's deal."

"Not Operation Lynchpin."

"*Omar's* idea? We're actually going to take something he said seriously? His idea of fighting back was to wear an owl costume and spray paint threats on buildings."

"That's not all he did, and you know it. Plus Ruston likes the idea. And Zane was on board from the start. Actually, we're going to need us a new Owl."

"Well, count me out. I ain't wearing that stretchy suit."

"I didn't expect you would. But someone will have to."

The question was, *Hoo?*

CHAPTER
2

"Liberated without delay?" Mason glanced at his little brother, who was secured to the seat across from him in the back of the prisoner transport van. Both had their hands and ankles cuffed, and the ankle restraints had been clipped to a bolt on the floor. Their trial had just ended. They'd been sentenced to premature liberation by the Safe Lands Guild. Maybe that was where they were headed now. "So, *without delay* as opposed to being liberated *with* delay?"

"It's perfect." A wide grin spread over Omar's face, which was sweaty and pale. Strange to see him smiling, since he'd just received the worst sentencing the Safe Lands had to offer. "Lhogan and Zane will see everything. And Zane can broadcast it as the Owl."

The contacts. Mason had forgotten he was wearing them. A little thrill shot through him at what this might mean. The greatest mystery in the Safe Lands, foiled by two rebel outsiders and some incredible technology. He couldn't help but return Omar's smile. Things might be looking up after all.

Omar waved at him. "Hello, Levi. Hello, Zane."

"They can't hear you," Mason said. "The contacts are visual only. No sound can be transferred."

"I know." Omar groaned and clutched his stomach. "It hurts, Mase."

"I'm sorry." It was all Mason could say, and he'd been repeating it for the last two days. Omar was suffering withdrawal from his chemical dependency to who knew what types of substances. Omar probably didn't even know.

To make matters worse, whenever Omar had screamed loud enough in the RC, the enforcers had come and administered what they called a "mercy vape." No more than one mercy vape per prisoner per day, but such *mercy* was counterproductive to Omar's recovery.

Since they'd gone to trial early this morning, Omar had not yet been given a mercy vape, and he looked it. Plus, daily meds were administered during dinner, so Omar was also currently without whatever mystery stimulant might be included in his meds.

Another groan from Omar, this one even more pathetic. Less than twenty-four hours without some sort of stimulant and his brother was falling apart. Mason prayed the deprivation wouldn't kill him.

"Where do you think they're taking us?" Omar managed to pant out. "We should have been back by now."

The ride *was* taking more time than it should. It had been a five-minute ride from the Rehabilitation Center to Champion Auditorium that morning. They'd been in the van twice that long already.

"It's been too long, hasn't it, Mase?" Omar asked. "If they're just going to kill us, the fact that Levi and Zane can see isn't going to be much help. And it's not like they can see where the truck is taking us right now."

"I don't think liberation is death," Mason said, though he had no evidence to support that theory. Liberation was a mystery in the Safe Lands. It happened to everyone at age forty, though some were prematurely liberated when they died, reached three strikes on their record, or if the Safe Lands Guild decreed it must be so. Omar had three Xs, or strikes, after this last infringement. Mason now had one. But the Guild had voted in favor of liberating Mason too. Lawten's idea.

"But what else can" — Omar sniffled and panted, having difficulty breathing again — "liberation be, though?" Another pant. "Seriously."

Mason didn't know, but he thought back to something he'd over-heard. "When we were at Champion House, Lawten told Otley that if Otley killed him, Otley would be liberated. Otley said he'd never be liberated. Then Lawten said, 'It's that or the Ancients.' As if Otley had a choice between those two things."

"Ancients?" Omar squinted at Mason. Could withdrawal affect eyesight? Perhaps it was a migraine. "Those guys in the hoods?"

Mason nodded. During their trial — or lack thereof — in the Champion Auditorium, there had been sixteen people sitting up on the platform wearing black hoods. Lawten had addressed them as the Ancients of the Safe Lands. "What if that's the ultimate promotion? Perhaps becoming a hooded Ancient is the only way to avoid being liberated at forty."

"Why would anyone want to wear a hood for the rest of their lives?"

"If liberation is death ..."

Omar rubbed his temples. "You're saying that a select few who know liberation is death have a way out by becoming an Ancient? Wouldn't everyone sign up?"

"I don't think they can. Lawten said that he doubted the Ancients would accept Otley, knowing how treasonous he was — as if he needed to apply. And such knowledge is likely only open to the top govern-ment officials of the Safe Lands."

"That's good stuff, Mase." Omar panted and sniffled. "The Owl should look into that." He looked directly into Mason's eyes. "Look into those hooded Ancients." He pretended to pull a hood over his head, but it just looked like he was scratching his head. Then he slouched back against the wall. "Still, where would they live? I've never seen any old people walking around the city."

"Maybe they're forced to live apart from everyone else?" Mason suggested.

"Maybe they're not old, Mase. Maybe they're young. Maybe Luella Flynn was under one of those hoods."

"Their voices sounded old." Though Mason had only heard a couple of them speak.

"I don't know, brother. I still think liberation is a firing squad."

"That would be too messy for the Safe Lands. Death by lethal vaporizer is more their style of execution."

"If they'd let me OD on brown sugar, it wouldn't be a bad way to go at all. It's almost like flying."

The comment pricked Mason's nerves. "Don't say that stuff, Omar. That's stupid."

"It just itches so bad. What if they don't give me anymore? What if—" Omar straightened. "We're stopping."

Indeed, the van had slowed down, and now it stopped suddenly. Mason strained to listen but could hear no voices. He did hear a garage door, though he couldn't guess whether it was opening or closing.

The back door of the van opened. It was darker outside the vehicle than inside. A single enforcer stood on the ground at the back of the van, visible from only the waist up.

"Welcome to lib prep." And he raised a SimScanner at Omar and fired.

Before Mason could think about offering sympathy to his brother, the enforcer shot him with the SimScanner as well. A pulse of electricity blossomed from the SimTag in his right hand and instantly spread through his body.

His muscles cramped at the electrical disruption of his nervous system. It hurt. Adrenaline rushed over his body like a flash of heat. He lost all motor control but could still see and hear. Being shot with the SimScanner didn't feel much different than when he'd been shot with a stunner. The only difference was the steady sting at the location of his SimTag.

The enforcer climbed into the back of the van. "Bring the stretchers." He unhooked Omar's ankle cuffs.

A second enforcer hopped up into the van, then turned and crouched to help a third enforcer with a stretcher. The front legs of the stretcher collapsed against the back of the van as the enforcers rolled it inside, inches above the floor and from Mason's toes. The two enforcers who were inside the van moved Omar onto it, strapped him down, then pushed it back out to the enforcer still on the ground.

They repeated the process for Mason, and soon he was being wheeled under a high concrete ceiling with round bay lights shining down on him. The current that had been pulsing out from his hand stopped sending its charge, and Mason's body relaxed. He still couldn't move, though, and his nerves seemed to throb along with the buzz of the overhead lights.

They wheeled him into some sort of laboratory, where two medics stripped off all his clothing and placed him on a paper-covered exam table. The table had no legs but stretched across the end of the room, attached to the walls at the head and foot. A circular indentation had been cut into the wall at Mason's feet. The circle was about a yard in diameter, and the end of his bed hit the wall in the circle's center. Tiny lights ran along the top quarter of the circle.

The medics strapped Mason to the table and left the room, closing the door behind them. Heat burned in Mason's chest and cheeks. He was mortified to be lying there naked. Movement had returned to his fingers and toes, and he wiggled them, hoping it might speed the recovery of movement to his limbs.

A mechanical hum throbbed from his feet, as if someone had turned something on. The tiny lights on the circle lit up. Something beeped. The circle emerged from the wall with a whoosh and stopped a few inches out, vibrating in the air. Narrow glass piping along the inner ring lit up bright blue. The circle moved out again, this time very slow and constant, sliding its way up and around Mason's body. It must have been scanning for something, though Mason couldn't imagine what.

When the circle passed over his head, it hissed, the lights went off, and it sailed back to the wall by his feet. The door opened and the medics returned.

"He has them too," one of them said. A male. Mid-thirties, perhaps? He stopped at Mason's side and looked down. "Nothing goes with you into Bliss. No need for SimSight there."

SimSight? The contact lenses. The circle must have scanned Mason's body for foreign materials and found the lenses.

The second medic — also a male, though slightly younger — stepped up beside the first and handed him a squeeze bottle. The first medic pulled on blue latex gloves while reaching for Mason's eye, soon holding the lid open and squeezing liquid onto the pupil.

Mason flinched at the coldness. The medic's finger easily swiped the lens to the side of Mason's eye and pinched it out. He repeated the procedure with the other eye, then handed the bottle and the lenses to the second medic.

So much for his friends being able to see what was going to happen to them.

"I'm going to unhook you now," the first medic said, pulling at the straps across Mason's chest. "There's a jumpsuit on the chair by the door. When you've got the feeling back in your body, put it on. Then we'll take you to the liberator."

Well, that certainly sounded foreboding.

The medic left, shutting the door behind him. Mason lifted his arm. It went only a few inches off the table. He turned his head and saw the chair by the door and the orange fabric folded on top of it.

Orange? A strange color choice for a journey to Bliss. It reminded him of what prisoners wore in all the Old movies he'd seen.

Was he still a prisoner?

He caught sight of a yellow camera in the top corner of the room, pointed down at the table he lay on. His nakedness was being recorded? Wonderful. That thought inspired him to try to sit, which he managed without too much difficulty. He swung his legs off the side of the table and found it was too high up for his feet to reach the floor. His gaze landed on the puckered scar on his thigh where Otley had shot him. Amazing what they could do with technology here. No stitches. It still hurt to walk, though. As if he'd been badly bruised.

Mason pushed himself off the side, and his legs buckled under his weight. He turned and grabbed the table to keep from collapsing on the floor. The concrete was cold under his feet. Once his legs felt stable, he limped backward toward the chair — childish perhaps, but he felt more comfortable with the camera behind him.

When he reached the chair, he picked up the jumpsuit and sat down. A pair of underwear fell onto the floor. He sighed. Safe Landers had not likely expected such humiliation as part of the exciting journey to Bliss. Though perhaps this was merely the journey for those convicted of crimes against the Safe Lands. Maybe upstanding citizens received better treatment.

Mason had barely zipped up the jumpsuit when the door opened. An enforcer stood outside, pointing a SimScanner at Mason and waving him out.

Mason limped into the corridor. A black rubber mat covered the floor and was warmer under his feet than the concrete had been. The enforcer had a partner, who was also pointing a SimScanner at Mason. With their blue uniforms and gray helmets, they looked identical. They didn't even have name patches.

The enforcers motioned Mason down the corridor. The walls were concrete, and bright bay lights and yellow security cameras hung down from the ceiling every few yards.

"Where's Omar?" Mason asked as they made their way along the endless hallway. "I came here with him."

"We can't talk to you, peer," one enforcer said. "Save it for the liberator."

The liberator. Of course.

The corridor finally ended in a T, and the enforcers prodded Mason to the left, where a doorway opened automatically. Inside was a chamber no bigger than the hallway's width squared. A closed door stood opposite the one he was looking though.

"This is where we leave you, peer," the enforcer said. "Find pleasure in life."

"Happy liberation," the other said.

The enforcers pushed Mason into the chamber and shut the door, which shook closed with a clank of metal against metal. Inside, Mason pushed against the door. It didn't budge. He tried the same on the other door. Nothing.

All right. What now? It occurred to him that maybe liberation was death, after all. Perhaps gas would filter in through the ceiling, and this little room would be where he died.

He stood in the chamber for a span of thirty seconds before the other door swung open. Mason walked out the doorway and met two enforcers — older-than-forty enforcers, if he wasn't mistaken. They wore green uniforms with brown helmets rather than the navy blue uniforms and gray helmets that the city enforcers wore. They had patches on their uniforms, though. One said Penn, and the taller of the two was Blake.

"Let's go, shell." Mason noticed Penn had a gray mustache. "Time to see the liberator."

Mason followed Penn and Blake down another corridor, though this one was only about ten feet long and ended with another automatic door. They passed into a small lobby.

An elderly woman was sitting at a counter, tapping on a GlassTop computer. She looked up, smiled, and pushed a SimPad his way. "Tap, please."

Mason set his fist against the pad and it beeped. The woman focused back on her computer. Mason's face came up on the screen.

"Oh, dear. You did get into some mischief, didn't you?"

No reason to pretend otherwise. "Yes, ma'am. I mean ... miss."

"No bother, boy. Have a seat there until you're called."

The enforcers led Mason to a row of chairs, and Mason went ahead and sat down, which made his gunshot wound twinge until his weight was off it. The enforcers stood out in front of the chairs as if Mason might make a run for it.

Mason studied the lobby. There were only four doors in the room: One behind the counter, one on each end of the lobby, and the one they'd entered through. A sign on the wall behind the reception desk said, "Taskers in this office may use sarcasm in a way you are not accustomed to. You might suffer severe mental damage."

Lovely.

The woman stepped back up to the desk. "The liberator will see you now, Mr. Elias."

"Let's go, striker," Penn said.

Mason got up, and the enforcers escorted him to the door on the left end of the lobby. Inside was a small office. It had concrete walls, a steel desk with a GlassTop installed in it, and a Wyndo screen on the wall behind it. It also had a yellow security camera in the corner of the ceiling. There was thin industrial carpet on the floor, white walls, halogen bulbs on the ceiling, and a big black swivel chair with a man sitting in it. He too was dressed in a green enforcer's uniform, though he wore almost as many bars and medals as General Otley once had. He was older — late fifties, perhaps? His salt-and-pepper hair was cut short, and he wasn't wearing a helmet.

"Another premie. Good. We could use some more muscle down here, though it doesn't look like you've got much, striker. That'll change in a hurry. Have a seat."

There were two metal chairs in front of the desk, so Mason pulled one out and sat down. His enforcer escorts remained standing behind him. "You're the liberator?" Mason asked.

"That's right. I'm General Dannen, head liberator for the Safe Lands. You were sentenced to premature liberation by the Safe Lands Guild, which, frankly, is not good. It makes you a striker despite the fact you never Xed out. You probably think that ranks you higher than your Xed-out peer. Not so. For some reason, the task director general wants the worst for you. Put you in Livestock. Sector five. Frankly, I don't think the Tasker G knows what's what down here. If it were me, I'd have put you in one of the slaughterhouses."

Slaughterhouses. A chill raced up Mason's arms at the very idea.

The liberator looked Mason up and down and sighed. "Life in the Highlands and Midlands, that's all about pleasure. Task a little bit, play a lot. That's all over for you. We task here so that the young can play. Since you're a striker, you get to live with the other strikers. And, lucky you, the Tasker G put you in the men's bunkhouse. That's about as bad as it gets down here, so I guess maybe he does know something about this place. You're in 2C. That's the second floor, block C. Bed 26. Your SimTag will let you in. Strikers have a curfew. You must be in your block by ten o'clock each night or your SimTag will shock you and let us know. You cannot leave earlier than five in the morning or the same will happen. Blocks are locked at night." He raised his eyebrows and looked Mason over again, and this time Mason shivered.

"Good luck with that. Women aren't allowed in the men's bunk-houses or striker residences, and men aren't allowed in the women's bunkhouses or striker residences. You got that?"

"Yes, sir."

"Good. When you're off shift, you can go most anywhere else, though, and even into private residences if you've been invited. If you're somewhere you're not supposed to be, we'll see you and your SimTag will let you know. Down here, we watch everyone through all these fine yellow cameras you'll see everywhere." He motioned to the one up on the ceiling. "If we see you messing up, enforcers will drag your sorry carcass to see your warden. And you don't want to see your warden. Ever. Got that?"

"Yes, sir."

"I like your manners. You should keep that up. Now, you get ten credits a day to use however you want. We've got stores and clubs and restaurants and theaters in Cibelo. That's the shopping district. You need something, tell the block enforcers or your task director, who is ..." He tapped on his GlassTop screen and squinted, pulled his head back like he needed glasses. "Gabon Gacy. He runs the cattle feedlot."

Mason was going to work with cattle? That wouldn't be so terrible. He'd worked with cattle back in Glenrock. "Are we still in the Safe Lands?"

The liberator grinned. "This is the Lowlands, shell. Welcome to the rest of your life." He looked over Mason's head. "I'm done here, so you can take him out."

Before Mason could protest, Penn prodded him out of the chair. "Let's go."

"Find pleasure in Bliss, shell," the liberator said as the enforcers ushered Mason out the door.

They left the office, walked down another long hallway, then took an escalator that emptied into some sort of train station.

This "train" was more like a tram. It had an engine on the front that looked like a miniature truck, and it had three cars attached to it, steel with no walls, just five benches in each car, all facing forward, all empty. The enforcers directed Mason into the front of the second car, then they climbed on three rows behind him, resting their SimScanners on the back of the seat in front of them. No one else got on.

The tram pulled forward and into a dark tunnel, which produced a cool breeze on Mason's face. Thirty seconds passed in the darkness until a light shone up ahead. It grew steadily until the tram passed through another station. There were a handful of people waiting, but the train didn't stop. Painted on the wall beside an escalator up were the words "Sector One: Drugs."

What could that mean?

A few minutes passed in the darkness until the tram sailed through "Sector Two: Produce." Since Mason was in sector five, which was Livestock, he surmised that each sector must produce some sort of raw materials for the rest of the Safe Lands.

It was even longer until "Sector Three: Textiles" flashed by, and it must have been five or six minutes until they passed through "Sector Four: Grains." Mason wanted to ask how many sectors there were, but he doubted the enforcers would speak to him. This must be some sort of working prison. *We task here so that the young can play*, General Dannen had said. Interesting.

To pass the time, Mason counted off the minutes, and just over ten passed before the tram started to slow. The smell of hydrogen sulfide gas that came from decompressed manure gripped him long before the tram stopped at the station for "Sector Five: Livestock." There had to be a lot of cattle up there to produce such a strong odor.

"This is your stop, shell," Penn said.

Mason got off the tram and limped toward the escalator. The station was empty. He and the enforcers rode the escalator up, which deposited them in the lobby of some sort of business building.

They left the building through a different door, which put them on a narrow sidewalk with a four-story brick building on one side, and on the other, a waist-high railing that overlooked a feedlot. The odor was intensely repugnant, and Mason coughed, though he'd never been hypersensitive to such things before. The sight staggered him almost more than the smell. Black and brown steers, as far as his eyes could see. Tens of thousands of them.

"Astonishing," he mumbled.

"I never get used to that stench," Penn said.

"They say it's not so bad depending on the wind," Blake said. "At least you're not in the slaughterhouse. I hear that's about as bad as it can get."

Mason didn't doubt it. He had seen enough animals butchered in his life to be able to imagine the horror of multiplying that times the number of cattle in that lot. What did they do with all the blood?

They walked the equivalent of two city blocks and entered a gray-brick building that said "Men's Bunkhouse" over the door. Inside was a small lobby with a scuffed tile floor. A hall stretched out straight ahead for what looked like the depth of the building. To the right was a stairwell and elevator. To the left, a door and a window in the wall that opened to a counter. Two enforcers sat at the counter chatting with each other. Behind them was an open room with desks and a sitting area.

Once the entrance door shut behind them, the manure smell diminished somewhat, but the smell of dirty humans instantly replaced the decomposing manure. It was disinfectant over sweat over urine over excrement. Oh, life had just become very unpleasant on many levels.

But at least it was still a *life*. So, liberation didn't mean death.

Mason's enforcers waved to the men at the desk, then took Mason up the elevator to the second floor. It looked identical to the ground level, with a scuffed-up lobby, the long hallway stretching back, and another window with two enforcers.

Penn stopped at the window and slapped his hand on the counter. Blake prodded Mason to follow. The enforcers behind the window wore the same green enforcer uniforms, without the helmets. Hays and Ebler, according to their name patches. Hays was totally bald and had tiny, sunken eyes. Ebler had black hair and a beard to match. He was a full head shorter than Hays, though if Mason had to choose one not to cross, it would be Ebler. He had a mean look to him.

"New resident," Penn said. "He's in 2C."

"Ooh." Hays winced at Mason. "That's a shame. That's Scorpion's block."

Ebler frowned as both he and Hays looked Mason over like he'd just lost a hand of cards.

"How old are you, kid?" Ebler asked. His beard was so thick around his mouth, Mason could hardly see his lips move.

"Eighteen."

Hays brushed his hand over his shiny scalp. "Dang."

"What'd you do to get the orange pajamas?" Ebler asked.

"Uh ... I made an enemy in Lawten Renzor."

Ebler snorted. "That wasn't smart."

"Yeah ... well, that's irrelevant at this point, isn't it?"

Ebler chuckled and glanced from Hays and back to Mason. "Scorpion will love that mouth, kid. You better learn to shut it."

Mason didn't want to be here. He'd never been one to spend much time out with the men, doing tough things, comparing muscles and who'd caught the biggest fish. And this seemed to be desperately worse than any of that. Not even comparable, really. Dealing with tough guys had never been one of Mason's strengths.

"Look, we do our best to crack down on violence in the blocks, but ..." Hays shook his head. "There's only so much we can do. If I were you, I'd cozy up to Rock Fist straight off. Him and Lethal are the only ones Scorpion won't mess with, but if you make a deal with Lethal, he'll own you, and you don't want that either. We haven't had any competitions for new arrivals in 2C since Rock Fist got here. That doesn't mean you're safe. But trust me, Rock Fist is your new best friend."

"Rock Fist," Mason said.

Ebler shook his head at Hays. "He doesn't understand."

"They never do," Hays said.

Penn squeezed Mason's shoulder, as if to offer some sort of support. "He will."

"Look." Hays leaned onto his arms on the counter. "Someone comes after you, yell out, 'I'm with Rock Fist.' And hope for the best. He sleeps in bunk three."

"It's all you can do," Ebler said. "And I'll tell the next shift to keep a close eye tonight."

That was comforting. Mason had started the day apprehensive about the trial, then he'd felt hopeless when he learned he was going to be liberated, hopeful when Omar had reminded him of the contact lenses, then he'd despaired when the lenses were taken, curious when he'd met the liberator. But in this place with these cryptic warnings ... he was terrified.

"We'll take him back to the block, then out to the pens," Blake said.

"Good Fortune, shell," Ebler said. "You're going to need it."

The enforcers led Mason down the hallway, where the stench of unbathed humans intensified. They passed two doors on the right — both labeled 2A — and two on the left — both labeled 2D. Each door had a window on the top half that was made of safety glass and a SimPad on the door itself. Inside, the rooms were filled with bunk beds. No people.

"Where is everyone?" Mason asked.

"Tasking," Penn said. "Most everyone in the Lowlands tasks from eight to six, except those who are on night shifts."

"But all strikers work days," Blake said.

"That's right," Penn said. "Every once in a while, they take a group of you strikers out to do some late-night task, but mostly, they want your kind locked up when it's dark out."

His kind. Strikers. Mason didn't like being lumped in with criminals. With the Safe Lands justice system, he wondered how many men in the bunkhouse were despicable and how many were merely as unlucky as he was.

They passed by the doors for 2B and 2E and found block 2C at the end of the hall across from 2F.

"Give your tag a try and make sure it works," Penn said.

Mason set his fist to the door and the entrance swung in. Nothing but bunk beds, three rows of them. One row on the front and back wall, one row in between. He quickly counted the bunks. Eight across ... must be three deep ... two beds per bunk. "Forty-eight people in this little room?"

"Naw, I don't think they put more than forty in a block," Penn said.

"And this is where I'm meant to live?" Mason asked. "For how long?"

"That depends on a lot of things," Penn said. "Your sentencing, your behavior, whether or not you work hard for your task director."

The smell wasn't so bad, though the room was empty. Add enough bodies, and it was sure to get far worse. "Where are the bathrooms?"

"In the back. I'll show you," Penn said, walking deeper into the room.

Mason followed and saw that the back row of bunks didn't have eight across, but six, separated by an opening in the wall that led to a tile room. Penn went inside, and Mason followed, stopping beside the enforcer. Ten shower stalls on the back wall — no curtains. He turned around. Four toilet-sink combos on one side of the entrance, four on the other. And on the ceiling, a yellow camera on each end of the room.

Blake was standing in the archway that separated the bunk room from the showers. He smiled wide. "Nice, isn't it?"

"Cameras in the showers?" Mason met Penn's gaze, and the look on his face must have showed his total horror because the enforcer jerked his head back to the bunk room.

"Don't let those cameras scare you," Penn said. "They're for your protection. And listen, a friend of mine started out in the bunkhouse.

Here's how he did things. He didn't shower here. He didn't use the toilets. He held it until his tasking breaks or his free time. And he only showered at the car wash."

"What's the car wash?" Mason asked.

"Mandatory cleaning for strikers," Blake said.

"It's a shower and change of clothing and a quick word with a medic to make sure you're okay," Penn said. "Get patched up, if need be."

Mason's stomach fluttered at those words. *Patched up, if need be.* "And that takes place ...?"

"Basement. Second floor goes on Thursdays, I think," Penn said. "The bunk enforcers won't let you miss it."

"I see." Mason glanced around the bunks. "Which one is mine? Twenty-six?"

"Numbers start on that wall, so ..." Penn pointed at the wall opposite the shower room, the one with the entry doors to the block. "Sixteen on the far wall, eighteen, twenty, twenty-two, twenty-four, twenty-six." He pointed at one of the bunks directly in front of the shower entrance. He walked toward it and moved a thin wool blanket off the bars on the end. "Twenty-six." He tapped the black number that had long ago been painted onto the steep frame.

"Someone's stuff is there," Mason said.

"Just claim an empty one later," Penn said. "After you find Rock Fist."

Mason had committed the name to memory. "Which is bed three?"

"Over there." Penn pointed to the corner by one of the entry doors, opposite the showers.

Mason walked that way and studied the bed. "You know him?"

"Naw. But you'd better, shell." Penn met his gaze, and the man's eyes were sympathetic. "You understand the gravity of the situation, I hope?"

"Yes," Mason said. "There is no doubt at all in my mind." It was going to be a long night.

CHAPTER
3

The enforcers showed Mason the striker's cafeteria in his building where he could eat for one credit a meal, then they took Mason out to the feedlot. Again he noted that the size of it was staggering. The cows were all brown or black, and the cattle in the pen to his right looked to be male yearlings.

They ended up in a red barn, where the enforcers introduced Mason to the yard foreman, Gabon Gacy.

"Glad to have another farmhand," Gacy said. "Have a seat, Mason."

Mason sat.

"You're on your own now, shell," Penn said. "Stay out of trouble."

"I'll try."

The enforcers left.

"I got a text tap on you this morning," Gacy said. "Said you tasked as a medic."

"A level two medic, yes."

"Well, the tap said you're to task in the pens as a farmhand. At some point, if you're good and lucky and the task director general thinks you've been punished enough, I could train you as a vet, since you have a medical background. You don't need to be a vet to learn how to vaccinate, though."

"Do the cattle have the Thin Plague?" Mason asked.

"Of course not."

"Then what are the vaccinations for?"

"Several things. They're vaccinated with a five-in-one for the clostridial diseases — tetanus, malignant oedema, enterotoxaemia, black disease, and blackleg. Clostridia are widespread in the lot, found in the soil and feces. We've got a separate vaccine for protection against botulism, if needed. We get a lot of BRD here — that's bovine respiratory disease. And we vaccinate for that, plus — "

"Why would cattle get respiratory diseases?"

"The lots are mud baths in wet weather and dustbowls in dry weather. Cattle catch colds. They're close together. They're stressed. So their immune systems are in high gear, trying to guard against everything that's coming at them. And other diseases crop up too. Besides vaccinations, since these animals are bred for meat we give them antibiotics to keep the liver functioning long enough to reach slaughter weight. And the females are on birth control to keep them from riding other animals and stirring up dust or bruising other animals.

"The vets keep a good watch on the animals, but that will be part of your job. You see a sick animal, bring it into a holding pen. I want it away from the others until a vet can take a look."

"What else will I be responsible for?"

"Moving the cattle for the vets, moving the cattle for cleaning the pens, watching for sick animals, watching for damaged fences, helping the penriders or vets when asked."

"May I ask, what is *your* job?"

"I oversee daily operations of the feedlot, monitor feed rations, animal health, fence building and repair. I also supervise thirty-some other taskers. That includes my assistant, the penriders, truck drivers, vets, farmhands, and maintenance workers." Gacy eyed Mason. "What do you think about working with cattle?"

Mason shrugged. "I like cattle. I took care of them in my village."

Gacy frowned. "You're an outsider?"

"Yes, sir."

"And you had your own cattle?"

"Not like this. Ours lived off grass."

"Is that a fact? Well, we don't have the space to let our cattle wander the prairie eating grass. We feed them grain with added growth hormones. How many head you have?"

"Head?"

"How many animals?"

"Oh, um, we had six milking cows, eight calves, six yearlings, and three bulls."

"Well, we've got about ten thousand head here. We've got fifty pens that house two hundred head each. You might have moved some cattle where you lived, but there's some things you need to know about the cattle in our pens. You need to handle them nice and quietly. Don't be rough with them. Cattle want to see where you are and will move accordingly. They'll want to go around you. They'll want to stay with and follow other cattle."

That sounded right to Mason. "I understand."

"Let's take you out and see how you do. You'll need a pair of boots. Check that room for your size and put them on." Gacy pointed at a closet by the entrance to his office.

Mason found a pair of boots, and they went out to the pens. Gacy showed Mason the setup. There were three rows of pens, each separated by the road for the feeding truck. As Mason and Gacy walked down one of the roads, the truck passed by, pouring grain into a trough that lined the outside of the pens. The cows had their heads between the bars and munched happily.

"Cattle need room to move or they get stressed, and that leads to illness or low weight gain," Gacy said. "We give the animals three hundred and fifty square feet each. It's our goal to maintain a low stress environment for the herds. Each pen needs to be safe and comfortable. We treat these cattle well. I see you shoving or beating an animal, I'll have you reassigned."

"I could never harm an animal," Mason said.

"Good. This first row has pens one through eighteen. The second" — he motioned to where the truck was dumping feed — "goes from nineteen to thirty-six. And the third row holds pens thirty-seven to fifty-four. We don't use those last few unless we need them. Off past the third row, that's where the manure stockpile is, and the terraces and retention pond. Down at the ends of the rows are the sick pens."

"Do you birth calves here?" Mason asked.

"Not on the feedlot. Calves spend six months with their mothers before being weaned. Then the trucks bring them here. We can finish a steer in twelve months. With the hormones in the grain, these animals gain an unnatural amount of weight in a short period of time. At eighteen to twenty-four months of age, the cattle are taken to the slaughterhouse."

When they reached the end, Gacy opened pen eighteen and they went inside. Two cows that were standing close to the door lumbered away.

"This will be your row. So every day you walk pens one to eighteen. I want you to become aware of what's normal so that you know when something is wrong. Watch their behavior. Look for depressed animals, droopy ears, excess salivation, shivering, panting, animals standing alone or reluctant to move or get up when others do. Look for animals that approach the feed bunk but don't eat.

"Watch their movement and how they look. Take note of limping cows. Check their legs for swelling. Lame animals might stand strangely or lean to one side or shift their weight from one foot to another. Watch for bloat. Look for restless, irritable animals. Are they swishing their tails or kicking their bellies?

"Watch for sickness. Count their breaths per minute in cold and hot weather. Be alert for short respiratory movements. Look up their noses. Get used to what's average for mucus. If an animal has more than the others, pull him out. A runny nose and short breath might be the start of a respiratory disease. Watch their dung. Look at the consistency and color. Pale dung or diarrhea may indicate feed problems or infections."

Gacy walked back to the gate they'd come in. "Farmhands task from seven in the morning to five at night. You get to take an hour lunch, but you got to work that out with the penriders. We like to have a penrider and a farmhand on each row at all times during the day. In fact, let me introduce you to the penriders and the other farmhands."

And so Mason met the two first row penriders, Coy and Brondon, who each rode glossy brown horses. He also met Wayd and Prezan, the other two farmhands for the first row. The vet, who was called Oakes Hackett, was busy working with the animals, so Mason was informed he would meet him later.

And with that, Gacy left Mason to it.

The cows were friendly, so Mason talked to them, telling them his woes of Glenrock and Ciddah and how he was worried about Omar. The rest of his shift dragged by. When a bell rang out, Wayd walked up to Mason.

"The bell means we're done for the day," Wayd said.

So Mason left the feedlot and followed the mob toward the city. He walked around Cibelo, which reminded him of the entertainment district in the Midlands. There were dozens of establishments, but everything looked a little bit rundown and careworn. Mason hoped he might become better acquainted with someone here soon. He could use a friend who could explain how things worked in this place. Unfortunately, he didn't think many people would want to befriend a striker. He wondered if he could get some other clothes. It would be easier to make friends without the orange jumpsuit.

He returned to the cafeteria for dinner. The establishment clearly wasn't used to vegetarians, forcing him to scrounge up a plate of droopy lettuce and some peas and carrots. Mason sat at a table near the entrance with his back to the door, hoping that would keep people from noticing him or picking a fight. A valid concern — the other strikers were loud and rowdy, and started two food fights and one fistfight while Mason ate.

He'd just about cleaned his plate when the SimTag in his hand buzzed, like a warning of some kind. A voice came over the speakers in the cafeteria.

"Ten minutes to curfew. Ten minutes to striker curfew."

Mason took a deep breath. Time to go.

He got up and turned in his tray, then walked upstairs slowly, feet dragging. It felt as if he were walking to his own execution. The warnings from the block enforcers had him scared out of his mind. Look for Rock Fist, he reminded himself. Rock Fist.

A mob around the elevator sent Mason to the steps. A river of men clad in orange jumpsuits flowed up each flight. Mason kept to the side, limping up the steps. People ran around him. A few bumped his shoulder on purpose. The smells of body odor were strong, though after the day Mason had experienced, he bet he was doing his part.

It surprised him to see the enforcer window closed as he and the mob walked through the lobby on the second floor, though he supposed the enforcers would be quite vulnerable in this crowd. They were likely watching through the cameras.

Mason studied the men's faces without trying to look like he was staring at any one person. The majority of the men seemed to be middle aged, though there were some younger faces and many older ones. Which was Scorpion? Lethal? Rock Fist?

He passed by the first door of block 2C and entered the second without drawing any attention to himself. He had thought this out all day. The second door opened right into Rock Fist's sleeping area. Bed three, Penn had told him, which was the bottom of the second bunk against the wall in the corner. It was currently empty. Mason walked into the narrow aisle between the first and second bunks and squatted against the wall, hoping no one would see him before Rock Fist did.

The men seemed to loom overhead as they filed inside, a mattress length from where he waited. Mason kept even his breath silent, but his position was making his sore leg ache. He shifted his weight onto his good leg, trying to get a little relief.

"Move it, Hobbles!" a loud voice jeered, every word a near scream. An elderly man stumbled into the entry door and grabbed hold of the post on the end of Rock Fist's bunk. A tall, skeletal man entered behind him. "Don't fall now, you ancient." He fisted the back of the old man's jumpsuit, pulled him off the bedpost, then shoved him forward, right in front of Mason, and onto the bottom bunk in the very corner.

The bully cackled as the old man's head struck the wall, but his voice tapered off when his eyes locked onto Mason's. "Who are you?"

Mason looked at the floor.

"What are you doing on the floor, sneak? You don't belong here." The bully lunged in between the bunks, hands outstretched.

Mason jumped from his crouch, but his sore legs didn't get him very far. He fell onto Rock Fist's bunk and wiggled over the bed until he fell out on the other side.

The bully darted back to the main row and cut Mason off between bunks two and three before Mason could get to his feet.

Mason stood slowly, then sat on Rock Fist's bunk like it was his.

That didn't faze the bully. He seized the front of Mason's jumpsuit in both hands and dragged him out like he weighed nothing. Mason grabbed the man's wrists and pushed them back, but that seemed ineffective. So he grabbed the man's throat and pressed his thumbs over the man's carotid arteries.

The bully's eyes bulged with fear, but only for a moment before he twisted over and threw Mason on the floor. Mason's back smacked against the tile and knocked the wind out of him. He tried again to get his thumbs on the man's neck, but someone else slid up beside him and pinned his arms against the floor — a small man with tiny eyes.

Lord, help me.

"What are you doing, Wicked?" a deep voice said from somewhere above.

"Block crasher," the bully said.

"Let's see him."

Wicked sat back, took Mason's left arm from the little-eyed man, and together they pulled him to standing while stretching out his arms.

A man pushed through the crowd. He was pale, bald, had horn implants, and his face was tattooed in hundreds of puzzle pieces. He had blue rings around his eyes that were inky black. Mason knew it must be due to contacts, but the effect was hideous. "Who are you?"

"Mason."

"You packing?"

Mason didn't understand the question.

"You come here to take Scorpion out?" Wicked asked. "Who sent you here?"

Ah, so this was Scorpion. "I live here now. Two C, bed twenty-six."

"A newman." Scorpion grinned, revealing teeth colored shiny black with SimArt. "Well, this *is* a celebration. Two C hasn't had a newman since Hobbles limped his way in here."

Men were still filing inside the room. Mason eyed the bed that was supposed to belong to Rock Fist, but it was still empty.

Scorpion leaned his face close to Mason's. "Now, what did you say, raven? Bed twenty-six?" He walked through the crowd, which parted for him like it was made of opposing magnets. The men holding Mason dragged him after Scorpion, who stopped at bunk twenty-six and tapped the side with his hand. "That's too bad. Strongboy sleeps in this bed. Where you at, Strongboy? You been holding out on me, peer?"

A man stepped into view. He was as big as General Otley, like someone had inflated him two sizes larger than everyone else. "Leave him be." His voice was deep and low.

"What'll you give me for him?" Scorpion asked.

Strongboy shook his head. "I thought we were done with this stuff."

"I like him." Scorpion looked back to Mason, slid his hand down the side of Mason's face. "Oh, I like him a lot. Maybe I'll trade you for Luella. Get me a new lifer."

"I'm with Rock Fist," Mason spat out.

Scorpion stepped closer, raised his eyebrows. "That so?"

"Yes," Mason said.

"Stimming block enforcers tell you to say that?" Scorpion jerked his head to the side. "Bring him."

The guys dragged Mason after Scorpion. When they made it out into the open space before the entrance to the showers, the little guy holding Mason's right arm screamed and released him. Then Wicked doubled over and fell to the floor. Both had clearly been stunned.

The enforcers were watching. Good.

Mason looked over to Scorpion, who stood at the foot of the bed in the opposite corner of the room from the place Hobbles had been thrown.

Scorpion straightened his spine, pointed to the bottom bunk. "You sleep here, raven."

But Mason knew he was safe, for the moment. "I don't think so." His legs were shaking so badly he thought he might collapse, but he backed his way past Strongboy's bunk.

A muscular guy tapped his shoulder. He had a thick, black chin beard. "Me and mine will protect you, peer. It'll cost you, but you'll be safe. They call me Lethal."

Mason shook his head and backed to the opposite corner of the room. "No, thanks. I'm with Rock Fist." He returned to where he'd started, crouched against the wall between bunks one and two.

"I'm-a get you later, raven," Scorpion yelled across the room. "The BEs can't be everywhere at once. Just you wait until dark."

Mason was certain his stress had blocked enough blood flow to his heart that the muscle could stop working at any moment. He took slow, calming breaths and thanked God for the yellow cameras. He didn't understand why Scorpion would claim anyone. It wasn't like these men were completely isolated. They were free to visit Cibelo like everyone else. Free to meet women.

"You okay?"

Mason looked to his left and the source of the voice. The old man named Hobbles. "Yeah. I don't understand, though. What does he want?"

"It's about power. Dominance. Plus, Scorpion can make credits off you."

A boy who looked younger than Mason hung his head over the bunk above where Hobbles sat. "You don't need him," the kid said. "You can sell yourself. Plenty will pay."

Mason wanted to puke. "Why don't they just go pay at a club in Cibelo?"

"Not enough women," Hobbles said. "They've got waiting lists. And most clubs don't allow strikers."

"Ah." So this was why Lawten had sent Mason here. Mason had underestimated him.

"Who's this?"

Mason looked up. A man stood in the opening between bunks one and two. He had chin-length graying black hair and a short beard. His hair was swept back over his head, making his forehead look nearly half the size of his face.

"Hay-o, Rock," the boy said. "This here's Mason. Scorpion tried to claim him, but he said he's with you."

"I don't know you," Rock Fist said.

"I realize that." Mason pushed to standing, wincing at the tightness in his thigh. "The block enforcers said you'd help me."

"I don't have any more beds for helping people," Rock said.

"I don't need a bed," Mason said. "I can sleep on the floor."

Rock Fist's hair fell into his eyes and he swept it back behind his ear. "I bet you can. What are you in for?"

Mason thought of the best way he could word this. "I stole Renzor's girl."

Rock Fist barked a laugh. "Oh, that won't do. You need to have a better story than that or the boys will start calling you love names. How'd you get caught?"

"I broke into Champion House and rescued her. She got away. Into the basements with Baby Promise and the latest Outsider Queen. Renzor wasn't happy."

A wide grin stretched across Rock Fist's face. "Your girl an Outsider?"

"A medic in the SC. I tasked there too."

"But you're an Outsider." It wasn't a question.

"What makes you say that?" Mason asked.

"You're far too pretty, and they don't sell roller paint in Cibelo. From which village?"

"Why would you assume I'm from a village? Why not Wyoming?"

Rock Fist merely waited for Mason to answer.

"Glenrock."

Rock smiled at that. "They liberate you as a rebel?"

"I don't know. They didn't say."

"Then they didn't. *Mason*." Rock Fist said the name as if many pieces of a puzzle had come together in his mind. He smiled again. "You're one lucky shell getting put in here with me, you know that?"

"That's become abundantly clear in the last ten minutes."

Rock Fist chuckled. "Mason. The smart one. The medic. Yeah, I'll claim you, boy. I got your back." And with that, Rock Fist turned around and shouted, "Listen up, you sick shells. This boy Mason is mine. You hear what I'm saying, Scorpion? *Mine*. Hands off. Don't even look at him. Don't even brush up against him while you're coming in the front door. You do, I will make you scream. That clear?"

Mumbles of affirmation rolled around the block.

A chill ran over Mason.

"Why you want his skinny butt anyway?" Scorpion's voice.

"That's not your business. It's just a fact. Deal with it. Now, I'm going to need a mattress over here, so someone better cough up."

Mason's gaze swept the room. No one was moving.

"I'm not going to ask again," Rock said.

Movement over by the first door caught Mason's attention. A man stood up and threw back the covers on his bed, revealing two mattresses stacked together. He pulled off the top one, dragged it between two bunks in the middle, and dropped it in the aisle in front of Rock Fist's bunk.

Rock Fist waved at the boy on the top bunk. "Get down here and help me, Teardrop. You too, Mason."

Mason jumped to standing. The boy climbed down, and he, Mason, and Rock Fist pushed the bunk over until it met the empty one on the other side. Then Rock arranged the mattress on the floor in the now wider gap between bunks one and two.

"Just until they get used to you being here," Rock Fist said. "Then we can find you a bunk."

"Thanks," Mason said.

"I hope you'll remember this, boy," Rock Fist said. "There might come a time when you decide you don't like me very much."

"I doubt that." But Mason wondered. Was this man only helping him in exchange for something? And if so, what?

CHAPTER
4

Omar was dying. At least that's how he felt. The medics who'd taken his clothes and the contact lenses had refused to give him his meds, saying someone would take care of that on the inside, whatever that meant. Then some enforcer peons took him to some enforcer rank who called himself the liberator, told him he was in a task prison, and that he would be tasking in the poultry slaughterhouse. When Omar had asked about his meds, the maggot wouldn't give him anything either.

Now he was riding with two new enforcer peons on some kind of underground train to who knew where. Sector six, the liberator had said, though Omar had barely been listening once he'd learned he wasn't going to get any juice.

He wondered what they'd done with Mason.

Omar turned in his seat on the train. "What about my meds?" he asked the enforcer peons. He had to lift his voice over the sound of the truck.

"Meds are distributed once a week when you check in for clean clothes," one of them said.

"Once a week? Are there stims here?"

"Sure, but you've got to buy them, and they're not cheap."

"How not cheap?"

"You get ten credits a day. A level one hit of alcohol will cost you five."

Two hits of alcohol a day? "What about brown sugar?"

"User, eh?" The peon shook his head.

"How much?" Omar asked again.

"Fifty for a level one, I think. Maybe five hundred for a level ten."

Walls! It would take Omar three weeks to save up enough credits for one vial of his usual. And he still needed to buy a new PV.

"Look, vaping that stuff will kill you," the peon said. "If I were you, I'd quit."

"Don't you mean it will liberate me?"

"We're past all that now, don't you think?" the peon said. "No one dies during liberation. There's no next life. Old people and strikers are exiled to the Lowlands to work the fields. That's where we'll all truly die. Surprise, surprise. Welcome to Bliss."

Well, that was one possibility Omar hadn't seen coming.

At the stop for sector six, they got off the truck train. The enforcers took him up to the ground level, where the awful stench of something rotten dominated the air. They went into a building with a sign that said Men's Striker Residence, which turned out to be his new home. He was in room 3 – 18, a closet with four bunk beds and a doorless bathroom with four doorless showers.

Whatever.

There was nothing Omar could do here. No way to continue being the Owl. No way to get the truth out to Safe Landers. No way to help Shay or ever see her again. The lenses were gone, so he couldn't show anyone what he was experiencing. He couldn't even vape himself to death, so he'd likely die in slow agony. It was over. Done. God had finally punished him for his sins. Justice had prevailed.

The enforcers took him over to the slaughterhouse. Omar had heard the word somewhere before, but he couldn't recall the source. Probably some Old movie. He discovered quickly this was the building where they killed chickens. There'd been no such place in Glenrock. Animals were killed when it was time and usually on the chopping block behind someone's home. They had no way to freeze meat, so they killed only what they needed and only when they needed it.

The enforcers left Omar in a dinky office with a grizzled man who called himself Taz Akers. Akers gave Omar a tour of the place. It was entirely automated. The chickens came in from outside in flat crates on conveyor belts, squawking and shaking. Omar was told these crates came in early each morning, after they sat for an hour or so to give the birds a chance to calm down before being slaughtered.

"Why?" Omar asked. "Seems like a waste of time."

"They need to settle for the taskers to be able to pick them up and hang them upside down on the rack."

In the first room, some taskers opened the crates and hung each live chicken by their feet onto metal hooks on a moving rail. That rail carried the chickens along, then dipped them into a trough of water, which Akers said was electrified.

"Stuns them," Akers said.

The rail rose up on the other side of the bath and carried the chickens through a hole in the wall, where a mechanical blade slit their throats as they passed by. Blood dripped down onto a shiny steel counter and drained into a trough that led to who knew where. And the rail kept moving, carrying the dead chickens into another room.

This second area was all machines with two guys who stood around watching and making sure nothing went wrong. First the chickens went through the scalding tank, where the birds were submerged in boiling "water," which was brown and filled with what looked like feces and floating feather shards. Akers said this scalded the skin and loosened feathers for plucking. Then it was on to new sections of the machine. Whirring rubber fingers ripped out feathers as the carcasses filed past, one part of the machine lopped off heads, another cut out their guts.

It was mad wild and gross at the same time.

When the tour was over, Akers took Omar out to the yards, which was a group of four barns filled with chickens. The stench horrified him, and he instantly wretched. He pinched his nose and breathed through his mouth, trying to calm his stomach.

"Walls, you're a weakling," Akers said. "Here. Put this on." He handed Omar a little U of plastic. "It's a nose clip." He pinched the bridge of his nose. "Slides right on."

Omar slid the U over his nose and the stench diminished. Much better.

In the first barn, trucks dropped off crates of baby chicks that were dumped into the yard to fend for themselves. The floor of each barn was a grid of steel squares that feces could fall through. Still, filth was everywhere. The barns had chickens of different ages. And each day Omar would have to wade through the chickens and choose which ones were big enough to be killed. Those he would gather and shut up in new crates that, when they were full, he'd set on the conveyor belt that carried them into the slaughterhouse.

Akers gave Omar a pair of thick boots and told him to put them on. Once he did, Akers led him out into the yard of Barn 2.

"Your job is to walk the pen and look for trouble. Pull out injured chickens or dead ones. Injured ones, if they're big enough, go in a crate for slaughter. Dead ones or ones that are too small go in the incinerator."

Omar followed Akers around the yard as the man showed him what to look for in regards to injury. "If you aren't sure, just ask one of the others. You'll get the hang of it."

"Why are their beaks cut off? And their toes?"

"To keep them from being able to hurt each other. Stressed-out birds have a short fuse and like to fight. This way, they can't do much damage to each other."

"Do we ever clean out the yard?"

"No point. The chickens are always being rotated in or out, so the yards are never totally empty. Plus most of it falls through the grid and gets washed out from below. It's really not that bad."

Oh, yes it was. Omar compared the life of the chickens they'd had in Glenrock to these. Back home, the chickens had lived in neat pens and could walk in the grass and sleep in little beds where they laid eggs. Here … there were no beds at all.

Akers left Omar to his new task. For hours, Omar kept his distance from the other men, not wanting to talk to anyone today. Though what if one of the men had a PV and would share a puff? Omar's bones were aching, and he felt cold despite how warm it was in the barnyard.

He walked around the yard "looking for trouble" of the chicken kind, until a whistle blew and the other men started for the exit. Must be end of the shift for the day. Omar followed them, watching as they clocked out at a SimPad at the end of the barn. Omar did the same and walked outside. He left the nose clip on and followed the men, not certain how he had gotten to this task or exactly where he was supposed to go next.

The men walked farther away from the buildings on the perimeter, though. And soon Omar saw the bright lights of a city. He removed the nose clip, and his temples throbbed. He could smell food. There would be clubs there too, he was almost certain. He thought back to what that liberator had said. Ten credits a day? He needed food, but it wasn't what he wanted. And he had a curfew of ten o' clock, meaning he was free until then. Free to find some clubs and make friends. Friends who might get him some juice.

But at the clubs he walked inside, he got thrown out for wearing the orange jumpsuit. "No strikers," both had said.

And apparently Omar was a striker. So how did strikers score juice? Should he use his ten credits on a beer? He wanted something, but a beer would only make him crave more.

He eventually bought a slice of pizza, which was the cheapest and biggest food he could find. He devoured it, then rejoined the flow of orange-clad bodies and stumbled to his new home. He hurt so badly, he hardly remembered most of the walk. He passed by the men's bunkhouse and entered the strikers' residence, and wondered briefly what the difference between the two was.

When he staggered into his room, he found that he wasn't the first to arrive. Three of the four beds had guys on them. They were all wearing the orange jumpsuit, though one guy with dark hair had stripped his off to the waist, showing off a muscled and hairy chest. The sound of water spraying in the showers told him it was occupied as well.

"Hay-o, newman. What's your name?" the half-dressed guy asked.

"Omar." Perhaps if he made friends with his new roommates, they would tell him how he could get some stims.

"I'm Prav," the hairy guy said. "This is Kurwin." He gestured to the bottom bunk across from his. "That shell over there is Jeorn, but he doesn't talk. Lost his tongue in a fight club that got ugly. You must be above one of our beds, yeah?"

Omar was staring at Jeorn, trying to decide if he should be afraid of the man or not. Prav looked much stronger than the mute. "Uh, I'm on five, I think."

"Yeah, okay. Bed five is over Kurwin."

Kurwin had white-blond hair that had been shaved so short that it looked like the fuzzy glow of a baby chick.

He shook the thought off. He'd seen too many chicks today.

"When do we get our meds?" Omar asked.

"We go to the car wash on Friday morning," Prav said.

"That long from now?" Omar winced at the whiny sound of his voice.

"What you in for, striker?" Kurwin asked.

"You don't have to tell us," Prav said. "Kurwin's a nosy shell."

Omar shrugged one shoulder. "I got on the task director general's nerves. Otley's too, but he's dead now."

"Stun me, Otley's dead?" Prav asked. "How do you know?"

"Saw him die. Bender shot him with an Old pistol. In the head. Guess they couldn't bring him back from that." Mason had told Omar that Papa Eli had shot Otley with his rifle, yet the MC had managed to save him.

"So you some kind of rebel?" Kurwin asked.

"Some kind. Not anymore, I guess."

"Yeah, ain't no rebels down here," Prav said.

"Why not?"

"'Cause enforcers are always watching. And if you get liberated as a rebel, they mark you. Two or more rebels can't be within two yards of each other for more than five minutes or their SimAlarms will go off."

"What's a SimAlarm?"

"You serious or just juiced up?" Kurwin asked.

"The stunner in your SimTag, peer," Prav said.

"Oh, right. I just never heard it called a SimAlarm."

"Well, that's what it is, and it hurts," Kurwin said.

"So what are you in for?" Omar asked Kurwin.

"Disorderly conduct." He cackled as if he'd made a joke.

"Kurwin gets drunk and acts like a shell. So the bouncers in the Highlands would throw him out, then he'd try to fight them."

"So, basically, you're an idiot," Omar said.

Prav and the mute laughed. Not Kurwin.

"Shut your face, shell," Kurwin said. "At least I don't hurt people." He gestured to Prav.

"I only hurt people who ask for it," Prav said.

It *would* be the strong guy who was in for hurting people. "How do people ask for it?" *So I can make sure I never do.*

"Prav gets credited by enforcers to bash faces," Kurwin said.

"We all have to earn a living down here," Prav said. "And ten credits a week doesn't cut it."

Maybe once Omar got to know Prav better, the guy would help him find a side job to make more credits.

There were seven men in bunk 3–18, which left one bed empty. Omar showered, but since he had no clothing to change into, he had to put on the same clothes again. His new SimTag hadn't brought back his SimArt. Omar missed it. He liked being able to put his feelings on his skin. Prav had SimArt down both arms, but whatever credits Omar made down here were going one place: in a PV.

He awoke that night, unable to breathe. He gasped and clutched his chest, turned on his side, and wretched over the side of his bed. The vomit splatted to the floor in the darkness.

"What the ...?" exclaimed Kurwin.

"Sorry." Omar fell back on his bed. He should get up. Clean that up before Prav found out and got angry. But all he could do was lie on his back and stare at the ceiling. His heart pounded against his chest, too fast or too slow. Too ... something. It wasn't right.

He was going to die for sure this time.

"Hey, shell. Here." Prav's voice.

The familiar cool metal of a PV pressed against his cheek. His lips found it and he inhaled. He could tell right away it was grass. A high level too. Glorious grass. He let it in, let it soothe the itch, though it still wasn't what he really needed to make him feel fully himself. It wasn't —

"What's your stim?" Prav asked.

Omar sniffled, unable to see Prav in the darkness of the room. "Brown sugar."

"Walls. That stuff's ranked. What'd you task before to make that kind of credit?"

"Enforcer."

"*You*, a force? Come on. I'm no dim."

"Does it really matter anymore?" Omar asked.

"Guess not," Prav said. "Look, I see you got two options. You can save up, and if you're smart you'll switch to grass before you kill yourself. Or you can do what we do."

"Which is?"

"Task for Rain in our free time."

"Is that the enforcer you beat guys up for?"

"Oh, no. This is different off-grid tasking. Both are special."

"Rain will like you, peer." This from Kurwin, from the bed below. "You look young. That's all she cares about."

"Meet us in Cibelo tomorrow night," Prav said. "Eight o'clock. Place called Fajro. And once you calm down, get up and clean this pile of puke. It reeks."

"Sure thing," Omar said, not wanting to anger his savior.

CHAPTER 5

S hh, it's okay." Shaylinn paced in front of the couch, bouncing baby Harvey with every step. She'd come to visit and had volunteered to watch the baby so Naomi could take a nap. But little Harvey wouldn't stop crying, and Shaylinn didn't know what to do.

Levi and Jordan acted like all should be well now that the children had been divided into homes and were, as they put it, safe. She didn't mean to make light of their living in the basements; she was thankful for it. What neither man seemed to understand was that this place was scary for some of the children, many of whom had just learned that their mothers had been liberated. And then there were the Safe Lands children, who knew only pleasure and had been dismayed to find no electronic toys here.

There was nothing to be done for any of it, though, but to pray and to comfort the grieving children and discipline the naughty ones as best they all could. Shaylinn hoped that school would be a positive distraction for the children and a constructive way to pass the day.

Little Harvey, however ... "Hush, baby. Your momma needs a nap." She bounced the boy, beyond frustrated. Maybe she should put him down. Maybe he didn't want to be held.

"He's not very happy, is he?"

Shaylinn spun around, startled, though she'd recognized Ciddah's voice. "You scared me." And Harvey cried louder, unhappy with the sudden movement.

"Sorry," Ciddah said. "Want me to take him a moment? Elyot is sleeping."

Elyot is *sleeping.* Shaylinn's cheeks flushed at the tone of her thoughts. It wasn't Ciddah's fault that Shaylinn was clueless with babies. "I guess you'd better, or Naomi won't get her nap."

Ciddah came and lifted Harvey into her arms. "Hello, my sweet boy. Are you unhappy? I'm so sorry. Yes, I am. But your momma needs some sleep. Yes, she does." Ciddah said all this in a gushy baby voice.

"I hadn't thought to talk to him," Shaylinn said. "He wouldn't understand me, anyway."

"Mason once told me that scientists of Old claimed that babies as young as six months can understand a wide vocabulary." Even as she said it, Ciddah kept talking in that gushy voice, looking all the while at Harvey. "He said that speaking to them normally could improve their language skills later on."

Yes, well, speaking normally. Not like the baby was a puppy. "Harvey isn't six months old yet. He's only a few days old." But Harvey wasn't crying anymore, just staring at Ciddah's face.

"I think I've intrigued him. You know, it might be my light hair. Your coloring is so close to Naomi's that maybe he thinks you're his mother and wonders why you won't feed him."

Shaylinn hadn't thought of that, either. "I don't think I'm going to be a very good mother."

Ciddah looked away from Harvey then, her cool blue eyes staring straight into Shaylinn's soul. "Shaylinn, you're so sweet, that's just not possible."

"But some people have difficult babies. My aunt Mary had a lot of trouble with Nell, so she knows. She told Jemma that Harvey was a good baby. I'll have two babies, and I don't know what to do anyway, so I'm sure I'll have trouble."

"I think you will learn quickly what to do."

"Jemma said my babies are hearing my voice all the time, getting used to the sound of me. Maybe that will help."

"I never thought of that. It's lovely."

"Shay."

Levi's voice made Shaylinn look to the doorway. "Hello, Levi."

"It's time to go."

"Already? That went fast." Jemma insisted that Levi escort Shaylinn back to their underground house, convinced Shay should not go out into the basements alone in her condition. Shaylinn walked toward the door and waved to Ciddah. "Good-bye, Ciddah. Thanks."

"Bye-o, Shaylinn."

Shaylinn walked beside Levi in silence in the creepy underground corridor. Shaylinn didn't like it here. She knew they were supposedly safe, but she missed the breeze and trees and sky. The air was stuffy down here. And even though she could walk around, she felt buried alive.

"Ruston and I have arranged for the children to go to school tomorrow," Levi said.

"How wonderful!" The children needed something to do. Being cooped up underground seemed to be making them all extra hyper.

"Eliza and Mukwiv are going to take the children," Levi said, "but I'd like you to go along. Ruston said they divide the children into smaller classrooms. And I don't want any of our kids to be without one of our adults."

Ah. She was going as a chaperone, not a student. "I'm an adult now?"

"Yes, Shaylinn. And I need you to be my eyes and ears."

She tried to hide her sigh from Levi. She would have to find books from the library if she wanted to keep learning for herself. "I will do my best."

The next morning, Shaylinn met Eliza and Mukwiv in the park. The other Glenrock and Jack's Peak adults brought children and left them in Eliza and Mukwiv's care for the day. Thirty children in all.

When everyone had arrived, Shaylinn took hold of Jake's hand on one side and Joey's on the other and followed Eliza through the dim corridor that separated the park from the school. They were all curious how this school worked and what would be taught.

The school door looked no different than any other door in the basements, though a sign hung on the door itself, some sort of sheet metal that had been screwed into the wood. Stenciled across the metal in black letters was the word SCHOOL.

They filed inside, into yet another corridor. But this one was a hallway inside a building. It stretched out before them, and Shaylinn could barely see the door on the other end over the tops of the heads of their group. There were doors between as well—three on one side of the hallway, three on the other. The walls were covered with the creations of children: coloring pages, paintings, and other assignments.

Their group was making a lot of noise, and Shaylinn shushed them as best she could. A door opened on Shaylinn's right, just a few paces ahead, and Tova stepped out. She surveyed them with a thin-lipped expression that made Shaylinn suspect that she might not want thirty new students in her school.

"Can you silence your children?" Tova said to no one in particular that Shaylinn could see.

Shaylinn shushed the kids again, Eliza put her fingers to her lips, and Penelope whistled sharply, like Jordan always did.

The noise died down instantly, though Tova frowned at Penelope as if she had done something wrong.

"The children must be divided by age," Tova said. "Five- to seven-year-olds will be with Samara in the first classroom there." She pointed to the door nearest Eliza. "Eight- to ten-year-olds will come into my classroom here. Eleven- to thirteen-year-olds will enter the class there." She pointed to the door on Eliza's other side. "And the older children, aged fourteen to sixteen, will go into this class." She gestured to the door across the hall from her classroom.

"Jake, you go in here," Shaylinn said, pushing him toward Tova. "Joey, go with Eliza."

"But I want to be with Jake," Joey said.

"You'll be with Weiss and Kaylee," Shaylinn said.

The frustrations continued as children were divided from friends and family. Mukwiv went in with the eleven- to thirteen-year-olds, as that was where his son Ian went. Eliza chose to go with the smallest children and her daughter Kaylee. And while Shaylinn was young enough to enter the fourteen- to-sixteen classroom, Eliza bid her go with the boys into Tova's class.

"Are you not still a child, Shayleen?" Tova said when Shaylinn came into her classroom.

"I'm here to observe," Shaylinn said, then swept past Tova and into the room.

Shaylinn found the outsider children — there were seven — standing in a line against one wall, looking uncomfortable. The classroom was furnished with two large GlassTop tables that already sat six students each — girls at one desk, boys at the other. There were no extra seats. A small GlassTop desk stood in the front corner of the room to the side of a Wyndo wall screen. The teacher's desk, Shaylinn assumed. Hadn't Tova prepared a place for the new children?

"Didn't you know we were coming?" Shaylinn asked Tova.

"My husband told me." Tova turned her back to Shaylinn and strode to the front of the class. "You may sit or stand in the back of the room."

Shaylinn's cheeks burned. But she needed to set a good example, make the best of things. Besides, maybe it was going to take time to find so many more desks. It was unfair for her to expect the Kindred to be able to provide for every need so quickly.

Shaylinn waved the children to follow her. "Come and sit," she said in a cheerful voice.

She settled them on the floor along the back wall, though she soon realized they were unable to see the Wyndo screen over the heads of the students. So she put the boys in one corner and the girls in the other where they could see down the space between the tables and the walls.

Tova sat at her desk in the front. "Open to page twenty-six in your history text. Resi, will you read, please?"

A little girl on the side near the door cleared her throat and wiggled in her chair. Shaylinn recognized her as Tova's older daughter. "Though Seth wanted to leave, he was now in prison, where he would remain for two years. When the day came that he was released, the fences around the city were now stone walls. He was trapped. But at least his son was free."

"Thank you," Tova said. "Hart?"

A soft voice came from the boy table. "Seth found a task as a car ... car-pen-ter. He learned to build many things. He made friends and met Syd-ney Williams. They got married and had seven children. In the year 2029, the Safe Lands Guild established a boarding school for all minors. Seth and Sydney did not want their children to go, so Seth made a way for his children to hide in their bass ... ment?"

"Basement. Thank you, Hart." Tova stood and walked to the center of the classroom. "That was the beginning of our people, the Kindred. For we were chosen to go below. We alone were saved from the evil that takes place topside. Thank the Lord and our Forefather."

"Thank the Lord and our Forefather," the children murmured.

"You weren't the only ones to be saved," Trevon said, sitting up on his knees. "We didn't grow up in the Safe Lands. We're from outside the walls."

"You will speak only when called on," Tova said.

Trevon frowned and looked to Shaylinn. "But she said a lie, didn't she?"

Shaylinn lifted her hand. "May I speak?"

Tova's body heaved up with an intake of air. She seemed to hold it, looking down her nose at Shaylinn from across the room. "You may not refute what I teach in my classroom, Shayleen. But if you have a question, I will answer."

My, my. Shaylinn phrased her question carefully. "Have you told your class who we are and where we came from?"

"You are refugees that our councils saw fit to offer asylum. You will learn our ways and adapt to them. Only if you are uninfected and join the Kindred may you marry with our people."

"Marry? These are only children, Ms. Tova. And we will not be here for long. Our elders will find a way out of the Safe Lands and we will return home to our village in the woods."

The children at the tables murmured.

"That was not a question, Shayleen," Tova said, her voice a scolding yell. "If you break the rules again, I will ask you to leave."

Shaylinn's eyes widened. How could anyone be so mean?

At that moment, the classroom door opened and Eliza leaned her head in the opening. Behind her, Shaylinn could see the outsider children filing past. "We are leaving. Shaylinn, bring out the children, please."

Leaving? Good. Shaylinn pushed herself to standing, which was harder than she had expected. Her body was getting heavy again. She ushered the children to stand.

"Where are you going?" Tova asked.

Eliza opened the door all the way and stepped inside the classroom. "Our children will not be attending your school," Eliza said. "We will not allow them to be treated as if they are of lower value. And we will not allow them to be lied to."

"Who has lied?"

"This is not the time." Eliza glanced at the children. "Samara can explain my concern, or I'd be happy to talk with you about your 'curriculum' later."

"This school is not yours to run," Tova said. "Our councils approve our curriculum."

"I mean no offense," Eliza said. "But why should your councils make the decisions for the children of Glenrock, Jack's Peak, or the Safe Lands? If you simply taught reading and math, we might be able to work together, but your righteous judgment is not acceptable."

"This is my school. I will decide what and how to teach."

"I thought this was the councils' school," Eliza said. "But never mind. We will start our own school."

"If you feel you must."

"You've given us little choice. Come, children!" Eliza waved the kids out the door. "We will learn in the park today."

They left the school and walked to the park, single file down dark corridors that smelled of soil, though Shaylinn saw no dirt. By the time she reached the park, the children had already raced ahead to the playground.

Eliza sat on a bench. "I'm going to let them play a bit. In fact, maybe we should bring them here during school hours so they can have this place to themselves. Then have our studies in the afternoon."

Shaylinn knew what Eliza wasn't saying. She wanted to keep the children away from the Kindred children as much as Tova wanted to keep the Kindred children away from them. It didn't seem right.

She sat beside Eliza on the bench. "Once we're free, we will all move away from this place, the Kindred included. Shouldn't we try to get along?"

"Once we're free, they'll find a place to build their own village," Eliza said. "They still won't want to live near any 'evildoers.' You should have seen what happened in that classroom, Shaylinn. Samara made our children stand in front of the class, then she told them that everything they had been taught up until now was a lie. As if she even knows what the children had been taught. Even Safe Lands children learn that one plus one is two. Is that a lie as well?"

Shaylinn shook her head. "Trevon spoke up to correct their history text that said the Kindred alone had been saved from evil." And Shaylinn shared how Tova had rebuked Trevon for speaking out of turn and what had happened when Shaylinn had tried to defend him.

"They've categorized everyone who is not like them as evil," Eliza said. "We're not people. We're different and therefore dangerous."

"I heard Ruston tell Levi that the Kindred believe in the Bible," Shaylinn said.

"Yes, I heard that too. But you have to watch their actions to see what they truly believe. So far, their behavior doesn't match the selfless love Papa Eli taught about," Eliza said. "They value control above everything else."

"Papa Eli did teach about selfless love," Shaylinn said, "but he was afraid of the Safe Lands too. He warned us never to come here. Yet we've seen good here, as well. Wasn't that fear as irrational as the Kindred's fear of us?"

"Papa Eli was warning us away from the thin plague. He was trying to protect us."

"But now we're here. And Omar and Mia have the plague. Does that mean they no longer deserve our love? The Bible says we're to love all people, not judge them because they are different from us. I still think we are supposed to love the Kindred, even if they treat us badly. We are to love Safe Landers, even if they have the plague. We are to love the people from Jack's Peak, even if they don't believe the same things we do. And love does not mean to be nice to their faces and judge them behind their backs or point out how we think they are evil and dangerous. It means to love them unconditionally. To accept them how they are and treat them no differently than we'd treat our own children."

Eliza wrinkled her nose. "It's not so easy to love people who hate you."

"No, I guess not. But we're supposed to do it anyway. And I don't think isolating ourselves from them is very loving. Look at how they treat Zane. Tova has exiled her own son, even after he came back and admitted that he made mistakes. We must show them that loving people is always the best way, no matter how they are different from us. No matter what kinds of mistakes they've made."

They sat together in silence awhile, watching the children play.

"The elder council will have to talk about this," Eliza said finally. "I'll ask Levi if you could come and share. I like what you said, and I know I won't be able to repeat it as well as you could."

"I'm too young to be on the elder council," Shaylinn said.

"Maybe," said Eliza. "But you're not that much younger than I am. And now that Mason is gone, well … we could use a logical perspective. You don't tend to get emotional like Mary and I do, and you know your Bible better than anyone I know."

The very idea of speaking to the elder council scared Shaylinn. But it also filled her with a surprising thrill. It was important to educate the children. But Shaylinn felt it was even more important, while they were in this place, to be an example of selfless love to the people in this place, be they Kindred or Safe Lander.

CHAPTER
6

When Omar awoke the next morning, he still hurt. The grass had only made him hungrier for the real thing. But he managed to get up and make it to the slaughterhouse by eight that morning. He had to task from eight to six with a one hour lunch break in the middle. And so he tasked. He must have boxed up a hundred chickens by the time lunchtime came. He'd put seven carcasses in the incarcerator too, and he sort of liked watching the iron door heat up until it glowed a reddish black.

Kurwin had told Omar about the strikers' cafeteria where the meals were only one credit, so Omar went there for lunch. He didn't see Kurwin or Prav in the cafeteria, so he ate as much as he could and wandered back to the slaughterhouse.

Another thing he was thankful for: working out in the yards. It stank. But with the nose plug, it was tolerable, and it wasn't nearly as bad as working inside the slaughterhouse would be.

Omar walked the yard. He found a dead chick and carried it to the incinerator. There was still ash inside from the last time someone had run it. So he set the dead chick on the floor, grabbed the hand broom, and swept the remaining ash into the ash pit. Once the inside was clean, he tossed the chick's body inside. Then he crouched down at the bottom of the incinerator and pulled out the sump trap. As many chickens as they burned, it needed to be emptied several times a day. By the time Omar had managed to pull out the drawer and carry it to the ash dumpster, his hands and arms — the whole front of his jumpsuit — was covered in pasty gray soot. Soot almost like charcoal.

It made him want to draw.

Could he draw with chicken ash? Was it unsanitary? He was already dying, so what was the worst that could happen?

Maybe he could find a container to collect the ash in. Then he could experiment with this new medium. He'd need black paper, though, since the ash was so pale in tone. Unless he could find a way to color the ash. An ink pen, maybe?

He tasked out at six o'clock that night, exhausted. His limbs trembled with every step he took away from the slaughterhouse. He hated feeling weak. What little muscle he'd built up wouldn't stay if he didn't get his act together. Did it really matter though? Was there any point? He was as good as dead here. At least he'd managed to free Shaylinn from Otley and Bender and Rewl and the Tasker General after they'd kidnapped her. He'd have to entrust her and the babies to Levi and Jordan. His babies, if Mason was right about the donor sample.

Levi and Jordan would do better for them than Omar ever could.

He sighed heavily, breathing out his depression and pain in one long exhale. He had two hours before he had to meet Prav and Kurwin to learn about the off-grid tasking, so he wandered the city called Cibelo, wishing he had the money to buy whatever he wanted. He'd come to the Safe Lands with millions of credits and big, naive dreams.

Now he was here.

He'd tasked two days now, so he should have twenty credits, minus the two credit slice of pizza he'd eaten last night and the one credit lunch he'd had in the striker's cafeteria. He was starving. For food and juice. And he no longer knew which was more important.

He was walking past a bar, smelling the hint of alcohol on the air, when he saw a man toss a half-eaten sandwich into the trash. He walked straight by the trash can and looked inside. The sandwich was just sitting there on the top, still partially wrapped in foil. It looked to be shredded steak with green peppers and onions. Omar snatched it out of the trash and took a bite.

It was still warm.

Afraid someone had seen him, he strode back the way he'd come, scarfing the sandwich down. He slipped into the narrow alley between a Sparkle cosmetics store and a SimSight dealer. He slid down against the brick wall of the Sparkle shop and savored the last few bites of the sandwich.

He was pathetic. This was what life had come to. The Owl eating trash.

The Owl was dead.

When he finished the sandwich and licked the juices from the foil, he folded the wrapper carefully and put it in his pocket. He might be able to collect ash in it from the incinerator.

He didn't know what time of night it was. And even though his stomach had been somewhat sated, his body sill hungered for brown sugar. Just thinking about it made his bones ache.

He finally forced himself to get up and walk toward the club district. He'd seen it last night. Heard the music and wanted to go. But he'd made himself stay away, afraid of what he might do in desperation.

He passed a Sweet Spot store, which sold a million types of candy. He went in and walked around. There were lots of machines where you tapped the pad to pay and the candy rolled down into a little slot. Omar checked all the little metal doors for any forgotten candy and found a gumdrop, a chocolate caramel, and a minty gumball. He was about to walk down the second row when a tasker from the shop walked up to him.

"Either buy something or get out."

"Sorry," Omar said. "I was just looking."

"I know what you were doing. Stop spending all your credits on juice and maybe you could afford to buy food."

The words shamed Omar and he left the store immediately,

chomping on the tiny bit of gum. The club district was quiet. Most places probably didn't open until at least nine or ten. Why had Prav told him to come at eight? Maybe that was when taskers got the club ready for the night. If Omar could get a second task, he might be able to afford what he needed to survive. Perhaps real tasks paid better than the measly credits strikers got. Would this Rain woman care that he was a striker? Prav didn't seem to think so.

He found Fajro, but it hadn't been easy. The place was deep in the heart of Cibelo, down several twisting roads and alleyways. Omar had had to ask five people to find the place, and several had given him a look — a glare, really — before answering. He figured it was the orange jumpsuit.

Fajro was a door in the wall between two bigger clubs. One called Ludo, which had a marquee with fuchsia and chartreuse neon lights that flashed silhouettes of curvy women. And the other called Zendax, which had piped stripes of white and black light alternating along the front, like pinstriped fabric. The lights moved too, flashing, which made it seem like the club front was made of water. It made Omar dizzy to look at it.

But Fajro was nothing more than a bright sanguine-red door, solid and glossy, set in a black wall. No lights. But the word "Fajro" had been painted on the black wall above the door in letters that looked like fire.

Someone might hire an artist to do such things in Cibelo. Maybe Omar could make credits doing some painting like this.

He knocked on the door, but no one answered. He looked for the SimPad but found none. It took him a blank moment of confusion before he saw the doorknob. He hadn't seen one since Glenrock. It seemed so foreign here.

He took hold of it and turned. It was unlocked, so he went inside.

It was dark, and though he couldn't see at first, the air smelled like incense and stims and alcohol and sweat, and Omar's stomach clenched at the very idea that he might find a breath of brown sugar here.

His eyes adjusted to the low red lights that edged the front of the bar that ran down one side of a very narrow room. No one stood behind the counter, but the shiny bottles of liquor made his mouth water, spoke to him. *Come to us, Omar. Drink us.*

He walked toward the bar.

"Can I help you?"

Omar jumped and clenched his fists. A woman had stepped out of a doorway at the back of the bar. Not a door, really, but an opening where a door should be. It was covered in shimmering red and orange and yellow strands of crystal beads.

"I'm looking for Rain," Omar said.

"Rain quenches fire," the woman said.

"Okay." Whatever that meant. "Do you know Rain?"

"You look too young for her. You look lost."

"I'm not lost, not literally anyway."

The woman cackled, baring a wide smile and very white teeth. "Aren't you funny? Who sent you?"

"Prav and Kurwin. They said to come at eight."

"It's only seven."

"I couldn't find a clock."

"How long you been here."

"In the club? I just walked in."

"In the Lowlands."

"Oh, this is my second day."

"Come on back here, where I can get a good look at you."

Omar walked the length of the bar. He tried not to look at the bottles of alcohol on display just out of his reach, but they were too beautiful.

He reached the woman and stopped. She was wearing a red and black animal-print dress. She was pretty, though desperately thin with a gaunt face and hollow green eyes. Too green. Fake. She reminded him of Red, back in the Midlands. All bones. Nothing soft left to her. Though unlike Red, she had thin, straight black hair that ran over her shoulders and curved past her breasts to her waist. Her skin was tan and flaky and decorated with lacy black lines. SimArt. Her lips were thin too, and painted maroon. The shade was off from the red in her dress. It was orangey, where the red in her dress was bluish.

73

She walked around him. Omar noticed she swayed when she walked. And when she stopped before him again, she reached out and touched his face with the tips of her fingers, which made him shiver. She was kind of creepy, for some reason.

"Walls, you're pretty," she said. "What's your name?"

"Omar."

"Can I get you a drink, Omar?"

"Can I get a vape of brown sugar?"

She stared at him a moment, then her lips curved into a slow smile. "Brown sugar is not a drink, sugar."

He swallowed, thirstier now that the options had been narrowed. "I'll have a drink. Anything is fine."

She swayed past him and behind the bar. She set two shot glasses on the counter and picked up a bottle of something clear. She filled only the bottom of the glasses, an inch of liquid, leaving most of the glass empty. He was an idiot. He should have asked for a beer.

She pushed one glass toward him. It slid across the shiny counter, scraping, the sound matching the ache in his bones. Her fingers were long and thin and tipped with red, which made him think of Belbeline.

He grimaced at the memory, grabbed the glass, and swallowed the contents. The liquid burned as it trickled down his throat. He set the glass on the counter and wiped his mouth with the back of his sleeve.

"You're a hungry one."

He didn't know what she meant, so he said nothing. "You're Rain then?"

"Like water from the sky, sugar."

Um ... okay. "Prav said I could get brown sugar if I tasked for you."

"If you task for me, you can get anything you want, Valentine."

She was teasing him. "So what's the task? Is there an application?"

"It's hardly a task at all, really." Rain scratched her fingernail along the neckline of her dress and looked deep into his eyes. "Women in the Lowlands are lonely, Omar. The men would rather go to the clubs and pay young striker women to play than look for companionship

74

amongst women their own age. Don't all women deserve the same pleasures in life? Hmm?"

What did that have to do with anything? "I suppose. But aren't there clubs for women to — "

"Yes, yes." She waved her hand. "They have them, of course. But women like being treated special. And those clubs ... It's shallow there, Omar. Women want more. I provide them with more."

Oh. He didn't like where she was going. "What exactly would I have to do?"

"Again, you're missing the point. You don't *have to* do anything. You have a right to enjoy life as much as the rest of us."

He was tired of her games already. "Stop saying nothing. Just tell me the truth."

"It's simple, really. I've created the ultimate dating service."

Omar's stomach tightened. "Would I get to pick who I date?"

"No, sugar. I pick." Rain pointed at her chest. "And only when I get confirmation from my client that things went well will I pay you."

Omar felt very small then. She would give him the stims he wanted — needed — but only if he traded paint with whomever she wanted. "Wouldn't that make me a ... uh ... prostitute?" He ran his hand through his hair, embarrassed. He'd never in his life heard of a male prostitute. He couldn't believe it was really a real thing. And that he was still standing there.

"Now why would you go and put a label on such freedoms?" Rain asked.

Label? "It is what it is. I mean, what's free about it? Nothing."

"It is what you make it, Omar. Good attitudes are contagious, you know. You don't have to be so negative."

He wasn't being negative. This was twisted. There was no way he could do such a thing. Unless ... "Could I vape first?"

Rain laughed, and it almost sounded like music. Omar bet she could sing. "My clients don't pay to play with juiced-up men. And you've already admitted to being a sweet tooth for brown sugar. That stuff makes you nod into a coma."

"I could do grass first."

"Not from me. My offer stands. Your choice. Take it or leave it."

Leave it, Omar, you fool. "Can I think about it?"

"Sure. Think all you need to, sugar." She reached under the counter and pulled out a PV, which she set on the surface and rolled from one hand to the other. He watched it. It was black and thick. A man's PV. He swallowed. He could take it from her. He had to be stronger than she was. He glanced around the room for yellow cameras and instead saw a black one looking down on him.

"You're not thinking of being naughty, are you, Omar? My body-guards wouldn't like that."

Omar looked into her eyes, winced a little as a bone-aching shiver attacked. He slouched onto the nearest barstool and watched the PV roll back and forth, back and forth. He wished Mason were here to haul him out of this place. He knew he should leave, but the PV had hypnotized him.

"I'll tell you what, sugar. You spend an hour with me, I'll not only give you a vial of brown sugar, I'll let you keep this here PV as a present. Do you like presents?"

"*With* you?"

"I have to know what my boys are capable of, don't I?"

Omar knew he should leave or pray or do something sensible. But all he could do was watch the rolling PV, the way the black cylinder reflected on the shiny gold counter. He felt sick in so many ways. Sick to his stomach, sick in his bones, sick in his mind, sick in his very soul. Sick at the arousal rising in him despite himself. He was dying. If she'd give him a ten, maybe if he took it fast he could end everything, finally be at peace. Unless he went to hell, of course.

He knew that Shaylinn would say that heaven and hell wasn't about his actions but his relationship with God. But maybe she was wrong. Maybe there was no hell. Maybe everyone went to heaven. Or maybe there was no heaven, no God, just nothingness. Darkness. Emptiness. Or maybe another life. Or maybe Bliss for everyone.

"Okay," he said, hating himself more than ever. He wanted to cry at that thought, but he shook it off. He didn't have to like himself. He just needed to survive long enough to get that PV filled with brown sugar.

She smiled at him, like she'd won a great victory, then came out from behind the counter and reached for his hand. She held the PV in her other hand where he couldn't reach it. Yet.

He slid off the stool and took her hand lightly, and she pulled him through the beaded curtain.

CHAPTER 7

Someone grabbed Mason's ankles and pulled. His body slid off the mattress and onto the floor. He looked up into Scorpion's angry, black eyes.

Mason's eyes flashed open, his pulse throbbing in his ears, his hand stinging from the effects of his SimAlarm. Time to get up. It had been a dream. Only a dream. Anxiety gripped him tighter than any man's fist, and he lay staring at the bunks above and the ceiling, breathing slowly to calm himself down. People were moving in the room.

"Time to get up, kid."

Mason's head twitched as he found the source of the voice. Rock Fist was sitting up on his bed, looking down on Mason from his bottom bunk.

Mason stretched until he could see the glowing blue digits of the clock on the center of the wall where the doors led into the room. It was 5:27 a.m. "I don't need to wake for another hour."

"We've got the car wash on Saturdays. It's mandatory."

"Oh." Mason sat up. "Where do I go?"

"Just follow the crowd."

Mason would follow Rock Fist, not the crowd. Many of the guys were already leaving. Mason made a project of making his bed, stalling in hopes that Rock would get up and walk to the door. But Rock appeared to have fallen asleep sitting up, which Mason found strange for the man who'd told him to wake up.

Then he saw the man's lips moving. Could he be praying? The very idea chastened Mason at how little time he'd devoted to prayer since they'd come to this place. Sure, he prayed continually, but they weren't prayers of devotion and praise or any sort of meditation on Scriptures he'd memorized. His were prayers of need, a string of selfish, "Help me with this" or "Help me with that." But before he had the chance to bow his own head, Rock opened his eyes and stood up.

He gathered the sheet off his bed. "Better go now, kid. Bring your sheet if you want a clean one."

Mason was already getting to his feet. He left his sheet, though. One night was clean enough for him.

He followed Rock out into the hallway and to the stairwell. They went down past the first floor and into the basement, stopping just past the cafeteria, where a line of men stretched to the end of the basement hallway.

Rock turned around in line and looked down on Mason. "Where you tasking, kid?"

"I'm a farmhand on the feedlot," Mason said.

"You know what time you take lunch?"

"I have to work it out each day with the others."

"Try to come eat lunch with me today," Rock said. "Eat late, if you can. At two. No one should complain about that. There's a Café Eat in Cibelo over by the entrance to sector one. Behind that is a place called the Get Out Now Diner. Meet me at the table in the back. I'll buy."

Mason wanted to refuse, but he couldn't think of a reason to, and he didn't want to risk angering his protector. "Okay." He only hoped that Rock Fist's ideas of payback were something Mason could agree to.

The line was moving fairly quickly, and soon Rock and Mason turned into a steamy room tiled in one-inch squares that were turquoise, white, or light blue. Inside the door, the line split into ten shorter ones that were queued up behind tile privacy walls. An enforcer stood at the door in front of a SimPad that was mounted on the wall.

Rock touched his fist to the pad. It beeped.

The enforcer read the screen and said, "Line three."

Rock Fist winked at Mason and walked to line three, standing behind four other men.

Mason stepped forward and touched his fist to the SimPad. It beeped, and the enforcer said, "Huh. Line one, shell, and don't forget to use soap."

Mason frowned as he walked past the enforcer and into line one. He counted the days since he'd last showered. It had to have been the morning before he and Omar had helped Kendall move up to the cabin. A full week ago, he guessed.

There were only two men ahead of him, lined up behind a semi-transparent shower curtain. He could see the peachy shape of a body inside the shower. A few minutes later the body moved out the other side. The man at the front of the line already had his socks and shoes off. They were sitting on the floor between his feet and a wadded-up bed sheet. He stripped off his orange jumpsuit and underwear, dropped everything in a chute before the shower, then went inside.

Car wash, indeed.

Mason wasn't thrilled with the idea of undressing in front of anyone — cameras included — but by the time his turn came, there was still no one in line behind him except the enforcer at the front door and the men being sorted into lines. He didn't know why his line was so short, but he was glad of it, at least for his first car wash experience. The camera, he'd have to get used to.

When he saw the man in the shower exit, Mason stripped off his clothes, dumped them down the chute, and went in, annoyed to see a camera overhead in the shower itself. Eyes were everywhere for the strikers. He quickly discovered the water was a single push button that sprayed high-powered streams of steamy water down on his head for ten seconds at a time. The soap was also a button that left a liquid stream on his palm. He lathered and rinsed quickly, then peeked around the second curtain into another curtained area with bins on both sides. Clean towels on the right, wet towels on the left. Then five bins of orange fabric on the right and five bins of white fabric on the left. Clean jumpsuits and underwear. Each bin was marked with a letter to indicate size. Then stacks of clean bed sheets.

Mason stepped out of the shower and grabbed a towel. He wrapped it around his waist, then grabbed a pair of underwear out of the medium bin. He hadn't bothered to check the size of the clothes he'd been wearing. He held them up and thought they looked okay.

Behind him, the shower started. Someone was coming through. He pulled on the underwear as fast as he could over his wet legs, then ran the towel over the rest of him and tossed it in the bin, not bothering to do a very good job. He was too panicked with the idea of someone stepping into his area of the curtain before he left it. He grabbed a medium jumpsuit and put it on. He'd barely zipped it up when the shower curtain behind him slid aside. Mason quickly stepped around the next curtain. The jumpsuit stuck to his arms and back where his skin was still wet.

In the next section, a medic was sitting on a small desk, swinging his legs. He stared at Mason a moment, then gestured to a SimPad on the desk. "Tap, please."

"Oh, right." Mason tapped his fist.

The medic watched the results screen and hummed. "No plague?" He looked up, his gaze roaming over Mason's body. "Wow, okay, then. No meds for you. Any health issues to report? Injuries?"

"No, sir."

"How long you been here?"

"Just one night."

"You okay in your bunk? No one assaulted you?"

Mason swallowed. "Someone tried to, but, uh, someone else helped me."

The medic hummed again. "Be careful making deals. Protectors usually want something in exchange for protecting you. Be sure to tell the enforcers if someone is harassing you. Most try to help if they can. This isn't a pleasant place to live, I'm sorry to say."

"You live here?"

"No. I live in a shoebox of an apartment two blocks away. But that's a hundred times better than what you've got."

That figured. *Lawten*, anyway. "Do you need more medics? I tasked as a medic in the Highlands before I came here."

The medic shook his head. "That's not for me to decide. They know your skills. They put you where they want to put you. Strikers don't get the luxury of retask testing. Work hard, and maybe they'll move you someday. I'm sorry, but you need to keep the line moving. Shoes and socks through that curtain."

"Thanks," Mason said.

"Find pleasure if you can," the medic said.

"Yeah, sure." Mason walked past the next curtain and found a bench on one wall and a metal door in the wall on the other side, like some kind of microwave oven. There was a SimPad beside the metal door, so he tapped his fist against it. Something in the wall ground together like gears shifting. There was a clump behind the door. Mason slid the door to the side. A pair of boots and a pair of socks sat inside.

Convenient. Mason grabbed the socks and boots and sat down to put them on. He was tying his second boot when voices rose in the medic booth behind him.

"Well, I need something! I can't take this anymore. Why don't you have mercy vapes here?"

"It will be better for you to get clean," the medic said.

"I don't want to get clean. I need some golden ice."

Mason thought of Omar then, and wondered if his brother's sessions with the car wash medic sounded similar. He stepped past the next curtain and found he'd reached the end of the car wash. A narrow corridor led back to the basement hallway.

Time to go to the feedlot.

It was his first full day on the field, and he didn't mind it at all. The cows were in good humor despite their crowded living conditions. He walked the first row from pen one to eighteen and back, checking the cows for sores, pink eye, or injury, trying to get a feel for what was normal behavior here. He found nothing odd in any of the animals.

He tried to forget about what the medic had told him about protectors wanting something in return, but he couldn't stop imagining all kinds of horrors that Rock Fist might demand of him.

The lunch hour arrived quicker than he expected. Coy and Wayd went first, and when they returned, Brondon and Prezan left.

Coy found him in Pen 6. "You can go to lunch now. Wayd and I can watch the pens."

"I'd rather wait until two, if that's okay." Though he'd rather not see Rock at all.

"Can you last that long? I hear the food in the striker's caf isn't the most filling."

"I can last," Mason said. "I'm meeting someone." Hopefully a friend and not a pervert.

At a quarter 'til two, Mason left. He found the Café Eat easily enough, but it took him longer to locate the diner. It was a dark doorway between a Lift and a place called Garrick's, which looked like some sort of dance club.

Mason slipped inside the diner, very much on edge. It was dark inside. A counter ran along the left-hand wall. Booths on the right. Only five. Small place. He spotted Rock Fist sitting at the booth in the very back on the side facing the door. He waved Mason back.

Mason limped toward the table. As he approached, he saw that Rock wasn't alone. He was sitting with two women, though Mason could only see the backs of their heads. He was three steps away when their heads turned.

Then he had to grip the booth not to fall over.

"Mother?"

And Shanna, who was Jordan's, Jemma's, and Shaylinn's mother. Alive and well? He could only gape.

"Praise God!" Mother jumped out of the booth and crushed Mason in a trembling embrace. Her familiar smell stunned him, for she couldn't possibly have access to the same soaps and herbs to clean her hair as she'd had in Glenrock, yet the smell was still there. His mother.

She pulled back and stroked his face, hair, shoulders. "You look well. Are you?" Her eyes were filled with tears. "Are you okay?"

"I'm fine. Terribly mortified at my new living arrangements, but Mr. Rock Fist has, thankfully, come to my aid." He gestured to Rock Fist, his arm trembling with adrenaline. He hadn't realized just how terrified he'd been of Rock Fist until now. But God was good. He'd given Mason a guardian angel.

Mother took hold of Mason's hand and turned to grin at Rock. "Yes, he's wonderful, isn't he?" And the sound of adoration in her tone gave Mason pause. "Sit down, here." Mother all but pushed Mason into the booth beside Shanna, who slid farther in. Then she sat next to Rock Fist, across from Mason.

"Mason, my children?" Shanna said. "Are they okay?"

"And Levi and Omar," Mother added. "Everyone, really. We never thought we'd see any of you again. Tell us everything."

"Okay, well, everyone is fine, the last I heard. Naomi had her baby. A boy they named Harvey."

"Oh!" Shanna cupped her hand over her mouth as tears materialized instantly and rolled down her cheeks.

"And Jordan performed a wedding for Levi and Jemma about a month ago."

"Good," Mother said. "Are the women still in the harem?"

"No, we helped the women escape the night of Lonn's liberation ceremony, which was almost two months ago."

Rock Fist grunted. "Two months ago?"

"That's right. And the children are free as well. We helped them escape from the boarding school just last week. Levi befriended some rebels, and though some betrayed us, some did not. Last I heard, everyone was moving underground into the basements."

"And Omar?" Mother asked.

"Omar is here somewhere, though they did not tell me where and

I haven't seen him in my building. We were liberated together. Omar is struggling. He's become addicted to vaping opiates. He's likely in a great deal of pain right now. He'd been suffering from withdrawal while we were in the RC."

His mother turned to Rock Fist. "Can we find him?"

"He won't be in sector six," Rock said. "They never put friends together."

"Is there anything worse than the feedlot?" Mason asked. "The liberator let on that the task director general was punishing us."

Rock Fist chuckled at this. "You lucked out then. The feedlot isn't bad at all. Though you do have the worst housing. As far as worst tasks, sewage cleaner or tasking in the waste treatment plant rank highest. Chimney sweep is a pretty rough job. And any slaughterhouse, I'd say. The dairy isn't too pleasant, either."

"What sectors are all those?" Mother asked.

"Dairy is eight and there's a slaughterhouse in five, six, and seven. Chimneys and sewage tasks in all of them."

"Is this just a prison for Xed people? Strikers?" Mason asked. "Where do the other liberated people go?"

"Everybody is here," Rock Fist said. "See, Loca and Liberté, the founders of the Safe Lands, wanted to be young forever. They were terrified of old age. Plus, no one wanted to work hard. People just wanted to play. So they decided it would be better to play when you're young, then work when you're old."

"Why were you and Omar liberated?" Shanna asked Mason.

"We were caught after breaking into Champion House. General Otley and a rebel named Bender had colluded to frame Lawten Renzor for several crimes. To do so, Bender had kidnapped Shaylinn to make it appear that Renzor was helping the pregnant Outsider fugitives get medical care. So we went in to rescue Shaylinn." And Ciddah.

"Shaylinn is pregnant?" Shanna asked.

"I'm sorry, yes," Mason said. "With Omar's twins."

"Omar?" Mother choked on her water and set down the glass. Rock rubbed her back

Mason berated himself for his lack of tact. "I'm sorry. I should have said that first."

"Omar and Shaylinn?" Shanna asked. "I didn't even know they were friends."

"It didn't happen like that," Mason said. "Shaylinn was in the harem. Omar was the donor whose sample they used to … create the children. He was the only man from Glenrock who complied. I expect at least one woman from Jack's Peak will be matched with his donation as well. The Surrogacy Center tries to vary the DNA pairings, though I checked Jennifer's chart, and she was not impregnated with Omar's sample. Nor was Mia."

"That boy," Mother said. "What has he done to himself? To all of us?"

Mason hadn't meant to make Omar look bad. "You should also know that Omar came back to us. It's still difficult for many people, Eliza and Jordan especially, but the new elders of Glenrock offered forgiveness to Omar and he's been working with us against the Safe Lands. Shaylinn's pregnancy has given Omar purpose, I believe. He risked his life to save her from the task director and General Otley."

"Did General Otley succeed in framing Renzor?" Rock Fist asked.

"No. A rebel named Bender shot and killed General Otley after Otley killed Bender's son, Rewl. And we helped Shaylinn and Ciddah and Baby Promise escape before Otley's men could confirm they were there. We took away all of Otley's planted evidence."

"Baby Promise is Kendall's child?" Mother asked.

"That's right," Mason said.

"And who is Ciddah?"

Mason looked at the tabletop. "She was the medic in the Surragacy Center."

"The blonde girl," Mother said. "I remember. She told me I was too old to conceive." Mother laughed. "As if I didn't already know that."

"This was your medic?" Rock Fist asked. "The one you stole from Renzor?"

Mason's cheeks filled with heat. He'd forgotten that he'd told Rock

Fist that he'd been liberated for stealing Lawten's girl. "Yes, I tasked under her in the SC."

"Who did you steal?" Mother asked. "What does that mean?"

"How did the medic play into Otley's plan?" Rock Fist asked. "And Baby Promise?"

Mason was happy to answer Rock's question over his mother's. "Right, well, Renzor had taken Ciddah to be his lifer — against her will," he added, reminding himself of the fact. "And Baby Promise is his own blood, a child he conceived with Kendall Collin after purchasing her from Wyoming. Ciddah says Lawten has always wanted to have a family of Old. Someone told me Lawten saw it as an experiment, though that doesn't make sense to me. Otley said that Lawten had the medic to provide medical care for the outsider women. And he said Lawten had kidnapped Baby Promise, but I don't recall the motive for that accusation."

"Who's the rebel friend Levi is working with?" Rock Fist asked.

"Ruston. And Zane."

Mother turned to Rock, her eyes searching his.

"Good men. Honest," Rock said to her, and she seemed to relax.

"Is anyone else pregnant?" Mother asked. "You said Mia and someone from Jack's Peak?"

"Yes. I don't know which of the Jack's Peak women, as I wasn't able to confirm that before I went into hiding. But Jennifer and Mia are. Mia by natural means, as she fell in love with a piano player, so she and her child are infected. Jennifer became impregnated because Mia refused to be rescued when we freed the women from the harem — Jennifer insisted on staying with her daughter. Jennifer's donor is from Wyoming, and I don't believe she or her child are infected."

"Foolish women," Mother muttered.

"Mason, I'm so sorry," Shanna said. "I know that you and Mia were to be married."

"Oh, I'm not sorry for that reason," Mason said. "My marrying Mia was my father's idea, not mine."

"And now you have the medic," Rock Fist said.

Mother looked at Mason, eyebrows raised. "You *have*?"

"No, now I am here," Mason said, hoping to change the subject. "So liberation is nothing more than a penal colony?"

"Someone has to do all the hard labor so that those in the Highlands and Midlands can task and play," Rock said. "Did you never find it odd that Safe Lands nationals only tasked four to six hours a day, four days a week?"

Mason had not, though he should have. He'd been too busy worrying about finding a cure for the plague to think about the economy. "I did notice the exorbitant wealth, but I did not take the time to consider where it was being manufactured. And Ruston mentioned factories in the Midlands, so I assumed ..."

"Oh, there are factories there, sure," Rock said. "We can't do everything down here. But we do the hardest labor. Without us, there would be nothing for the people to find pleasure in."

"Mason, you need to eat," Mother said. "And then I want to find Omar. He might not be as lucky as you to find a rebel in his prison block."

"Wait, you're a rebel?" Mason asked Rock Fist. That explained how he would have known Ruston and Zane.

"He was their leader!" Mother exclaimed, her expression beaming with pride. She clutched Rock's arm, and understanding settled over Mason with a chill. His mother and this man were together. Romantically. A couple.

"Rock Fist isn't my name, kid. Scorpion and the rest of 2C, they give everyone nicknames. I got mine when Scorpion tried to claim me and I turned his face into road kill."

Mason shuddered at the very thought. "So your name is ...?"

"Richark Lonn."

Mason limped back to the feedlot in a daze. Rock Fist was Richark Lonn, the Safe Lands rebel he had been researching back in the

Midlands. Worse: His mother was romantically involved with Richark Lonn. He wanted that story, for sure, but there was so much Mason wanted to ask the man about the thin plague and why he'd been fired from his medic task, and what he'd been looking for in the MC, but they'd taken too long reminiscing and there hadn't been time. Lonn had said Mason would get in trouble if he were late to return. So Mason had left with plans to go back for dinner.

He was making his way up the feed alley between the first and second rows when he caught sight of a penrider in row two. A bald one. With SimArt all over his head. The closer Mason got, the clearer the artwork became. Puzzle pieces.

It was Scorpion.

Mason stared across the pens, shocked to see the bully outside their bunk. And then Scorpion looked his way and grinned. Not in a friendly way.

"That's one you don't want to mess with," someone said.

Mason looked behind him and found Wayd standing beside a wheelbarrow, holding a shovel.

"Who is he?" Mason asked, curious to learn how those outside bunk 2C viewed the man.

"Score Pinion. But people call him Scorpion."

Mason shuddered at the sound of that name. "Does Gacy like him? I mean, he got promoted to penrider, right?"

"I don't think anyone likes him. But believe it or not, he's a hard worker." Wayd scooped up a shovel full of manure and dumped it into the wheelbarrow. "I heard he was a murderer in the Midlands before coming here. And not because he was angry or vengeful. He just likes killing. Be thankful you're not in the second row."

Mason was desperately thankful he wasn't in the second row and that Richark Lonn was in bunk 2C, and he spent the remainder of his shift telling God just how thankful he was.

Mason returned to the Get Out Now Diner for dinner, where Lonn had promised to show him something worthwhile. Mason didn't think anything could top the discovery that his mother was alive and well and romantically linked with the leader of the Black Army, but who knew? He wasn't about to spend another meal in the striker's cafeteria when he could be with his mother.

Mason entered the diner and found his mother, Shanna, his aunt Janie, and Lonn in the back booth. Had they even left?

"Sit, Mason," Lonn said. "I want to explain how our rebellion works in the Lowlands."

Mason sat beside Shanna. "You have a rebellion here?"

"Of course. But they make it difficult. Were you told about rebel tags?"

"Only when you asked me if I'd been tagged a rebel."

"Rebel tags keep rebels from gathering at once. If two or more rebels are within ten yards of one another for more than ten minutes, their SimAlarms will go off."

"Must make going to the movies troublesome," Mason said.

"Most theaters will let a rebel know if another rebel bought a ticket before you," Lonn said. "But you get the idea. It's rather unpleasant, and it's forced us to get creative."

"How?" Mason asked.

"By some miracle, you outsiders weren't tagged rebels, not even after you broke into Champion House. That's fortunate — for all of us."

"Did you find Omar?" Mason asked.

"He did." Mother beamed at Lonn.

"He's in poultry. Sector six," Lonn said. "And he's living in the sector six Strikers' Residence, which is safe compared to where we live. I'm going to try and contact him over the next few days. Just need to figure out where they have him tasking."

"Why did Mason get put in maximum security? Omar had three strikes, right, Mason? And you only have one."

Mason didn't answer. His feelings for Ciddah were private. He'd acted like a fool in front of Levi when he'd thought Ciddah's life was in danger, but now he was just embarrassed that he'd said anything.

"Task director is punishing him," Lonn said.

"Why? What did you do to make him so angry?"

A smile broke out on Mason's face. He tried and failed to fight it. It was kind of funny, he supposed.

"He stole Renzor's girl," Lonn said. "Like we said at lunch."

"*You* stole a girl?" Shanna shot him a skeptical glance.

For some reason that comment made Mason defensive. "She likes me. Is that really so difficult to believe? She's a medic, if that helps you."

"That does, actually," his mother said. "But Mason, a Safe Lander? You don't actually care for this girl, do you?"

Mason was pretty sure he loved Ciddah Rourke, not that he was experienced enough in such things to know for certain. But he wasn't about to tell his mother any of it. "So how do the rebels make plans if you can't meet?" he asked Lonn.

"The conversation about the medic is not over," Mother said.

Lonn chuckled. "It's not easy. Everything takes a very long time. But we've set up a meeting chain. Each rebel is assigned another. When a message needs to be spread, it starts at the top and works its way down."

"Does it work in reverse as well?" Mason asked. "If someone wanted to talk to you?"

"Yes," Lonn said, "though it's not as fast that way. There are no transmitters down here. Reputables can communicate through their Wyndo wall screens, but everything is monitored heavily. So those with Wyndos can make plans to meet through the wall screens, but no one passes messages that way. We've learned the art of patience. We're working on a plan now, but it's taking awhile to get everything in place."

"What's the plan?"

"Trucks take raw goods into the Midlands for distribution. From what I've learned, those drivers only move the goods as far as the wall. Then there are the turnstiles."

"Which are what?"

"Think of that chamber the Midland enforcers put you in, that the Lowland enforcers took you out of when you came here. The one with a door on each side. Like that, only big enough for a truck. They use the turnstiles to keep Lowlanders from speaking with anyone else. They're what keep us from getting back to the Midlands. There are no other doors. There are no storm drains down here, at least not big enough to walk through. And we can't get into the tube."

"What's the tube?" Mason asked.

"The road that cuts through the Lowlands from the entrance to the Safe Lands to the Lowland/Midland Gate. The Lowlands is a prison, even for the reputables. And the Safe Lands government can't afford to let that secret out, or their way of life is over."

"You said that before. What's a 'reputable'?"

"Someone who was liberated at forty," Lonn said. "Or in your mother's case, because she was an outsider and could no longer bear children."

"I see. So you plan to sneak into one of the turnstiles?"

"We figure one of us can hide in the back of a truck, buried under lettuce or something. As long as we cut out our SimTag first."

"Someone must have tried that already."

"People have cut out their SimTags, yes. They've tried to sneak through the turnstiles. And they've even tried to scale the walls, but there are motion detectors on them. And they're much higher here than in the Highlands and Midlands too. But from what I've been able to learn, no one has tried to hide in a truck. So we're going to."

"When?"

"In a few weeks."

"And who are you going to send through?"

"Guy by the name of Grady. He was one of my men. Liberated a few years before me. He's high up in the rebellion down here. Earned the right to be the one to go."

"I hope it works," Mother said.

"I think it will. Unless there is technology I don't understand or know about, which is always a possibility."

Mason ate his salad in silence for a few bites and thought about the technology in the Safe Lands, which made him think of the advanced health care and their failure to find a cure for the thin plague. "I have a lot of questions for you," Mason said to Lonn.

Lonn narrowed his eyes. "About what?"

"Why you got fired from the MC. What you were looking into. And what part Lawten Renzor played in the whole thing."

"Later," Lonn said, tapping the location of his SimTag. "It's almost time to go."

Sure enough, a few bites of salad later, Mason's SimAlarm warned him that it was ten minutes until curfew. He stood to leave. Shanna and Janie followed him to the door. And when Mason turned back, he saw Lonn and his mother lingering beside the table, holding hands and talking to each other. Then Lonn quickly kissed his mother on the lips and they embraced.

Mason could only stare.

"I know it's only been a few months since Justin was killed," Shanna said, "but ... Rich is very good to her."

Rich? Mason glanced at Shanna, eyebrows raised.

"It's only that Justin ..." Shanna frowned. "He never ..." She twisted her lips. "Sometimes arranged marriages are difficult, Mason. I'm glad you didn't have to marry Mia, though I'm sorry over what's become of her. But perhaps you both have a chance at happiness now."

Happiness? Mason didn't want to be negative, but he doubted such a thing was possible anymore. He'd been liberated, for crying out loud. Though as he looked back to his mother and Lonn and saw the man hold one side of his mother's face in his hand, smiling as he spoke to her, their foreheads touching, her lips curved in a smile, Mason did wonder. He couldn't recall ever seeing his parents kiss, though they must have since they produced three sons.

Much had changed about romance in Mason's mind, though he

still had much to figure out. But if his mother could choose love with a Safe Lands national, why couldn't he?

For one simple reason. Because he was here, in the Lowlands, and Ciddah was not.

CHAPTER
8

There's wisdom in your words, Shaylinn," Aunt Chipeta said. "But I still don't feel comfortable letting our children go to their school. Not if the teachers belittle them."

"I agree," Levi said. "Can you ladies create your own curriculum?"

"We'll manage," Eliza said. "But we should heed Shaylinn's advice and find other ways to befriend the Kindred."

"Think on it, all of you. And I will as well." But at the moment Levi couldn't really be bothered with whether or not the Kindred liked him. He had more important things to worry about. They'd combined their elder council meeting with the rebel meeting because the only time the women could all get away was at night, and that was also when Zane and Ruston were free. "So now that moves us to the subject of the Jack's Peak women in the harem."

"We need someone who's been there," Zane said. "I mean, even if I could turn off the cameras, I don't know my way around there. None of us do. How will you know where to go?"

"I know where to go," Jemma said. "I could come with you and — "

"No." As if Levi would put his wife in danger.

"Don't just say no without thinking it through," Ruston said. "I realize the idea of sending any of the women back there is not a pleasant one, but she could be a great help."

"*No*," Levi said. "That is not an option. Can we find a way to communicate with them?"

"There's no way to communicate with them," Zane said. "Not secretly. Everything is monitored."

"Who else can go, Levi?" Jemma said. "Hazel needs Chipeta. Aunt Mary's knees are too bad. Eliza's children need their mother. Naomi has the baby and is still recovering from childbirth. And Shay . . . she can't go back there, Levi. I'm the only option. Unless you're willing to use Ciddah."

Levi gritted his teeth. "We can't trust Ciddah."

"I think we can," Naomi said. "She's been such a help with the babies. And she's so sweet."

"She lied to Mason, and very convincingly, if I understand things correctly," Levi said. "She's good at what she does. She stays here."

"Then let me help," Jemma said.

Levi glared at his wife. "We'll talk about this later."

"I want to get my wife out now," Beshup said. "It might already be too late for her."

"I agree," Mukwiv said. "My wife is not as young as the others. If something goes wrong, she could be liberated."

"And now that they took the lenses from Mason and Omar," Jemma said, "we still don't know what that means."

Levi shook his head at his wife. "Jemma can draw a map. Then we'll know where to go and she can stay here."

"Levi, I can't draw."

"It doesn't have to be like Omar's art. Just a simple map with arrows and stuff."

"I promise you, I can't," Jemma said.

"Between the six of you, I'm sure you can," Levi said.

Jemma glared at him, and he knew she wanted to go. Why she wanted to go, however, he couldn't guess.

"Let's try a map first," Levi said. "Please."

And so the women set to work drawing a map, and when it was complete and they all somewhat agreed on how it looked, they handed it over to Levi. The only problem was that no one knew which rooms the women might be living in. According to Jemma, there were two floors with suites.

"It's silly, Levi," Jemma said to him that night. "Just let me come with you. We'll be twice as fast with me as a guide."

"You're not coming with us."

"Why? Why do you get to decide?"

"Because I'm the village elder and I'm your husband."

"And that makes you my boss?"

"Yes! I mean, no. I just … don't want anything to happen to you."

"You're a liar. You think you can control me. Keep me here. You think I should obey your every word."

"I don't think that."

"So you are going to become just like your father, is that it? Are you going to hit me too?"

Levi could only stare at her. He was so angry he wanted to shake her. Did that prove her point? So he left the room, then the house.

He stormed through the corridors, so desperately angry. And hurt. He knew people had talked about his father's temper. But he really thought no one knew that Elder Justin had ever struck his wife. And he hadn't … often.

Maybe his mother had told someone.

But that didn't mean Levi would harm Jemma. Ever! Why had she said that? Did she think he would? Was she afraid of him? Had he given her reason to fear him? He hadn't. Had he? Surely he hadn't.

He couldn't fathom why she'd said such a thing.

Hours later, when he was certain he'd walked every inch of the underground corridors, he ended up at Ruston's house. The man invited him in, gave him a piece of some kind of cake his wife had made. Levi ate it in silence.

"I like to go on walks when Tova and I have a fight."

"What makes you think Jemma and I fought?"

Ruston chuckled. "Didn't you?"

"She said so many mean things."

"Women do that. Some men do too, I suppose, but men are usually quiet in a fight. The women do most of the talking."

"Yelling, you mean. She cut me with words. I swear I must be bleeding." Levi looked at his arms, turned his hands over.

"I doubt she meant any of it. Women, they get emotional. Half of the fight takes place in their imaginations."

"Yes. She yelled at me for things I hadn't done."

"But what is she really angry about? That's all you need to focus on."

"She's mad I won't let her help with the harem rescue."

Ruston smiled at him kindly. "And why won't you?" At Levi's glare, he added, "Humor me."

"Because she could get hurt or arrested. I could lose her. I lost her once. It was agony."

"What do you love about her?"

Levi frowned. "What's that have to do with —"

"Humor me again, please."

Levi sighed and rubbed his temple. "Fine. Jemma, she's kind. And smart. And when I look at her, it's always a shock that *she* loves me. Such an amazing, beautiful creature … and she's mine."

"And you're hers."

"Yeah, so?"

"You're a team. That means give and take. Why should you get to be the only brave one?"

"I told you, it's not safe."

"Nor is it safe for you."

Levi had no reply to that.

"You're going to have to let go of control, Levi," Ruston said. "That can be a difficult thing. And I'm not necessarily saying that Jemma should come with us. But if you want to have peace in your house, if you want to *keep* that woman in love with you, you're going to have to trust her. Otherwise, her love will slowly turn into resentment."

So Levi went home. The lights in the house were all out. He walked carefully so he didn't wake Trevon and Grayn, who had taken to sleeping on the couches to be apart from the little boys in the boys' bedroom.

The lights in his bedroom were off as well. He changed in the dark and climbed into bed, trying not to wake his wife.

"Where have you been?"

So much for not waking Jemma. "Walking. Went to Ruston's house."

"Why?"

"Don't know. He says I need to let go of control."

A pause. "Interesting."

"You think I'm controlling?"

"I think you worry too much."

Levi stared into the darkness above. "The village elder has a lot of responsibilities."

"Yes, I know. And you handle them well. But fretting isn't going to change anything. It's only making you cranky and impossible to be around. Trust God to take care of us. He will, you know."

But Levi didn't know about that. Sometimes people died, like his father and uncles and Papa Eli. Like Susan and little Sophie. "Why do you want to come on the harem rescue?"

"Because I can help. My presence can shave ten minutes off your time. I promise you."

"That's it? You just want to help us be fast?"

There was silence again for a long moment, and Levi wondered if his wife had fallen asleep. But then she spoke. "I'm trapped here, Levi." And there were tears in her voice, like she was struggling to say these words. "I want to help. And this is a place where I can help. I'm the best one for the job. Me. Only me."

"It means a lot to you? To come?"

"Yes."

Levi felt like the next words might kill him, but he said them anyway. "Then come.

99

"I don't like it," Levi said. He and Jemma were in the nest with Zane, sitting in chairs beside him, looking at his GlassTop computer screen, where Zane had somehow pulled up a real floor plan of the inside of the harem.

"It's the best we can do," Zane said. "I can't find a camera for that back stairwell. So that's how you go in. Jemma leads the way. Once you're inside, you might have to stun the matron and an enforcer or two, so be ready. Then you come out the way you went in. It's pretty easy, really. What don't you like about it?"

What Levi didn't like was having Jemma involved, but it was too late to change that. "Why wouldn't they have put a camera there after two escapes that way?"

"I don't think they know," Zane said. "The first time, the girls didn't get caught until they were in the gardens. The second time, they never got caught."

"Still, after losing the entire harem, you don't think they'd investigate, see how the women had escaped?"

"The power was out. It was chaos. By the time they thought to look, the women were gone without a trace. They likely assumed the women had gone out the front doors."

"It'll be fine, Levi," Jemma said. "I'll be beside you the whole way."

Which made him useless. How could he be alert and watching for enforcers when he'd have his eyes on his wife? "How many men do we have?"

"All five from Jack's Peak, plus you and Jordan, and Farran and Nash."

"And we're looking to free how many women? Ten?"

"Eleven," Beshup said.

So that was fairly even. Still, that Jemma was leading the way, that his wife would be in danger ... He couldn't imagine any of these other men allowing their wives to come along.

The whole scenario was completely unfair. Levi had raged about it for the past week, but God had offered no alternative. His instincts told him that he'd rather have Jemma home and resentful he was keeping her away than with him and happy that she'd tried to help. But he had made his choice, and he couldn't go back on it now.

That night in the library, after Zane and Levi gave instructions to the group, Levi gave one more. "If anyone is captured" — he looked at his wife — "do whatever you can to stay out of prison. Pretend to switch sides, offer false information about the rebels, make the best of living your life as a good Safe Lands national, whatever it takes. We'll come for you when things calm down."

"What false information can we give?" Beshup asked. "Anything we say will be tested."

"Theater nine still hasn't been discovered," Zane said. "I could take some supplies over there and set up a fake rebel headquarters. I could even set up a spot that looks like where we film the Owl. And Omar had a mask that didn't turn out well. I can leave it there as a clue."

"Good," Levi said. "Do that. But if you're caught, don't give up the theater right away." Again he looked to Jemma. "Hold out for a day or two, like it's important information. Delay long enough for Zane to get the theater set up. Don't let them torture you, though. Just let them ask a few times first. Understand?"

Jemma smiled and nodded along with the others. She wouldn't get caught, though. Because Zane had reassured him that this would be easy.

Ten rebels entered the Safe Lands through a storm drain in Champion Park. They walked in pairs out to Gothic Road, spaced out a few yards from each other. Levi walked hand in hand with Jemma, following

Nash and Farran. Behind him were the men from Jack's Peak: Beshup, Mukwiv, Tupi and the teenaged boys Nodin and Yivan.

They followed Gothic Road into the downtown Highlands. Zane and his father were watching through the street cameras, though Levi couldn't speak to Zane since he'd never gotten a SimSpeak implant. Zane had offered to take Levi to get one, but Levi didn't want any Safe Lands technology in his body. But that put him at Nash's mercy.

Levi's senses screamed at him to turn back. He felt like he was walking into a den of mountain lions with no weapon. They were carrying stunners, but for some reason he still felt on edge.

It was Jemma's presence that had him mad wild, he knew. What kind of man would risk his wife in such a way? He should have insisted she stay behind, no matter what. He hoped she knew how much this was killing him.

As per the plans, Dayle should have parked a Department of Public Tasks truck beside the Green Cactus Grill. Farran and Jordan split off to walk that way — they would drive around to the back of the harem. The other men continued to walk.

Nash stayed at Levi's side, repeating to Levi everything Zane said. Beshup walked on Nash's other side. Levi knew his friend from Jack's Peak wanted to be in charge of this operation as much as Levi did. Working with so many leaders was more difficult than Levi would have ever imagined.

When Zane agreed the roads were clear, Jemma led them to the loading dock and into a warehouse of sorts. They moved quickly, through the warehouse and to the stairwell, then up they went — all but Jordan and Farran, who were hopefully parking the truck to wait for their exit. Levi wanted to tell Jemma that he could find the way from here, make her go back and wait with Jordan, but he knew where that would get him.

They climbed to the fifth floor and Jemma stopped at a door. Locked, of course. While Nash and Zane talked about reprogramming Nash's SimTag to get the door open, Levi grabbed hold of his wife, slid his arms around her waist and pulled her close.

"I'll be fine," she said.

But Levi didn't want to hear her reassurance again. He just wanted to hold her. He buried his nose into her neck and hair and prayed that God would keep her safe.

Papa Eli would have said that God would do what he would do and no amount of begging would change that. But Levi also knew that God heard his prayers, so he begged anyway, pleading that God would grant this request, then put an end to all their misery and let them escape this place so they could be free to live their lives the way they wanted to.

The door clicked open. "We're in," Nash said. "Jemma?"

Levi fought back a sigh and released his wife, took hold of her hand.

She pulled him through the door and into a dead-end hallway. She motioned to another locked door on the right.

"This door leads into the back of the kitchen."

Another chance for Levi to hold his wife while Nash and Zane worked on the lock. He reached for her, but whatever magic Zane had worked on the last lock was still in Nash's SimTag. He set his fist against the SimPad and the door clicked open.

And into a kitchen they went.

The room was dark, lit only by the glowing green exit sign over the door they'd entered through as well as a white light over the stove. Jemma pulled Levi across a tile floor to a set of two-way swinging doors. She pushed them open enough to peek through, then she and Levi slipped inside the harem.

It too was dark, though street and city lights from outside cast their glow through a wall of windows on the left that stretched three stories high. Even in the dim light, Levi could see the extravagance. The place looked like a palace. Thick white carpeting, draping crystal chandeliers, gold sconces, elaborate paintings, fancy furniture.

Jemma pulled him toward a staircase that ran along the wall opposite the kitchen doors. Nash remained in the large living room to act as a scout. The rest followed Jemma. Up they went, the stairs creaking underfoot. Jemma had said the matron lived in the suite under the stairs, on the fifth level, so he hoped the creaking stairs wouldn't wake her.

Since they didn't know who was where, the plan called for Jemma to go to the top of the stairs, hoping to avoid Mia's room the longest since Mia had been on the sixth level before.

The seventh floor was a long hallway with two doors on each side. The doors had nameplates: Black Sapphire, Citrus Blossom, Fire Opal, and Imperial Topaz. Jemma knocked softly on the door that said Fire Opal.

"Beshup," she whispered, "you knock on one of these other doors, but be ready with your stunner just in case it's someone you don't recognize."

So Beshup knocked on the Imperial Topaz door and waited. Still no answer from Fire Opal.

Beshup's door opened first. "Beshup?" The voice was female and high-pitched.

"Shh," Beshup said. "We've come to free you of this place. Where is Tsana?"

Levi did not recognize the woman speaking to Beshup, but she looked to be near his own mother's age.

"Tsana is downstairs in the Moonstone suite. Must we hurry?"

"Yes, but do you need help?"

"No, I'll get Paa and Kwis."

"Kwis is in there?" Tupi asked.

"What other rooms are our people in?" Beshup asked.

"Kwis is in here with me. Ani, Sunki, and Mamaci are in Fire Opal." She nodded across the hall to the door Jemma had knocked on. "The others are downstairs in Moonstone and Blue Diamond."

Beshup turned to Mukwiv. "Then we should go down — "

"Jemma!"

Levi turned back to the Fire Opal door and there stood Jennifer, hugging Jemma.

"You've come for Jack's Peak, haven't you?" Jennifer said.

"Won't you and Mia come too?" Jemma asked.

"Mia won't come. In fact, you shouldn't be the one to go after our girls in Blue Diamond. Send one of the Jack's Peak's girls after them instead. If Mia should see any of you, she might call for help. And there's Faeryn in Moonstone as well. A Safe Land national who is pregnant. We should try not to wake her."

Jennifer waved Jemma inside the Fire Opal suite. "Go and wake the women. They're all from Jack's Peak in here. I'll go down to the Blue Diamond Suite and wake the girls there. Hopefully Mia will stay asleep. Levi, you and some of the men could come with me."

"I'll not leave Jemma, but Beshup, will you send some men down with Jennifer?"

"Where is Samantha?" Mukwiv asked.

"Down in the Moonstone Suite with Tsana."

Jennifer, Beshup, and Mukwiv went back to the staircase.

Jemma went into the Fire Opal Suite. Levi made to go after her, but she turned and stopped him with her hand against his chest. "Wait here. There is only one exit from this suite. I don't want you scaring these women in their beds."

So Jemma was separated from him, just as he'd feared. He waited outside as instructed, but he was unhappy about it. Yivan stood beside him, an eager look on his face. Nodin paced the hall behind them. Tupi stood outside the door to the Imperial Topaz room.

Seconds later, the Imperial Topaz door opened again and Chowa returned with two other women. Tupi embraced one of them. The couple looked no older than Jordan and Naomi, though Levi knew they already had three children.

"Take them into the kitchen and be quiet," Levi said. "Nodin and Yivan, stay with me."

Tupi led the women toward the stairs.

Jemma came out of the Fire Opal suite with two older women and a young girl who looked no older than Shaylinn. Yivan greeted the young girl by taking her arm and whispering to her. She hugged his waist.

"That's all," Jemma said. "Let's go."

"Gladly." Levi took Jemma's hand and motioned for the women to go first. "Into the kitchen as silently as you can go." He and Jemma brought up the rear.

"Where is Alawa?" Nodin asked the girl.

"She's not here. She's in the doctor place."

"Why?" Nodin asked. "Is it far?"

"Shh," Levi said. "Wait until the kitchen to talk."

They reached the sixth floor, and Jemma tugged him to stop. "I need to make sure they got everyone from here."

Levi frowned and let Jemma pull him into the sixth-floor hallway. Beshup and Mukwiv were waiting in the hallway.

Levi joined his friends. "Well?"

"The one called Jennifer came out of Moonstone and went into Blue Diamond along with Ani, whose daughters are in there." The Moonstone door opened. "Ah, here comes someone."

"Beshup!" It was Tsana. And another woman who ran to Mukwiv and embraced him.

Reunions everywhere. But it was past time to go.

Finally the door to the Blue Diamond Suite opened, and an older Jack's Peak woman came out, helping a young girl along.

"I want to stay with Alawa," the girl said.

The woman didn't answer. She simply continued to help the girl along. Jemma ran to the girl's other side and supported her.

"Is she okay?" Jemma asked.

"She and her sister had an allergic reaction to something in the meds. Shootsi has mostly recovered, but her sister is still in the SC."

Levi's heart sank. They had no way to get to the SC tonight, and enforcers would increase security once they learned of the escape.

Jemma and the woman helped the girl toward the stairs. Finally, they had everyone. Levi followed and waited at the top of the stairs for the ladies to start down.

"*Behne*, Levi."

He nearly jumped out of his skin. He turned around. Kosowe stood just outside the Blue Diamond suite's door, her dark eyes fixed on his.

"Head on down the stairs," Levi said. "That's the last of you. Right?"

"Jennifer and Mia are in there." Kosowe walked toward him.

He backed against the wall and waved her past, not wanting to touch her. He was overreacting, sure, but he knew well that she was trouble. And the history the two of them shared …

She walked past, and he followed her slowly, wishing she'd move faster. "Hurry, Kosowe. There's not much time."

She turned around, facing him. "But Jennifer and Mia — you can't leave them."

"They're not coming," Levi said. "They don't want — " Something tickled his waist. He reached down, patted his hip. No gun. He spun around.

Mia was grinning at him. His own stunner trained on his chest.

What? Why? "Mia, don't be — "

She fired. The stunner cartridge blasted against Levi's chest and knocked him back a step. He slammed against the wall and slid down it like a broom handle, stiff and hard, sharp pain immobilizing his body.

"What are you doing?" This from Kosowe.

"You wanted him, didn't you?" Mia said. "Well, I want her. So help me get her."

Levi was stunned and couldn't move, but his ears worked just fine. *Her?* Who was her? Not Jemma. *Please not Jemma.* Levi lay staring at the ceiling, straining to hear the whispers of Mia and Kosowe from the doorway. Kosowe stepped over him and walked toward the stairs.

Mia's face appeared over his. "You left us here, like we didn't matter. Mason told me they made you elder, and then he left us too. But Kosowe told me all about the terrible things you did with her, *Elder* Levi. Not so perfect, are you? Wait until I tell Jemma what I know about …"

Mia vanished.

"He's here on the floor." Kosowe had returned. "He fell over."

"Levi!" Jemma knelt at his side, took his hand in hers and pressed her other fingers to his neck.

He tried to open his mouth to speak. He could see Mia's shadow shifting on the wall. *No! God, help her! Please!*

But God did not. Jemma gasped as the stunner's cartridge struck her back. She stiffened and fell on top of him. He could smell her hair under his chin.

Mia dragged Jemma off of him and into the Blue Diamond suite. "He's all yours," Mia said, then she shut the door.

Jemma!

Kosowe grabbed Levi's ankles and pulled him toward the stairs. His body tugged over the thick carpeting, four inches at a time as Kosowe dragged him along.

Beshup arrived at the top of the stairs. "What happened?"

"The one called Mia had a weapon. She shot Jemma and Levi. She has Jemma in her room and said she was calling the enforcers to come. I could not open the door."

Beshup looked down on Levi, his eyes wide. Shocked. Filled with conflict. Levi knew what he was thinking. Save the women or go after Jemma? Enforcers on the way. What to do?

Levi needed his body to move. Now! At least to speak. He willed his voice to make sound. To fight the numbness. It ignored him. All but a tear that rolled down his cheek and pooled cold and wet in his ear.

Useless tears!

"I'm sorry, my friend." Beshup crouched and lifted Levi's limp body over his shoulder. He carried him down the stairs, into the kitchen, out into the dead-end hallway, and down the dark stairwell, with Kosowe following. Down, down, down, leaving Jemma — his life and heart — behind.

CHAPTER
9

Shaylinn went with Eliza, Chipeta, and Aunt Mary to Jordan and Naomi's house to pray for the harem rescue. Though the night wasn't going as Shaylinn had expected. Naomi had taken Harvey out to feed him, and Ciddah and her parents were in their rooms. Everyone else had somehow drifted off topic and were discussing the school situation again.

"We need to get started teaching," Eliza said. "I love having my kids back, but with the three additional Safe Lands girls, it's pretty wild in my house. They need something to do all day."

"The boys are driving Levi crazy," Shaylinn said.

"He should send them to the park," Chipeta said.

"He did," Shaylinn said, "but they left the park and got in trouble, snooping around the greenhouses. Someone complained to Ruston, who passed it along to Levi, and now Levi's grounded them to the house."

"Oh, dear." Aunt Mary frowned at Shaylinn. "It's got to be hard on the older boys, who had so much freedom in Glenrock."

"There are plenty of books in the library," Eliza said. "Why not assign them all books to read and report on?"

"It might be worth trying. Though they're such a wide range of ages," Shaylinn said. "I mean, how will I know if the book is too easy for them?"

"How fast they read it," Chipeta said. "But honestly, if they're quiet and happy, I wouldn't worry about it. Let them read whatever they want."

"And don't forget, we won't be here much longer," Eliza said. "Once the Jack's Peak women arrive, we can focus on getting outside the walls."

"But we still don't know the secret of liberation," Shaylinn said. "Don't forget my mother and Omar and Mason."

Eliza looked like she was trying to find a way to say something delicately. "Shaylinn, no one knows what liberation is. Not the rebels, not the Kindred, no one. We'll likely never know. Don't you think we'd be wise to consider them lost?"

"I will not!" Tears filled Shaylinn's eyes. "I can't." The very idea of never seeing her mother again. Never seeing Omar. "I *won't* give up hope, and neither should you."

"Your tone, Shaylinn," Aunt Mary said. "You must not speak disrespectfully to your elders."

"I'm sorry," Shaylinn said. "But I can't just forget about them! We have to believe they're okay, that they're being protected ..."

"Let's pray again," Chipeta said. "I fear we've gotten distracted from our purpose."

And so they went back to praying for the rescue, and not stopping until Naomi returned, carrying little Harvey in her arms.

"Is he sleeping?" Chipeta asked.

"No, just waking up," Naomi said.

Shaylinn watched Naomi with her child, and fear overwhelmed her at the knowledge that she soon would have two babies to care for.

What if she couldn't do it? What if she failed?

The front door opened then, and Jordan and Nash entered, carrying Levi between them. Levi's head was limp and he was muttering, whimpering. A beautiful, dark-haired woman came in behind them. She looked like someone from Jack's Peak.

Shaylinn stood to make room for Levi on the couch. "Someone should get Ciddah."

"I will." Chipeta jumped up and ran to Ciddah's bedroom.

Jordan and Nash settled Levi on the couch.

"What happened?" Aunt Mary asked.

Ciddah's bedroom door opened and she ran out.

"He was stunned," Jordan said.

"How long ago?" Ciddah asked.

"An hour? A little less maybe? Kosowe said it was Mia."

Mia? Shaylinn looked to the Jack's Peak girl, Kosowe. "Why would Mia do that?"

"I know not," Kosowe said, "but I was the last to leave. I blame myself. I will care for him as a debt."

"That's not necessary," Jordan said. "He has a wife to care for him."

Shaylinn looked back to the front door, saw it hanging open, then walked to it and looked out into the dark corridor. Empty. She closed the door and walked back to the couch. "Where's Jemma?"

"Jemma," Levi said, his lips still not fully working. "Mia Jemma. Mia Jemma."

"Finally, he's talking," Jordan said.

"Relax, Levi." Ciddah knelt on the floor beside the couch. "Your voice will come back and then you can tell us everything."

Shaylinn frowned, overcome with emotion she could not explain. She grabbed Jordan's arm. "Where is Jemma? Jordan, can you tell me?"

"I don't know."

"What does *that* mean?" Naomi asked.

"It means I don't know." Jordan was stormy, his eyes dark and angry. "I didn't go inside. I was waiting in the truck with Farran when they all came out. Beshup and Mukwiv were carrying Levi, and there was no time. Kosowe said Mia had stunned Levi and called the Enforcers."

"Mia also stunned the one called Jemma and took her into the room," Kosowe said.

"Could have opened the room." Levi's voice was hoarse but clear and accusing. He glared at Kosowe. "You had a SimTag. It was your room."

Kosowe shook her head. "There was no time."

"Get her out, Farran," Levi said. "Take her to Beshup. Tell him to keep her away from our people."

"Levi, what has she done?" Naomi asked.

"You heard the man. Let's go." Farran stretched his arm toward the door and waited for Kosowe to move, but she did not.

"I owe you my life, Levi of Elias," Kosowe said. "I will pay my debt."

"You owe me nothing. Get out."

Shaylinn's eyes widened at such harsh words. Finally Kosowe turned and walked out the door, head held high.

"I'll check on you later," Farran said, closing the door behind him.

"What happened?" Jordan asked.

Jordan's eyes were wild and angry, but Levi's were fire itself, blazing as he looked around the room. "That woman. And Mia. They tricked us. Me. I turned my back on the room and Mia must have come out and taken my stunner. She stunned me. Told me she wanted Jemma. Then Kosowe lured Jemma to me, to help me, and Mia stunned her as well. Once Mia dragged Jemma into a room, Kosowe moved me toward the stairs and told Beshup that Mia had Jemma and was calling the enforcers. Beshup made the choice to carry me out. I don't blame him. He didn't know."

"Why would Kosowe help Mia do that?" Shaylinn asked.

Levi sighed, palmed his face.

"Kosowe has wanted to marry Levi for years," Jordan said. "Does she really think she can steal you like this?"

"I have a wife!" Levi screamed. Then he sat up, or tried to. Jordan lunged forward and helped him. Once he was upright, he scowled and stretched out his arm, moving it in an arc, pointing at everyone in the room. "None of you believe her lies. She's got a ton of them. Listen to me and know I speak the truth. One night in Jack's Peak, Beshup and I found a case of alcohol. It should have been given to our elders, his or mine, but we kept it for ourselves and we drank it with Tsana and Kosowe.

"Omar was there as well, but he was off with Nodin until much later. He came back and found us silly with the drink. The five of us slept in Kosowe's teepee. And Kosowe … she led me to believe that something happened between us that night. That I should marry her because of it. She told Beshup, and they both threatened to tell my father. But Omar said she was lying, that we had only kissed. Regardless, I'm sorry for my behavior and for keeping it from you."

"It's not our business to know, Levi," Chipeta said.

"Does Jemma know?" Naomi asked.

Levi closed his eyes, shook his head. "Mia said she would tell her." He looked at Jordan. "But what she'll tell her are Kosowe's lies. And my wife will hate me. And she'll feel even more alone in that place. I never should have kept this from her. If I'd told her, at least she'd know the truth."

They stood there staring at Levi, who was staring at his hands, face pale. The fire had gone from his eyes and left them glassy.

"Levi?" Chipeta sat beside him and patted his leg. "Jemma knows you better than you think she does. Trust her for that."

He startled, his shoulders raising like a scared cat's. "I've said too much. Forgive me." And he stood and walked unsteadily out of the house. The front door shut with a loud clump behind him.

For a moment everyone remained still. Shaylinn looked from face to face, but everyone seemed to have taken great interest in things like the rug, the ceiling, and the wall fixtures. Jordan was picking at his hand. Then Aunt Mary started to cry, which made Shaylinn cry too.

Jemma gone. In the harem again. It was really too much to bear.

Shaylinn and Penny did all they could to keep the children quiet and give Levi space. But Shaylinn couldn't just sit and stare as Levi did. Didn't he know that she was sad too? That she loved her sister?

Shaylinn decided to visit the library. She needed something to read, to distract her from her sorrow. Ciddah had also asked to go, so

Shaylinn went to Jordan's house to fetch her, since Ciddah still needed an escort to leave. When they walked inside the library, Tova was there.

"Good afternoon to you, Shayleen. Who is your friend?" Tova seemed to be overly cheerful today, though she was giving Ciddah a wary glance. It was probably Ciddah's flaking skin. There was no Roller Paint in the basements.

"This is Ciddah. Ciddah, this is Tova, Ruston's wife. Ciddah is a medic."

"I see," Tova said.

"Nice to meet you," Ciddah said.

Ciddah walked over to the nonfiction books. Tova just stood there in the middle of the room, holding a book, but Shaylinn couldn't see the title. Shaylinn turned and wandered to the fiction section. Oh, they had Jane Austen books! Jemma would have been so excited about that.

"I've been meaning to apologize to you," Tova said.

Shaylinn looked over her shoulder at Tova. "Really? What for?"

"My husband was not pleased that your people left the school and so soon. I should have tried to mend the argument. And I did not speak kindly to you, either."

Well, that was nice of her to say. "I'm sure our being here is difficult for you." It was difficult for all of them.

"Yes," Tova said, "but it is good too. It will be, anyway. Once your people understand what's at stake and agree to our terms, you can apply to become Kindred. Did you know that?"

"No." But why would they want to? The Kindred wanted to stay underground forever. Who could agree with such terms?

"We should have started there, I think," Tova said. "If we teach you what it means to be one of us, you can choose to be cleansed."

Cleansed? As if Shaylinn were dirty? Inferior? Was she referring to the biblical baptism? But that was done between a person and God. Who did the Kindred think they were to have the power to clean any person? "But why must we conform to your ways? We have no intention of staying here."

Tova laughed. "You are in denial, I think. It's not possible to leave this place, unless you are a man looking to bring back food."

"What about the rebels?" Ciddah asked. "They come and go."

Tova's face went stony. "To rebel against our safety here is to rebel against Providence. Our home is a gift. We were chosen to live here, free and away from the evils above. Those who leave are not welcomed back."

"But isn't Ruston, your own husband, one of them?" The leader, if Shaylinn wasn't mistaken.

"My husband, *Shane*, speaks with the rebels, but he takes no part in their schemes. He helps where he can but does not put himself in harm's way."

Yet Ruston had gone with Levi and Mason the night they'd freed the children. And according to Jemma, he'd also gone out to help Omar and Mason borrow the invisible suits. Could Tova not know? Shaylinn didn't dare get in the middle of this woman and her husband's communication problems, so she tried to end the conversation. "Well, thank you for apologizing, but I still don't think we will be attending your school or participating in your Kindred cleansing."

Tova raised an eyebrow. "In time you will, Shayleen. Or you will be asked to leave. We will not tolerate anyone living here who refuses to seek the truth."

"What truth? Yours?" Ciddah said. "Truth to you may not be truth to me."

"There is only one truth," Shaylinn said. "If truth is what each of us believed, and we each believe differently, there would be no such thing as truth. Truth stands against what is false. If there is no true and false, light and dark, right and wrong, then there is nothing to guide human morality."

Tova and Ciddah were staring at Shaylinn, but this topic always annoyed her, so she pressed on. "I know what you're thinking: to each her own, right? Well, I'm tired of such nonsense. The world isn't filled with endless pleasure. There's evil in this world, and it's real. There's evil in our hearts, and it's real. You may deny that, but I won't. So if you want our people to swallow *your* truth, Tova, you'll have to back it up with the Bible. Because I won't take authority from your *feelings* on what's right or wrong. Feelings change. Truth does not. And my authority comes from my Creator. Anyone else, and it's nothing more than each man's pleasure."

"You speak in riddles, Shayleen," Tova said. "But I accept your challenge. I'll use the Bible to show you truth."

"I look forward to seeing your claim," Shaylinn said.

Tova left the library.

Shaylinn felt as if she'd been attacked. What right did that woman have to judge her? She had hurt no one. Still, this was their home, and they had shared it freely with the outsiders.

"You really believe in one truth for everyone?" Ciddah asked.

"It depends on the statement," Shaylinn said. "If I say, 'Spinach is disgusting,' you may disagree, and that's a matter of opinion. But if I say, 'Ciddah does not exist,' you know that is false, since there you stand. On the important things, there is only one truth."

"You sound like Mason," Ciddah said. "He loves to argue about such things."

"I hate to argue, actually," Shaylinn said. "But I can't stand by and let someone hurt another. And the Kindred are hurting people with their 'truths.' Zane, for one. They've appointed themselves judges over people's behavior. If I can convince Tova that the Kindred truths come from fear and their desire to control behavior, then I might truly have a purpose in this place."

"I'd like to see how you convince her, if you don't mind," Ciddah said. "Mason talked about the Bible, and I'm curious what you all think is so great about it."

"We believe it's the Word of God, who is somewhat like what you call Fortune, but also very different." Shaylinn located a section in the library that was filled with Bibles, and she looked through them until she found one that had wordings she was familiar with. She gave Ciddah a similar one. "If you want to know what Mason believes, you'll find it in here."

Then Shaylinn found some picture books for the children and Ciddah found a book about herbal medicine, and they left.

The library entrance was only two doors away from Levi's house, but Shaylinn had to walk Ciddah back to Jordan's home, which was farther down and around a corner. As they rounded that bend, a man was coming toward them. Though it seemed silly, Shaylinn panicked. Cold fear trickled up her spine and down her arms, pooled in her belly. The interaction with Tova had taken all her effort. She didn't want to have a run-in with a Kindred man too. She stepped closer to Ciddah, which gave her a bit more comfort, until she recognized the man. It was Nash. Ruston and Tova's eldest son. Oh, good.

Nash stopped and smiled at them both. He looked like Zane in the shape of his face and the color of his eyes, though Zane often dyed his hair strange colors like blue and orange. Nash's hair was a natural brown, as were his eyes. He was a few inches taller than Zane, though Shaylinn remembered that Nash was the elder of the two.

"Hello," he said. "We've not officially met. I'm Katz, though you probably know me as Nash."

"Yes, hello," Shaylinn said. "This is Ciddah, and I'm Shaylinn."

"Do you prefer to be called Katz?" Ciddah asked.

He shrugged. "I answer to both, though don't call me Nash when my mother is around." He raised his eyebrows, flashing his eyes wide as if to hint at the danger such a mistake might lead to.

"I don't think your mother likes me," Shaylinn said. "Any of us, actually."

"She's afraid. If enforcers were to find this place, it would be the end of our way of life."

Shaylinn knew that was true, but it didn't seem like an excuse to be judgmental. Nash/Katz wasn't being judgmental. He was very friendly. "Do you like living here?"

"I like being free from all the Safe Lands regulations. But I like the breeze too, and the feel of my feet in the bottom of Lake Joie, and the sun shining on my skin. And I like watching birds fly. They get down here sometimes and flutter about until one of us takes them to the dumpsters and helps them out before they die. I guess I'm like the birds: I know that this isn't where I was created to live."

"That's very wise," Shaylinn said. "Do you go to the school?"

"I'm twenty."

"Oh." He didn't look that old to Shaylinn, but Zane was eighteen and Nash was older, so ...

"Is twenty bad?" Nash asked, wincing slightly with a cute expression.

"Not at all. You look younger, that's all."

He smiled, had a nice smile too. "You look older than ... fourteen, right?"

"Fifteen in another month." Why had she said that? Did it really matter?

"Almost a grown woman," Nash said. "With me looking younger than twenty and you looking older than fourteen, we're almost the same age."

The comment made Shaylinn blush, and she suddenly felt uncomfortable again. "We should go." She looked at Ciddah, whose eyes widened, as if getting Shaylinn's hint.

Ciddah smiled at Nash. "Good-bye."

"Good-bye," Nash said.

And they hurried on. Shaylinn looked back over her shoulder. Nash was standing in the corridor, watching them. "He's watching us."

Ciddah looked over her shoulder. "He likes you."

Shaylinn almost tripped over her own feet. "Me? Why?"

"Why not?"

Shaylinn all but ran the rest of the way to Jordan's house, eager to put a door between her and Nash. She didn't know why she'd wanted to get away. But Nash had made her uncomfortable. And now she missed Omar more than ever.

CHAPTER
10

Omar stood in front of the incinerator, feeding dead chickens into it one at a time. He wasn't supposed to let it burn with the door open, but he liked the heat on his face and the way the feathers shriveled into flame and ash. Some of the smaller feathers didn't burn right away, but danced around in the hot air above the flames, the heat making them float.

It reminded him of a story Jemma had once told the children, about a balloon that flew through the sky and carried people. He remembered the debate Mason had gotten into with Uncle Colton when the older man had mocked the story as impossible. Mason had disagreed, said that hot air was lighter than cold air, or some such scientific answer. Omar didn't understand it, but he wondered if such a thing might help the Owl fly again.

The Owl. He should forget all about such fantasies. The Owl was dead. As was Omar. The sooner he resigned himself to that, the better. Hope was deceitful. Hope was for fools.

Yet he watched the feathers fly, wondering. For hope was also tenacious.

When his shift ended for the day, he trudged along with the

other strikers to the strikers' exit. There was segregation in this place. Strikers' bunkhouses and residences, strikers' exits, strikers' restrooms. There were even some restaurants, shops, and clubs that prohibited strikers from entering. They were filth here. Criminals. Failures. Like they hadn't all been duped by the Safe Lands government. If only the Owl could fly over that wall and tell the truth to the people.

Liberation wasn't death, but it was a prison sentence, even for "reputables."

Outside the gate, Omar headed for the cafeteria in his residence. He'd decided to spare one credit a day for a meal. Eating out of the trash was too low, and Omar felt low enough as it was. He staggered across the street to the sidewalk that would lead to the striker cafeteria, and a man stepped in his path. A large man in orange. Omar made eye contact with him and was startled to find a pair of dark eyes already fixed on his.

Omar stepped aside and muttered, "Excuse me."

But the man turned and walked with him. "You Omar?"

Omar stopped walking. "Who wants to know?"

"Tamera of Elias."

The words froze time. His mother's name? Omar's mouth opened, and it took him a moment to formulate a reply. "You know my mother?"

"She tasks in sector one. Wants to see you."

His mother was alive?

"Come with me," the man said.

Omar nodded dumbly and followed the man. "How do you know her? And how did you find me? How did you even know to look for me?"

"I live in the sector five bunkhouse with your brother Mason. He told us you were here. As to how I found you, that's my business."

Sure. "But how do you know my mother?"

"I first saw her in a café. A man started choking and she helped him. I'd tasked as a medic for years, so I recognized her medical training and decided to strike up a conversation. That's how we met."

Which only left Omar with more questions. "When did this happen?"

"The end of June. I'd been here for just a few days when we met. And she hadn't been here long before me."

That fit the timeline.

His mother was alive!

"Why does she want to see me?" Omar had enough problems. He didn't need to add motherly lectures to that list.

"Your mother loves you. Isn't that reason enough?"

"How could she? After everything I've done?"

"How badly do you want an answer to that question?"

Omar stopped walking. "This is my punishment. I deserve to be here. But my mother doesn't. And Mason doesn't. Seeing them ... It will only make me feel worse. Tell them I'm sorry." And he turned to walk away.

But the man grabbed Omar's arm, his grip squeezing to the bone. "I'm not asking if you want to come, boy. You'll come. And you'll be respectful. You hear me?"

The man had such intensity that Omar could only say, "Yes, sir."

The man shook Omar's arm. "You going to walk on your own, or do I have to drag you?"

"I can walk fine." But the fright had unnerved him. That, coupled with his fatigue from a long day's work in the pen, brought on the shakes. And he'd left his new PV at home where it wouldn't be vaped all at once.

The man released his arm and nudged Omar to a nearby bench. "Hey, take a seat."

Omar sat.

The man stood over him, looking down. "What's your juice?"

"Brown sugar."

"Walls, boy. Best to let go, okay? Don't go looking to find more. I've worked with a lot of addicts. The good news is, it's hard to get the stuff. So that'll help you get clean."

Omar looked at his shoes. The thought of losing his PV was more than he could bear. He wouldn't tell this man about the PV or Rain or the deal he'd made with her or what he'd already done. It would be his secret. He'd had to ration the vial of brown sugar she'd given him. But one vape a morning wasn't enough to keep the shakes from coming late in the day. He needed to earn more, but he really didn't want to do it Rain's way.

"I know," the man said, "you don't want to get clean. But you'll be happy when you do. Trust me."

When his strength returned, he followed the man into Cibelo. "Who are you, anyway?"

"My name is Richark Lonn. Most people call me Lonn."

"No way! The rebel leader? We saw you get liberated!"

"That's right kid. And the rebels haven't stopped fighting."

Really? Omar hadn't thought there was a way to fight from down here. He wondered what Lonn had meant by that. Was it a chance for the Owl to soar again?

Lonn opened the door to a diner and held it, motioning Omar to enter first. He stepped inside, thankful for the cool air-conditioning.

"Omar!" Mason stood from a table in the back and strode toward Omar, smiling. He gripped Omar's shoulders and squeezed. "Come on." He pulled Omar back to his table, but their mother had stood and was already running toward them.

She met them halfway and embraced Omar, squeezed him. She smelled vaguely like some kind of stimulant, though he couldn't name it. Behind her, Shanna and his aunt Janie stood beside the table, staring at him.

Tears flooded his eyes. He was guilty. They all thought so. And he couldn't deny it. Their husbands were dead because of him. And they were in this place because of him.

His mother kissed his ear, his cheek, his forehead, then pulled back and took hold of his cheeks and really looked him over. She looked well. Healthy. Her eyes were filled with tears, some of which had already spilled down her cheeks. She was tanned, as if she'd been working outdoors every day all summer long. "My son," she said.

Omar shook his head. "I'm sorry. I'm so sorry."

She took his hand and pulled him toward the table. "Sit here." She pushed him into the booth. There were white paper placemats on the table and Omar longed for a chance to draw on them, the first paper he'd seen in days. "Shanna? Will you order Omar a chicken dinner? Chicken was always his favorite."

"Not chicken," Omar said. "I'm working in the slaughterhouse now and ..."

"Say no more," Mother said. "What would you like to eat?"

He was tempted to ask for a salad, which was the only meal he could think of that might be created in a way that wasn't horrifying. But he was too hungry for lettuce. "Is there soup? Tomato, maybe? And some bread rolls?"

"I'll ask," Shanna said.

Aunt Janie slid into the booth across from him. She reached across the table and squeezed his hand. "How are you, Omar?"

"I've been better."

"Is it bad in your bunkhouse?" Mason asked.

Omar frowned at his brother. "Not really. I'm in the residence, though. You're in the bunkhouse?"

"The liberator told me Renzor wanted the worst for me," Mason said.

What did *that* mean? "Is it that bad?"

"Yes," Mason said. "But thankfully Lonn is there to act as my guardian angel."

"God is looking out for us, still," Mother said. "Don't give me that look, Omar. I have seen things you wouldn't believe. God has not abandoned us. In fact, I think he brought us here."

"What?" Omar couldn't believe it. "Why would you say that?" Omar's selfishness had brought them here. Nothing else.

"These people are trapped," Mother said. "But we came and reminded them that there's something else out there. Hope."

There it was again: hope. It was haunting him. Omar wanted to say, "Hope for what?" but he held his tongue. He didn't want to fight.

Shanna returned with a bowl of red liquid and a plate of bread. She set it before Omar, then sat next to Aunt Janie.

"Thanks," Omar said, tearing off the end of the bread and dunking it in his soup. He bit into it, and the warmth and tartness of the soup was delicious.

Lonn sat down and told him about the rebels and their plan to try and get a man into the Midlands.

"I think that going over the wall is a better plan than trying to sneak through the turnstiles," Mason said.

"Your brother doesn't like my plan," Lonn said. "But there is no way to get over the wall."

"If only the Owl could fly," Omar said.

"The Owl?" his mother asked.

Omar and Mason told them of the Owl, and what Omar had done in a few short weeks before being caught and liberated.

Then Omar thought about the feathers in the incinerator. "If we could make a balloon with hot air, I could fly over the wall."

Mason grinned. "That's a great idea, Omar. Perhaps we *could* make one."

"A balloon can't lift a man," Lonn said.

"So we make more than one," Omar said. "Or we attach a rope to it, and it carries the rope up the wall. Maybe with a grappling hook on it."

"There are no grappling hook stores in Cibelo," Mason said. "Plus there are motion detectors on the wall. Still, a hot air balloon — or a collection of small ones somehow bound together — could be done, in theory. It would be a lot of work."

"We have a plan," Lonn said. "And it's a good one."

And no more was said about hot air balloons.

When it was time to leave, Omar collected the paper placemats from the table and carried them outside the door of the diner. Mason had stopped, so Omar stopped beside him. He looked back through the glass door and saw Lonn and their mother back at the table. Then Lonn kissed their mother.

What? "They're together?"

"Strange, isn't it?" Mason asked.

"Beyond so." Omar shook his gaze away. "Why are we standing here?"

"I don't dare enter my bunkhouse without Lonn," Mason said.

Omar wanted to ask why, but he wasn't certain he wanted to know. "Meet me tomorrow at one? If you come to the poultry slaughterhouse, I can show you the incinerator."

"How do I get there?"

So Omar explained where the strikers' entrance to the chicken yards was and where to find Omar.

"I'll come tomorrow, brother," Mason said. "I'd like to see how you got your idea."

While Omar wanted to obey Lonn's advice and refrain from brown sugar, he could not. When Prav and Kurwin left for Fajro that night, Omar went with them.

There was a back entrance to Fajro that led into a private restaurant and an area with changing rooms. Rain made them change clothes when they arrived. She didn't want her customers knowing they were playing with strikers, though she didn't try to hide the Xs on their faces or hands.

Omar found a pair of black pants and a dark brown satin shirt that made him think of Shaylinn's eyes. Burnt umber. All the men's clothing in Rain's closets was flamboyant and lacked buttons that normal shirts had. The shirt had only three buttons at the bottom. Ridiculous.

There weren't many customers at Fajro that night. Two men sat at the counter, apart, one drinking, the other vaping something with lime green fog. Omar sat with Kurwin at a booth in the corner, as he had every night since his encounter with Rain last Saturday. Every night Prav had gone out with a woman. Kurwin and Omar had not. Where Prav's muscles had intimidated Omar at first, he was glad for them now since the women always chose Prav instead of him. Hopefully they'd continue to choose Prav and leave Omar alone.

Though he wouldn't earn any brown sugar that way.

"Do you get chosen much?" Omar asked Kurwin.

"Two or three times in a weekend. That's when the reps come out. Rarely on a weeknight."

"Oh." Today was Wednesday. The weekend was coming. Omar took a gulp of his beer, trying not to think of Friday night when the reputables would come looking for pleasure.

The mere thought didn't at all feel *reputable* to him.

Rain let her ravens — as she called them — drink as much as they wanted, so Omar was drinking, trying to keep his mind off the half-full PV in his pocket. He needed to make it last until he could afford to fill it himself. So he sat drinking and trying to think of ways he could earn credits without being one of Rain's ravens. Maybe he could sell some art or learn how to apply ash ink tattoos to strikers. They might pay him in vials of brown sugar for such things.

Or maybe Mason would see the feathers and know how to make a hot air balloon, and they'd all fly away.

"What's so bad about the bunkhouses?" Omar asked, thinking of Mason.

"It's the maximum security cage," Kurwin said. "Where they put the real rotters. Be thankful you don't live there, peer. They're a nightmare. And it's even worse for the strikers in sectors five and eight."

Mason was in sector five. "Why?"

"Cows, peer. They're heavy. Like fifteen hundred pounds. This one time, a cow busted through the ground, which was the ceiling of the top floor of the Strikers' Bunkhouse in sector five, and killed three men in their sleep."

"No way."

"That beast crushed them in their beds. Sector six is safe, peer. Ain't no turkey that big."

"Omar."

He jumped at the sound of Rain's voice and looked up.

She was standing across the table, looking at him. "I have a customer for you."

A chill ran up his arms. "For me? But it's only Wednesday."

"Why does that matter? Come." She turned and walked away.

"Well, there you go," Kurwin said, elbowing him. "Have fun."

Omar felt dizzy. He downed the remainder of his beer and slid out of the booth. Rain was waiting for him beside the beaded curtains. When he reached her, she remained standing before the doorway.

"She's new," Rain said. "And she's scared. She only wants to talk to someone, so I figured it would be a good first for you. I didn't charge her the full price, but I'll pay you in full, if you make her happy."

"What does that mean? What do you want me to do?"

"Just make her happy. You figure out how." Rain pulled the curtain aside. "She's in the booth in the back. Wearing a blue shirt."

Omar nodded and ducked under the beads. He found the lady in the blue shirt easily enough. She looked about his mother's age. She was pale and very thin, and she watched him approach with wide eyes.

Omar sat across from her. "Hey."

"Hay-o," she said. No smile.

What am I doing here? He stared at her for too long, until she looked to her lap. Then words came out of his mouth. "What's your name?"

"Cacia."

"I'm Omar. Where do you task?"

"Sector three. Textiles. I like your shirt."

Of course she did. "Are you sad, Cacia?"

"Why do you ask?"

He shrugged, feeling like Mason trying to be a doctor of the brain. "Something in your eyes."

She blinked, and tears fell to her lap, tears that hadn't been there seconds ago. "I just feel really alone."

"Yeah, well, this isn't a world that encourages real friendships."

"That's so true," she said, suddenly eager. "I thought I had a friend, but she wasn't."

"What happened?"

"She blamed me for something that went wrong at the office. She did it because our task director liked me, but she liked him. So she made me look bad to make herself look good. And he believed her. And I was demoted." She gasped, choking back a sob.

"I'm sorry," Omar said. "That's horrible." And it was. People here didn't care about anyone but themselves.

"They were both my best friends, but she betrayed me and he believed her. So I never really had any friends, did I? It was all a lie."

Omar shrugged one shoulder. "I don't know. Maybe not a lie. And he'll find out what she did, eventually. Liars are always caught at some point. Then he'll know he can't trust her."

"But that won't fix things with me."

Yeah. "Probably not."

"So what can I do?"

Omar recalled the advice Zane had given him a few weeks back. "Forget them. You have to decide who you want to be. And you have to like that person and believe in that person no matter what anyone else says." He paused, thinking over how that had sounded. How like Zane. Omar added his own thought. "But you need to find true friends. There's no pleasure in a life lived alone."

"Being alone means you have fewer problems," she said.

"Then why are you here?"

Cacia smiled through the tears. "Because I wanted some company."

She'd come here and paid for company. That was so sad. Though not as sad as the guy who got paid to hang out with people because he was hooked on stims. "I used to think being alone was good because I could do what I wanted and I didn't have to answer to anybody. But looking back, my family was only trying to protect me."

"I don't understand that word. Family."

It was so easy to forget just how different these people were. But they were still human. "In the Safe Lands, everyone lives alone. Everyone seeks their own pleasures, no matter who gets hurt. This nation is fragmented. There's no community here. Have you ever experienced true intimacy? I don't mean sex. I mean knowing a person. Loving that person more than you love yourself. Being vulnerable to that person. I have, I think." He pictured Shaylinn and all the ways he'd hurt her and how she'd always forgiven him. Did she believe he was dead right now? "It's painful sometimes, but in a beautiful way. She loved me despite my mistakes. She loved me anyway. She forgave me."

"You think I should forgive them?"

"Maybe. Because when you live without friends, you become selfish, concerned only with your own needs or rights to have your needs met. And you can come here and pay to be with a man. Or you can go on the grid and tap someone and get your thrill that way. But it's an imitation of real love. It's easy. And cheap. And shallow. And selfish. And if that's all you want from this world, take it. Have a party.

"But *I* want more. I want to know people. To see them and touch them and speak to their faces. I want to live with them, fight with them, and apologize to them. I want that pain and joy and difficulty — because it's real. What you have here in the Safe Lands, it's a mockery of what is real and good and hard and deep."

"But relationships are fragile," she said. "My co-taskers hurt me. I can depend on myself. If I task hard and save, I can create security for myself."

"So again I ask, why are you here?"

"Because I want to feel better. My neighbor came here and told me the pleasure would cover the pain."

"It won't. There's nothing lonelier than living only to please yourself. I've taken from others all my life. And I whined. 'Poor me. Look at what everyone else has.' But in my search for gaining the world, I lost what little good I had. Don't you see? Life is about giving, not taking. It's about loving others more than you love yourself."

Cacia sniffed. "You're so weird. There's no such thing as love."

"No such thing? Love covers all wrongs. Love is kindness and patience and discipline and trust. Waters can't quench it or wash it away. It binds us together in unity. It covers endless amounts of mistakes. And perfect love — ah, perfect love drives out even the darkest fears. Love ... Cacia, love never fails."

She laughed. "You're a songwriter, raven. How can you be so young and so wise?"

"Because I've made a ton of mistakes. And people love me anyway." Shaylinn, Jemma, Levi, Mason, and now Mother, Shanna, and Aunt Janie. They shouldn't love him, but they did. They'd forgiven him. Why?

Because they had love.

A verse came to him then from deep inside his memory. *"We love because he first loved us."*

"Let me tell you a story," Omar said. "Once upon a time there was darkness. And a voice came out of that darkness and said, 'Let there be light.' And there was light."

"Light? Had the power gone out?"

"Cacia, just hush and let me tell the story, okay?"

"Okay. Gosh."

And Omar told the story.

CHAPTER
11

It was time for all the cattle to be vaccinated, so Mason started at Pen 1 and drove the cattle, six at a time, out of the pen and into the cattle lane. They were good-natured and went where Mason urged them to go, but it was tricky to get them into the cattle lane gate. Once he did, however, they moved quickly down the path, past all eighteen pens, all the way to the end of the row.

He saw Scorpion on his enormous black horse in the second row, but thankfully Scorpion's back was to him. Mason couldn't bring more than six head at a time into the crowding tub, because if it was too full, the cattle couldn't move. When the first cow reached the tub, Mason had to squeeze past them all and open the door. The heavy iron half door squeaked as he pushed it. Its hinges were rusted and could use oil.

Once the door was open, Mason herded the animals inside. The bang of cattle bumping against the chute walls sounded like the tribal drums from Jack's Peak. Once each cow was inside, Mason shut the door behind him and chased them into the chute system. This wasn't difficult — the cattle knew where they were going. Mason squeezed past them again, opened the alley gate, and the first cow ambled through. The others followed.

The hum of the hydraulic chute motor purred like one of the Old generators in Glenrock. Wayd was ahead of Mason and helped move each cow up to the chute. Over and over, a cow ran inside until his head came out the other end, where the press caught him and held him until the vet could check him over and administer the vaccine.

Then the vet released the cow and Wayd steered it back into the cattle lane.

The repetition meant the hours passed by quickly, and soon Mason was on his way to sector six to visit Omar at the poultry slaughterhouse.

Mason had been tasking in the feedlot for nearly a week now, and he'd just about gotten used to the smell of cow manure. But sector six had a different stench. The chicken manure wasn't pleasant, but there was a rotting smell too. A smell of death that hung on the air.

He had to ask several people before he found his brother. As Mason walked over, Omar was wrestling some chickens into a flat rubber crate. Every time he tried to close the lid, a bird escaped and he had to chase it down. With Mason's help, he managed to wrestle the lid shut. Then Omar set it on a conveyor belt, which pulled it inside a dark chute that went into the building.

"Where does it go?" Mason asked.

"The slaughterhouse. Trust me, you don't want a tour, Mr. Vegetarian."

"I'll take your word for it. So where is this incinerator?"

Omar pointed to the far corner of the yard. "Over there."

They crossed the strange metal floor, which Mason soon figured out was a grid that allowed feces to fall beneath the surface. The incinerator was a bright red barrel the size of a Safe Lands car, with a hinged black door. Blue and silver pipes curled out from the incinerator's sides and toward the ceiling.

"This is good timing," Omar said as he put on a pair of thick gloves. "We burned some birds a while ago, so it's cooled down enough that I can open it." Omar gripped the handle, pulled down until his actions produced a loud clank, then opened the heavy metal door.

Inside was a chamber of smooth, dirty steel walls, like some sort of massive oven. There were two holes in one side and a rectangular hole in the very front bottom. Light gray ash was scattered on the bottom in clumps.

Omar gripped the rectangular hole with his gloved fingers. "This is the ash pit." He grabbed something that looked like a large hoe, poked it inside the incinerator, and scraped the ash into the ash pit. The hoe made an awful sound scraping over the steel surface. When he got most of it, he traded for a hand broom and brushed the rest into the hole. When he finished, he crouched on the side of the incinerator and pulled out a long drawer. It too scraped as he pulled it out. It was filled with gray ash. Omar carried the drawer over to a dumpster and emptied it, tapping it until all the ash fell out. In the sunlight that beamed through open windows above, Mason could see the particles dance in the air around his brother.

"They use this ash to make cinderblocks," Omar said.

"That's interesting." And disturbing. That some of these buildings could be made from the remains of chickens and who knew what other animals. And he'd never seen a graveyard in the Safe Lands either, so they likely cremated people as well. Mason shuddered.

Omar carried the drawer back and replaced it. Then he walked around Mason to a waist-high bin on wheels. He wheeled it over to the incinerator, and Mason saw that it was full of dead chickens or chunks of dead chickens. Omar tossed a few handfuls into the incinerator and wheeled the bin out of the way.

"Back up." Omar pulled Mason away until they were a good ten feet from the open incinerator door. "Stay here." Then Omar walked over to the side of the incinerator. "Okay, watch this." He pressed a button.

The incinerator growled, then flames gushed out of the side of the chamber. It sounded like a waterfall of fire and looked like an oversized blowtorch. Omar released the button, but inside the birds still burned.

"Come closer now," Omar said.

Mason inched toward the open door.

His brother stepped up beside him. "See it? See the feathers?"

Mason did see. Bits of feathers and ash circled in the air above the flame, the hot air a current for them to ride on.

"Well?" Omar asked. "Do you know how to do it?"

It tickled Mason that Omar had put on a full demonstration to show Mason something he already understood. "In theory, yes. But it will take some trial and error. And I'm not sure where we'd get the supplies. We'd need a lot of fabric."

"But it's a good idea, isn't it?"

Mason patted Omar on the back. "It's a great idea, brother. Let me think on it."

When Mason's task shift ended for the day, he went into Cibelo and to a G.I.N. store there. He'd been tasking only six full days now, so he didn't have many credits to spend. But he didn't need much. Just enough to test the theory for Lonn.

Smoking was illegal in the Safe Lands, but he did find a small box of matches on the cooking aisle next to the birthday candles. He recalled an Old book of children's experiments that Papa Eli had given him for Christmas one year. Mason had done them all many times. He felt fairly confident that he could find what he needed. He bought the box of matches, a box of the birthday candles, a box of bendable drinking straws, a roll of tape, and a package of dental floss. It all came to eight credits, nearly a full day's task credits. He sighed, hoping this wouldn't be a waste of time.

As he paid, he asked the clerk for a few extra plastic bags. The clerk was more than generous, shoving a handful into the one holding Mason's purchase.

Mason carried it all to the Get Out Now Diner. The place was empty for the moment, so he sat at the table in the back and ordered a salad, which would likely be put on Lonn's tab. Mason wasn't sure how Lonn paid for all the meals here. Maybe the cooks were rebels too.

While he waited for his salad, he started his balloon. He took five straws, pinching one end of each and tucking it into the open end of another, then bending the straws until he had a misshapen ring. He then ripped off four foot-long strips of dental floss, tying one end of each evenly spaced around the straw ring. Next he taped the ring around the opening of one of the plastic bags, pleating the excess bag here and there, careful to leave no holes.

His salad arrived then, so he took a break and ate. When he was done, he tore apart the box that held the birthday candles until he'd removed the back. He used a tine of his fork to poke a hole in each corner. Then he tied the other end of each piece of dental floss around each hole.

He'd just completed that step when Lonn and his mother arrived.

"What are you doing?" Mother asked.

"An experiment." Mason looked to Lonn. "Do you think the cook would mind if I lit a few birthday candles?"

"No. What kind of experiment is this?"

"You'll see." Mason used his fork to poke four closely spaced holes in the center of the cardboard. He pushed a birthday candle through each until they were about halfway through. Then Mason slid out of the booth, pulling his "balloon" with him. "Will you help me, Mother?"

Lonn got up so that Mother could get out.

"What am I doing?" she asked.

"Hold the top of the bag, please, while I light these candles." Mason pinched the top of the bag to show her what he wanted, and she took it from him. Then he grabbed the matches from the table and squatted under the bag. By then, the waitress and chef had come out around the counter to watch.

Mason put his hands near the candles and struck a match. He had two candles lit before the match burned too close to his fingers, forcing him to drop it on the floor. He lit a second match and lit the other two candles. "Okay, give it a moment," he said, taking the bag from his mother.

He let go of it and it sank, so he grabbed it again and waited longer. He continued to release and catch the bag until it hovered in place. He stepped back and watched as it slowly rose into the air and finally bumped against the ceiling.

The waitress and cook cheered and clapped for the balloon. Mason grinned at them.

"It flies," the waitress said.

"You wanted to show this to me?" Lonn asked. "Omar's balloon?"

Mason sat down across from Lonn and leaned over the table. "What if we could build one big enough to lift a man? Carry him over the wall where he could get a message to the rebels in the Midlands?"

Lonn didn't look convinced. "How big would it have to be to lift a man? And how would you get the controlled flames big enough?"

"I don't know yet," Mason said. "But I think it's possible."

"I can see that it *might* be possible." Lonn gestured to the balloon, which was already starting to sink. Mason saw the bag had shriveled, meaning the flames had gotten too hot. "But I think it's unlikely to work. Might be just as likely to kill the man inside as lift him."

Mason pursed his lips, then got up and blew out the candles on his balloon. He wanted to say that he felt Lonn's plan to sneak a man through the turnstile was also unlikely to work, but there was no point in that. Lonn would do what he would do. And so would Mason.

"You have no objections to me trying, do you?" Mason asked.

"Of course not. Just don't get caught."

Mason grinned. The game was on. He wadded up the remains of his balloon and put them in the trash, then came back and sat across from his mother and Lonn. As he watched the two interact, he realized he still knew very little about his guardian angel — and possible step-father. "Why did you get fired from the MC?" he asked Lonn. "What were you researching?"

Lonn's eyes bored into his. "What makes you think I was researching anything? Or that I got fired?"

"I read your bio in the History Department. They didn't say you were fired, by the way. It says 'forced retirement.'"

"Forced." Lonn huffed a laugh. "It was indeed forced."

"What happened?" Mason asked.

"I'd been doing experiments. And I hadn't told anyone about them."

"Not even Lawten?"

"Not at first. It all started with Martana's death in sixty-eight. She was hypoxic, and I felt like she wouldn't have had an oxygen deficiency if she'd been healthy. The plague causes anemia, which decreases the amount of red blood cells in the body and therefore decreases the amount of oxygen in the blood. So I set out to find a way to increase red blood cells. I got nowhere for the first few years, and most my free time was spent with the growing rebellion anyway.

"But I got thinking one day about trying to filter blood. To create a sieve. We did that for dialysis patients, so why couldn't we do something similar for the plague? I started talking with a man in technology design. I also brought in a biologist, and we used a dialysis machine as a prototype. Together, we found a way to filter the virus from the blood."

"That's amazing!" Mason said. "Why wouldn't they want that?"

"Well, it didn't work. I mean, it did, but the problem was that the blood is not the location of the infection. Blood carries the infection throughout the body. It's a transmitter of the virus. But the replication of the virus happens in the lymph nodes and the spleen. So transfusion might have filtered the virus from the blood, but it didn't stop the virus from entering the blood all over again."

Oh. That made sense. Frustrating, though. "So what did you do?"

"I tried another theory. I tasked in the MC, and we occasionally worked with bioengineering on transplant patients. My first instinct was to grow new organs — a spleen, lymph nodes, intestines, whatever was needed — to flush out the plague. I hoped that the combination of new organs with filtered blood would provide the cure. We could rebuild the body, so to speak, replacing the infected areas one at a time."

The very idea enthralled Mason. "How can you grow a new organ?"

Lonn smiled at his mother. "You ask the same questions Tamara asked. Another time on that one, okay? It's a complicated procedure. If we ever get out of here, I'll take you both over to bioengineering. You'll love it."

Mason already felt a tinge of excitement. "So, your plan didn't work?"

"The virus is too complex. It latches on in so many places that what works for one person might not for another. And growing organs is time-consuming, and transplants are hard on patients. None of this was ideal. So I came up with yet another idea: Grow a womb."

Mindboggling. "You can do that?"

"I didn't see why not. Now, whether or not the womb could grow a child to term, well, it would have been an experiment. I approached the bioengineering department about it, and it turned out they'd been trying to do this for a few years. They had successfully grown and implanted a womb for a woman who couldn't conceive, but it did not keep the virus from the fetus. Learning this sent me back to the virus itself and the meds we were already using."

"And you found out there was a stimulant in the meds?"

Lonn's eyebrows sank. "No. What makes you ask that?"

"That's kind of how I got here," Mason said. "Ciddah learned that there was a stimulant in the meds, and she and I were testing my blood to find it."

"Why your blood?"

"It was just a wild guess on my part. She told me she'd tested a variety of blood types, but it was all infected blood."

"And if the meds catalyzed with the virus, it would be impossible to detect what was in the meds."

"Exactly."

"But they stopped you before you could do this test?"

"Almost. The enforcers came just as the blood meter was running the blood. I hid in the closet while Ciddah went out to talk with the enforcers. They took her away but didn't find me. And when I came out, I checked for a result. The blood meter said Xiaodrine."

Lonn wrinkled his nose. "Odd. Why put that in the meds?"

Lonn knew the med? Maybe Mason would finally get some answers. "What is it?"

"It's an amphetamine designed to fight obesity. It speeds up the metabolism. The plague does slow the metabolism, but I'd think Xiaodrine would be a dangerous combination with the plague."

"Why?"

"Xiaodrine is processed in the liver. It would interact with other medications and reduce the benefit of the antivirals in the meds. Plus, I've read studies from bioengineering that say dependency on amphetamines has a physiological impact on the immune system."

"So why put Xiaodrine in the meds?" Mother asked.

"I don't know. Whose meds were you testing?"

"Ciddah's old prescription. Once she learned about the stims, she started compounding her own meds."

"Clever girl."

Mason thought so and couldn't help smiling.

"It never occurred to me to ask to compound my own meds," Lonn said. "I'm surprised they allowed it."

"Why?" Mother asked.

"Because meds for the plague aren't compounded in a regular Pharmco. They're made in the compounding pharmacy located in the main lab. Every medic knows that. How would she have gotten the recipe?"

A connection clicked in Mason's mind and his heart sank. "This was the Pharmco in City Hall. And Ciddah ... she's ... she was together with Lawten Renzor."

"Ahh ... yes. Renzor's girl. The plot thickens. That Pharmco ... and the SC ... things go on there that no one is supposed to talk about. Some do, of course, which only adds to the legends. If this Ciddah was one of Lawten's femmes, he'd probably let her do whatever she wanted."

"But she stole things from the Pharmco to compound meds for her parents, and then Otley came asking questions."

"Well, sure. Otley's been after Renzor's job for a while now. He was just waiting to catch the man doing something wrong."

Like letting his girlfriend take unauthorized meds.

"Well, the two of you got further than I did," Lonn said. "I'd tried to take a closer look at the meds, but I didn't have any reason to wonder what was in them so much as to wonder why every patient's prescription was so different."

"I don't understand," Mason said. "You don't write the prescription? Aren't you the medic?"

"You just asked one of the biggest questions every medic has, Mason. We write prescriptions for everything *but* meds for the thin plague."

"Then would they have let you compound your own?"

"I wish I'd thought to try compounding my own. But, again, I don't think I would have been allowed. I think that was a privilege granted to someone Renzor highly favored. A golden ticket of sorts."

Wonderful. This conversation might be getting them somewhere in regard to the meds conspiracy, but it wasn't giving Mason any confidence that Ciddah truly cared for him. "Fine. But you believed there was some difference to the recipe other than the volume of compounded suspension based on the patient's weight?"

"It's obviously more than simply consulting a dosing chart. Some of my patients had to vape meds three times a day. Some only once a week. And some patients were far healthier than others. I wanted to find out why."

"But that wasn't a safe question to ask," Mason said.

"It was not. And I made the mistake of talking about it with Lawten one day. He brought it up too. Looking back, I know they put him up to it. They'd been watching me. I didn't know either, fool that I was. And when Lawten and I had that long conversation about the meds, he recorded it. He took the recording to the Guild, and I was — how did you put it? — promoted to 'forced retirement' for task infraction."

"What's task infraction?" Mother asked.

"All taskers sign an oath when we graduate from our mentoring programs," Lonn said. "We're not to ask questions outside our task. We are not to meddle in another task area. And that's what I'd been doing. I wasn't tasked as a bioengineer or a technology designer, after all. I was fired. And Lawten got my job."

"And a seat on the Safe Lands Guild," Mason said.

They sat silently for a moment, until Lonn said, "We need to find a way to test more meds. A wider variety. See if they all contain Xiaodrine. See what else they contain. I wish we could talk with your Ciddah."

Your Ciddah. A nice thought. He wondered if she was grieving him, believing him dead. Was she still with Levi and the others? "I wish we could visit the compounding lab."

"You know, I've never been there. To the blood lab, either," Lonn said. "I'm sure you know that medics take a blood draw of every patient at every visit."

"Yes. Why?"

"Again, I don't know. I always assumed they were monitoring the meds to make sure they'd prescribed the best dosage. But who's to say that's what they're doing."

That thought was a little scary. "What else could they be doing?"

Lonn chuckled. "Oh, Mason, it won't do to have you trust our government so easily. The fact is, they could be doing anything."

CHAPTER
12

Jemma woke in the Rehabilitation Center, inside the same cell she'd been in last time: cell 40, at the very end. She had a wall to her left, and the cells on her right and across the way were empty. Her nearest neighbor was four or five cells away. She didn't bother trying to speak with him. She didn't see Levi. She hoped he'd gotten away.

The first night in the RC, she'd wept. Why had Mia betrayed her in this way? It had been Mia's choice to remain in the harem. Yet she had said such hateful things to Jemma after she'd stunned her. Mia blamed Jemma for something, though Jemma did not understand what it might be.

After she'd tired of her anger toward Mia, she'd remembered Levi's instructions before leaving the basements that night. She was to pretend to betray the rebels. She was to give up the location of theater nine as a rebel meeting place. But not at first. Not until Zane had time to prepare it. She had to hold out for a few days, then she could pretend to switch sides in order to protect herself.

Protect her from what, though? They wouldn't kill her. They'd put her back in the harem and make her pregnant.

Again she wondered why Mia had done this to her. For a reward, perhaps?

She'd spent the next day and night in the RC as well, and woke on the third day shortly before an enforcer came for her and transported her to the lobby, where Matron Dlorah was waiting with Ewan, one of the harem enforcers.

"Hello, Jemma. We have a meeting with the task director general," Matron said. "We mustn't be late."

"What does *he* want?" Jemma asked.

Ewan held open the door and Matron waved for Jemma to exit first. "You'll find out when he tells you," she said.

A quick ride in a black car brought them to City Hall. The task director general's office was on the top floor of the building. An elevator took them there far too quickly.

Jemma had never been in the task director's office. It had the same opulence of the harem, though the colors here were black and red with dark hardwood floors. Three of the four walls were made of floor-to-ceiling windows that offered a splendid view of the city and surrounding area. And as her gaze fell to the fourth wall and the man sitting between it and a large desk, she almost felt as if she were standing in a throne room.

Jemma had seen Lawten Renzor before, in Champion Theater right before the entertainment orientation. He looked older now, though he wasn't wearing makeup like he had been the night he'd been on the ColorCast. He was a hunched man with flaking skin and a large nose that claimed most of his face. The size of his nose made his dark eyes seem smaller and more intense. A pale number nine glowed on his cheek.

Kruse, whom she remembered was the personal assistant to the ruler of the Safe Lands, stood next to the task director general's desk. He was bald with smooth pinkish skin and a funny black SimArt tattoo that looked like a hand slapping the side of his head.

"Ms. Levi, welcome," Kruse said in a happy voice. "Please have a seat." He gestured to a chair in front of the task director's desk. "Matron Dlorah, would you mind waiting outside?"

Matron shot Kruse an indignant glare. "Ms. Levi is my charge. What concerns her, concerns my harem."

"If there is something you need know, Matron, I will inform you," the task director said. Where Kruse's voice was pleasant, the task director's was grating and deep.

Jemma shivered at the looks Matron and the task director exchanged, but Matron turned to leave the room without saying another word.

"Ms. Levi, you and your rebel outsider friends have deprived our nation of nine surrogates," the task director said.

"Ten," Jemma said, lifting her chin. She must stay confident and proud. This nation had no right to imprison people.

"Perhaps you didn't factor yourself into my equation," the task director said. "You helped ten women leave the harem, indeed, but you remained behind, a valuable surrogate and a replacement."

"I will not be a surrogate," she said, though she knew there was little she could do to keep from becoming one.

"You *will* carry a child. I leave the method of conception to you. In fact, I'm personally happy to oblige should you prefer more natural methods over the SC's embryo transfer program."

Jemma gasped at his rudeness. "I would never do anything with you." But she was supposed to be playing along. How could she give the location of theater nine if he did not ask? And why would he make such a lewd offer, anyway? Did he no longer care about producing uninfected infants?

"I think that, in time, you'll change your mind. I can be very persuasive."

She didn't want to encourage this man's advances, but she held back her revulsion in an effort to do what Levi had asked. Perhaps if she were able to befriend this man, she could learn more about his plans. Though she did not think she could succeed at such an endeavor. "What do you want from me?"

"You will be a queen, of course. But since the leader of your outsider clan claims you as his, I will claim you as mine. In this, I will show my people that no outsider or rebellion is greater than that which we offer our people. And there's still no greater privilege for a woman than bearing a child for the Safe Lands."

That was what they'd wanted from the Glenrock women from the start. But allowing the task director general to claim her? Perhaps this was the way to turn this in her favor. To make herself appear to be the traitor Levi wanted her to be.

"I will be your queen, on one condition."

The task director raised his eyebrows. "A condition? I'm intrigued."

"I want to be the only queen. Mia does not get to be on the ColorCast, nor does Jennifer or any other pregnant woman. Only me, until I deliver my child."

He sat back in his chair, folded his arms. "Why do you ask this?"

"Because Mia betrayed me. And if I'm going to have a baby, I want to be the famous one. I want to be the one on all the posters and ColorCast programs."

"All our queens get that," Kruse said.

"But not Mia," Jemma said. "Not anymore."

"Why should I agree to your condition?" the task director asked. "You'll do what we say when we say it."

"I know you can trick me into saying whatever you want. But that way is a lot more difficult. Wouldn't you rather work with someone willing?"

"Mia has been very willing," the task director said. "I don't see that you have any right to make demands."

Now was her chance. "What if I give you something?"

The task director chuckled. "I like your bargaining spirit, Ms. Levi. What will you give me to leave Mia off the ColorCast?"

Jemma swallowed, and her eyes filled with tears, which she hoped made it look like the decision had been a difficult one. That her desire for revenge was stronger than doing what was right. "I'll tell you where the rebels meet in the Midlands. I'm not very good with directions, but I know enough that your enforcers will be able to find it."

The task director raised one eyebrow. "Why would you give this information?"

"Because they haven't helped us!" Jemma yelled. "And they won't help us. We just wanted to get outside of these walls, back to our home, but the rebels have their own plans. The Owl. Taking over the government. We don't care about your political problems. We only wanted to leave. But now I'm back in the harem, because the rebels wanted to free the other women and because Mia stunned me. So the rebels and Mia ... they ruined my plans. So now I'll ruin theirs."

"Very well," the task director said. "Where do they meet?"

Jemma shook her head. "First, you make me queen."

"You aren't even pregnant yet," Kruse said.

"Your people are living with the rebels, you said?" the task director asked. "You're dependent upon them?"

"Yes," Jemma said, not understanding why he would ask such a thing.

"I'll need time to think this over. For now, you'll move into the harem. You'll have your appointments in the SC. Then we'll talk again."

Matron took Jemma directly to the SC for an appointment. Rimola was still there, and she seemed to be doing Mason's old task as well as her own. But now instead of Ciddah, a man worked there as the medic. Medic Vallen, Rimola called him. When Rimola took Jemma into the exam room and asked her to put on the blue robe, Jemma looked out at the new medic and refused.

"Why are you being difficult?" Rimola asked. "Matron said you were eager to become queen."

"I'm not being difficult. I just don't want to have a male doctor." And she winced at her words. She'd always been supportive of Mason's interest in medicine. But she was not pregnant yet and did not require a doctor. "Is there no female medic?"

"Not since Ciddah left. If you won't cooperate, I'll have to stun you."

Tears flooded Jemma's eyes. She didn't want to get stunned, but maybe that would be better. Then she wouldn't remember what had happened.

But that was cowardly. "I'll do it." She snatched the blue gown from the exam table and waved Rimola out the door.

"Thank you," Rimola said, as if they were friends.

Jemma changed into the robe and fought back tears. She didn't want to do this, but if she were going to be convincing as a Safe Lands queen, she'd have to do a better job of acting.

Rimola came back and took Jemma's weight and blood pressure, then asked her to go to the bathroom and urinate in a plastic cup. Once Jemma did all that, she was sent back to the exam room to wait, and dread, the medic's arrival.

He came finally, dressed in a bright blue shirt and pants. He looked to be in his early twenties. Short with a square face and green eyes. But Jemma's eyes were drawn most to his skin — it was flaking, and he hadn't bothered to use Roller Paint.

"Ms. Levi, hay-o." He was too busy reading the CompuChart to look at her. When he finally did look up, his eyes widened and slid across her entire body. "*Hay-o.*"

She tried not to express disdain at the sultry tone of his second greeting. "Hello."

He swallowed, his throat bobbing. "I ... You ... I'm sorry." He actually flushed and looked back to the chart, scratched the back of his head. "It, uh ... may interest you to know that you're pregnant."

Pregnant? "But you haven't done anything to ..." Her words trailed off as understanding settled over her. "On my own?"

"Yes, well done." He smiled. He had very small teeth. "Procedure dictates that you ask the donor to come in so we can check his blood and DNA. If we can get you on the right combination of meds now, there's a chance we can stop the virus from reaching the child. It's a new procedure. Still being tested. So far there have been no successes, but we're hopeful that — "

"My husband and I are not infected," Jemma said. "I won't take any meds you offer me. Nothing, is that clear?"

"*Not* infected?" Medic Vallen looked back to the chart, scrolled back a page. "Oh. Forgive me, Ms. Levi. I didn't think to check that. I apologize." He looked at her again, frowning. "Both of you uninfected? Are you certain? Men sometimes say things that aren't true to, you know, to ..."

Jemma beamed at him. "I am positive." Pregnant! Praise the Lord! There would be no embryo transfer procedure for her, no having to deal with Lawten's suggestions. Wait until she told Levi! She tried to imagine the look on his face. Surprise first. Then a wide smile.

"Well, I, uh, I see Rimola didn't fill in the last date of your menstrual cycle. Do you remember? It will help me to determine the birthdate. An ultrasound will confirm it, but it's a little early for that."

"I don't know." Jemma tried to remember. "I was here. In the harem," she said. "I was only days away from an embryo transfer appointment. That's probably written in your chart."

He frowned and studied the CompuChart, tapped around a bit. "Ah, yes. You've skipped, it looks like ... two. That puts you seven or eight weeks along. We *could* do an ultrasound, but we won't today, of course. I'll need to notify the task director first." He looked up at her and smiled wide. "Congratulations, Ms. Levi."

Jemma couldn't help but return his smile. "Thank you. And it's *Mrs.* Levi.

Jemma entered the Blue Diamond Suite, furious that Matron Dlorah had put her in the same area as Mia. She wouldn't be here long. Not if she could negotiate a room change with the task director. She hoped he'd go for her deal-making. There were plenty of empty rooms in the harem now.

Only one person was sitting in the living room when Jemma entered. A very young girl with long, dark braids. From her coloring and hair, Jemma guessed she must be from Jack's Peak, though she knew very few women from that village. She'd met Tsana before. And she knew of Jack's Peak's medicine woman, Shavingo'o, and of course Chief Kimama.

The girl jumped up and ran to meet Jemma by the door. "You're Jemma, aren't you?" the girl said. "You're the one Levi of Elias chose."

That brought a smile to Jemma's lips. "Yes, that's right."

"I'm Alawa. My mother and sister were here too, but they escaped when I was in the SC." Her voice became wistful and tears filled her eyes. "Mia has been telling me that you were coming. I'm sorry you're here, but I'm glad."

Jemma took hold of the girl's hand and squeezed. "It's nice to meet you, Alawa. How old are you?"

"Seventeen." She took a deep breath. "Jemma, can I ask you a question? Did you see any of my people, besides the women and girls in the harem, I mean. The men and boys?"

"I've seen many of them. Is there one in particular you're curious about?"

"My brother Yivan and his friend Nodin."

"Yes, I've met them both. They helped rescue the children from the boarding school, and they were here the night we freed the other women — all except you and me, that is."

Alawa gasped, a huge smile on her face. Tears rolled down her cheeks. "Oh, thank you, Jemma. I was so worried about them. I-I saw my father die. He was so brave. But when I was taken, Yivan and Nodin were still fighting."

"I'm glad to be able to tell you that they are well — though missing you, I'm sure."

"Nodin and I were planning to get married," she said. "But now ..."

"You mustn't give up hope," Jemma said. "We won't be here forever."

"But they made me pregnant with another man's child! What will Nodin say when he learns that? Why would he still want to marry me?"

"If he loves you, he'll still want to marry you."

"Sure he will. Jemma has a lot of silly ideas about men and love."

Mia's voice. She was standing at the mouth of the hallway, leaning against the wall, arms folded. She looked lovely and not at all pregnant, though she wasn't any further along than Shaylinn.

"There is nothing silly about a man who loves a woman, Mia," Jemma said.

"Men are incapable of loving one woman," Mia said.

"Did your piano man hurt you?" Jemma asked. Maybe that was why Mia was trying so hard to ruin Jemma's life. Could she be jealous that Jemma had a husband who loved her?

"No," Mia said with a hint of disgust in her voice. "I didn't want him anyway."

"If you're patient and wait for the right man," Jemma said, "you'll find one who will love only you."

"Like you can talk," Mia said. "Levi can't decide whether he loves you or Kosowe."

Jemma straightened her posture. "Who?"

"Kosowe is from my village," Alawa said. "She has always longed to marry Levi."

Jemma had never even heard Levi mention this Kosowe before. "Was she in the harem?"

"You met her," Mia said. "Last night. She was pulling Levi toward the stairs when you came to help. Or should I say, when you came closer to the stunner."

Jemma could hardly breathe. Had Mia and this Kosowe woman conspired against Levi and Jemma? "You did this to break up our marriage?"

"Oh, you got married?" Mia chuckled, as if it were very funny. "I don't think it will last. Kosowe is gorgeous. And Levi loved her long before he loved you."

Though Jemma tried to fight it, tears filled her eyes. "That's not true." But it could be true, couldn't it? Levi had spent a lot of time trading in Jack's Peak. No. Surely it wasn't true.

"Why do you think he was always going out on those trips, spending the night? He was sleeping with her."

Heat flashed through Jemma's chest. "Mia, you are a horrible person. I can't imagine how being this cruel could give anyone joy. I feel sorry for you." She turned and tried to open the door, found no knob, remembered the SimPads. She slammed her fist against the wall and the door popped open. Jemma wrenched it open wider, faster, and fled down the stairs and across the main sitting area until she was standing at the vast picture windows that overlooked the harem gardens.

And she cried.

She didn't know how to respond to any of Mia's declarations, and could only pray God would send her the strength and conviction she didn't feel. One thing was certain: Jemma would not stay in the Blue Diamond Suite. And she would take Alawa with her.

CHAPTER
13

A bang jerked Levi from sleep. He sat up on one elbow and blinked, confused. It was dark, but a bright light was streaming in the open doorway. Someone stood there, silhouetted in the doorframe.

"Time to get up, you lazy maggot."

Jordan. Levi rolled over and pulled the pillow over his head. "Go away."

"I don't think so. I've let you waste enough time moping around like a girl. You're going to get up, you're going to eat something, then we're both going to go talk with Ruston and Zane and figure out how to get her back."

"You know we can't go get her." After losing ten harem women, there was no way they'd give up the last few they had. "They've probably got enforcers sleeping outside her bedroom door now."

"You think I'm not hacked about this? She's *my* sister. If we can't get into the harem, then it's time to put this psycho nation down. The sooner we do that, the sooner we all go free."

Free. As elder of Glenrock, this was Levi's job. He couldn't afford to hide in his cave and mourn the loss of his wife. He had people looking up to him. And he'd wasted three days.

"Okay." He rolled over and threw back the covers. "I'm getting up."

"Mad good. Shay and Nell made breakfast. Come eat."

And so Levi found himself at the table, eating pancakes with his household, minus one.

Minus Jemma.

"Good morning, Elder Levi," Trevon said, and the other children around the table parroted him.

"Good morning," Levi said, looking around at their faces. The table was surrounded with boys, except for little Carrie, who was squeezing chunks of pancakes into mush with her fists. Trevon, Jake, Joey, Grayn, and Weiss all watched him with wide eyes, like he might explode at any moment. So he looked to his plate, which was empty. "Did someone give thanks?"

"Jordan did." Shaylinn walked to the table, holding a frying pan and spatula. She scooped a large pancake out onto Levi's plate. "We didn't know if you'd be joining us. It's nice to see you."

Levi nodded, glanced around the table again. "Well? Go ahead and eat then." And the children all started shoveling food into their mouths.

Levi didn't feel comfortable at the head of the table without Jemma here. What if they never freed her? What if they never learned what liberation truly was and his mother and aunt Janie were gone forever? What if he had to raise his cousins without a wife? He was suddenly thankful they were mostly boys. He could raise boys, but Naomi or Shaylinn would have to help with Carrie.

Levi had never felt so defeated, and the feeling was not one he liked. Let the women care for the children for now — he and Jordan were going to war against this place. And he would get his wife back.

When he finished eating, he showered and dressed, then went with Jordan to Ruston's house.

Tova opened the door and, not surprisingly, did not seem pleased to see them. "My husband is not here."

"Can you contact him?" Levi asked. "Tap him?"

"We don't allow the technology of the devil in the basements."

"Even the stuff Zane makes safe, like the Wyndos and GlassTops?" Levi asked.

Her face flushed then. "Whoever wants to be a friend of the world is an enemy of God."

Wow. The rage in Tova's expression and tone chastened him for his fears of flakers. Had Levi ever been so judgmental toward Zane? He hoped not.

"Zane isn't a friend of the Safe Lands, Tova," Levi said. "He's a rebel. And anyone who stands against those psycho Safe Landers is a friend of God."

"You know not of what you speak. The Kindred know we are from God and that the rest of the world lies in the power of the evil one."

"You're as psycho as they are," Jordan said. "Last I checked, you're not God."

"He who is spiritual judges all things, for we have the mind of Christ."

The crazy woman was twisting the Bible to make it say what she wanted it to say. Levi wished he could quote verses as well as Shaylinn or Jemma could. He'd like to see one of them take on Tova.

"Is something wrong?" a male voice said from behind Levi. He turned and saw Nash standing in the corridor behind him.

Thank goodness. Sanity had arrived. "We were hoping to speak with your father," Levi said. "Tova says he's not home."

"Come with me," Nash said. "I'll take you to him." And he stepped past Levi and into the house.

Tova backed up a step, out of her son's way. "I'll not have my home turned into a common passageway."

"Of course not, Mother," Nash said, "but we must be flexible in this transition time."

"This is not a transition. All will return to normal soon enough. I will not have these upsiders putting ideas into my children's heads."

Nash pulled his mother aside and waved Levi toward the door that led to the gate to Zane's Midland house. "Peace, Mother. Perfect love casts out all fear."

Levi and Jordan stopped at the gate and waited for Nash.

"Don't talk to me about perfect love," Tova said. "I have loved you all, and what has it gotten me? You all go upside, against my wishes!"

"Mother, please. We'll talk more on this later." Nash kissed her forehead and joined Levi and Jordan at the gate. "Didn't my father teach you how to open a gate? It's quite simple." He grabbed the wheel and turned it to the left until it clicked. "Once you hear the gears shift, you turn it back the other way until it opens." He did this, and the door clicked again and popped away from its frame. Nash opened it and the hinges creaked with the weight of the iron door. "After you."

Levi, Jordan, and Nash followed the corridor to Zane's basement. From there, they moved the shelves and curtain and went into the nest, where they found Ruston and Zane hunched over the GlassTop computer.

"Hello," Ruston said, straightening to greet them. "Levi, it's good to see you awake. How are you?"

"As well as any man whose wife has been taken to that place," Levi said. "I don't suppose there is any hope of going back for her?"

Zane twisted his chair around. "It's not looking good. They've installed cameras in all the rooms now, added an enforcer shift inside the harem, and they've sealed off that door in the kitchen. I guess they don't care if there's a fire exit or not. Now, if we had those SimSuits, we might have a chance. But Lhogan is not returning our taps."

"I owe him now," Ruston said, "and he's not eager to take such a risk again if he doesn't have to."

"Could we start a fire? Then try and free them when they're outside?" Levi asked.

"I wouldn't want to risk them getting trapped in there," Zane said. "It's too dangerous."

It was. "So we focus on Omar's old plan: Operation Lynchpin?"

"The sooner we can take down the government, the sooner you can get to Jemma," Zane said.

"But this isn't a thing that can be rushed," Ruston said. "We've been working toward this for years."

"And what have you learned?" Levi asked.

"Much about enforcer protocol, how enforcers get their orders from the guild," Zane said.

"What do you know about those hooded people?"

"The Ancients?" Zane turned back to his computer and pulled up a map. "They live in Teocalli Manor — a mansion in the forest at the northern curve of the bell." He zoomed into the location and pointed to it on his screen. "They're not allowed to come and go as they please. They have servants who see to their needs and enforcer escorts for when they are permitted to leave the manor."

"So they're prisoners too," Jordan said. "Who are they?"

"Safe Landers believe they're the wisdom of the past," Ruston said. "They've forsaken moving on to the next life in order to stay here and advise the people."

"But what about what Ciddah said Mason overheard Renzor say," Levi said. "That they wouldn't have accepted Otley? Do you think they become Ancients to avoid liberation?"

"It makes as much sense as anything," Ruston said.

"So that means liberation is death," Jordan said.

"Or something unpleasant," Zane said. "It doesn't seem pleasant to have to keep your face hooded and live in confinement. Yet these people choose it."

"We've tried to figure it out for years," Ruston said. "But we've never known what to look for. Now that we know liberation ceremonies are prerecorded and that those who go through it are taken directly from the Champion Theater to wherever they're liberated, perhaps next time we can have some vehicles waiting to follow the van when it leaves the amphitheater."

"I wish I would have thought to follow the van back to the RC on the traffic cams," Zane said. "Then I could have seen where it went. I just assumed they were going back to the RC."

"Next time," Ruston said.

"Isn't there a liberation tonight?" Jordan asked.

"Liberation ceremony, yes," Zane said. "But it is only the recording.

And there are never trials at night. We need to monitor the trials somehow. Then we can try to track the vehicles that leave the amphitheater."

"We can't wait around until then," Levi said. "What about the Owl? The kids are still talking about him. Did it have as much success with adults?"

"At first," Zane said. "But the ratings are dropping fast. I've had to cobble together different videos and backgrounds to make it seem like new material, but the people are on to me. We need a new Owl."

"I'll do it," Levi said, feeling reckless and desperate to do something. "What do I have to do?"

"I'm not sure you'll fit in the suit," Zane said. "Omar's a lot smaller than you."

"Where is it?" Levi asked.

"Upstairs. After Otley died, I went to Omar's apartment and grabbed whatever I could before they came and cleaned it out. I went to Mason's too, but he didn't own anything but a suit and some medic scrubs." Zane shrugged. "I thought Omar would want his paintings."

Such a thing had never occurred to Levi. "Thanks for doing that for him, Zane. What else did Omar have? Any weapons?"

"No. He had the Owl costume and a bunch of art and paints, brushes, and canvasses. A few letters from Shaylinn."

"What kind of letters?" Jordan asked.

"I didn't read them. They were from the Messenger, which I know was Shay, so … you know how she is."

"No, I don't," Jordan said. "She never mailed me any Messenger letters. Why would she mail some to Omar?"

"So if I can fit into that suit," Levi said, hoping to distract Jordan from his nonsensical issues with Omar, "what do I have to do?"

"We'll make a plan for what to have you say," Zane said. "We can add some of what we saw happen through the contact lenses. That Mason was liberated with only one X, that they were given no liberation ceremony. Stuff like that."

"And for Operation Lynchpin?" Levi asked. "What can we do to move that along?"

"All the food comes from the Lowlands," Ruston said. "We'll need to figure out how to stop the shipments. The water comes from the dam."

"So we drive down there and see what's what," Jordan said. "See what we can burn."

"We don't want to *destroy* the food or the water," Levi said. "I don't want to be responsible for thousands of people starving to death this winter. We just need to take control of them somehow."

"It won't be easy," Ruston said. "No one just drives to the Lowlands, not the way Highlanders can come into the Midlands, anyway. The road to the Lowlands leads outside the walls, so it's heavily guarded."

"Can you make fake SimTags with Lowlands information?" Levi asked Zane.

"Conceivably," Zane said. "I've never seen a Lowland SimTag, though. I'll ask my contact in Registration."

"Do you have any friends up at the dam?" Levi asked.

"We've never had a man at the dam," Ruston said. "They're so far away from where we recruit that none of us have ever gotten to know anyone who tasks there."

"So we've got three goals," Levi said. "The Owl, the Lowlands, and the dam." It felt good to have a plan.

"It's a start, at least," Ruston said. "And if Jemma gave them the information about the theater, that should distract them from what we're really working on."

Levi took a deep breath through his nose, hating that Jemma had been the one to get caught. He should've insisted she stay behind. He shook his head—no use going over that territory again. She'd wanted to go. Now he wondered if she had given up the information on the theater. They'd better not have hurt her.

"Let's go see if you can fit into that suit," Zane said.

Levi followed him upstairs. The Owl suit was tight, but Omar had made it from an Old wetsuit, which was stretchy. Levi fit into it and was able to move surprisingly well. Once it was clear the headpiece fit as well, he and Zane went back down to record a new statement.

"I'll broadcast it tonight, in the middle of the liberation ceremony," Zane said. "The task director general will *love* that."

A chill ran up Levi's arms. This month's ceremony should include the prerecorded footage of Mason and Omar. And Bender and Rewl and General Otley, as well. Time was going by faster than Levi wanted it to. They'd been in this place for two and a half months already.

"Make sure to interrupt someone we don't know," Levi said. "I'd like to watch this one." Though he didn't know why. It would only make him upset.

He and Jordan returned to the nest to watch the liberation ceremony that night. Levi sat in a chair beside Zane and focused on the big screen.

Finley and Flynn were wearing matching purple outfits with silver hair, which meant that by tomorrow morning, purple would be flooding the streets and storefronts. Levi was glad to be underground.

Luella Flynn opened with a tribute to Kendall Collin. Dozens of pictures flashed across the screen as Finley and Flynn took turns talking about the great times they'd had with the former Safe Lands queen. It was tragic that she'd been liberated so young, they said, but being a number one, she had many more lives to get it right. Best of luck to Kendall Collin in the next one.

It had been two and a half weeks since Levi's brothers had been captured. And he knew from what they'd seen through their contact lenses that they'd been sentenced almost two weeks ago. But to everyone else watching, it was as if they were just liberated.

Levi's hands were shaking. Watching this would provide no clue as to his brothers' whereabouts, yet he stared at the screen, eager to see their faces.

"Maybe we should kidnap Luella Flynn and see what she knows about liberation," Jordan said.

"Now there's an interesting idea," Zane said. "Maybe the Owl should pay her a visit."

"I'm game," Levi said.

Luella brought out a man named Garber Bloom, who had been a dancer who had taught Maroz Zerrik everything he knew, whoever Maroz Zerrik was. She introduced a video montage that showed clips from movies he'd been in, dancing and singing.

"Why are we watching this dung?" Jordan said.

"It might be your last chance to see Mason and Omar," Zane said.

Jordan grunted, and Levi knew what he was thinking. "We saw the last we're going to see of them," Levi said. "If by some miracle liberation isn't death, and if they're still alive, until we can learn the mystery of liberation, we can't help them." And maybe never could. Maybe whatever lay beyond liberation was a death camp like in that Schindler movie. Welcome to Bliss. Mass murder. "But I still want to watch. That way I can know how to word what I say as the Owl so I'm contradicting what they've said here."

"Fine," Jordan said. "It's a lot of fluffy nonsense, though. I can't imagine Luella Flynn would have interviewed Mason or Omar."

"She couldn't have. You never saw anything like that in their contacts, did you?" Levi asked Zane.

"Nope. They weren't important to the Safe Lands," Zane said. "They'll show their faces at the end and that's about it. They don't usually interview Xed people. Lonn was an exception."

"More like a warning," Levi said.

"Liberation has to be death," Jordan said.

It can't be death, Levi thought, trying to convince himself.

They suffered through another twenty minutes of the dancing man before Luella Flynn brought out a woman who'd tasked as a costume designer for twenty-two years. She got a standing ovation.

Jordan threw an apple core at the screen. It bounced off and left a wet mark across the glass.

"Whoa!" Zane said.

"*Jordan*," Levi said.

"I'm sorry, but why does this place think dancing and acting and fashion is better than every other job? Seems to me it's more work to task in construction or street cleaning or picking fields in the

Lowlands. Why don't we ever see a pig farmer getting interviewed by Luella Flynn, huh?"

"Because pig farming and construction and street cleaning aren't glamorous," Levi said. "And perception of pleasure is all that matters here. So they show us what's perceived as glamorous, hoping the viewers will love it and not ask where bacon comes from."

"That's not exactly true," Zane said. "There are some who are that naive, of course, but most know the guild is hiding things. But they go along with it because it's in their best interest not to ask questions."

"The truth is your best interest," Levi said. "And we have to find it."

"Shh!" Zane said. "It's General Otley."

A still image of Otley's face filled the screen. "Tyr Otley," Finley Gray said. "Best known as the young enforcer who took down the rebel group VIRUS in 2076, Otley kept our land safe as Enforcer General for the past nine years."

Jordan groaned. "And I wasted my apple core on the fashion lady."

"You could use it again," Zane suggested.

"Why is Otley so far down the list?" Levi asked.

"Don't know," Zane said.

"Because he doesn't sing and dance," Jordan said.

Finley went on for a long while about how great Otley had been and how much the Safe Lands would miss him. Levi wondered how many Safe Landers were secretly glad that Otley had been premie libbed.

When the Otley tribute ended, the camera showed a close-up of Luella Flynn's face. Her skin was silver and glittery, her eyes lime green. What a freak.

"Safe Landers, join me in a moment of silence to honor the nationals who have passed on to the next life, including some nines who are entering Bliss. We send them our love and know that we will see them soon."

Luella faded away, and the camera showed a wide shot of the amphitheater and the distant Wyndo stage screen, slowly zooming back in. The first face appeared on the screen. A man with dark hair and SimArt lines on his forehead.

"Jesmin Harres, six," Finley Gray said, "tasked in engineering and design. The Safe Lands bids you pleasure in the next life, Mr. Harres."

"August Liv, three," Luella said, "tasked as a level sixteen medic in the Men's Health and Wellness Department. The Safe Lands bids you pleasure in the next life, Mr. Liv."

"This is stupid," Jordan said. "How long are they going to make us wait?"

"I told you, they'll be on last," Zane said. "Nationals are ranked by celebrity status, so the Xed come at the very end."

"Bertram Grice, five," Finley Gray said, "enforcer, wall patrol unit. The Safe Lands bids you pleasure in the next life, Mr. Grice."

"Nella May, two," Luella said, "tasked as an educator in the Safe Lands boarding school. The Safe Lands bids you pleasure in the next life, Ms. May."

"Leon Jaff," Finley Gray said, "tasked as an educator in the Safe Lands boarding school. The Safe Lands bids you pleasure in the next life, Mr. Jaff."

"Do you think all those teachers got liberated because we took the kids?" Levi asked.

"I wouldn't doubt it," Zane said.

Levi didn't know if he should feel sorry for them or not. He guessed not.

"Angel White," Luella said, "tasked as a matron in the Safe Lands nursery. The Safe Lands bids you pleasure in the next life, Ms. White."

"A nursery worker too," Levi said. "I bet she was the one who killed Kendall."

"More likely she's the one who didn't. Killing Kendall would have been seen as heroic by the guild," Zane said. "I doubt they liberated whoever did that."

Jordan looked at Levi and frowned. "Can you believe that?"

In this place, Levi could believe just about anything.

Then Omar's face claimed the screen. The picture had been taken back when he was wearing an enforcer's uniform, complete with hat. It reminded Levi of the Old Colorado State Patrol hat Omar used to wear every day. The look on his face was smug, back when he thought this place was best for Glenrock.

"Omar Strong, nine," Finley Gray said, "tasked with the enforcers, in SimArt design, and in construction. The Safe Lands bids you enjoy Bliss, Mr. Strong."

"Cavek Rose," Luella said, "tasked as a cook for Café Eats. The Safe Lands bids you pleasure in the next life, Mr. Rose."

"That's it for Omar?" Jordan said. "He deserves more words than that! Those stinking maggots and their — "

"Jordan, look!" Levi gestured to the Wyndo screen.

"Bender," Finley Gray said, "a known rebel from the Midlands. No tasks on file, no full name, no number. The Safe Lands bids you pleasure, Mr. Bender, wherever you next find yourself."

"Wow," Levi said. "Not a word about his killing Otley." This place was bizarre. He'd never understand it.

Then Mason's face filled the screen.

"Mason Elias, nine," Luella said, "tasked in the Pharmco Pharmacy and as a level two medic in the Surrogacy Center. The Safe Lands bids you enjoy Bliss, Mr. Elias."

Tears filled Levi's eyes, and he blinked them back. He never should have let them go after Shaylinn without him. He'd known they weren't ready. But Ruston had convinced him. What did Ruston know about anything? His people hid underground with no desire to leave. Levi hadn't wanted Jemma to go on this last mission either.

From now on, Levi would trust his own instincts.

"Time to interrupt this broadcast," Zane said, tapping on his GlassTop keyboard.

The liberation broadcast blinked to black, then the Owl filled the screen — Levi, the Owl. Zane had given him a video background of the footage captured through Omar's eyes just before he was liberated as he got stunned in the back of the truck and taken out on a stretcher.

"This is not an error," Levi's distorted voice said. "The Messenger Owl has truth to deliver to the people of the Safe Lands. Truth brings freedom. Listen well. Liberations are not peaceful. You are taken to a facility where you are strip-searched before being taken into the unknown. This ColorCast you were watching is a tool for the Safe Lands Guild to tell lies. The Messenger Owl speaks the truth. There are not nine lives, but only one. Make yours count."

And behind Levi, the video through Omar's eyes continued to roll as he was set on the strange exam table and the enforcers started to undress him. The footage faded to black just as Levi stopped talking.

Zane tapped back to the liberation ceremony where Finley Gray was talking.

"On this, the first day of September," Finley Gray said, "there are still fourteen people in the Safe Lands who will be celebrating their liberation in what remains of 2088. If you know one of them, take the time to enjoy them while they're here. For it won't be long until they head into the next life."

"From us to you, Happy Liberation Day, Safe Landers," Luella Flynn said. "We'll see you next month. And as always, find pleasure in life."

Zane muted the volume as the broadcast went to commercial.

"That was outstanding," Jordan said. "What you did with the contacts video ..."

"It looked really good," Levi said. "Surely it made Renzor mad."

"Well, it's all we had," Zane said. "I can use it again with different words, but you're going to have to find something just as good to keep people watching."

"Don't we have what Mason's eyes saw?"

"Lhogan isn't answering my taps. So I only have what was on my screen at the time, which was Omar's."

"I'll find something to show them," Levi said. "We must have missed Rewl. Bender was a natural, and they put him on."

"As a warning," Zane said. "And because he was alive when they recorded this. Rewl is a dead ghost that no one will miss."

Which was what they'd all be if they got themselves killed.

"Levi!" Shaylinn jumped up and ran toward him as he entered his underground house. Her face was tear-streaked. "The liberation ceremony was on. We watched it on my Wyndo. They showed Omar and Mason and Bender and Kendall."

Levi looked around the living room. Everyone was sitting on the couches, staring at a portable Wyndo that was propped up on the coffee table. "All of you watched it?"

"I thought they might have said something about the Owl," Trevon said, "but then the Owl came on! That means wherever Omar is, he's okay!"

Levi bit his cheek. Should he tell the kids that he was Omar's Owl now? No, he couldn't take away their hope. "Listen, I don't want any of you watching the ColorCast. There's not supposed to be any technology down here unless Zane has modified it. It could be dangerous."

"I'm sorry," Shaylinn said. "I didn't know I was supposed to give it back."

"Ruston didn't say, but you need to be responsible with it, and showing the children the ColorCast wasn't a responsible thing to do."

Tears pooled in Shaylinn's eyes. "I wanted to see Omar."

"I understand," Levi said. What else could he say? "But I don't want anyone watching any more Safe Lands TV. Including you." He snatched up the Wyndo from the coffee table. "I'll just hold on to this and see what Ruston says. He may not want us having them down here. I know his wife wouldn't!"

"But how will I research people to send messages to?"

"Shaylinn, take a break from sending messages for a while, will you? Focus on helping Eliza teach these kids."

"Okay." But her voice sounded so desperately sad that Levi felt like a jerk. Still, he carried the Wyndo into his room and tossed it on the bed. He needed to keep his people from indulging in Safe Lands entertainment. The more they liked this place, the harder it would be to leave when the time came, which, Levi hoped, would be very soon.

CHAPTER
14

That Friday night, Omar climbed into his bunk and pretended to be sick. He didn't want to go to Fajro, but he was too chicken to just up and quit.

Pretending wasn't all that difficult. He'd earned a second vial of brown sugar from Rain last Wednesday for talking with Cacia. So he'd let himself finish off his first as a reward for a job well done. But that had only increased his craving, and he hadn't loaded his new vial yet in fear he'd down the whole thing. Instead he'd spent all his credits on a level two of grass, which he'd nursed for the past two days and was almost gone. The aches and trembling had returned as his body cried out for the sugar.

Kurwin peeked over the side of Omar's bunk. "Did you already vape your whole vial from last weekend?"

Omar answered with a pathetic moan.

"You can't just skip. Rain isn't going to like it. Prav either."

Prav? What did he have to do with it? Omar wanted to ask. Instead he waited, praying Kurwin would leave and give Rain the message that Omar was ill.

"You better not make a habit of it." And Kurwin left.

Omar stayed in bed, taking little puffs of grass and letting it calm his nerves. He didn't dare leave the room in case someone saw him out. He was exhausted anyway, so going to bed early was probably for the best.

He lay there savoring each breath of grass and thinking about Shaylinn, wondering where she was, how she was doing, if her belly had grown yet, if the babies were okay, if they were boys or girls or one of each.

He fell asleep with those thoughts lingering in his mind, thoughts of Shaylinn and children and a life he'd never live.

"Get up, you shell!"

Something struck Omar's face. He rolled onto his side and opened his eyes. Prav was leaning over one side of his bed, hand raised to strike again.

"Don't!" Omar said, shrinking against the safety bars on the far side of his bunk.

"Don't you tell me don't, you lazy juicer." Prav settled both hands on the safety bar, holding himself up. "I don't care if you're puking your guts out. Tonight, you come to Fajro. No excuses."

"*Okay!*"

Prav gave him one last glare before jumping back to the floor. Omar watched him walk into the bathroom. Walls, that guy was intense.

Omar's SimAlarm buzzed, telling him he had ten minutes to be up and out of the residence. No time to shower. He'd slept in his jumpsuit, so he climbed down and shoved his feet into his boots.

"You shouldn't have skipped," Kurwin whispered. "I told you Prav wouldn't like it."

"Why should he care?"

"Because he brought you to Rain. He stuck his neck out for you, and she's invested in you. If you turn out to be worthless, she gets mad at Prav for wasting her time."

"Oh." Omar didn't want to be anywhere near Prav right now. "See you later then." And he darted out the door and into the hallway. His stomach roiled with hunger. Credits were applied each morning for the previous day's work, so Omar jogged down to the cafeteria and went through the line for two dry pancakes and a banana. He ate them on his walk to the pens.

It looked like he was going to have to go to Fajro tonight. That, or deal with Prav. Neither option sounded very pleasant.

When Omar entered Fajro that night, he was surprised to find it crowded. He stood in the doorway, paralyzed, uncertain if he should stay or run. Maybe if he stayed out past curfew the enforcers would take him into custody. Maybe they'd give him a mercy vape.

"Omar, come."

He jerked out of his daydream and his gaze fell on Rain. She was wearing purple tonight, and once again her lipstick didn't match. That suddenly annoyed him. Why couldn't she see how the shades clashed?

"Come."

Omar stepped deeper into Fajro, following her, not knowing what else to do. He didn't want to be here, but he didn't know how to leave, either.

She held aside the beaded curtain and his steps slowed. Go back there? Already? He glanced back to the table where he and Kurwin always sat and drank. It was filled with people he didn't know. Customers.

It was busy tonight.

He ducked under the doorway and Rain let the beads fall shut. They clicked against each other and the doorframe, oddly sounding like rain on a window.

"She's waiting for you," Rain said, nodding across the room.

Omar followed her gesture to a booth where Cacia sat. Omar sighed as weight melted away from his heart. Another night of talking? No problem.

He walked over to the booth and sat down. "Cacia."

"Hay-o, you." She grinned and bounced in her seat. Omar didn't like her flirty tone. She hadn't been like that on Wednesday. "I'm feeling better tonight, thanks to you."

"That's good."

"So I thought tonight we could go out. There's this dance club I like called the Dexx. Then we can go back to my place."

Omar tried to keep his face calm, but he felt his eyes swell. He hoped she hadn't noticed. "Uh, I haven't been feeling well. I'd hate for you to catch something."

She narrowed her eyes. "I'm not that old, you know."

"Old? I never said you were old."

"I know an excuse when I hear one. Well, guess what, raven boy? I paid for you, and I paid for the whole night."

Oh, walls. Omar's stomach turned to stone. He gritted his teeth. "My mistake. Dancing it is." He got up and strode away, pushing through the beads. He stopped at the counter and ordered a beer. The barkeep had just pushed it toward him when Cacia appeared at his side with Rain.

Omar picked up the beer and took a big gulp. He held the glass at his stomach and looked at the women. "What? I need a beer before I dance, okay?"

Rain raised one eyebrow, then glanced at Cacia. "He'll behave."

Behave. As if this woman owned him. She may as well get a collar and leash.

He finished his beer and left the glass on the counter. "So where are we going?" he asked Cacia.

"I told you. The Dexx. It's on the classy side of Cibelo."

Omar went with Cacia to the club. It was dark, with red lights shining down from the ceiling onto a packed crowd, the silhouettes of waving arms and bobbing heads all facing the stage where a live band was playing.

Cacia took his hand and pulled him along the back of the crowd. "The dancing is over here."

He plodded along after her, but his attention was on the stage. There were four in the band. Two men and two women, all in their mid-fifties, perhaps? They had chartreuse-and-violet FloArt tattoos that glowed like light under their skin. The three who were standing played guitars, though these guitars looked nothing like the one Uncle Ethan used to play in Glenrock. These were thin glass and looked like toys. The fourth band member — a woman — was sitting down at a GlassTop, tapping her hands on the surface in the rhythm of the percussion. They all must have had some sort of amplified SimSpeak, as their voices rang out from all sides of the club.

Cacia stopped suddenly and started to dance — at least that's what Omar suspected she was trying to do. He tried not to laugh at her obvious lack of rhythm. She wiggled and kicked and shook her arms, but it looked more like she was trying to shake out an itch than dance.

She looked happy, though. Maybe if he could keep her here long enough, she'd forget about going back to her apartment.

So Omar tried to enjoy himself. And there were moments — brief ones — where he completely forgot that he'd sold himself for brown sugar. Like when he thought about Shaylinn or when the band played a slow song and the man's voice seemed to carry him into a dream.

But then Cacia said she wanted a drink, grabbed his arm, and dragged him toward the exit.

"But the bar is that way," Omar yelled.

"I have drinks at my place," she said. "We're running out of time."

Right. Because Omar had a curfew. If he wasn't back at a certain time, Cacia would have to pay more.

Omar followed her, dumbly, a slave to his stupidity. Would he never make the right choice?

Her apartment was small — all in one room. But it was clean and she didn't have to share it with anyone. Not like Omar did, anyway. Or poor Mason.

She gave Omar a bottle of beer from her fridge and urged him to sit on the couch. They sat side by side, drinking their beers.

Omar stared straight ahead. He wanted to leave, but how could he?

What were his options? Stay with her and get paid with a vial of brown sugar, or leave and get beat up by Prav — and get no brown sugar.

There had to be another way.

She took the beer from his hand and set it with hers on a table beside the couch. Then she turned back to him. "Kiss me."

To be fair, she wasn't ugly, not like some of the women he'd seen Prav leave Fajro with. Maybe if he didn't think about what he was doing ... Or he could pretend she were someone else. Shaylinn?

No, not Shaylinn. Someone who didn't matter. Red or Belbeline. If he pretended he was with one of them, perhaps he could get through this.

He closed his eyes and pressed his lips against hers. She grabbed his head, his neck, his shoulders. Her hands were clammy and bone-like, and he recoiled at her touch.

Lord, help me, please. I'm sorry I got myself into this.

Cacia pulled away from him and groaned like he was the most disappointing date she'd ever had. "Don't just sit there. Do something. Why are you such a prude?"

He stood up. "I'm going to leave."

"What? Why? You can't."

"I'm sorry, Cacia. You're a nice person, but I just can't do this. Besides, I like someone else."

"You like someone else?" Her tone dripped with disbelief. "I paid good credits for you. I own you for another forty-five minutes."

"Nobody owns me." Omar walked to the door and opened it. "I'm sure Rain will give you a refund." And then have Prav turn Omar's face into a pile of guts worthy of the incinerator.

He slipped out into the hallway and quickly shut the door behind him. He grinned, which was stupid, because now he was in trouble.

The door to Cacia's apartment opened and Omar jogged down the hall.

"Get back here!" she yelled after him.

But he slipped down the stairwell and out of sight. He didn't slow down. He had no desire to have her chase after him and make a scene.

What now? He headed across Cibelo on his way to the strikers' residence. But going back would only put him in Prav's path. He wandered around, trying to decide what to do. Maybe he should just go back and tell Rain he quit? Take his beating and be done with it.

He found himself outside the Get Out Now Diner, but he didn't recognize anyone inside. He wondered if any of them were rebels. The thought made him think of the RC. If he missed curfew, they'd take him there, right? He'd have a private cell and maybe even a mercy vape.

He never thought he'd actually look forward to spending a night in prison. But right now, prison looked pretty good.

He entered a club and watched people dance, knowing it was close to curfew. He sat at the bar, but he didn't want to spend what little credits he had on anything, so he went back to the dance floor rather than have to deal with dirty looks from the barkeep.

He wished he had his PV. He'd left it in his pillowcase so he wouldn't be tempted to finish it, saving his meager puffs for when he was lying in bed each night. But he was wound up now from stress and fear and the not knowing what was going to happen when he didn't go back to his bunk.

His SimAlarm pulsed with the ten-minute warning. Ten minutes and he'd break curfew. Thankfully he wasn't wearing an orange jumpsuit, so he wouldn't stand out as a striker to the reputables if he were out late. But where should he go?

He decided on a bench at the end of a narrow street of shops. Most were closed as they weren't the kinds of shops that got a lot of shoppers at this time of night. A cleaner, a cosmetics store, and a messenger's office. If he was someplace secluded when he got stunned, he wouldn't make a scene.

He thought of Shaylinn and wondered if she was still sending her messages. He suddenly ached with indignation at his lot in life. Sure, he'd done it to himself. But he'd been trying to fix his life and now he was here. And Shay was there. It was probably for the best. He'd hurt her enough. He hated the idea of her raising the babies on her own, but maybe Nodin would marry her. Or Yivan. They were decent-enough fellows.

The SimAlarm went off then, delivering as much current as any SimScanner or stunner could. Hid body seized, and he fell onto his side on the bench. Little grunts came out of his throat, though he wasn't trying to make any noise. He closed his eyes and pictured Shay's burnt-umber eyes until he passed out.

"Hey! What's the problem here, shell? You OD?"

Omar opened his eyes and found an enforcer looking down on him. He jumped, slid on the bench a little, and pushed himself up. He could move. What time was it? How long had he been here?

The enforcer held out a SimScanner and Omar heard it beep. "Omar Strong. He's a striker."

"Where's your jumpsuit, striker? Those are awful nice clothes."

"You got a girl buying you nice things? Or are you a streetman?"

"Can't you talk?" the other said. "Stand up. We need to search you."

Omar pushed up on shaky legs. The weakness hadn't fully faded yet.

The enforcer patted Omar's body, running his hands along Omar's back, sides, hips, pockets, and legs. "No PV. No vials either. Shame, I was looking to help myself to some treats tonight, striker boy."

"He can still buy us something," the other enforcer said.

The one with the SimScanner read his SimTag again. "He's got nine credits."

"That's it?"

"Strikers don't get paid much, but that's pathetic. You spend it all on that fancy outfit?"

"I thought you were going to take me to the RC or something," Omar said.

"Oh, you want to go to the RC, is that it? Someone back in the bunkhouse have you scared?"

"No. I just thought that's what happens."

"What's your address, shell?"

Omar didn't say anything.

"Stupid, stubborn strikers."

The other chortled. "Say that three times fast."

The enforcer used his SimScanner again. "Sector six. Strikers'

Residence. 318. Cohabs are Vita, Jeorn, Arling ... Prav." He grinned. "Oh, yes. It's Prav who's got you scared, I bet."

"Then let's take him to Prav."

"What? No! I missed curfew, and the liberator told me I'd have to see the warden."

But the enforcers didn't care. They dragged Omar to the strikers' residence and right up to the door to his room.

Where Prav was waiting.

"Missing someone?" the enforcer said.

"Yes, actually," Prav said. "I've been waiting for the little guy."

"You want to do it out here?" the enforcer asked.

"Do what?" Omar said. He caught sight of Kurwin's wincing expression through the cracked open door.

Prav held out his hand. "I would, thanks."

"Do what?" Omar asked. "Prav, what's this about, peer?"

The second enforcer used his SimScanner on Prav's hand, and Prav walked out into the hallway. His SimAlarm didn't go off for being out of his room after curfew. Why not? Omar swallowed as the door fell closed.

"Prav, come on, peer. I just can't do it, okay? I tried but ..." Omar tried to pull away from the enforcer. He pushed. Grabbed at the man's hands and pried his clamped fingers open. Just as he slipped free, Prav grabbed Omar's shoulder, turned him, and his fist shot out and struck Omar's jaw.

Omar's head jerked back like bone breaking. Throbbing fire engulfed his face. He stumbled against the wall and grabbed it to keep from falling.

Once his footing was steady, he palmed his jaw. Okay ... nothing seemed broken. He glanced up.

Prav was staring down, a sneer on his face. "You don't get off that easy."

Omar lifted his arm to block his face, and Prav's fist rammed into his stomach. Omar groaned and doubled over, hugging his gut. He gasped for breath, but had barely managed to inhale when Prav struck him again, this time in the side. Omar tottered, off balance, and fell on the floor. The cold tile felt nice on his cheek but stank of urine and bleach at the same time.

Why did the enforcers just stand there? And why did no one watching through the yellow cameras come to help?

"You're pathetic," Prav said. "Aren't you even going to try to fight back?"

"Do what ... you have to." Omar choked in a breath. "I'm not working for Rain again."

"If you insist." Prav grabbed Omar's sleeve and dragged him into the middle of the hallway. "Why don't you give me a hand with this, peers."

The three men beat him with their fist and feet until every inch of him had been bruised or jabbed or clawed or kicked. Without mercy, they showered him with blows. He curled into a ball and tried to make himself smaller, but that didn't end the pain.

At some point he awoke. He was being carried through the door of his room. The enforcers had his legs, Prav the underside of his arms. They pushed him up onto his bunk and left him there. The door opened and closed. Then the lights went off.

Omar lay in the darkness, listening to his own choked breaths and Prav settling into his bunk. He dared not move. His body felt like someone had peeled off the skin and rubbed salt over his rawness. He burned. He ached. Something was bleeding. He was pretty sure he was dying.

Why die in pain when he could fly?

Though his muscles protested, he reached up inside his pillowcase and found his PV and the vial of brown sugar he'd earned last week talking to Cacia. He couldn't see, but he'd done this enough that he didn't need light. He popped out the nearly empty vial of grass and replaced it with the brown sugar.

He couldn't take it all in one breath, but two should do the trick. Then it would all be over. His hand was shaking as he lifted the PV to his lips.

Good-bye, Shay-Shay.

His first vape was long. He breathed the juice all the way into his toes. He held his breath through the nausea, waiting for it to carry him into the blissful warmth. The rush had never been as good as that first time, but when it finally came, it melted all the pain off his body. He was safe in this place. Nothing hurt here.

A flash of white mist formed around him, so thick he couldn't see past the edge of his bed. Above, the ceiling sparkled and glitter began to rain down. He closed his eyes and he was driving his old motorcycle down the forest road toward Glenrock. Going home. The sky was white above stark branches. Suddenly the road was covered in snow.

Up ahead, a man was standing on the road. Not a man, but a face. A giant face twice as big as Omar was tall. It was God's face, he somehow knew, frowning, daring Omar to stand before him and be judged. A path branched off the road and Omar steered the motorcycle onto it, leaving God behind him.

Something clumped on the floor across the room. He opened his eyes and found himself still shrouded in white mist. His bed shook. Someone was climbing up. No! He would do this his way. His heart fluttered, and he vaped another long drag.

As he clenched against the nausea, the white mist darkened to gray. Then black. Smoky tendrils drifted toward him, coiled around his legs and arms, his waist. He thought about his motorcycle again, closed his eyes, tried to picture the road in the forest.

The tingling came, and he was riding again down the dark road. Something was racing him, trying to fly past him. An owl? It was big and black. Not a bird. It had arms. The sky was black now and there was no snow. He sped down a dirt path, his headlight casting a faint glow. And still the creature came, sometimes on his right, sometimes on his left, sometimes above, behind, down by the tires. A flying, hooded shadow. Faceless. Chasing him. Reaching out.

The road vanished and the motorcycle dove into a chasm. The chasm was the shadow monster, arms grasping, prickly and clawed.

And Omar saw no more.

CHAPTER
15

I don't understand why you're so upset." Penny was sitting beside Shaylinn on a bench in Kindred Park, watching the children play. "You never really watched the ColorCast, did you?"

"No," Shaylinn said. "But I used it to research people so I could write them messages. And now I can't." Levi had taken away her link to the Safe Lands. Writing messages had given her a sense of purpose and meaning in this place. Granted, she hadn't written any in a few weeks. The move and the drama with Tova had distracted her. But now that she couldn't, she was angry.

"Just tell him you want it back."

"I tried. He said I didn't need to be writing messages anymore."

"Sounds like *he* needs a message," Penny said. "It's not fair. He treats us like children, but he makes us take care of the little kids. We're doing the work of mothers, but we're not getting any of the respect. He never used to be like this."

"I think he's afraid. For Jemma. For all of us. And fear makes people do strange things. It makes them paranoid and irrational, stubborn and domineering. They think if things are done a certain way, then bad stuff won't happen. But that's silly, because bad stuff happens anyway. We just have to live each day as best we can, treat others the way we want to be treated, and trust that God knows best."

"Like with Omar," Penny said. "Did he really kiss you?"

"On my forehead, like I told you."

"Right. And he kissed Kendall the other way. Do you think he loved her?"

"No. I don't think so. He said he didn't. But, Penny, it doesn't matter. He's been liberated. Maybe he really is dead." Shaylinn didn't want to talk about this again, but Penny kept bringing it up.

"Of course it matters! You have to have faith, like you said."

"I have faith ... mostly. But if he isn't — Until Omar comes back, there's no point in dwelling on everything that's happened. That would be like torturing myself." Not that she hadn't been, but she was trying not to. "That's why I need to write messages. Even if I take care of the children all day and help Eliza teach and cook all the meals for Levi's household, there's that time when I first wake up or right before I go to bed. I could write messages then. I want to."

"Then do it for the people you've already written to. Don't worry about trying to find new addresses. Just be loyal to the ones you've got."

That was a good idea. "But how will they get delivered? Levi won't help me. And forget Jordan. He thinks I should be sewing baby clothes for my children twenty-four seven. And I already used the entire bag of fabric Omar gave me."

"How many clothes does Jordan think a baby needs?"

Shaylinn shrugged. "Plus, I'll have his son's hand-me-downs."

"Why don't you ask that guy to help you?" Penny pointed at the playground. Just on the other side of the slide, having just walked in through the corridor on that end, was Nash. He stood talking to Trevon and Grayn.

"Zane's brother? I suppose I could." But Ciddah thought Nash liked Shaylinn, so she didn't want to encourage him. The few times they'd met, he'd been overly friendly.

He saw them, then, and waved, though he continued talking to the boys. Shaylinn waved back.

Penny grabbed Shaylinn's arm. "He'd be perfect, Shay, because he can go upside but he's not from Glenrock."

Which likely meant he wouldn't feel obligated to tell Levi. Not that Omar had told Levi about Shaylinn's messages, but that was because Omar had liked keeping things from his brother.

"He's coming!" Penny whispered. "Quick, talk about something interesting."

"What do you mean? Was I boring you before?"

Penny started to laugh, a strange, fake laugh that was overly loud and turned the heads of most of the kids on the playground.

Shaylinn stifled a groan. "You like him, don't you?" Penny used to act this way whenever Levi had brought Nodin to the village. "What about Nodin? I thought you liked him."

Penny's eyes bulged. "Shhh!"

Shaylinn couldn't believe how silly her friend was being. "Hello, Nash," she called out. "We were just talking about you."

"No!" Penny tried to put her hand over Shaylinn's mouth.

"Stop it." Shaylinn shot Penny a glare. Why would she assume Shaylinn was going to try to embarrass her?

Nash stopped in front of them and looked from Penny's face to Shaylinn's, back and forth. His lips curved in a slow smile. "It was all good, I hope?"

"We weren't talking about you." Penny's cheeks were beet red.

"Penny suggested I ask you a favor," Shaylinn said. "When I was in hiding in the Midlands, I wrote messages to people who'd expressed interest in the rebellion. They were generic messages, but I wanted to do something that would cheer and inspire and give hope to those who needed it. Omar delivered them for me, but now that I'm down here and Omar ... I have no way to deliver them."

"You're the messenger girl?" His eyes lit up and his smile grew even wider, though that didn't seem possible. "Zane told me and Dad about you. I think that's amazing. I'd love to help. On one condition."

Shaylinn held her breath and glanced at Penny.

"You have to write me a message too," Nash said. "I want to see for myself what's so powerful about these words of yours."

"Of course I'll write to you. Thank you."

Again the wide smile. "Well, my mother is waiting for me, so I should go. But, hey, I have my own house. It's in block eight, between the greenhouses and the gym. The number is 8–2. Bring your letters by anytime. I don't lock the door."

"Thank you," Shaylinn said, excited that she'd have a way to deliver her messages again.

"I look forward to that message." He winked, then waved and walked away.

" 'I look forward to that message'," Penny said in a mocking voice. " 'Bring your letters by anytime. I don't lock the door.' "

Shaylinn glared at her friend. "Why are you doing that?"

"Because it's obvious that he's in love with you."

"He is not."

"Is too."

"Penny, I can tell that Nash likes me a little. But he doesn't know me at all."

"He wants to."

"Perhaps. But that's not love. Jemma told me love is hard work, not just thinking someone is cute. I love Omar." And that *was* really hard work.

"No one will ever love me," Penny said. "Nodin is pledged to marry Alawa, and Nash likes you."

And Shaylinn suddenly understood why she was so frustrated. Shaylinn had changed but Penny hadn't. Shaylinn's time in the harem, the babies, Omar ... those experiences had forced her to grow up sooner than she might have liked. But Penny had gone to the boarding school with the other children and had seen girls and boys in superficial relationships. While Shaylinn could try and offer advice, she wasn't sure Penny had the maturity to understand.

"Penny, listen to me. Love isn't all butterflies in your stomach and staring into each other's eyes. Eventually, one of you will mess up. And that hurts, trust me. To love someone is to accept him, faults and all. And you have lots of time to find that kind of love."

"Don't lecture me, Shay. I'm not stupid. Just don't steal Nash from me. I saw him first."

Which was totally untrue. Shaylinn had seen Nash while Penny was still living in the boarding school. "I have no intention of stealing Nash. I told you: I love Omar."

"I know. But Omar is ... But if Omar doesn't come back, you'll want a husband to help with the babies."

"Stop it! You already promised to help me with the babies. Why are you doing this?"

"Don't yell at me. You're not that much older."

Shaylinn took a deep breath. "I'm sorry I yelled. I promise I won't steal Nash, okay?"

"Thank you. And I'm sorry I said Omar might not come back. Hug?"

Shaylinn accepted Penny's peace offering and the two embraced. It seemed to heal all of Penny's worries, but for Shaylinn, it only confirmed how much they'd changed. The thought made her feel tired and lonely. But at least she'd have her messages to occupy her mind.

Shaylinn wasn't supposed to wander the basements alone, but she couldn't risk anyone knowing what she was doing—especially not Nell, who couldn't keep a secret to save her life. From the tour Levi had given when they'd first come to the basements, she remembered that she could get to the gym from the corridor by Ruston's house. So she walked that way, seeking to avoid the park and school and the other houses that people from Glenrock were living in.

Unfortunately, there were boys in the gym playing basketball. Shaylinn recognized some of the older boys from her day in the Kindred school. She clutched her package of letters tightly and jogged across the center of the gym.

Someone whistled, which made the hair stand up on the back of her neck.

"Hey, upsider. Over here!"

But Shaylinn didn't stop, didn't look his way. She reached the other side of the gym and yanked open the door. Once she was on the other side in the dimness of the corridor, she relaxed. She hoped no one had recognized her or would tell Ruston they'd seen her.

The first alcove on her right was numbered 8 – 8. Then 8 – 7 on her left. She passed by 8 – 6 and 8 – 5, then 8 – 4 and 8 – 3. She could see the door at the end of the corridor and the word GREENHOUSE written above it, but right before it was the final alcove and 8 – 2 on her right. She stepped into the alcove and knocked, hoping Nash wasn't home and that she could slip inside and leave the letters on his table or something.

When no one opened the door, she turned the knob. Sure enough, the door opened. Shaylinn went inside, but she couldn't see. She caught the door that was swinging shut behind her and held it open until she found a light switch beside the door and flipped it up. The lights flickered on over her head and she found herself in an enclosed entryway. She let the front door shut completely and stepped inside.

It was no bigger than a half bathroom, and had a coatrack on one side and shelves on the other. There were two coats on the rack and a pair of boots on the floor under them. The shelves were filled with cowpots and planters in dozens of sizes. There must have been a thousand the way they were stacked and crammed on the shelf.

There was a second door, so Shaylinn knocked on it before entering. She cracked the door a little, and a sweet and powerful smell engulfed her. "Hello?"

This next room wasn't dark, but it glowed with electric white light. She crept inside and lost her breath.

Flowers and plants. On every surface, in pots on the floor along the walls, and even hanging from the ceiling. The heady smells of blossoms mixed with the tangy scents of greens. She could smell hyssop, basil, and lavender the most. She wandered inside, scanning the room for the purple blossoms she loved so much.

She found a pot of lavender hanging against the wall where the kitchen counter ended. She buried her face in the slender stalks and breathed them in. Lovely.

She stepped back and tried to take in the house itself. The first thing she noticed was that it was clean. Spotless, really. Not a dish in the sink or the dish rack. The floors were swept, even under the plants on the floor that were growing in big pots of soil. Grow lights lit the room in a soft white glow. Some hung from the ceiling, some were floor lamps, some hooked to the wall with cords running down to the plugs that were closer to the floor. There was no Wyndo wall screen here. No electronics of any type.

She wasn't sure what she'd expected Nash's house to look like inside, but this wasn't it.

Curiosity pulled her feet to the bedrooms. There were three. Two had no furniture and were completely filled with plants. She passed a tidy bathroom that had green and brown towels in it. For some reason that made her smile.

And the last bedroom must be where Nash slept. It had only two plants. A green fern-like tree in one corner and a potted freesia plant on a table beside his bed, which was covered in a homemade quilt of small red, black, and green squares. The bedroom was also spotless. She walked inside and bent to smell the freesias. There was a portable Wyndo sitting beside it on the table. She'd thought such things weren't allowed down here.

"Hello?"

Shaylinn screamed and dropped her package of messages. She spun around and saw Nash standing in the doorway to his bedroom.

"Shaylinn, I'm sorry." He lunged to her feet and picked up the package of messages. She'd wrapped all thirty-two envelopes in a scrap of the ducky fabric that Omar had given her. Nash held out the package, but she waved him back.

"Those are my messages. I'm sorry I came in here. I was snooping. Your plants are all so beautiful, though. Did you grow them yourself?"

"Yes. I picked this place since it was closest to the greenhouses. I work there when I'm not running errands for my dad or Zane. Or my mother."

"How long have you lived on your own?"

"Two years. Since I turned eighteen."

He was twenty. He'd told her that already. He was six years older than Shaylinn. Five and a half, really. It was still a lot. But Eliza had married Mark when she was eighteen and he was twenty-seven. That was nine years' difference.

Why was she thinking about that? Penny had turned her back into a silly child. "Do you have any favorites? Of the plants, I mean."

"These two. That one there is my ficus. It was one of the first things I ever planted myself. It's sort of my baby. And the freesia. I had two that turned out that nice. Gave the other to my mother."

"It's really beautiful."

"Thank you. Did you see my lavender plant?"

"I did. Lavender is my favorite, so my nose led me right to it."

"You should take it, then. I doubt there are any plants in Levi's house."

"Oh, I couldn't take your plant."

"Don't you think I have enough?" He winked. "I'm happy to share. Come on."

Shaylinn followed Nash back to the living room-kitchen. He set the package of messages on the kitchen table and walked straight to the lavender plant. He unhooked it from the ceiling then turned and set it on the low table between the couch and chair.

"There. You take that with you when you leave."

"Thank you." She should leave now, but she didn't want to be rude.

"So, show me these messages," Nash said. "And you have one for me, right?"

"Yes." She walked to the table and pulled the yarn string that she'd tied the package together with. Once she'd loosened it, she unwrapped the stack of letters. "Yours is on the top, but you can't read it while I'm here."

"Then I'll wait." He took the letter in his hands and stared at the front. It was a plain white envelope like all the others, but rather than an address on the front, his simply said "Nash" in Shaylinn's loopy handwriting. "Shaylinn, I wonder if you'd be willing to write to my brother."

"Zane?"

He flashed his wide smile. "Well, him too, if you'd like, but I meant Tym. He's at a fragile age, and he's being pulled between my mother and father and his love for Zane. I'm not asking you to take sides, but you said you like to give hope and encouragement, and, well, I think he could use some."

"I'd be honored to write to him. Do you think your mother would mind?"

"She won't know. And even if she finds the message, she won't know it's from you."

"Will you at least ask your father?" Shaylinn asked. "I don't know if it's appropriate for me to write messages to children I don't know personally."

"I'll ask him." He set down his letter and met her eyes. "I appreciate your caution. Down here, most people are concerned with the rules but not because they care about people's feelings. They only care about obedience. But you care about people. I like that."

Shaylinn blushed. "Rules aren't bad. I just find life so much easier to live when I worry about the greatest two."

"Which are?"

"To love God and to love others before loving yourself."

"That, Shaylinn, is something you do very well."

CHAPTER
16

Before he could start building a hot-air balloon, Mason needed to determine two things: what type of fabric would work best and how much of it he would need. The ideal fabric would be lightweight, nonporous, and heat- and flame-resistant, like the kind of fabric once used in tents or umbrellas but with protection against fire.

Mason had no idea where he could get such a fabric.

And then there was the amount. He needed only to lift the weight of one man and only as high as the wall, which he estimated to be about one hundred feet high. There were a lot of other factors that would need to be considered as well, like the temperature outside, the wind, how the rider would keep the balloon from rising too high, and how he would land it.

But for now, he concentrated on the size of the balloon. It was September, and while it was still rather warm during the days, the nights were cool. Yet it would take some time, at least a month, to sew together the balloon, and the October nights would be even colder. Mason guessed it would be between 20°F and 30°F. Such cold nights should make it easier to fill the balloon with warmer air. It didn't have to be extremely hot. Cold air would also affect the lift rate of a hot-air balloon.

It took Mason much longer to work out the equation to determine the size of the balloon. But after much trial and error, he determined that the volume of the balloon that would lift one man would need to be about $500m^3$. That would give him a radius of about 4 meters, which would give him a surface area of around $200m^2$.

That was a lot of fabric. And Mason had no idea how to get so much of it, short of purchasing two hundred umbrellas and dismantling them.

That was a lot of umbrellas too.

He went back to the G.I.N. and scoured the store. There was no fabric at all. Plenty of umbrellas though. But then he spotted one item that might change everything: waterproofing spray. It wasn't cheap, and it wouldn't protect against fire, but perhaps Mason could use it on cotton bed sheets. It would be heavier than the nylon, but it just might work.

A week later, Mason was walking Pen 12 when a human scream rose over the braying cattle. Mason scanned the browns and blacks until he caught sight of an orange jumpsuit on the ground in the second row, surrounded by four-legged animals.

He ran out of Pen 12, climbed over the cattle lane, and sprinted across the feed alley. The man was in Pen 30. Mason slipped inside and crossed the pen, taking a wide berth from the man in hopes that he wouldn't herd the cows closer to him.

"What happened?" a farmhand yelled, running up to the fence between Pen 29 and 30.

Mason hadn't met either of these men. He knew only the taskers in the first row. "I heard a scream and saw him on the ground. I don't know what happened."

"Miks ran for help, but I didn't hear what he yelled at me. I'm Crag."

"Nice to meet you."

Mason reached the fence on the far side, the one the man laid next to, and started along it. Cows ambled out of his way. As he closed the gap between him and the injured farmhand, he heard the moaning. The man was alive and conscious. Then he saw the familiar tattooed head. The sight stabbed a thrill of fear into Mason's gut. Scorpion.

He crouched at the man's side. He couldn't see any injuries at first glance. There was no blood. No tears in his jumpsuit or dirty hoof prints. "Where does it hurt?"

"My foot."

"What happened to your horse?" Crag asked.

"Miks needed a hand with a steer that had its leg caught in a coil of wire," Scorpion said.

"Which foot did you injure?" Mason asked.

"My right."

Mason took a good look at his boot. It was flattened at the heel. He didn't dare try and take it off. He needed to get Scorpion out of here. But did he really want to help *this* man? He bit back his hesitation. It didn't matter who was hurt. Doctors took an oath to help others. And Mason was no different.

"We need to get you out of here."

"Shouldn't you take off his boot and see what's wrong?" Crag asked.

"No," Mason said. "His heel looks crushed. I don't want to touch anything until a medic can take a look. And we need to get out of the way of the cattle. Let me try and help you up." Mason moved to Scorpion's left and put his arm around the man's waist. He pushed against him. Thankfully, Scorpion used his good leg to heave himself up, because Mason didn't think he would have been able to lift him on his own.

Scorpion had to hop, but they moved, slowly, toward the fence.

Gacy was waiting for them. "Should I call Enforcer 10?"

"No!" Scorpion said. "I'm not that bad off."

"He's pretty bad off," Mason said.

"Then you take him to the MC," Gacy said. "I'll drive you to the tram."

"What sector is the MC in?" Mason asked.

"No sector. It's in the wall. Just get on the tram and get off at the stop after sector eight. That's all there is to it."

So Mason helped Scorpion into Gacy's truck, then Gacy drove them to the sector five tram station. Then, step by step, hop by hop, Mason helped Scorpion to the tram. Once they were settled on the tram and had some space between them again, Scorpion spoke up.

"How'd you know not to take off my boot?"

"I tasked as a medic before."

"Ah."

And Scorpion said no more the rest of the ride. The tram started to slow at the Midland Gate. The sign gave the impression that anyone might travel through the gate and right on into the Midlands, though Mason knew that wasn't true. They got off and took the escalator up to the ground floor. There they followed the signs to the MC — step-hop, step-hop — which turned out to be on the second floor. Mason appreciated the crowded elevator that kept him from being alone with Scorpion.

Inside the MC . . . chaos. Medics bustling to and fro, some pushing wheelchairs, some clutching CompuCharts. Mason helped Scorpion to the nearest desk.

"Excuse me, but this man is injured. A steer trampled him."

The woman at the GlassTop glanced up, looked Scorpion up and down, then motioned to the elevators. "Take him to General. It's on four." She looked back down to the GlassTop. "Midland Gate Emergency Medical Center, how may I help you? . . . Is he breathing? . . . What's your sector?"

Mason helped Scorpion back to the elevator. It took them another ten minutes to reach what Mason guessed must be General. The waiting room was overcrowded, four rows of chairs — all filled. There must have been fifty people waiting. Another dozen were in line at the counter where a frazzled-looking receptionist was sitting. Behind her, a single medic in blue was bustling from bed to bed. Not even private exam rooms here?

"Will anyone give up a chair for this man?" Mason shouted. "He can't stand."

No one moved.

"Will you shut it?" Scorpion hissed.

But Mason tried again. "His foot was crushed by a steer. A cow. A thousand-pound cow."

A woman three rows back stood. "He can sit here."

"Thank you," Mason said, helping Scorpion in that direction. It occurred to him then that they were wearing the orange jumpsuits that marked them as strikers. Perhaps that was why the people had been hesitant to help. Perhaps not.

Once Mason had settled Scorpion into the chair, he went up to the counter to check in. The woman in line ahead of him was clutching her arm and sniffling. She glanced back at Mason, wide eyes taking in the color of his jumpsuit. Her eyes were bloodshot. Dried tears streaked down her cheeks.

"May I ask what happened?" Mason asked.

Those wide eyes settled on his again. She glanced down at her arm, then quickly moved her other hand off the wound and back in a flash. A gash, three inches wide. It hadn't looked terribly deep, though Mason had seen it for only a quarter of a second.

"Where did it happen?"

"Sector seven. Salmon packing plant."

"Was it a knife?"

She shook her head "The blade on the gutter."

"So, clean, though likely not sterile."

"I don't know."

There was no reason for this woman to wait in line when Mason could easily assist her. He looked to the front of the line, then over the counter, his gaze searching for what he needed. He spotted a box of alcohol pads on a counter against the wall. Liquid adhesive was likely nearby ... There. He spotted the familiar purple tube sitting on the shelf below the counter. And a bottle of sterile water to clean it. Excellent. Now, if only the receptionist would not panic.

He left the line and darted through the swinging half door that separated the waiting area from the medical area. He had the bottle of sterile water in hand before he heard the first protest.

"Excuse me, you can't be in here."

He grabbed a pair of gloves, the liquid adhesive, and the box of alcohol swabs, then jogged back to the swinging door. The receptionist was standing beside her chair, scowling at him.

"I tasked as a medic before," he said. "I can help shorten your line." Then he pushed through the door and set the materials on the counter.

"Sir, that's really not necessary," the receptionist said.

"I tasked as a medic in the Highlands," he told the injured woman, pulling on the gloves. "Would you allow me to help you?"

The woman glanced at the line, then at the receptionist, then back to Mason. "I guess."

Gloves on, he waved her to him. "Come here, please."

The woman walked to his side. Mason took hold of her arm and set her elbow on the counter. He turned her hand, palm side up, which revealed the still-bleeding cut. Mason squirted sterile water over the wound, then opened an alcohol swab and wiped the cut. It wasn't deep. The liquid adhesive would be enough to heal it without a scar. Mason pinched the wound closed with one hand and squeezed the tube of liquid adhesive over the cut with his other.

He met the woman's eyes and smiled. "Now we count to twenty. It dries quite fast."

"He just took things and started to help that woman." The receptionist's voice, behind him. "Said he tasked as a medic in the Highlands."

Mason looked over his shoulder. The receptionist stood with the medic, a man with white hair and a tired but curious expression.

"This is your friend?" He nodded to the woman Mason was helping.

"No, sir," Mason said. "My, uh, friend's foot was crushed by a steer in sector five. I saw how long your line was and thought I could be of some help."

"Where did you task in the Highlands?"

"The SC. Under Ciddah Rourke."

"Never heard of her, but I've been here for fifteen years. Who's your task director?"

"Gabon Gacy in the sector five feedlot." The adhesive had dried, so Mason released the woman's arm. "That should do it. I could wrap it in gauze if you'd like. It would keep you from scraping the cut until it has time to fully heal."

"Yes, please," the woman said.

Mason looked to the medic. "May I fetch some gauze?"

The medic nodded. "Reena, tap Gabon Gacy at the sector five feedlot and tell him that I am borrowing his ...?"

"Farmhand," Mason said, pushing though the swinging half door to find gauze.

"I'm borrowing his farmhand for the rest of the day. See if he cares and let me know."

And so, for the rest of the day Mason went to task in the Midland Gate General Medical Center under the medic, Kam Cadell.

Mason helped administer meds to bedridden patients, patched up a dozen more cuts, helped Cadell wrap Scorpion's foot until he could be sent for surgery, and took vitals on dozens of patients until Cadell could manage to see them.

"Mason, get a blood sample and test for opiates on bed twelve."

Mason took a vial of blood, then located the blood meter. As he waited for the results, he recalled the experiment he and Ciddah had been doing when the enforcers had come for her. Lonn wanted to try to test more patients to see what stimulants were in their meds. Could Mason steal the supplies for that? He didn't see how. The orange jumpsuits had no pockets.

He tapped the results from the blood meter into the CompuChart, then cleaned up his mess. This area was like some sort of indoor triage area. He counted sixteen beds, all of them full. Where would they put the rest of the patients who were sitting in the waiting room?

Cadell walked up to him. "An aide is here to move bed six down to long term. I can't go with him right now. Can you walk down and make sure everything is hooked up correctly? They're busy down there too, and I don't like moving someone like this without a medic involved."

"Sure. But can you show me what I need to hook up?" Mason had never moved beds before. There had never been a need in the SC.

Cadell waved him over to bed six. Mason followed. As he neared and the person in the bed came into view, he slowed to a stop.

Omar.

His little brother lay there, unconscious and intubated. A nasal cannula delivered supplemental oxygen through his nose. His face was covered in bruises and cuts that had been patched up with liquid adhesive.

"The beds have everything the patient needs," Cadell said. "They even have a small battery, but it won't last long. The patient's SimTag is registered to the bed, so if the breathing or heart stops, it will set off an alarm and the medics will come running. Still ..." He tapped the top side of the bed. "The cords are here. Just wheel the head up against the wall and plug it in. Be sure and bring me back an empty bed to replace this one."

"What happened to him?"

"OD'd. Can't be sure, but his bunkmate who brought him in thinks he was trying to end it. Took a whole vial of heroin at once. That's not smart."

Oh, Omar, you fool. "What about the bruises and cuts?"

"Someone beat him up pretty badly. But he did worse to himself with the PV."

Indeed. "He's comatose?"

"Yes. He should recover once the substance clears his system, though."

Relief flooded through Mason. "How long will that take?"

"Most overdose comas last between two and four weeks, but sometimes longer. Recovery is usually gradual. The patients become more aware over time and will wake for longer periods. His coma scale score was an eight, so that's not terrible. Since he OD'd, and likely on purpose, I'll probably keep him sedated for four weeks, then see if he'll wake on his own. I like to detox juicers. Force them to get clean. What he does after that is up to him. Now take him down there for me, will you? And hurry back."

"Yes, sir."

Mason and the aide moved Omar's bed down to the third floor and made sure the bed was plugged in. When the aide left, Mason prayed for his brother, that this was a good thing, that being here would keep him away from the stims and that his body would heal and when he woke up, all the cravings would be gone.

When lunchtime came and Cadell told him to go eat, Mason went to the diner and told his mother the news.

"He tried to kill himself and you think it's a good thing?" she asked.

"Just that when he wakes up, it'll be completely out of his system. He'll have a new start," Mason said. "He wanted to beat it, but I saw the cravings in his eyes. He would have done anything to get more. It was scary."

"My poor boy. We all have a time in our life where our curiosity is stronger than our common sense. But I've never seen anyone take it as far as Omar has."

"He's not as lost as you think, Mother," Mason said. "He intended to help Shaylinn however he could. If we ever get out of here, I think he'll turn out fine."

"Lonn's plan is almost ready. If we could get just one person to the other side, he could take the truth to the people."

"Yes, but, Mother, their plan is reckless. I'm working on Omar's balloon idea. I've been taking three bed sheets instead of two when I visit the car wash. It's not the ideal fabric, but it should work with the waterproof spray I saw at the G.I.N. If you guys would help me gather bed sheets, I could have the balloon ready in another three or four weeks. There's no need to risk any lives."

Mother sighed and took hold of Mason's hand. "Lonn doesn't believe your balloon will lift a man. I've tried to tell him not to underestimate how clever you are, but his mind is set. He's going to do this. We must pray that it will succeed."

"And if it doesn't?"

"Then we pray that no one will be hurt."

"Mother, my idea risks no one." But Lonn arrived before he could say anything else.

"Mason worked in the MC today," Mother told Lonn.

"Really? How?"

Mason relayed the morning's events and how Kam Cadell had called Gabon Gacy and gotten permission for him to stay.

"This is excellent," Lonn said. "You have access to meds there. You could test them."

"I thought about that, but it's only for today," Mason said. "I don't think I could manage to do any tests there with us so busy, and I have no way to steal the supplies, either."

Lonn grabbed Mason's shoulder. "You've got to try, boy. You've got to! This chance might not come again."

When Mason returned to the MC, Cadell had a surprise for him.

"You've been reassigned," he said. "You're my assistant now."

"What? No more feedlot? How?" It was too good to be true.

"It was purely selfish, I promise you," Cadell said. "I've been asking for another assistant medic here for ages, but medics don't tend to be prematurely liberated, so … I'm sure the liberator was simply tired of hearing me whine. But I couldn't let someone with your skills and bedside manner be wasted on cows."

"Thank you," Mason said. "I greatly appreciate what you've done." For sure he could find a way to conduct tests now that this was his permanent task.

"I wasn't able to move your residence, unfortunately. I'll keep trying, though. Striker bunkhouses are filled with disease. If you're to work with me, I need you healthy."

Mason hadn't minded tasking on the feedlot. True, the smell was horrible, but he'd been getting used to it. But this news took off the pressure of trying to steal meds and a blood meter this very afternoon. He now had time to conduct his investigation. And being here would allow him to check up on Omar as well.

This felt like a new beginning. He and Lonn could look for a cure for the thin plague. And if they found one, it would change everything.

CHAPTER
17

The day the task director learned that Jemma was pregnant, things started to happen quickly. She met with Tyra to discuss wardrobe, a makeover, and to schedule initial ColorCast interviews with Luella Flynn. Jemma demanded that she and Alawa be moved into their own suite, and Matron Dhlorah gave them a tour of the rooms. Jemma and Alawa chose the Citrus Blossom room on the seventh floor, as the colors were bright and cheery and it was completely empty, so they didn't have to share it with anyone.

The first actual ColorCast appearance for Jemma was that very afternoon. Tyra took her to a hairdresser in the morning, then Matron and Ewan escorted her to the ColorCast Studio lot and into a sound stage. There was a small theater with maybe fifty seats. Only the first two rows were filled.

Matron took Jemma to a dressing room where a red ball gown hung on the wall, with a V waist and a full skirt that poofed out and swept the floor.

Jemma tried to hate it, but it made her feel like Cinderella in red.

Once she was dressed and a woman had painted her face with makeup, Matron led Jemma back out to the stage. There were two little white couches in the center, angled so that they faced each other. Lights from the ceiling were pointed down at the couches, making them glow in comparison to everything else.

"Jemma, lovely!" Byran Kester, a director, walked out on the stage and greeted them. Two kisses for Matron and two more for Jemma, who felt strange to greet this man like they were friends when he had betrayed her the last time they'd met.

Byran was a short man with dark hair and a scruffy face. As per the current mimic trends, he wore a loose purple shirt with several thick silver chains around his neck.

"I hope you plan to film an honest interview today, Mr. Kester," Jemma said.

Byran chuckled. "Now, where's the pleasure in that?"

Jemma glared at him, and his expression sobered.

"In all seriousness, this will be a very simple interview. Your words are on the teleprompter. Just read what's there. Try not to adlib. We'll do it once and then maybe run a few places where I think we need a little something extra."

Jemma knew all about the something extras they used here. The last time she had acted for him, they'd edited the footage to make it seem like she was being held hostage. Then they'd used it to blackmail Levi.

Well, they didn't have Levi this time, so she doubted they could do anything too terrible.

"So I just need to read the teleprompter. That's it?"

"Mostly. Luella will come out first. She'll introduce you both. You'll come in on the right, Mr. Renzor will enter on the left. I'd like you to take hands when you reach the center of the stage, right in front of the two couches. Take hands and smile. Act like you like him. This is to show the people that the rebels aren't what they claim to be, so you need to look thrilled to be here. Think you can do that?"

"Yes," Jemma said, knowing she would truly have to become an actress to pull this off.

"Once the applause dies down, you'll sit together on the couch on the left, on Mr. Renzor's side. Luella will sit on the other couch. Then just follow her lead and read the prompter. If Mr. Renzor touches you, don't move away. Look like you want to be here."

Jemma fought back a sigh. "I understand."

"Great," Byran said. "We'll get started soon."

"Ready in five!" a man yelled from the back. A cameraman.

"Well, there you go." Byran walked to the end of the stage and jumped down.

Matron led Jemma over to the side of the stage, similar to where Naomi had stood a few months ago and when she'd been introduced as the Safe Lands queen.

A burst of spicy perfume clouded around Jemma. "Hay-o, femmys!"

Luella Flynn walked up the three steps to the side stage. She was wearing a very tight black skirt that ended just below her knees and a fluffy purple top that made it look like she had climbed inside a gigantic rose. Her hair was silver tinsel and must have been some kind of wig.

Luella kissed them both on the cheeks and looked Jemma up and down. "My, don't you look gorgeous! Lawten chose that dress, you know. He has a thing for red. I wouldn't be surprised if you gain some mimics over that outfit."

"We're on in sixty!" the cameraman said.

"I'll see you up there, femmy!" And Luella trotted past Jemma on spiky platform heels.

Jemma felt nervous. She didn't want to be on TV. She wished she were in the basements with the others, taking care of Shaylinn. She said a quick prayer for her sister, wondering how she was coping with her morning sickness and being alone with Levi and all those kids. She hoped Levi was being sweet to her little sister.

Levi.

"In five, four, three, two ..."

Luella Flynn was standing in the center of the stage, touching her ear with one finger. She released it and beamed at the center camera. "I'm right here, Finley. And I'm simply juicing to introduce you all to our brand-new Safe Lands Queen. But she's not alone today. She brings with her a very special guest, our own task director general. Please welcome Ms. Jemma Levi and Task Director General, Lawten Renzor!"

Music burst out from overhead speakers. The crowd clapped. Matron nudged Jemma and her feet started to move. She walked across the stage toward the couch. On the other end of the stage, the task director walked toward her. They met in front of the couches, and Jemma let him take her hand. He held up their joined hands, faced the crowd, and waved. Jemma waved too. The applause increased.

He lowered their hands, Luella gave them both cheek kisses, and they sat down, Jemma and the task director on one couch, him still holding her hand, and Luella on the other.

"Jemma, darling. Tell us, how far along are you?" Luella asked.

"The medic said I was eight weeks along," Jemma said.

"Tell us what this means for you," Luella said.

"I'm very excited," Jemma said.

"And isn't it true that this is a miracle baby? Conceived in the natural way?"

"Yes." Jemma looked into the camera and said, "You're going to be a father, Levi!"

"Indeed," the task director said. "Levi served as the best kind of donor. He's an example to all of us. But the child belongs to the Safe Lands. The baby is ours." Lawten put his arm over Jemma's shoulders and squeezed.

Jemma gritted her teeth.

"Jemma, why did you return to the harem?" Luella asked. "Weren't you in hiding?"

Why did she return? Because Mia had stunned her. She suddenly remembered the teleprompter and read the words there. "I felt it would be a good gesture to the people to show my support of the Safe Lands government. I was a rebel, but I am no longer."

"I'm very glad to hear that, Jemma," Luella said. "Rebellion tears our nation apart where we should be trying to work together."

The interview went on. Lawten explained that this pregnancy meant good things for the future of the Safe Lands, which to Jemma meant they intended to steal her child. Luella gushed over Jemma's dress, and just as Jemma started to get comfortable, Luella said good-bye.

"Clear," the cameraman said.

"Oh, well done, Jemma," Luella said. "She's going to do fine, Lawten. Much better than the others."

"She's humble," Lawten said.

"The audience loves humble," Luella said. "Especially after that Mia. Oosh."

Kruse walked up to the stage from the audience, looking short the way he stood below them. "Mr. Renzor, you have an urgent tap."

"Excuse me for a moment, ladies," Lawten said, and he left the stage, leaving Jemma alone with Luella Flynn.

"So, this wasn't really live, was it?" Jemma asked.

"Not this time, femmy, no."

"So when will it air?"

"Byran? When will this air, trig?" Luella yelled.

Byran's voice came from the back of the room. "On tomorrow's morning show. Then we'll run it again throughout the day."

"Tomorrow morning you can watch," Luella said, then raised her voice again. "Are we done?"

"I'm taking a look at the footage," Byran said. "Just hold tight for another couple minutes."

"Hold tight, hold tight," Luella muttered to herself. "So, Jemma. You must know the identity of the Owl, no?"

"Who?" Jemma had said it too quickly, though.

Luella grinned, knowingly. "His little broadcast interrupted this month's liberation ceremony."

"I didn't see it."

"Oh, well, you missed something spectacular, then." She lowered her voice to a whisper. "The Owl had footage of two outsiders being liberated. It was *incredible*."

Jemma's eyes widened. "Which outsiders? What is liberation, anyway?"

"No one knows," Luella said. "Lawten keeps it from me. But that footage was more information that I've ever gotten with Alb. And it was footage of the two outsiders who share the same donors as your lifer. Surely you know who I mean. They were liberated for crimes against the Safe Lands? One was the medic who tasked in the SC."

"Mason and Omar," Jemma said. "They're Levi's brothers."

"Yes, well, the Owl intrigues me. I'd love to do an interview with him. Think you could put in a good word for me?"

"I don't really know who the Owl is," Jemma said. "I'm not sure that it's one person." That much was true. Omar had been liberated, so someone else had to have put on the costume and done that recording.

"Of course," Luella said. "That's truly brilliant. A flock of owls. Oh, I love that."

"Luella, femme," Byran called, "I'm going to need you for a few more shots. But Jemma, you're free to go."

Jemma stood, anxious to be away from Luella Flynn and all of her questions. "Good-bye."

"Yes, indeed, bye-o, femmy. I'll be seeing you soon enough, I'm sure."

Jemma tottered across the stage on the heels that had started to pinch her feet terribly. Matron was waiting.

The next morning, Matron escorted Jemma and Alawa to the main sitting room to watch the broadcast. The massive wall of picture windows had already been converted into a Wyndo screen, which, combined with turning off all the lights, made the sitting area dark. The Finley and Flynn show was on, muted, though Jemma recognized it as yesterday's program, which always aired before the current day's show.

The other harem women were already seated, though with the ladies from Jack's Peak set free, there were only four others: Jennifer, Mia, and two Safe Lands women Jemma had not yet met.

"Why do we have to watch this?" Mia asked. "I wanted to sleep in this morning. This pregnancy has me exhausted."

"Because this is a historic occasion," Matron said, "and because the task director demanded it."

"He demanded we all watch Finley and Flynn's morning ColorCast?" Mia asked.

"Yes," Matron said. "I think it will be the best way to show you what's possible to achieve with your position here."

"Cryptic," Mia murmured to Jennifer, her mother.

"It's starting." Matron tottered on her high-heeled shoes to her chair and sat. "Wyndo: Volume: Twenty."

The opening music and montage began, showing candid clips of Finley Gray and Luella Flynn on various interviews or with Safe Lands celebrities. When it ended, the screen flashed to Finley Gray sitting behind his desk.

"Good morning, Safe Lands nationals. We have an incredible morning planned for you. Bick from the To Dye For Salon is here to give my hair a new style. I've got to say, I can't wait to see what he does. It's time for a new look. We're also going to hear from *Big Is Beautiful* star Melana Georjan. I just love her show. Look, I'm even wearing my *Big is Beautiful* T-shirt." He opened his jacket, revealing a white shirt with two fancy letter Bs on it. "Decked, isn't it? But first we're going to go live to the ColorCast Studio, where Luella is waiting to introduce you all to a very special guest. Luella? You there, femme?"

The image on the screen switched to Luella, who was standing on the stage in the ColorCast Studio in front of the white couches. "I'm right here, Finley. And I'm simply juicing to introduce you all to the brand-new Safe Lands Queen. But she's not alone today. She brings with her a very special guest, our own task director general. Please welcome Ms. Jemma Levi and Task Director General, Lawten Renzor!"

"What?" Mia shot Jemma a glare.

Applause and whistling came from the speakers as the camera angle changed to show a packed auditorium, way larger than the amount of seats that really existed in the ColorCast theater. The crowd was clapping and cheering, some on their feet as in the distance on the stage, the task director general and Jemma walked out.

"That's so weird," Jemma said. "There were only a few people there. How'd they make it look like so many?"

"You probably didn't notice," Matron said. "Nerves and all."

"I *did* notice," Jemma said. "There were only twenty people in the crowd."

"Shh." Matron waved her hand at Jemma and looked back to the wall screen, where Jemma was walking across the stage in that gorgeous red dress. She took Lawten's hand, and the two of them stood there. Jemma hadn't paid all that much attention to what the task director had been wearing, but she did now. He was in a white suit with red accents. They matched. Like a couple.

Her stomach churned as she watched them sit side by side on the sofa across from Luella.

"Jemma, darling," Luella said on screen. "Tell us, how far along are you?"

"Just a few weeks," Jemma said.

The real Jemma froze. "What?" That wasn't what she had really said.

"And isn't it true that this is a miracle baby?" Luella asked. "Conceived in the natural way?"

"Yes." Jemma smiled.

"The baby is ours," Lawten said, and his hand lowered onto Jemma's shoulder. The camera zoomed in on the task director's lined face. His eyes were teary, as if he were emotional over the news.

"No!" Jemma shook her head in horror. "That's not what I said. I said it was Levi's baby." Why had they done this?

The camera flashed back to Luella. "Tell us what this means for you."

"I'm very excited," Jemma said.

And back to Lawten, the close up on his face. But his eyes weren't teary now. "I know there's much controversy over the subject of lifers. But Jemma and I, we share a bond that's stronger than pleasure alone. This child. We created this child through our passion for each other."

At the harem, Jemma cried out and stood, horrified at what he was saying. "That's not what happened!"

"Jemma, please sit down," Matron said.

On screen, the task director said, "In fact, I am so in love with this woman, I want to exchange vows with her."

Jemma lost her breath and sank back into her chair, staring at the screen, horrified at what was happening.

"What kind of vows?" Luella asked.

"In the Old days, couples who wanted to spend their lives together exchanged vows of promise before witnesses," the task director explained. "Jemma and I have decided to do this."

The camera switched to Jemma's face. "I felt it would be a good gesture."

No! "They've twisted things around. That's not how it happened." Even in her horror, she realized that she should've seen this coming.

On screen, Luella looked into the camera. "And so, Safe Landers, we're going to have a party. The date has been set. January twenty-fourth. You won't want to miss it."

Then the camera changed to a view of the couches with the task director holding Jemma's hand. Animated letters flew across the screen like a spilled puzzle and arranged themselves to say "Vow Exchange, January 24, 2089. Don't miss it."

"That's not the way things went!" Jemma cried. "They changed things. He made it seem like I'm going to marry him." Tears rolled down her cheeks at the thought of Levi seeing what she just saw. "Why would he do that?"

"I don't understand," Alawa said.

"How could they change it?" Jennifer asked. "It's recorded, isn't it?"

"And why would they bother?" Mia asked.

"I don't know, editing?" Jemma wrung her hands together. "The people who filmed us. They rearranged the things I said. And they changed the task director's words. That part when they zoomed in on his face, they must have recorded that another time. And they played the things I said out of order to make it sound like I said things I didn't say."

"You should be happy," Mia said. "You like romantic things."

"This is *not* romantic."

"Sure it is. It's like that story in the Bible you like so much. You know, the orphan Hadassah, living in exile with her uncle in Susa after King Nebuchadnezzar conquered their home."

"That's romantic?" Alawa asked.

"Only because of how the story ends," Mia said. "Hadassah becomes Queen Esther, marries King Xerxes. He chose her out of all those others."

Jemma glared at Mia. "This is *not* the same. Hadassah wasn't married. I am. And this baby is Levi's, not the task director's."

"It really doesn't matter who the donor is," Matron said. "It belongs to the Safe Lands."

This comment poured ethanol on Jemma's anger. She wasn't acting like a prisoner. She was failing to play her part. "He could have at least told me what he was going to do." Jemma stood up. "I want to talk to him. Take me to the task director's office. Now."

"You can't see him without an appointment," Matron said.

"I am the new Safe Lands Queen. I can do whatever I want."

Matron's eyebrows furrowed as if she wasn't certain what to do. "Jemma, dear, let's not get upset. Why don't you use the Wyndo wall screen in your suite to tap him? That way, you can talk to him right away or at least make an appointment. He's a very busy man."

"But I don't know how to tap anyone," Jemma said.

"I'll help you. Come along."

So Jemma let Matron escort her up to the Citrus Blossom suite. Inside, Matron walked up to the wall screen.

"Wyndo: power. Tap: Lawten Renzor." The screen faded into white with text on it. "Wyndo: zoom. Wyndo: zoom" The text got larger, then larger again. It said:

Renzor, Lawten. 79 Summit Road.

Renzor, Lawten. City Hall.

Renzor, Lawten. Safe Lands Guild.

"Wyndo: select: City Hall," Matron said.

The wall screen went black and the logo of the Safe Lands rotated on the dark screen.

Then a woman's face appeared on the screen, slightly misshapen as if the camera was at an odd angle. "Lawten Renzor's office, City Hall. How may I help you?"

"This is Matron Dlorah at the Highland Harem. Our queen, Jemma Levi, would like to speak with the task director. Might we set up a tap appointment?"

"Just one moment and I'll see if he's available," the woman said.

The screen went black and silent again, and the rotating Safe Lands logo filled the screen.

"See now?" Matron said. "Isn't this easier than driving over there?"

Jemma shrugged, though she had to admit it was. She wondered if there was any way to talk to Levi on this contraption.

The task director's face suddenly appeared on the screen. "Jemma, shimmer, I thought I might hear from you. Hay-o, Matron."

"Hay-o, Lawten. I hope you're finding pleasure this day."

"Indeed, I was, until this tap came through. My queen's expression weighs heavily on my mind. She seems upset. Would you give us some privacy, Matron?"

"Of course." Matron nodded to Jemma and left the room, closing the door behind her.

"Why did you do that? You said so many lies!" Jemma yelled.

"Everything I did was for your benefit, shimmer."

"Don't call me that! You don't have any right to call me anything."

"I don't understand why you're so angry. You asked to be the Safe Lands Queen."

"Then you lied! And you made it sound like I'm going to marry you. I'm already married to Levi."

"Oh, that doesn't matter."

"Of course it matters!" She stopped talking and took several deep breaths. How could she do this? Share her anger yet still play the part of a rebel who'd changed sides? "I might not believe in the rebel cause, but I still love my husband. I mean to see him again someday."

"You will, shimmer. This whole broadcast was for his benefit. When he sees it, he'll have no choice but to comply with my demands."

"What demands?"

"That's not your concern. If there's nothing else, I have much to do."

Questions jumbled in Jemma's mind. "Nothing else now, no," she said, almost to herself.

"Then we understand each other. Good. Oh, and don't wear that muddy color again. It completely washes you out."

The screen went blank. She glanced down at her shirt. It was dark tan, almost the color of her skin.

Why did he think he could tell her what to wear? She sat on the couch and thought over what had happened. The task director was up to something. He was using her to blackmail Levi, but why? How could he even communicate with Levi?

She still smarted over Mia's comparing this to the story of Esther. Mia had no doubt said it out of her own anger of Jemma having taken her place as queen, but what if there was some truth to it? If Jemma could play this role of Lawten Renzor's lifer, perhaps she could learn things that not even Luella Flynn knew. Like what he wanted from Levi and maybe even the truth about liberation. Maybe Jemma could use her position to save her people. Maybe she had been brought to the harem for such a time as this.

CHAPTER
18

W here did you get this?" Levi asked Zane. He and Jordan had come to the nest the moment Nash had brought word that Lawten Renzor had left them a package. It was an envelope made of gold foil with Levi's name on the front in black type. Inside was a little square of plastic with a metal strip on one end, like a tiny Old video game cartridge.

"It was left in theater nine," Zane said. "We decided to open it there just in case there was some sort of tracker on it."

"You sure it's safe?" Jordan asked.

"I looked it over, shot it with a SimScanner, put it in an off-grid GlassTop to scan it for spy adds. There's no other way I can think of to put a trace on a data card. It's clean."

"So, what is it?" Levi asked.

"It's a video — two, actually. One is footage from this morning's *Finley and Flynn Morning Show.* Jemma was on it. The other is a message to you from the task director general. He's trying to blackmail you."

"How?"

"He wants Ciddah. Best if you watch." Zane took the plastic from

Levi and inserted it into a slot in his GlassTop computer. A few taps later and the video filled the GlassTop screen. Another tap and the video appeared on the wall screen as well.

Jemma had been a special guest on the ColorCast program. They'd dressed her up in a fancy gown and had her sitting with Renzor. And Renzor was touching her. Holding her hand and putting his arm around her. Levi's stomach clenched. Then that Luella woman said Jemma was pregnant with Renzor's baby. And Jemma looked happy about it.

Why would she look happy?

"That scum-licking maggot," Jordan said.

Then Renzor announced that he and Jemma were lifers and were going to exchange vows. "This isn't real," Levi said. "Right? Tell me this is a fake. How could she be pregnant already? She's only been there a few days."

"They made Shaylinn pregnant after a few days," Jordan said.

"Thank you for pointing that out," Levi said.

"The video is fake, sort of," Zane said. "But it's what they showed the nation this morning. Jemma was there when they recorded this, but there are discrepancies. Like when they zoom in on Renzor's face, the lighting is off, as is the position of his body. I don't think Jemma was sitting beside him when they shot those lines."

"Just like those videos they made of Jemma and Naomi," Jordan said. "The ones they showed us in the RC. Naomi told me she never said those things, that they'd been told they were acting a part in a play."

"Jemma told me too," Levi said. "You think they edited this to make it say something different than it did in real life?"

"They always do that to a certain degree," Zane said, "but that would make the most sense."

"So she's probably not pregnant." Levi grabbed a chair and sat down, relieved. "He's just messing with me."

"Let me show you the second file." Zane tapped around his GlassTop, and soon Lawten Renzor's face replaced the image of Jemma.

"Mr. Elias, it pains me to greet you in such a way after I've taken your lifer from you. I'm sure you'd like her back. So, I propose an exchange. Your Jemma for my Ciddah. It's that simple. Leave your reply by Monday morning in the same place this package was found."

The screen went dark.

A chill ran up Levi's arms. "That's it? He wants Ciddah?"

"Do it," Jordan said. "And send her *donors* along. I'm tired of having to watch them."

Oh, how he wished he could. "I'd love to trade, but it's not that easy, brother. She knows too much. Everything. She could lead them right to us, and we still don't know that her presence here wasn't Renzor's plan from the start. Plus, Shaylinn needs her."

"The other women delivered Harvey Jr. just fine on their own," Jordan said.

"But they had Jemma, who was learning about that stuff from my mother," Levi said. "Jemma's not here. And Shay's been glad Ciddah's here because she was worried about the twins coming early."

"Why would they come early?" Jordan asked.

"I don't know," Levi said. "It's just something she said. Look, none of that matters. I don't trust Renzor. What's to say he'd really give us Jem? Or if he might give her up, but hurt or even killed? If he does have her ... pregnant already, then she's important to them. They're not just going to give her up."

"So what do we do?" Jordan asked.

"We've got to get her out of there," Levi said. "That video said she was at the ColorCast Studio. You think that was true?"

"It looked like the studio to me," Zane said, "only the theater doesn't seat that many. They could have faked that too, though."

Levi thought that over. "So maybe she leaves the harem sometimes to do this stuff. And if they've made her queen, she'll have to leave more often, right?"

Zane nodded. "I guess."

"So we attack when she's in a vehicle," Levi said. "There can't be more than two enforcers that would go along. We could take down that many."

"Yeah, but I can't sit here twenty-four seven waiting for her to leave the harem," Zane said.

"I could," Jordan said.

"You have a wife and kid, brother," Levi said. "But we could take shifts. Can't you train someone else to watch the cameras?"

Zane sighed. "My father won't let just anyone have access to this room."

"What if you and your dad and Nash helped out, just for a day or two of constant surveillance?" Levi held his breath. *Please say yes.*

"You're going about this the wrong way," Zane said. "We need to get her schedule — or better yet, Luella Flynn's schedule. She'll be doing all the ColorCast interviews monitoring the pregnancy. If we can get a peek at her schedule, we'll know when and where she'll be seeing Jemma."

A surge of hope swelled in Levi's chest. "How can we get it?"

"We break into the ColorCast Studio offices," Zane said.

"*We* do?"

Zane tapped Levi's chest. "You do. I'll help."

Levi batted Zane's hand aside. "Yeah, that's what I figured."

"And for fun," Zane said, "why don't you go as the Owl?"

Nash dressed in an enforcer uniform. Levi dressed as the Owl. He also had a tiny device inside his ear that allowed Zane to speak to him. Zane had found it after Levi had again refused a SimSpeak implant.

They'd come through the storm drains into the Highlands. The night air was icy and the sidewalks slick under Levi's feet. The nights were getting cold. Winter was coming. Halfway up Snowmass Road, they picked up one of Dayle's DPT trucks, which Nash drove to a garage near the back of the ColorCast Studio lot.

"I'll be waiting right here," Nash said. "Don't take your time."

"Don't worry." Levi climbed out of the truck and crept through the dark garage. There were only two vehicles inside, and the one they closely passed by was covered in a layer of dust.

At the back of the garage, he found the corridor that led to the studio. He walked quickly, but as Zane suggested, didn't run. Zane had taken over the camera feed to the Surveillance Department, but later, the enforcers would be able to play back the footage and witness the Owl's confident entrance. To make this look like just another Owl act, Levi would spray the Owl's mark on the set of *The Finley and Flynn Morning Show*. Either Luella Flynn would leave it for shock value or she'd have it painted over before the show aired tomorrow. Either way, Zane was recording the footage to play later on one of the Owl's broadcasts.

He reached the back entrance to the studio and stopped at the door there. No handles.

Levi touched his gloved fist against the SimPad and the door popped open. Thank goodness for the ghoulie tag. "It worked."

"I see that," Zane said.

Levi slipped inside. So far he'd seen no one. It was dark, and he stood still for a moment while his eyes adjusted to the darkness. He stood in the corner of where two hallways intersected. An emergency light down the left hall was the only light that was on.

"Walk into the light," Zane said in a low singing voice.

"Ha, ha." Levi crept toward the light, and when he reached it, he was in another corner. But this turned into the back stage of the theater.

"Go ahead and leave some marks on the stage," Zane said. "Maybe a nice big one in the middle of that white couch."

So Levi climbed onto the stage and set to work, using cans of spray paint and Omar's Owl stencil. When he finished, Zane directed him up the center aisle of the theater and out the front doors. That led him to a lobby with red carpeting and white walls.

"Take the elevator to the fourth floor," Zane said.

The elevator opened to another lobby, though this one was more of a waiting room filled with chairs and a reception desk. A sign over the desk said Communication Department.

"Walk right past that desk and down that hall," Zane said. "Now, I'm not sure which office is Luella's, since there are no cameras in any of the offices. But I've seen her enter two rooms more than any other. The third door on the right. And the one across from it."

Levi walked past the reception desk and down the hall. He passed one door, a second, and stopped outside the third. It wasn't locked and the door was open. He went inside. The room was long and narrow. One long table sat in the center of the room and was surrounded by chairs. A large white board covered one wall and was divided into a four-month calendar. Levi caught sight of Jemma's name on the wall and paused.

This appeared to be what they were looking for. "I found something," he said to Zane. "A show schedule. It's a four-month calendar and Jemma's name is on it in dozens of places."

"Use the camera and take a picture," Zane said. "But if it's only the schedule for when episodes air, it's not proof enough of where Jemma will be for each filming. We need exact locations. See if you can find Luella's office next."

Levi pulled Zane's tiny camera out of the satchel on his Owl belt and took several pictures of the calendar. Then he walked across the hall and into the office there. It had two desks, a round table, and some couches over by the windows. He paused at the first desk, looking over the papers on the desktop. He spotted the name Finley Gray on a nameplate, then walked to the second desk. He scanned for a similar nameplate and found it on the very back of the desk. Luella Flynn.

"Here we go."

"What?"

"Luella Flynn's desk. And her calendar." Levi took a picture of the open desk calendar, which was for the month of October. He flipped the page to November and photographed that page too. He kept going until there were no more entries. Then he flipped back to October and found the entries with Jemma's name. "I think some of these will work." There was an appointment at the To Dye For Salon next Friday and a shopping spree scheduled for two Saturday's from now. But there were weekly appointments at the SC.

Jemma really was pregnant.

"Great," Zane said. "Time to go."

Levi pocketed the camera. "On my way."

"Who *are* you talking to, trig?" a female voice asked.

Levi jumped. He squinted, his eyes seeking out the bearer of that voice.

A click. A lamp lit the room. Luella Flynn was reclined on a couch on the other side of the table.

Maggots! Levi backed slowly toward the door.

Luella straightened but didn't stand. "Don't leave so soon! Are you looking for something particular? I was asleep when I heard you talking, but I missed the beginning of your conversation with yourself."

"Get out of there," Zane said. "She's trying to stall you."

"What's liberation?" Luella asked him. "At least give me a clue."

"Don't *you* know?" Levi asked.

She shook her head. "It's the one story that's always evaded me. Well, that and you, now. But here you are. What do you say? How about an exclusive? We could do it now. I just need to tab Alb. He's my cameraman."

"No thanks," Levi said, inching toward the door. "I'm well aware of how your exclusives are edited."

"Only when Lawten insists," she said, "or when the camera makes me look fat. A girl has a right to look her absolute best, you know."

Levi sidestepped toward the door. Two more steps and he'd turn and run.

"Just one more question!" She scooted to the end of the couch. "How did you get that footage of Mason Elias and Omar Strong? Did that happen in the RC?"

"You'll have to wait and see like everyone else," Levi said, then for the sake of the fake mission added, "The Owl sees all. Trust the Owl." And he ran out the door and to the elevator.

"Take the stairs this time," Zane said. "That cameraman of hers is waiting for the elevator."

Levi slowed in the reception area until he saw the glowing green exit sign in the opposite corner. He ran to it, bashed his glove against the SimPad, and it swung open.

Down, down, down he went. He paused to make sure the lobby was empty, then ran back through the theater and out the long corridor to the garage, where he found the Highland Public Task truck. The passenger door was already sliding above the roof.

Levi climbed inside.

"You get it?" Nash asked.

"Yeah, I got it. Luella Flynn was there, though."

"I swear I saw her leave earlier today," Zane said through Levi's earpiece. "I'm really sorry."

"You think that's true what she said?" Levi asked Zane. "That she really doesn't know the truth about liberation."

"Sure," Zane said. "The woman can't keep a secret. If it wasn't worth telling, she'd know. And if she knew, so would everyone else. Which means it must be a big secret."

But there was nothing big around here, not outside the Safe Lands walls, anyway. Whatever liberation was, it happened inside. And if it was inside, they could find it.

They got back to Zane's house, and Levi changed out of the Owl costume. Then Zane loaded the images Levi had taken onto the Wyndo wall screen and they studied them.

"Lots of opportunities," Zane said. "But I don't like any of these locations. Except that one. On December twenty-six."

"Dedication of the Prestige?"

"They've been rebuilding it for the past year in the old Entertainer building," Zane said.

"But that's two months away." Levi didn't think he could wait that long to see his wife.

"The Midlands is my backyard," Zane said. "I can help you here much better than I can in the Highlands. I mean, we could try to hijack her car as they head to any of these other appointments, but they're all during the day. If there's a chase, there's no place for us to go. The only storm drains I trust in the Highlands are nowhere near these places."

Levi understood. If they tried to rescue Jemma and failed, the security around her would increase. They might not get a second chance. She was already pregnant. She'd be safe for two more months.

Though Levi might go insane.

CHAPTER
19

Shaylinn sat on her bed holding the letters Nash had given her. Letters that had been sent to the messenger. Three of them. A thrill pulsed inside her. What was she waiting for? She should open them.

She ripped the first envelope and found a single card inside, the same size as the envelope.

To the Messenger —

> *Who asked you? Don't send your sentimental musings again.*

C. Hydel

Shaylinn's breath shuddered. Tears flooded her eyes. She hadn't expected such a response. Had she been wrong to write people? Omar had liked her letters. But he'd known they were from her.

She wasn't sure she wanted to open another one, but she did it anyway.

> *Are you spying on me? Is this Ranj? Leave me alone. My life is none of your business.*

Tears streaked down her face. These people hadn't liked what she'd had to say at all. She tore open the last one, eager to get it over with.

Mystery Messenger,

Thank you for your note. It made me cry. In a good way, though. I do feel alone, but not so much now that I know you're out there. Please write back.

Your friend,

Elani

Shaylinn cried even harder, though it was relief to know that she'd connected with someone.

She immediately got out her paper and wrote back to Elani. Without her Wyndo, she couldn't remember which person Elani was, though. She sat pondering what to say when it suddenly occurred to her that Levi had gone out with Zane.

She quickly walked out of her and Penny's room and tiptoed across the living room where Trevon and Grayn were sprawled out on the couches like shirts to dry.

It felt wrong to invade Levi's bedroom. But she did it anyway, quickly spotting her Wyndo on his bedside table. She sat on the edge of his bed and the smell of his room made her wrinkle her nose. A pile of laundry against the wall and the smell of his sheets were the obvious culprits. She would offer to do his laundry tomorrow. The poor man was hopeless without Jemma.

She powered on the Wyndo and was surprised to find that it was not off but only asleep. Levi must have been using it.

The screen faded into view on the grid page for *The Finley and Flynn Morning Show.* The title said "Safe Lands Crowns New Queen," and there was an image of Luella Flynn, the task director, and Jemma sitting on two couches.

Jemma ... pregnant?

She couldn't help herself, she tapped play. The volume came through low enough that no one could hear outside the room. What she saw was horrible — couldn't be true. Why would Jemma ever look happy holding that man's hand, claiming to carry his child?

She didn't understand.

"What are you doing?"

"Oh!" Shaylinn jumped, shocked to not have heard Levi open the door. He was staring at her. But his face didn't look angry.

"This can't be true." She held up the portable Wyndo.

"Give it to me." Levi walked to where she sat and took the Wyndo away. "I asked you not to look at this thing anymore."

"I needed to learn something about someone I wrote a message to. She wrote me back, see?" She handed Levi the letter and wiped her eyes. "That's not true about Jemma, right?"

"Zane says they faked some of it. There's no way to know what was really said until Jemma tells us."

Shaylinn sniffled. "So you're not mad at her?"

"Mad at Jem? How could I be? She's only doing what I asked of her."

"What do you mean?"

"If any of us got caught, we were supposed to pretend to switch sides, to try and learn anything we could about the government or liberation. Anything."

And now Jemma had to play the traitor. "I'm sorry, Levi.".

"It's fine. Just, please don't come in here again."

"No, I mean, I won't. I meant that I was sorry this happened. To you and Jemma."

"I'll get her back."

And Shaylinn knew he would.

The next morning, after she'd started Levi's laundry and she, Penny, and Nell had taken the kids to the park, Shaylinn walked to Nash's apartment, let herself into his foyer, and knocked on the inside door.

Nash opened the door wearing a tank top and shorts. His feet were bare, and his hair was sticking up. He also had creases across his face.

Oh, dear. She'd awakened him. "Were you sleeping?"

"Just got up seconds before you knocked. You want to come in?" He stepped back and opened the door wider.

For some reason, she felt embarrassed. "Um … I was hoping to borrow your Wyndo."

"Electronics aren't allowed below."

"Yeah, but I know you have one. I saw it in your bedroom."

He pursed his lips and cocked his head to one side. "And that's what I get for letting a girl into my bedroom."

Was he mad? "You didn't let me in. I let myself."

He smirked and folded his arms. "What do you want it for?"

"The answers you gave me? The answers to my messages? One of them wants me to write back, but I couldn't remember who she was and wanted to refresh myself with her story so I could do a good job writing to her. I wanted to look up her profile on the grid."

"Only one wants you to write back?"

"Yeah … The others weren't very happy with my letters."

He waved her inside. "I hope you won't let that discourage you."

"Only from writing to them again." Shaylinn walked inside, greeted by the sweet smells of the garden inside.

"I have another letter for you. From Tym. You've really lifted his spirits." Nash walked into the kitchen and handed her the message.

She took it and smiled at Tym's childlike handwriting. "Do you mind if I read it now?"

"Not at all. Sit down, though. Here, let me move that." He darted past her and moved a stack of cowpots off the couch and set them on the floor.

Shaylinn sat, feeling shy since he was staring at her. Why did he always have to stare? Was it wrong for her to visit? He was the only person willing to help her with her messages. What else was she supposed to do?

She opened Tym's letter.

Dear Messenger,

Thanks for writing to me. Where I live is probably different from where you live. I can't say more than that, but I'd like to leave someday. Not forever. I just want to know what's out there. Does that make sense? Sometimes I feel really alone here.

My mom doesn't understand. I know my dad will support me whatever I decide, but not Mom. She's stubborn about anyone leaving. She doesn't trust me at all. I know nothing's going to happen to me. But she thinks I'll mess up like my brother. So she's always watching me. I feel like a prisoner. I can't do anything without her thinking it's bad.

I'm not a bad person. Just curious. Is it bad to be curious? I know we're not supposed to think about the world above. And Mom says God hates that world and thinks it's evil. But I found a place in my Bible that says that God loved the world so much he gave up his son. Don't you think those things contradict each other? I've been wanting to ask my dad, but I haven't yet.

One other thing. I met a really nice girl. She's pretty too. But I know my mom wouldn't want me to talk to her. I said good night to her once when I saw her walking with her friends. And she said it back. Anyway, I'm afraid my mom will be angry if I make friends with her, since she's not like us. What do you think I should do?

Write back soon!

Tym

Sweet Tym. She ached for him, but she also understood Tova's fear. It must have crushed her when Zane left home. But when she found out he'd contracted the thin plague … Shaylinn couldn't imagine a mother getting such news.

She wondered what girl he'd met. "I'll write him back tonight," she told Nash. "Now, could I use your Wyndo, please? I left Penny and Nell alone in the park with all the kids, and I don't want to be gone too long."

Nash went into his bedroom and handed Shaylinn his Wyndo. "Best hurry." Once again, he gave her that wide smile.

Shaylinn looked down, focused on finding Elani on the grid. She recognized her face right away. She was the girl who'd been depressed, who'd suffered two miscarriages. Shaylinn would write back tonight — Elani *and* Tym — and she'd bring both messages to Nash first thing in the morning, before the kids awoke for breakfast. Her morning sickness was still waking her early enough that she had no doubt she'd be back before anyone missed her. But maybe she shouldn't bother Nash so early. Perhaps she'd just slip the messages under his door. That way —

"Hello, Katz? Are you here, son?"

Tova.

Nash looked over to the door, eyes wide as his mother's voice came from his foyer. "Oh … She won't be pleased to find you here."

Shaylinn scooted to the edge of the couch. "Should I leave?"

"It makes no difference now."

Oh, dear. "I'm sorry."

His eyes latched onto hers. "Absolutely not your fault. I won't hear of you blaming yourself."

The inner door opened and Tova let herself in.

"Hello, Mother," Nash said. Shaylinn started to stand, but Nash waved her back in her seat. "Please don't trouble yourself, Shaylinn. You should rest whenever you can."

"I'm not an invalid, you know."

Tova stopped in the opened doorway, staring at Shaylinn. "What is *she* doing here?"

"She's borrowing my … uh …" His eyes narrowed, looking at the Wyndo in Shaylinn's hands.

Shaylinn shoved the Wyndo under a couch pillow.

"She's just visiting, actually," Nash said.

Well, that hadn't been at all suspicious.

Tova slammed the door. "This cannot be, Katz. I will not have my son breed with an upsider."

Breed? Shaylinn's cheeks burned.

"*Mother!* Please. You're embarrassing yourself."

She walked up to him. "I'm making myself clear. Haven't I lost enough? If you do this, what will Tym do? With two older brothers leading him astray? Becoming exiles?"

"Mother, Tym won't go astray. Nor will I."

She poked his chest. "You both must obey the law. Only then will God protect you."

"That's not true," Shaylinn said. "Kindred laws are not all the same as God's laws."

Tova turned her angry glare on Shaylinn. "Don't you tell me about the law. I know the law."

"Your law, perhaps. But nowhere in the Bible does it say that a man must live underground all his life."

"The law protects our people."

"I understand that. But stop judging your sons for sins they haven't committed."

"You have no right to speak to me that way, Shayleen, especially about my children."

"You're right. Forgive me. I was out of line. Nash, I'll visit you another time. Thank you for your help." Shaylinn stood and walked to the door. Tova was standing in her way. Shaylinn looked into the woman's eyes. "Excuse me, please."

Tova pursed her lips and stepped aside. And Shaylinn left.

She chastised herself on the walk back to the park. She shouldn't have fought with Tova. She shouldn't have spoken to Tova at all. For some reason, that woman continually needled her.

Lord, help me to love Tova. Help me to see the good in her and not only her faults. I know I have faults enough of my own. And thank you for Elani, that she wrote back. Help me encourage her to make the most of her life. And help me make the most of my own, with or without Omar.

Shaylinn suddenly found herself at the door to Levi's house. Why had she come here? She went inside and put her letters in her room, then pulled out a chair at the kitchen table and flopped down onto it to rest a moment.

And she sat in a puddle of water. She jumped back up and looked at the chair to see what she'd sat in. Water trickled onto the floor from the chair, and her pants were soaked.

The babies. Her water had broken! And it was way too early.

"Hello?" Her breathing grew agitated as the fear settled over her. She was alone in the house. Everyone was still at the park. Should she move or sit down? She felt no pain and didn't think she was in labor. But this wasn't supposed to happen. She knew that much.

She'd just have to go and fetch Ciddah. She took one step toward the door. Her pants clung to her legs, feeling thick and heavy. She pushed down her fear and inched her way to the door. She'd just about reached it when someone knocked.

"Shaylinn? It's Nash."

"Come in!" The door opened and she grabbed hold of the end of it to steady herself.

Nash towered above her. She'd never been so close to him before, and he smelled like a garden. "Hey, I'm sorry about my mom." He smiled down on her and his expression quickly faltered. "What's wrong?"

"I think my water broke."

"Water?" He glanced at the kitchen.

"I think the babies are coming."

His eyes focused on hers, wide and bulging. "Now?"

"Can you go and find Ciddah or one of the women from my village?"

He stepped back, then forward again. "I don't want to leave you here."

"Please hurry!"

"Okay." He backed out into the corridor. "I'll be right back." And he ran away.

Shaylinn shuffled back to the kitchen, searching for a towel to clean up the mess she'd made. A small kitchen towel hung from the oven. She inched toward it, knowing it wasn't nearly big enough.

"I've never seen this happen," Ciddah said, "but I believe you've experienced a premature rupture of the membranes."

Eww, Shaylinn thought. "What does that mean?"

"That your water broke prematurely," Ciddah said. "Most often, the water breaks at the end of the first stage of labor. Sometimes it breaks before a woman goes into labor. When this happens, most women will go into labor on their own within the next twenty-four hours. But if the water breaks before thirty-seven weeks, it's called preterm premature rupture of membranes."

It was like she was reciting from a textbook she'd memorized. No wonder Mason liked her. "Is that bad?"

"It can be. But for you, yes. It's far too early for the babies to be born. They need more time."

Shaylinn's chest burned. "Why did it happen? Did I do something wrong?"

"Not necessarily. You're having twins, and that can put more pressure on you. But so far, you've not gone into labor. But with your water having broken, the longer it takes for labor to start, the greater the chance of infection. So I'm putting you on bed rest. That means you stay in bed until the babies come."

To bed? "But that could be months!"

"I know, and I'm sorry. But the babies will do better if their lungs have more time to grow before they're born. I wish I had some steroids to help them grow faster or even antibiotics to prevent infections. I'd like you to last at least until thirty-four weeks."

"But that's what you've always said. That's February! I can't stay in bed until then. That's over four months away!" Why was this happening? What was she going to do?

"I'm sorry, Shaylinn. If I could take you to the MC, I could do some tests and give you the right antibiotics. And steroids would help the babies grow faster."

"I don't want to give my babies steroids. I want them to have the time they need."

"Then you need to stay in bed, Shaylinn. I'm sorry."

Shaylinn hugged herself. It was like she'd just been sent to prison. She was sorry too.

CHAPTER
20

Eight weeks had passed since Omar had tried to take his life. Medic Cadell had taken Omar off the sedation at four weeks, but Omar had yet to wake up.

Mason had kept busy. He'd spent the last two months helping his mother sew together a balloon made of bed sheets at her apartment. When they'd finished it, he'd spent almost all his credits on water-proofing spray. Then he needed to find a way to fill it with hot air. He'd been unable to find a way to build a burner, but he thought it might work to fill it with chimney smoke.

So, as soon as it got dark one night, he snuck up to the roof of the steel plant in sector three with enough cement blocks to equal a man's weight. He'd tried to fill the balloon, to test it. It had been working too. The blocks had lifted off the roof, but the fabric at the base of the balloon had caught fire, and he'd barely managed to get it put out without going up in flames with it.

It was damaged now. His mother was working on sewing patches over all the burned spots. And Mason was working on a way to keep that from happening the next time around.

"I've got an injured enforcer here," the receptionist called.

Enforcers were always priority patients in the GMC. "I'll be right there." Mason finished the blood draw he was taking from the man in bed seven, then jogged to the reception counter.

She pointed to the enforcer, who was standing against the wall. "His name is Gryffel."

"Mr. Gryffel?" Mason said, looking toward the man. "Come on back." The man followed Mason to station fourteen. "Have a seat on the table, if you don't mind."

"I'd rather sit in the chair, thanks. It's not a big deal. I'm only here because my captain insisted."

"The chair is fine," Mason said. "What seems to be the problem?"

Gryffel slumped into the chair and held up his right hand, which was already wrapped in gauze. "Stimming rebels, that's what. Five of them jumped me in the bathroom, cut out my SimTag. But they didn't get far."

Mason's pulse rose. This must've been Lonn's escape plan. And it sounded like it went badly. "Five of them? They were captured?"

"Not at first. They knocked me out, see, so I didn't know what happened until I came to and the guys on my squad filled me in. One of them took my clothes and somehow used my SimTag as his. Stuck it in a glove, so my squad told me."

Mason unwrapped the gauze from the cut, which was unnecessarily big and deep for simply removing a SimTag. "To what end? What did he try to do?" Mason knew, but he was hoping to learn that Lonn's man had made it through.

"He didn't do anything, that's the problem. It's my squad's job to inspect the trucks, and my job to do the back. One of his rebel buddies had sneaked into the back of an onion truck. So the shell who took my SimTag, he let the truck pass through, said the back was clear when it wasn't."

An onion truck. "What happened?"

"He got caught. I guess the trucks are inspected again before they go into the Midlands. And once they caught the guy, they used the cameras to trace the guy who took my tag. They've got them both in the RC now."

Mason cleaned out the cut, but it needed stitches. Even though Mason knew how, he'd have to call Cadell over to finish since only level six medics or higher were permitted to do any type of surgery. "But didn't they see them attack you on the cameras?" Lonn didn't have the ability to take over the cameras down here like Zane could in the Highlands and Midlands.

"Naw, cuz I was in the bathroom."

"But aren't there cameras in the bathrooms here?"

"In the striker bathrooms, yeah. But not for reputables."

Mason called Cadell to sew up the wound, and when the medic finished and sent the enforcer on his way, he came over to where Mason was gathering materials to administer meds to the patient in bed four.

"Did you hear what that was all about?" Cadell asked.

"With the rebels, yes."

"I know it's a hopeless cause, but I admire their spirit. The way the government lies to us, it's not right. I fear I'll die here with more questions than answers."

Mason had never heard Cadell say anything so subversive, but he'd worked with the man for over two months. He had no love for their situation down here. Maybe it was time to sniff around to see whether or not Cadell could be of any help.

Mason looked at the vial of meds in his hand. "You know, part of why I was liberated early was because I was looking for answers."

"What kind?"

"Firstly, I was looking for a cure for the thin plague."

The medic snorted. "Well, there's your first mistake. There is no cure."

"Perhaps not. But it all started with this." Mason held up the vial. "Did you know there are stimulants in the meds?"

Cadell looked skeptical. "Surely not. Why would there be?"

"That's what we wanted to know."

"Who's 'we'?"

"Ciddah. The medic above me. She discovered it and had started compounding her own meds as a result. We had an idea to test the meds to find out what was in them. That's what we were doing when the enforcers came for us. They arrived just as we were conducting the experiment, which leads me to believe that we were on the right track."

"What was this experiment of yours?"

"We'd mixed a sample of my blood with Ciddah's old meds to try and identify the stimulant."

"Now, why would you do that?"

"Because Ciddah had found nothing when she tested her own blood. The theory was, perhaps the stimulant converted in some way when it reacted with the virus and that's why Ciddah had been unable to isolate it. So we decided to test it on my blood, since I'm uninfected."

"Uninfected? How can anyone be uninfected?"

"Because I'm an outsider. Safe Lands enforcers raided my village and took the young women into the harem."

"I'd heard there were fertility problems up there lately, but all we get is all hearsay from the newly liberated."

"I'd give more credit to hearsay than anything the task director general approves as news."

Cadell smiled ruefully. "Yes, I suppose there's truth in that. So what about your medic friend? She down here too?"

"No, she got away. Went to live with rebel ghosts in the Midlands."

"Too bad. I could use someone like her." He waved his hands at Mason. "Not that you aren't great, but it would be nice to have another surgeon."

Mason thought of Lonn then. He hoped Lonn wasn't the second rebel who'd been caught. Cadell would love to meet him. Maybe he could get Lonn assigned here. Mason realized he had no idea where Lonn tasked.

"I guess I don't understand the point of your investigation," Cadell said. "Even if you did learn something, what good would it do? We're still here. They're still there. We're trapped in this place, slaves to a system that has been working for the past fifty-some years. You heard what happened to those rebels who tried to get out today. How can any machine so tightly oiled break down?"

"Truth has a way of changing everything," Mason said. "We must never give up hope that the truth can set us free."

"Yes, well, right now we have work to do. Give that man his meds, please."

"Yes, sir."

And Cadell walked away, leaving Mason wondering whether he'd found an ally in the man or not.

Once his shift ended at the MC, Mason ran all the way to his mother's apartment building in sector one, slipping every few steps on the icy sidewalks. The snow had come and with it a coldness that Mason's striker coat didn't ease much. But at least the coat was brown and not orange. Cadell had given him several pairs of scrubs to wear at the GMC, and Mason hadn't worn his orange jumpsuit since. He doubted many people in sector one would like having a striker in their midst.

His mother opened the door, and before he could speak, she asked, "Is something wrong?"

"That's what I came to find out." He came inside the warm apartment and shrugged out of his coat.

Lonn was there, sitting on the armchair in the living room.

"Oh," Mason said, "you're okay." He fought to catch his breath. "I heard about the mission. An enforcer came into the GMC today. The one who'd had his SimTag cut out."

"It's awful," Mother said, closing the door.

"It was a setback, Tamera, but we can try again," Lonn said.

"How? Show Mason your neck. Show him."

Lonn and Mother stared at each other. Mason walked behind Lonn's chair, and Lonn lifted the hair off the back of his neck.

Mason leaned close and examined the red welt on his skin. "A SimTag?"

"A SimTag. Our punishment for trying to escape," Lonn said.

"And everyone is to get one," Mother said. "There will be no escaping now. I'm a doctor, and I wouldn't dare try to cut a SimTag out from behind someone's spine."

Mason couldn't have imagined a bigger blow to their plans. To his plans. How was anyone going to ride in his balloon now? "When do we get them?"

"Strikers in the car wash," Lonn said. "Everyone else in their weekly medic appointments."

Within a week, the entire population of the Lowlands would have unremovable SimTags.

But there was still one option. "Omar," Mason said. "I bet they won't administer new tags to coma patients until they're released."

"But he's unconscious," Mother said. "What can he do?"

"Nothing yet," Mason said. "But when he wakes up, he can ride in my balloon."

Lonn's jaw hardened.

"You didn't see the first one, but it lifted the cement block straight up into the air." Until it caught fire.

"No, I didn't see it. No one did," Lonn said.

"Well, take my word for it. I don't lie."

"That much is true," Mother said.

"Mother is patching it up now. I bet we could be ready by the end of next week," Mason said.

"You have one problem, *boy*," Lonn said. "Omar is in a coma. What makes you so sure he'll ever wake up?"

"*Richark*," Mother said.

"I'm sorry, I'm just being honest here, because that's what Mason likes."

"He might not wake up in a week, but he *will* wake up. And when he does, we'll be ready."

Lonn looked to Mason's mother. "What do *you* think?"

"You already know what I think. I've told you all along not to doubt Mason. He's very clever."

"Fine," Lonn said. "We'll try it your way. What have we got to lose?"

"Thank you." Mason couldn't help it. He smiled so wide he chuckled. "It'll work. You'll see."

The next day was Saturday, and when Mason went through the car wash, the medic was waiting with a SimTag gun. It stung worse to get a SimTag in the back of the neck. As Mason sat to put on clean socks and shoes, the thought occurred to him that he would likely have this SimTag for the rest of his life, even if they escaped.

That evening after his shift, Mason went to the G.I.N. store and bought a pencil and a blank card that had a picture of Joie Park on the front. He took it to the Get Out Now Diner and sat down to write Ciddah a letter that he would ask Omar to deliver.

Ciddah,

> *I hope this letter finds you well. You'll be pleased to know that I have befriended Richark Lonn. He is a good man, and he is still running the rebellion even from here.*

No. It wouldn't do to send his brother with a letter that divulged any information on the Lowland rebels, in case Omar were caught. He erased the last two sentences and tried to be more careful with his words.

Ciddah,

> *I hope this letter finds you well.*
> *Liberation is not death. We are in work camps. You'll be pleased to know that I have befriended a certain medic. One*

whom we once researched together. He's an interesting man. I'm also close to again donating my blood to a good cause.

He wanted to tell her that the stimulant in her meds had been Xiaodrine, but he wasn't sure how he could manage such a thing, so he ended the card with:

I don't know what the future holds, but I hope that you are part of it.

Love,

Mason

CHAPTER
21

T here. His eyes twitched."

"I didn't see it."

"See that? Oh, yes. Here he comes."

Omar opened his eyes to bright light. Shut his eyes. Why was it so bright? Even with his eyes closed, the light made his eyelids red.

"Omar? Are you there, brother?"

Mason's voice. How had Mason gotten into his bunk?

Omar opened one eye, squinted it, then blinked rapidly to get used to the brightness.

He wasn't in his bunk at all. This looked like some sort of medical center. Sure enough, a medic was standing across the bed from Mason.

Apparently he hadn't died.

"Wh … wha …" His voice didn't work. He cleared his throat and tried again. This time his question came out in a whisper. "Where am I?"

"In the Lowlands MC," the medic said.

"You OD'd," Mason said.

Why was it always Mason who delivered that news? It was so like his brother to rub it in.

"Why'd you let me live?" Omar asked.

"That kind of a question doesn't deserve an answer," Mason said.

"I'll leave you for now," the medic said. "I'll be back to check on you later."

"Can't wait," Omar said.

"Yes, well. Good day." And the medic left.

"Don't be rude, Omar," Mason said. "That man saved your life."

"Not really. He only prolonged my death," Omar said. Mason folded his arms and shot Omar a dirty look. Oh, he hadn't liked that comment, huh? "You forgot I'm already dying, did you?"

"Omar, I'm not here to talk about your death wishes. Whether or not you care, there have been some developments while you've been sleeping. I'd like to convey those to you."

Omar rubbed his eyes. "How long was I out?"

"Ten weeks. The Lowlands have a forced detox program. You shouldn't be craving stimulants anymore. Do you?"

Forced detox? "Seriously?" Omar thought about it. He was hungry, but it was all in his stomach. He didn't feel that ache for brown sugar. "Why don't they do that in the Highlands?"

Mason shrugged. "Forced detox isn't very fun, I suppose? You're lucky you were in a coma for it. Now, listen. I need you to try and stay here as long as you can."

"Why?" If Omar had been in bed for two months, he probably needed to learn to walk again.

"Remember Lonn's escape plan?" Mason asked.

"Yeah. The turnstile thing."

"Well, it didn't work. Two rebels are in the RC. And not only that, but they've reapplied SimTags to all Lowlanders. In the back of the neck, right along the spine and deep enough that I wouldn't even try to cut one out of anyone."

"Walls." No more walking around off grid. No more Owl.

"Yeah, *walls*. Anyway, the good news is, because you've been here, you haven't gotten the new tag yet. They gave them to us at the car wash."

"Okay ..." His brother was working up to something, Omar could tell by his agitated tone.

"You remember my special project? Your idea."

"The balloon? You got it to work?"

"Just about. Mom says there's a little sewing left. I've made friends with Medic Cadell, and he says that when you're ready, he'll help you leave at the right time."

"At night."

"Yeah. So, no hurry or anything, but with the new neck tags, there isn't anyone else who can go over. You're it. Everything depends on you. So, I know you wanted to die, but we need you to live a little longer. Think of all the people stuck in the Lowlands. Think of Shaylinn and your future kids stuck underground somewhere. Get better, Omar, and help us."

"Yeah." For Shay. For his kids. "Okay, brother. I'll do it."

Four days later, Mason was ready. And so was Omar. Medic Cadell came to his room after dark that night, moved Omar to a chair under the room's security camera, and cut out the SimTag in his hand.

"I guess this officially makes me a rebel now," the medic said, applying a bandage to the small cut. He wrapped Omar's SimTag in a cotton ball and used some medical tape to stick it on the backside of the chair. "I brought a set of clothes for you. They're on the chair by the door. Change into them and I'll take you out."

Omar changed into a black shirt, black pants, and black shoes, then came back out into the main room. "Won't I look suspicious dressed like this?"

"Oh, right. There's the coat." He pointed at a brown coat hanging on a hook beside the door. "There's a pair of leather gloves in the pocket. You'll need those."

Omar put on the coat, and Medic Cadell walked him down to the front entrance of the building that let out into the tram station.

"So where am I going?"

"To the bottom level of sector one, though I don't recommend you take the tram. At this hour, it would be only you on it, and if an enforcer should try to ID you and find no reading, he might ask questions. Take Circle Drive. It's about seven blocks to Sigland Street. Your mother lives in the Borderland Building. You should be able to tap her through the gate outside. She lives in apartment 212. That's all I know."

"Thank you." Omar held out his hand to the medic, who grasped it tightly.

"You just come back for the rest of us, you hear?"

"I'll do everything I can. I promise."

"I'll hold you to that."

Omar headed down the street at a brisk pace. It felt good to walk again. His legs were stiff and his muscles sore from so many days in bed. It was freezing outside. His breath puffed out before him, and soon his cheeks and ears were hurting from the cold. He wondered if there was snow aboveground.

He'd never walked in this part of Cibelo. Sector one was a lot cleaner than sector six. He didn't see any strikers' residences, either. Maybe they didn't have strikers in sector one.

He spotted Sigland Street up ahead on his left. Halfway down the street, he came to the Borderland Building. He punched the numbers 2, 1, 2 into the gate.

"Hello?"

"It's Omar."

"We'll be right out."

A few minutes later his mother exited the gate, followed by Lonn, Mason, and some old guy who walked funny. Mason was carrying a thick blanket under one arm. Lonn was wearing a backpack that hung low on his back.

His mother kissed him. "You look well. How are you feeling?"

"Good. Where are we going?" Omar asked.

"Sector three," Mason said. "Steel factory."

"Steel?" What was Mason talking about?

"It will be better to walk to sector three underground. There's more people for us to blend in with," Mason said.

And so they walked through Cibelo, and Omar's stomach growled at the smell of food as they passed various restaurants and clubs.

At the sector three tram station, they took the escalator up to the surface. An icy wind clapped around him as they stepped outside into the dark night. A soft layer of fresh snow blanketed everything, though it wasn't snowing now.

He supposed he *had* been out for two months. "Is it December?"

"Yes, the twentieth," Mason said.

Months of his life gone, given to too much brown sugar. Well, never again. It was time to make things right.

He followed Mason and Lonn. Their steps left shallow footprints in the fresh show. Omar squinted into the distance and could just see the red lights that edged the Lowland-Midland wall. "Shouldn't we launch closer to the middle wall?"

"Nope," Mason said. "We need the steel factory. Plus the wind will help us tonight."

Omar didn't know what the wind had to do with anything. They walked down a narrow street that cut between a row of buildings that Mother said were where they wove fabrics. Apparently Grandma Sarah tasked in one of them. At the end of the street they turned, walked another two blocks, then turned again, approaching a big building with multiple chimneys on the top that were pouring white smoke into the dark sky.

They passed under a streetlamp, and Omar caught sight of a yellow camera on the front of the building. "Aren't they going to see us?" Omar asked.

"They might," Mason said. "But we hope they won't pay too close attention since it's before curfew and we're just walking. And there are no cameras in the back alley, believe it or not. That's why I chose this building. That and the chimneys."

Again Omar wanted to ask why they needed a chimney, but Lonn said, "Quiet now," and Omar said no more.

Mason led them around to the back of the building. There they turned into a narrow alley that separated this building from the back of the one behind it. The snow was deeper here where there was no reason to shovel a path. They trudged through it for about fifty yards until Mason stopped at a metal ladder that ran up the side of the wall.

"Up we go," he said, then started to climb awkwardly with the blanket pinched under his arm.

Omar watched him, then looked to Lonn. "Is he kidding?"

"Shh." Lonn motioned for Omar to go next, so Omar started climbing. He wished Mason would have bothered to clue him in on the plan. None of this made sense.

Once they were all on the roof, Lonn slipped off his pack and Mason unfurled the blanket, which Omar saw wasn't a blanket at all, but an oblong shape.

The balloon. "Why's it so big?"

"It has to be big enough to lift you," Mason said.

"Are you sure it will work?" Omar asked.

"Mostly," Mason said. "I *did* test it. And tonight the wind is blowing the right way." He crouched and held out a harness for Omar. "Put this on. Legs in the smaller holes."

Omar stepped into it, then took it from Mason and pulled it up his legs. It was orange. Looked to have been made of a striker's jumpsuit.

Lonn, along with the old guy who walked funny and their mother, spread the balloon out beside a smoking chimney. Mason tied a bunch of knots on Omar's harness and held up a long rope. "This is for us to hold, to keep the balloon from going too high and to pull it back to us once you're on the wall." He hooked a coil of fine rope to the back of Omar's belt. "This is for you to use to rappel down the wall into the Midlands. These two here ..." He grabbed a wide strip of orange that was part of Omar's harness and raised it until it was up near Omar's eyes. "There's one on each side of you. See the black X?"

"Yeah."

"That's where you're going to have to cut it. On both sides."

"I'm sorry, what?"

Mason crouched back by the pack and pulled out a knife. "I got it from the diner. The knife goes here." He slid it into a sheath on Omar's leg. "When you are about to crest the wall, catch the railing if you can. Then cut yourself free. If you go too high, we'll try and pull you back. But you'll need to either take off the harness completely, or cut it. Whichever is easiest."

"Easiest. Right."

Mason removed a folded piece of paper from his pocket and held it out. "This is for Ciddah. Would you mind?"

"Not at all." Omar took the paper, which was actually a card, and stuffed it into his pocket.

"Now put on the gloves," Mason said. "You're going to need them to rappel down the wall. The rope will burn your hands otherwise."

Omar dug the leather gloves out of his pocket and pulled them on. Mason went to Lonn's pack and dug out a coil of wire. He started to unfold it, like he'd already shaped it into something once, but it had gotten squished. "The wire will get hot, so try not to touch it. It shouldn't be anywhere near you, really." He carried his wire sculpture to the balloon and began attaching it to the narrow end, which tugged at Omar's harness. Whatever he was doing slowly added a third dimension to the fabric, but it didn't look like a balloon to Omar. It looked more like the floppy hat of a giant.

Mason picked up the base of the floppy hat. "Follow me, Omar." He walked over to the chimney. "Sit now, close to the pipe, but don't touch it. It's hot and will burn you."

"Gee, really? I wouldn't have guessed." Omar sat cross-legged near the pipe, which warmed his right arm and cheek. Mason was holding the balloon behind Omar, opposite where the pipe was. "Why am I sitting here?"

"Because we need to fill the balloon with hot air, and it will help to have you out of the way. Lonn, Mother, Hobbles? Come and hold the ties."

The old guy's name was Hobbles?

The four of them each took hold of a different long strip of fabric, each evenly spaced around the sides of the balloon. The way they held it, spread out between them, Omar could actually see that there was indeed a balloon there. Mason's wire had put a round shape in the narrow bottom of the balloon, making a stiff circle. Another piece of wire stuck up inside the balloon, holding the fabric up and away from the bottom hole.

"Okay, let's move it over the chimney on the count of three," Mason said. "One, two, three!"

They moved at once until the hole was over the smoke pipe. The chimney smoke started going up inside the balloon.

His brother was filling the thing with chimney smoke? Huh. Omar wasn't at all convinced that it would work, but to his surprise, the fabric started to swell and take shape.

Mother giggled. "It's working!"

"It's huge," Lonn said.

It was. As the balloon started to fill out, Omar could see that the thing was easily twenty feet wide at the center. And the fabric was white.

"They're going to see that," Omar said.

"They're not going to be looking for it," Mason said.

"But on the wall. The patrols will see it."

"We're just going to have to hope they don't," Mason said.

Omar wanted to argue, to say, "Really? That's your plan?" But it would serve no purpose at this point.

The first tug took him by surprise. It wasn't until then that he realized he didn't really think Mason's plan would work. But the force of that tug ... He was really going to do this. Like it or not, the Owl was going to fly.

The balloon was huge now, a lightless moon over his head. It suddenly lifted Omar off the ground. Just a little bounce. He put down his hands to steady himself. "It picked me up."

"Lonn, grab the tether," Mason said.

Lonn left his post on the side of the balloon and studied the pile of rope. "Where's the end? I don't want to tangle this."

Mason left his post as well and grabbed the coil. "It's on the bottom. It should unwind as he rises. Just hold this end and don't let go."

Any second now and the Owl would take flight. "How much longer?"

"When you're floating up the wall, you'll know," Mason said.

And then Omar rose off the ground. Another bounce, but this time he bounced again and didn't land. He put down his feet and stood on the air.

Mason took hold of the tether rope and Omar's waist and ran a few yards of it through his hands. "Mother, Hobbles, let go of the balloon. Let's see what happens. I've got the tether, so he won't go far."

Mother and Hobbles let go. The balloon rose slowly until the cords attached to Omar's harness pulled taut and his feet left the ground. His stomach flipped, and he grabbed the harness cords for lack of anything else to hold on to. But he stopped a few feet off the ground, held by Mason's tether.

"Okay, I'm going to let go," Mason said. "The wind should take you right up over the wall. We're going to hold the tether and try and keep you low until you get there so you can unhook yourself. Once you're off, we'll pull the balloon back."

"I'm ready," Omar said.

A hand touched his leg, then foot. Mother. "I love you, son. I'll be praying for you."

"Thanks." Omar wanted to say he loved her too, but he was trying to look brave and too many words would reveal the quaver in his voice.

Mason let go, and Omar rose up in the darkness, much slower than he'd imagined. The wall stood about ten stories high. The factory roof was two stories, so they'd gotten a head start. Omar was already about four stories up. He looked down and could see nothing at all, his companion's faces obstructed by the darkness and distance that separated them. All around, sparse lights of the Lowlands were divided by acres of black fields. Maybe no one *would* see him.

He looked up, but all he could see was the balloon overhead. The queasiness left. He was flying. He was the Owl, and the Owl was coming back.

Back to save the people.

CHAPTER
22

Omar continued to rise, but in the darkness it was impossible to know how high he was. He decided to look for the red lights that were spaced along the top of the wall. Once he located them, he had his bearings. He wasn't far from the top now, and he was really close. The balloon was actually taking him the right way. Mason was a genius.

A set of headlights swept past him as a patrol turned around at the northernmost corner of the wall. He watched the vehicle, surprised that the wall didn't go all the way around. He shouldn't have been surprised, but this was a problem. The wall that separated the Midlands from the Lowlands ran across the road too, so that patrols from the Highlands and Midlands couldn't drive into the Lowlands and vice versa.

So how was he going to get over that?

He was headed to the side wall, but maybe if he let himself drift a little farther, he'd get over both, and when Mason started to pull him back, he could catch himself on that inner wall.

He didn't see any other way.

He swung his legs and even tried swimming with his arms, but it didn't seem to help his trajectory. So he waited and drifted higher until he sailed right over the side wall. Sure enough, he felt a tug on the tether rope. They were trying to pull him back, but the rope must have been sagging, because he was well out over the forest before he stopped.

If only he knew how to make the thing sink a little.

He'd started to move back toward the wall again, from Mason and whoever's pull. He needed to cut a hole in the balloon somehow. That should make him sink.

He dug the knife out of the sheath and pulled at the harness that was attached to the balloon. He stuck the knife in his teeth and pulled with both hands until the balloon's opening was within arm's reach. One of the safety holds from the side of the balloon slid past his face, and he grabbed it and let the harness go. The sudden rise of the balloon made him jerk to the side. Once he was steady, he pulled the safety hold, hand over hand until the side of the balloon was within arm's reach.

He held tight with one hand, grabbed the knife with the other, and stabbed it into the side. He had to really push to get the knife to pierce the fabric, but when it did, he sawed down about a foot then released the safety hold.

Again his body jerked as the balloon rose up. He looked around. The balloon was still being pulled back, but it was falling too. And the inner roadway wall was coming at him. He was just slightly lower than it — and on the Midlands side too.

He struck the wall much harder than he'd expected. But then started to rise. No, stop! They were still pulling him. He had to cut himself free before they pulled him back to the Lowlands side, but he was a good twenty feet above the roadway. Too high to fall. He needed the balloon to let him down slowly.

Maybe he could cut the tether.

But then Mason would lose his balloon.

Omar getting to the rebels was more important than the balloon, right?

No time. He started sawing at the tether rope. Mason's pulling lifted him to the top of the wall that crossed the roadway. He grabbed it with one arm, trying to hold himself there long enough to cut the tether.

Just a little bit more.

The tether pulled him to the very top of the wall. He scissored his legs over the top, one on either side and squeezed with his knees. He sawed frantically.

And the knife severed the rope.

The tether fell away. Overhead, the wind blew the balloon, pulling him with it. He found a way to keep his hold on the wall. He couldn't afford to have it blow him over the side now.

He slid the knife back into the sheath, then twisted himself around on the top of the wall until he was lying on his stomach and had his legs on the Midland side. Behind him, the balloon was lower than it had been. He let himself slide over the side until he was holding the wall with his hands, hanging there. Time to let go and hope for the best.

He let go and slid right down the wall a good six feet before the balloon caught him and pulled him away, back from the surface. But he was sinking fast, more like a guy in a parachute. He jerked at the harness above, hoping to keep himself over the road.

He was so close.

The tips of his shoes slid over the asphalt, but he was going sideways. The balloon was way ahead of him, pulling him fast toward the side of the wall. He just managed to hook his foot around the guard rail to stop himself.

He reached down with his hands until he got them around the guardrail too. Both arms and legs hugging that metal like it was life. He let go with one arm, slipped the knife out of the sheath, and started cutting the harness.

His hand was shaking, but he managed to cut through the first tether. The balloon continued to tug at him. It was sinking, but it was still stronger than he was. A few seconds later, he cut through the second, and the balloon sailed away into the dark night.

Omar let himself fall onto the icy roadway. There were streetlamps along the top of the wall, and they lit the road enough that he could see.

He'd made it. He'd escaped the Lowlands. Mason was a genius. Sort of.

He could see the city too, glittering and bright. He used to obsess over that city, desperate to come in and experience it.

It had nearly killed him, but he wasn't dead yet.

Omar got up and jogged across the road. He removed the coil of rope from the back of his harness and tied one end to the guardrail. Then he climbed over.

But when he got his body over the rail, lying on his stomach, legs dangling over the edge, he found it hard to go all the way.

The Owl wouldn't hesitate, he told himself.

He tugged on the cord, making sure it was securely attached and that he had a good grip, then slid back. The guardrail caught on his coat, snagging a bit, but he pushed past it until his body was completely over the side and he was holding his own weight by his grip on the cord.

He moved his feet until he got his toes on the wall, then let himself down a hand. His feet slipped, and he tried to get them on the wall again. No use. It was coated in frost and too slippery. So he twisted his body around until his back was against the wall, then he lowered himself, hand under hand, toward the ground.

When he reached the ground, he couldn't tell exactly where he was. Way past Midland West. Could he take the train? Were there still ghoulie tags in locker 127? He sure hoped so.

Omar knocked on the door to Zane's house in the Midlands. His heart was beating so hard, he wished he has his PV. But he was done with that now, and, hopefully, very close to seeing Shaylinn again.

Would she forgive him?

He heard footsteps behind the door. A deep mumble. The door swung in.

Zane. Looking totally shocked. Like he was seeing a ghost. "Now, I was *not* expecting you. How?"

Omar grinned wide. "Unhappy to see me?" He darted inside and Zane shut the door behind him.

"Omar?"

Omar barely saw Levi coming before he was tackled in a tight embrace. Levi's body trembled, but it was laughter that he heard, not tears. When Levi finally released him, he looked around the room. Besides Levi and Zane, Ruston stood staring.

"Hello, Ruston."

The man blinked and shook a smile onto his face. "Omar, you're not dead! I mean, you are very welcome here."

"But I don't understand," Levi said. "Where have you been? You were liberated, weren't you?"

The three men stared at him, eyes eager for the answer to the biggest mystery in the Safe Lands. "Yes, but liberation isn't execution. Everyone who gets liberated gets sent to the Lowlands."

"The Lowlands?" Levi and Zane exchanged a look of confusion. "But ... doing what?"

"Have any of you ever tried to visit the Lowlands? You can't. Because it's a task prison. Mason called it a penal colony."

"*Penal?* What's that mean?" Zane asked.

"Something to do with punishment, Mason says. As, of course, he knows more vocabulary than any normal person." But Omar was thankful for his brother's knowledge and the wisdom to apply it.

"Liberation is only punishment?" Ruston asked.

"It's where they send strikers and old people — they have for decades. They task so the young people up here can play. And, Levi, everyone is there. Our mother and Aunt Janie, Avaci, Grandma Sarah, Grandma Marian, some older men and women from Jack's Peak. Mom said Chief Kimama was down there with Shavingo'o. And Elsu too."

"Elsu!" Levi cackled and clapped his hand. "That's wonderful. Beshup will be thrilled."

"And Richark Lonn is there," Omar added.

"Lonn is alive?" Ruston said.

"And still running the rebellion. And guess what, Levi? Him and mom are, you know, together."

Levi's face went slack. "Together?"

"To-geth-er." Omar crossed two fingers and held them up. "Yeah. Weird."

Levi frowned and looked at Zane, who shrugged. "But — "

"If it's a prison," Ruston asked, "how did you get out?"

All three men looked at him, mouths gaping slightly in anticipation. Omar couldn't help but smile, knowing what he was about to say would sound impossible. "I flew. Mason sent me over the wall in a hot air balloon he and Mother made."

Zane's eyes narrowed. "I don't even know what that means."

And so Omar did his best to explain how Mason's balloon had worked. And then Levi insisted they go down to the basements right away so that everyone could hear the good news.

Omar followed Levi, Zane, and Ruston down to the basement where they entered a second secret storm drain. While they walked, Levi told Omar that Jemma had gotten caught.

"We're planning a rescue, though," he said. "Soon. And now that we know the secret of liberation, the Owl can tell the people. Oh, this will be good."

"I don't even have my costume," Omar said.

"No, we've got another Owl."

"What? Who's running around in my costume?"

"Me." Levi offered a sheepish smile. "It's actually kind of fun."

Omar gave Levi what he hoped was a stern look. "That doesn't sound very practical or safe."

"I know, but desperate times … Once they'd taken you and Mason, and once Jemma was caught, it was the only thing I could do."

Ruston stopped at a watertight door and began turning the handle. They all stopped behind him, and Omar squeezed Levi's shoulder.

"I was joking, brother. I'm sure you make a fine Owl."

The door seal banged, and Ruston pulled open the door. They all walked into someone's living room. The space included an open kitchen on the other wall, separated by a counter. A woman and small girl stood behind it.

"Father!" The girl ran up and hugged Ruston's waist.

"This is Ruston's house," Levi said. "His real one."

"Another one?" This from the woman, who was glaring at Omar.

"Omar, meet Tova, my wife," Ruston said. "Tova, this is Levi's youngest brother, Omar."

"The father of Shayleen's babies?" She squinted at him and her mouth quirked up at the corner. "Good. That's excellent news."

Omar looked to Levi. "Is Shay okay?"

Levi patted Omar's shoulder. "She's fine. Let's go say hello."

They made plans to meet up with Ruston and Zane in the morning to discuss what to do next, then left Ruston's underground home and walked down a manmade passageway. Energy-saving light bulbs hung from the ceiling ever four or five yards. They passed little indentations with doors that likely led to more underground homes. The doors were labeled such things as 17 – 4, 16 – 2, and Library.

At 16 – 1, Levi went inside. It was dark, lit only with a pale light over the kitchen stove. This home had a similar setup to Ruston's, though the kitchen was partially hidden by a short wall rather than an open counter. There were two couches in the living room, and sleeping bodies occupied both. Omar recognized Trevon but not the other boy.

Levi nodded at the door behind Trevon's couch. "That's Shaylinn and Nell's room there."

Omar skirted the couch and peeked inside. The dim light that seeped through the door's opening barely illuminated two forms under blankets on a narrow bed.

He closed the door. "I'll wait until morning."

"He's not really the Owl."

"Yes, he is! And he's my cousin too, which means we're related."

"What's related?"

"I swear you don't know anything."

"He looks dead."

Omar opened his eyes to a pair of blue ones with thick lashes. Jake.

"Hello, Jake." Omar rose up onto one elbow and saw another boy peek out from behind Jake. A littler boy.

"Trevon said you were bad because you brought the enforcers to Glenrock," Jake said, "but he then said you tried to fix it by being the Owl. Is that true?"

"I suppose it is, though Levi has been the Owl lately, since I've been gone."

"Levi?" Jake practically screamed.

The front door opened then, but it wasn't Levi who came inside. It was a woman with blonde hair.

"Ciddah?" The medic.

She scanned the room. "You? You're not dead?" She walked to where he lay on the floor and crouched at his side. "Is Mason alive too? Did he come with you?"

"He couldn't," Omar said.

"But he's alive? He's okay?"

"Yes. In fact, he sent a letter for you." Omar sat up and reached into his pocket. He had to lie back down to pry the envelope out, and when he sat up and handed it to Ciddah, it was all bent out of shape. "Sorry. I didn't want to risk losing it."

She took it from him gently, like it was fragile in some way. "Thank you." And then she stood and left the house, clutching the letter to her chest.

"Girls are weird," Jake said.

"Sometimes," Omar said.

"Not nearly as weird as boys."

Omar twisted around. Nell stood behind the couch that Trevon was still sleeping on. "Good morning, Nell."

"Levi just told Jordan that you're back. Ciddah and her parents live at Jordan's house, so that's probably why she came looking for Mason. Shaylinn said she loves him, but Levi doesn't believe it."

"Why would Ciddah and her parents live with Jordan?" Omar asked.

"Because Levi and Jemma had all these kids to take care of, and someone needed to keep an eye on Ciddah in case she's the task director general's spy. Jordan thinks they're all spies."

"Ciddah is not a spy," Omar said.

"How would you know? Shaylinn is waiting for you, by the way. I told her you were back. She's in the bedroom but she's awake. She can't get out of bed, though, so you'll have to go see her."

"Why can't she get out of bed?" Omar pushed up to his feet, a little dizzy with the sudden movement.

"Her water broke and Ciddah put her on bed rest because if the babies come early, they'll probably die."

"What?" Omar walked around the couch, but Nell was standing between him and the door to Shaylinn's room.

"Did you know Jemma got taken?" Nell said. "It was Mia's fault. She stunned Levi so Kosowe could have him. Kosowe wants to steal Levi from Jemma, but it didn't work. He made her go live with her brother and won't talk to her."

Trevon threw the blankets off his head. "Stop gossiping."

"He should know what's going on," Nell said.

Omar grabbed Nell's shoulders and twisted around so that they traded places. The door to Shaylinn's room was open a crack, so he knocked. "Hello? Shay?"

"I'm here."

Her voice brought goose bumps all over his arms. He pushed the door in and peeked inside. Shay lay in bed under a thin blue-gray blanket, her belly a small mountain. The painting of Shay, Nell, and Penny hung on the wall over the bed.

He swallowed. "Can I come in?"

"Of course."

He closed the door behind him and walked to her bedside. "Shay, what did you eat? Something doesn't look right."

"Ha, ha."

She looked different. Rounder everywhere. "How much longer?"

"Well, they're not supposed to come until the second week of March, but Jemma said your mom told her that twins are always early. And Ciddah says that she normally induced labor with twins at thirty-seven weeks, so that would be the last week of February. But then my... I had a problem, and Ciddah said it's way too early, so I have to stay in bed until they come. It's so boring."

"Shay, I know you think I — "

"How are you?" she asked. "You look tired."

"I am. But I'm good. I got clean. From the PV."

"That's wonderful. Nell said you were in the Lowlands?"

"Yeah." And he explained a bit more, how Shanna was there and excited about her three new grandchildren."

"You really saw my mom?"

"She's fine, Shay. And I'm back to tell everyone the truth. It won't be much longer until we're all free."

"And then what?"

"I know you think I... that I cared about Kendall."

"You kissed her."

"Yes. I told her to stop, but she said you and I wouldn't work. She said you wouldn't want to be with someone who was infected."

"That's my choice, not Kendall's or yours."

"Not Kendall's, true, but it is mine. Shay, I couldn't live with myself knowing I'd infected you. I already have so much guilt. Those who died in Glenrock. But to see your face every day, to see you get sick and know that it was my fault... I didn't think I could handle that."

"So you were going to pick Kendall? Because of that?"

"No. But that's why I let her kiss me. She got me thinking about what it would mean to marry you. And I was scared. But mostly I was stupid. I should have been stronger. And then you were there, and I'd hurt you again. So I just …"

"Ran."

"I was a coward. I'm sorry. Everything was just so intense. And I didn't know how to handle it." His time with Rain came back to his mind, but he couldn't tell her about all that yet. It sent another stab of guilt through him. "But I've been thinking a lot about it. About … everything. And I want to be there for you. I want to be a father to these babies. But I'm dying and I … I can't ask you to die with me."

"Omar, I'm dying too."

His heart hitched at her words. "What do you mean? Mason said you weren't infected."

"The moment we're born, we start to die. So you have an infection. So you might die younger than me. I might die younger than you. You never know."

"*Shay.*"

"You don't know. So why live your life in dread? Embrace life while you have it. Trust that —"

Someone knocked on the door.

Not now! Omar gritted his teeth.

"Yes?" Shaylinn said.

The door opened and a man stepped inside. Nash.

"What's wrong?" Omar asked.

Nash brought his hand out from behind his back. He was holding a bunch of bright orange and yellow flowers. He stepped past Omar, and the nectar from the flowers filled the room with sweetness.

"Oh, thank you." Shaylinn took the proffered flowers and smelled them. The colors were amazing next to her tanned skin. Omar wished he could paint her like that, eyes closed, nose buried in blossoms. She opened her eyes and they were focused on Nash. Not Omar. She did glance his way, though.

"Nash tasks in the greenhouses," she said. "You should see his apartment. It's filled with plants and flowers."

Omar's stomach tightened. Shaylinn had visited Nash's apartment.

How foolish of him to assume she'd be waiting for him all these months. "Oh," he said. "I see. I, um ... I'm going to go." Omar pointed at the door, backed up a step.

Shaylinn frowned, reached out a hand. "No, Omar, please stay."

"Yes," Nash said. "You were here before me. Don't leave on my account."

"Really, it's okay." Omar's chest felt thick somehow, like a weight had been pressed down on it. "You two talk."

"*Omar.*" Shaylinn's voice was deep and firm.

But Omar was already out the door. A breath shuddered past his lips. It was better this way, really.

"Omar!"

He ignored Shay's yell, strode through the living room, dodged little Carrie, who toddled out of nowhere.

"Omar, Shay's calling you," Nell said.

He pretended not to hear, opened the front door, slipped into the cool corridor, shut the door behind him.

He stood in the alcove, shaking. He patted his pockets, looking for his PV. No more PV. Sober. Clean. He had to deal with pain and disappointment on his own now.

The door opened, striking the backs of his shoes. He lurched out of the way and turned around to see who was coming out.

Nash.

He shut the door, grabbed Omar's shirt, and pushed him against the wall.

"Whoa!" Omar grabbed Nash's wrists and tried to push them away. The memory of Prav hitting him flashed through his mind. "What is this?"

"I have a message from Shaylinn for you. You ready?" He gave Omar a little shake. "You listening? Because I'm only going to give it once, then you're on your own. Because I love that girl. And I think I could make her happy."

Omar didn't want to hear this. Who did Nash think he was, shoving Omar around like this and saying such things? "Then you should marry her. Shay's a nice girl. She doesn't pair up or anything like that." Could someone even do that when they were pregnant?

"Shut up." Another shake. "You're an idiot, you know that?" He released Omar with a shove. "Shaylinn doesn't love me. She loves you. Do you even get what that means?"

What? No, he was wrong. Omar had seen the way she'd brightened when Nash had given her the flowers. "You said Shaylinn had a message for me?"

Nash shot Omar one last dirty look, then grimaced. "She said, 'Don't you dare run away from me again.'"

The words were like a punch to the gut. Omar closed his eyes, wanting to defend himself. He met Nash's dark eyes. "I just thought she was better off with you, you know? Without me."

"Yeah, well, I do too. But you don't get to decide that, unfortunately." He opened the door to Levi's house and pushed Omar back inside. "Be good to her." And he slammed the door in Omar's face.

Well, then. That was nice and awkward. And so would be going back to Shay.

So Omar didn't go back. He stood, leaning against the front door, watching Joey and another boy play the Owl. Joey was the Owl, of course, and the other boy was an enforcer.

"You won't get away with this!" the boy said.

"Enforcers can't stop the Owl!" Joey said. "The Owl speaks the truth. Trust the Owl!"

Omar smirked, a little twinge of pride swelling in his throat.

A booming knock on the door made Omar jump. He turned and opened it.

Ruston's wife pushed past him. "Where is she?" The woman shook a crumpled piece of paper in his face. "Where is that girl?"

"Which girl?" Omar asked.

"Shaylinn. I will speak to her right now."

"She's in bed like always," Trevon said.

The woman started toward the couch, but Omar grabbed her arm. "Wait. What do you want? Tell me first."

"Remove your hands from me this instant!"

Omar let go, taken aback by the anger in the woman's voice. She strode through the kitchen, past the couch, and knocked on the door to Shaylinn's bedroom.

Omar chased her.

CHAPTER
23

A wave of aching pain pulsed through Shaylinn's abdomen, starting in her back and ending at her belly button. She gritted her teeth and wondered what Nell had put in her oatmeal this morning that had given her such indigestion.

Omar had better come back. She'd hoped for so long, and now he was here, back from the dead, but also back to being flighty. She wanted to talk to him. Needed to.

Someone knocked on her door. Omar! Good. "Come in." She smiled, glad that Nash had persuaded him to return.

But when the door flung wide, it was Tova who came inside. Stormed inside was a better description. The woman's face was red, her lips pinched in a snarl that bared her teeth.

"Good morning." Shaylinn caught sight of Omar behind Tova and her heart quickened. He *had* come back!

Tova swept into the room until she stood over Shaylinn's bed. She held up a crumpled piece of paper. She recognized the bits of blue handwriting. It was one of her messages. "Don't be friendly with me, you little wretch."

"Hey! Don't talk to her like that." Omar wedged himself between Tova and Shaylinn's bed, pushed the woman back. "Just calm down."

"She's been writing letters to my son." Tova shook her fist, the paper still clenched inside. "She has no right!"

Omar looked down on Shaylinn. "You wrote to Nash?"

"Yes," Shaylinn said. "That was our agreement if he was going to deliver my messages. I needed someone to."

Tova walked to the foot of Shaylinn's bed, uncrumpling the letter. "This is *not* to Katz." She held it up, turned it so Shaylinn could see.

Ah. "That's to Tym."

"You have no business poisoning a thirteen-year-old boy's mind with your worldly ideas," Tova said.

"I didn't. I was very cautious in what I wrote. Nash asked me to do it. He even asked Ruston's permission first, to make sure it was okay."

This only seemed to anger Tova further. "You encouraged Tym to write to Dathan!"

"They're brothers," Shaylinn said.

"Dathan has been exiled. He's no longer a member of our family. We don't communicate with him."

"Who's Dathan?" Omar asked.

"Dathan is Zane's real name," Shaylinn said to Omar, then addressed Tova. "From what I read of Kindred policy in the library, if a prodigal returns and asks forgiveness, he's to be forgiven and welcomed back. It's your *law*."

"The Old ways are not practiced here. Not when the thin plague is rampant. We cannot let offenders back into the community to spread the disease."

"I have the disease," Omar said, setting his hand on Tova's shoulder.

The woman shrieked and flew back from Omar.

Shaylinn tried not to laugh. "Tova, you can't get the thin plague from touching someone."

"You have no right to meddle in my family's business."

"You're right. I'm sorry. I just figured that everyone has a right to know they are loved, especially around Christmas. And Tym wanted to tell Zane that he loved him. What's wrong with — Ahh!"

Another wave of pain surprised Shaylinn, squeezing, burning the back of her spine. She held her breath through it.

Omar leaned over her. "Shay, what's wrong?"

"I have a bellyache," Shaylinn said. "I think I ate something bad."

"What did you eat?" Tova asked.

"Just oatmeal."

"The kids ate the same oatmeal and they seem fine," Omar said.

"But they're not pregnant. Everything about me is strange right now."

"How long have you been hurting?" Tova asked.

"Off and on since breakfast," Shaylinn said.

"Contractions," Tova said.

"No, it's too early," Shaylinn said.

"They start in your back and wrap around you."

Cold fear made Shaylinn shiver. They couldn't be contractions. She was only at week ... She couldn't remember what week it was, but she knew it was much too early. She tried to sit and reach for her journal.

"What do you need?" Omar asked.

She pointed. "That red book."

He handed it to her and she flipped to the calendar in the front, quickly located December 21. "Twenty-nine weeks." Tears flooded her eyes. "It's too early."

"I will help you, Shayleen," Tova said. "Though I don't have any obligation to do so."

Tova help her? Anything but that. "No, that's okay. Omar? Will you go find Ciddah, please?"

"You bet." He turned and ran from the room.

"You need crampbark and fennel," Tova said. "We grow it in the greenhouse. I'll send Katz to get some. Until then, roll onto your hands and knees. Rest your head on your arms. Put your backside up in the air. That will help the babies move closer to your lungs."

Shaylinn couldn't help it. She giggled. "Gravity?"

Tova nodded. "To be certain. Now do as I say. I'll return shortly."

Tova left, but Shaylinn did not roll over and put her butt in the air. She wasn't even certain she was in labor. It was likely only indigestion from the oatmeal.

Omar returned with Naomi and Ciddah, both of whom shooed him right back out of the room.

"Do not let anyone come in here until I say so," Ciddah said. "Do you understand? I'm going to check her."

Omar looked past Ciddah and met Shaylinn's gaze. "Check her for what?"

"To see if the babies are coming," Ciddah said.

Omar's face paled and he inched back a step. "What, uh … How long will it take?"

"Not long. Now, out!"

One more glance from Shaylinn and he pulled the door shut.

"You poor dear." Naomi sat on the edge of Shaylinn's bed, swept the hair back from her forehead. "Are you all right?"

"I'm fine." Shaylinn would never get to finish her conversation with Omar at this rate. "Ciddah, I really don't think I'm in labor. Tova thought so, but — "

"Tova has birthed five children, Shaylinn," Ciddah said. "I think that gives her some level of expertise."

"I guess."

Ciddah examined Shaylinn, and halfway through, another cramp seized her body. This one hurt more than the others.

"Ohh, Shaylinn," Ciddah said. "Yes, you're in labor."

Shaylinn took long breaths through her nose to try and ignore the pain. "Really?"

"I'm afraid so. Oh, I really need some meds! What if Levi took me to a Pharmco? We could steal some."

"If he won't trade you for Jemma, he won't take you out for meds," Naomi said.

"Then he's a fool!" Ciddah tucked Shaylinn back under the blankets. "I've never tried to stop labor without meds and my equipment."

"I'll fetch Chipeta," Naomi said. "She might have some ideas. She's miscarried several times."

"Miscarry!" The word shot fear through Shaylinn's heart.

"Don't worry." Naomi jumped up. "I'm simply hoping she remembers what Tamera tried to stop early labor."

A knock sounded on the door.

Naomi was already halfway to the door and opened it herself. Tova swept inside, holding a fabric bundle. Omar was right behind her. Naomi left and shut the door behind her.

"Why are you on your back?" Tova asked. "Roll over, Shayleen. Now!"

"What do you mean roll over?" Ciddah asked.

So Tova explained how the position could help the babies fall away from the birth canal.

"It's worth a try," Ciddah said, nodding to Shaylinn. "If the babies come now, they'll be too little, and I have no way to help them."

Tova instructed Ciddah and Omar to help Shaylinn roll onto her face, then supervised how to get her into the correct position. Shaylinn felt so fat and heavy and embarrassed that Omar was seeing her like this. She wanted him to leave, but she was afraid that saying so would hurt his feelings.

"Fifteen minutes, four times a day," Tova said. "I'm going to make you some tea that will also help."

"What kind of tea?" Ciddah asked.

"Crampbark and fennel."

Ciddah frowned. "You grow those here?"

"For medicinal purposes, yes." And Tova left.

"Omar, will you watch her?" Ciddah asked. "I need to find Levi. If he won't get me any meds, he needs to get an incubator. Preferably two, but we could make do with one."

"What's an incubator?" Omar asked.

"It's a special bed … box … for premature babies," Ciddah said. "It helps them stay warm and finish growing. I hope that Tova can help slow the labor, but if not, we need to have a place ready for those babies."

Once Ciddah was gone, Omar came and sat on the edge of the bed. He had to duck his head to look into her eyes. "How do you feel?"

"Stupid."

"You? Never! Why?"

"Because I'm in a really strange position and all the blood is rushing to my head."

"I could draw you, *Shayleen*," Omar said.

She reached out and tried to poke him in the side. "Don't you dare!"

"I promise I'd make it favorable."

"Omar, no."

He chuckled. "Well, it would make you laugh, anyway. Things are way too serious in this room."

"Speaking of which, we never finished our conversation," Shaylinn said.

"The one about you dying?"

"Yeah, that one."

He took a deep breath. "I don't know if now is the best time."

"Of course it is!"

He set his hand on the back of her head. "Hey, listen. We're both really young, and weird things are happening to us. There's no one I'd rather spend my life with than you, Shay, but we don't need to rush into anything. Until we're all free, we should just relax and not worry about the future."

"You have someone else? Someone in the Lowlands?" A thought occurred to her with a jolt. "Was Kendall there?"

"Kendall is dead, Shay. There's no one for me but you. And that's how I want it."

"Really?"

"Yeah. But what about you and Nash?"

"I think he likes me. But he's only my friend."

"Yeah, he likes you." He gave her a strange smile. "Okay, then. I like you and you like me. So let's get through this war they're planning and get you and the babies safe, and then if you're interested, maybe we can see if Levi will mentor us."

Again all she could say was, "Really?"

"You may not want to after going through labor. I've heard my mom tell stories."

"As long as you give up the PV. Do you think you can?"

"I already have."

"But for good?"

He chuckled. "Am I so unbelievable today?"

They sat together quietly for a time. Then the door opened and Tova came in with a mug that was steaming. "You can roll over now. It's been fifteen minutes."

Omar helped Shaylinn get settled upright in the bed again.

"Can I get you anything, Shay?" Omar asked.

"An incubator, I guess."

He leaned close and kissed her forehead. "You got it."

CHAPTER
24

W ell?" Cadell asked.

Mason looked up from where he was stocking the cupboard with medical supplies. Cadell watched him, his expression curious, eyebrows wrinkled, lips pursed in a flat line.

"We're pretty sure he made it."

"Pretty sure?"

Mason knew how that had sounded, but he could only guess what had happened with the balloon. From what he'd been able to see, Omar had gone too far. They'd tried to pull him back, but he'd cut the tether. He wouldn't have done that unless he'd had to. "There's nothing to do but wait and see."

"Wait." Cadell's posture slumped. "I'll be sixty-two in three weeks. I've already been waiting a very long time."

"So what's a few weeks more, right?" Mason said. "There's more we can do, you know. We could try and find some answers."

"You said there hasn't been a natural pregnancy in years?" Cadell asked.

"That's right. Not in the Safe Lands," Mason said. "Ciddah said infertility started showing up five years ago and spread rapidly."

"What changed, do you think? The thin plague has been around since the Great Pandemic. Why, after so long, would fertility problems suddenly become rampant? Something must have happened five years ago. A new antibiotic, perhaps? Or a mutation in the disease?"

Maybe that was when they had started putting stimulants in the meds. "I don't know of anything. I'll ask Lonn."

"Richark Lonn?"

"He used to be a medic," Mason said.

"I know him. Fastest twenty rank in the history of medics. He's here?"

"In my bunkhouse. He was liberated a rebel, so that makes him a striker. I found out he tasks in the cattle slaughterhouse."

"Richark Lonn in a slaughterhouse." Cadell shook his head. "That's really something, you know. No one saved more lives than that man. Until he became a rebel, I suppose."

"He's still trying to save lives." Saved Mason's life every night in their bunkhouse.

"It was never reported why he was fired from the MC," Cadell said. "But word got around. They wanted us to know his behavior wasn't acceptable. Still, I used to dream about finding a cure. I was too scared, though. After what happened to Lonn. But I'm old, Mason. And I don't care anymore. Before, there was the threat of premature liberation to keep me in line. Now, what can they do to me?"

"Move you to the strikers' bunkhouse and make you task in the cattle slaughterhouse," Mason said.

Cadell laughed. "True, that. I suppose they might." He put his hands in his pockets. "I wish I would have taken more risks back then."

"It's not too late," Mason said. "If Omar made it ... If he got word to the right people ..."

"I asked about compounding my own meds. I was told no." Cadell withdrew a vial of meds from his pants pocket and set it on the counter. "Thought maybe you'd like to mix this with your blood and see what's in it."

"Is it yours?"

Cadell nodded. "You might set up shop in exam room two. We rarely use those rooms, so as long as we keep one open you should be safe. And you might prepare an extra vial of meds for the patient in bed five." He gestured to the bed as if he were giving Mason instructions. "There's an extra blood meter in the cupboard above the sink by bed six."

Mason stared at the man, shocked in more ways than one. "Thank you."

He started to walk away. "You just make sure you share your results. I'm curious to see what you find out."

Between patients, Mason set up his laboratory in exam room two. It wasn't going to be easy to take his own blood, so he waited until his lunch break, got a sandwich from the GMC cafeteria, and brought it back to his lab. He spent the rest of his lunch drawing his own blood and eating his sandwich while he rested. By the time his lunch was over, he and his testing were in good shape.

He made two mixtures: One with his blood and Cadell's meds, and one with his blood and the meds of the patient in bed five. He tested Cadell's blood first. The tick, tick, ticking of the blood meter drew out the suspense.

Then it beeped. Mason read the display.

Inergia.

He'd never heard of it. He wrote it down on a slip of paper and tested the second sample. Xiaodrine, like Ciddah.

He recorded his data, frustrated that he had nothing more to test today. He cleaned up his mess, stored his blood samples in the mini fridge, and went back to work.

If he was going to do this well, he needed to get a lot more meds.

Mason had barely laid down on his mattress on the floor that night when the sounds of a fight made him sit up.

Shadows danced on the tile wall in the shower. He couldn't see who it was, but Lonn had gone over there. Surely Lonn could beat any man in a fight, though. That was why no one bothered him. Right?

Mason prayed God would protect Lonn, but he felt like a hypocrite, knowing he was truly afraid for only himself.

Then he heard it, the sound of SimAlarms stunning their victims. The SimAlarms made no real sound, of course, but the sounds of the fight ceased and were followed by soft grunting and some sort of a keen.

Someone on one of the bunks snickered.

Mason looked up to Hobbles. He was lying down on his side, his eyes wide and fixed on the showers. Mason looked back just as the door to their block pushed open and enforcers ran inside. Six of them, all holding stunners in hand.

"Everyone stay in bed or you'll be stunned," one of them yelled.

Mason didn't move. No one did. But someone was still snickering.

Four of the enforcers carried two big men from the showers. One was Strongboy. The other Mason Beckott. They carried them into the hallway, then came back in. Next they carried out Scar and Dash. Four against Lonn? Why? And why had the enforcers waited so long to stun everyone?

Lonn was the last to be carried out. As two enforcers carried him past where Mason sat on the floor, Lonn wrenched free and grabbed hold of the side post on his bunk bed.

"Hit me," he growled at Mason. "Now, you stupid shell!"

A third enforcer ran inside the room and pried Lonn's hand off the bunk.

"Attack one of the enforcers, then, boy!" Lonn yelled. "Do something."

Attack an enforcer? Mason didn't understand. The enforcers managed to get Lonn out the door before any more clues could be offered.

Why would he tell Mason to attack anyone?

The outer doors closed with a bang. Mason could hear the footsteps of the enforcers in the hallway, retreating from bunk 2C.

That's when they came for Mason.

Like the shadows of hawks they flew across the room, flew toward his place on the floor, looking to devour him. He understood Lonn too late. If Mason had joined the fight, he would have been stunned and taken to the warden. Now he was alone with evil men and no protector.

Mason slid underneath Lonn's bunk and grabbed the bedsprings above. Big hands snaked under the bed, grabbed him, pulled.

Save me!

His body slid out from under the bed. He wrapped his arm around one leg of the bed, bent his elbow, and clutched his opposite wrist with each hand.

Still they pulled until the bed slid out from its place and struck the one in the next row over. Someone grabbed Mason's waist, squeezed and yanked. Mason felt like he might rip in half at his hip bones.

"I got this," a deep voice said. And suddenly the bed tipped up and his anchor was no more.

They lifted him then, like the enforcers had lifted the others. Only Mason was not going to see the warden. Mason was going to the opposite corner of the room. To Scorpion.

When they got there, they tipped him on his feet so that he was standing in the gap between Scorpion's and Wicked's bunks. Scorpion was sitting up in his bed, looking surprised. Wicked had a hold of Mason's right arm. Mason didn't know the names of the others. He didn't recall ever seeing some of them spending time with Scorpion *or* Wicked, though for the right price in this place, almost anyone could be bought.

"What's this?" Scorpion asked.

"You wanted him," Wicked said. "I got him for you."

"You arranged this?" Scorpion asked. "Even the guards?"

"It took some careful negotiations," Wicked said, "but I did. I figured if Lonn was gone, we could get him without too much trouble."

"I'm impressed," Scorpion said.

The guards were involved? Why? Mason wanted to die. *God, take me to heaven. Don't make me live through this. Please.*

"What shall we do with him?" Wicked asked. "We have all night."

Save me from these wicked men. Have I not tried to serve you? Have I not done my best?

Scorpion pointed. "Take him back."

"Back where?" Wicked asked.

"To his bed," Scorpion said. "Take him back."

"What? Are you crazy?" Wicked's eyes flashed. "Do you know how many credits it took to pay off everyone?"

Scorpion was watching Mason, expression stoic. "I appreciate what you did tonight, Wicked. And there's no way you could've known it, but I'm in Raven's debt."

Wicked's voice rose an octave. "Since when?"

"You helped me," Scorpion said to Mason. "And now I'm helping you. This time, you go free. We're even now. Next time, I'll owe you nothing."

Bile squeezed up Mason's throat, and he swallowed it, trying not to let his fear and horror show. "We're even," Mason said, surprised at the sureness of his own voice when he was a pool of quivering fat inside.

"Good." Scorpion waved his hand at Wicked. "Let him go."

Wicked practically threw Mason across the room when he released him, which was just fine. Mason forced himself to walk back to his mattress on the floor, like he wasn't completely terrified. His bunk-mates were all staring, and Mason doubted anyone had ever gotten away from Scorpion like that.

He lowered himself to the floor and pulled the blanket over his body.

Hobbles whispered and it barely reached Mason's ears. "How did you do that?"

But Mason couldn't answer. He was too busy thanking God through his tears.

CHAPTER
25

"Ciddah, just say it plainly. What do you want me to do?" The woman had come to Levi yet again, this time ranting about Shaylinn's labor like it was his fault. He didn't like feeling attacked.

"I need to get her out of here," Ciddah said.

"Not happening." He knew it sounded mean, but he couldn't risk moving her.

"Then take me to a pharmacy where I can get her what she needs to save her babies."

Levi fought back a sigh. "I can't take you to a pharmacy."

"If it was Jemma in there, you'd do it," Ciddah said.

Low blow. Levi sat back on the couch. Was he being coldhearted? What would Jemma say? "Ruston said his wife has things under control."

"Yes, but for how long? If those babies come this early, they'll die."

"What do we need to help them live? Meds?" Maybe the Owl could break into a pharmacy and get whatever meds were needed.

"Meds might keep the babies from being born early. But if they're born early, I'll need an incubator."

"Like for baby chicks?"

"I don't know what that means," Ciddah said. "An incubator is a bed for a premature infant. It's enclosed and the temperature is regulated. It also monitors the baby's heartbeat and internal temperature. It filter's the air and protects the baby from infection."

O-kay. "Where would I find one?"

"Various places. Certainly in the MC. And in the nursery. And I suppose they must build them somewhere," Ciddah said.

If Ruston could find invisibility suits, he should be able to dig up an incubator bed. "I'll get one as soon as I can."

"Get two if you can, since Shaylinn is having twins."

Determined woman. Levi didn't understand how Mason could put up with her. "Two. I'll try to get two."

"Thank you, Levi." And Ciddah left.

There were twice as many men than usual at Thursday's rebel meeting, all of the newcomers Kindred. Levi wondered if they'd come because he was related to Seth McShane or because of Shay's letters. Maybe both.

Maybe neither.

"Operation Lynchpin won't work without the Lowlands, which we now know is where everyone goes when they're liberated," Levi said. "So the question is, how do we communicate with them?"

"Can't someone sneak in? Rappel down the wall or something?" Nash suggested.

"If they did it at night, it should work," Jordan said.

"No, they've got motion detectors on the walls," Omar said. "Maybe if we shot out the transformer like you did before. But we'd still have to get onto the Lowlands side of the wall, and it's not easy."

"What's it like down there, Omar?" Levi asked. "Can one of us blend in? Or does it have to be you?"

His little brother sighed. "It would be faster if it was me, but I've gone missing down there, so they're probably looking for me. One of you might not be noticed during the daytime, but you could wander into trouble trying to get to Lonn."

"It shouldn't be Omar," Nash said. "Shaylinn needs him."

Levi gritted his teeth. Nell, of all people, had filled him in on the fact that Nash and Omar both liked Shaylinn. Levi didn't have time for that kind of drama right now. "It's best for Omar to go back because he knows what he's doing."

"But how will we know if he gets the message to Lonn?" Ruston asked.

"Because I'll be listening." Zane tapped the place where his ear once was.

"I thought SimTalk doesn't work in the Lowlands," Levi said.

"It doesn't. But from what I can see, that's because there are no terminals down there to provide a signal to his implant. So I'm going to send him with a cube."

"Which is?" Levi asked.

"A portable terminal."

"I don't like that," Ruston said. "What if people start tapping old friends and telling them they're alive and slaving away in the Lowlands before we can make our move?"

"I don't think that will happen," Zane said. "People think there's no SimTalk down there, right? So why would they even try to use it?"

"It's a risk," Omar said. "I tried it several times, once when I was juiced and just not thinking straight. So that could happen. Plus, any newcomer would try to tap someone."

"It would be great to send the Owl down there right at launch time," Zane said. "I could use the block to hack the Lowlands ColorCast and send in our message — tell people that their SimTalk implants are working again. So just as we reveal the truth to people in the Highlands and Midlands, people in the Lowlands can start making taps and verifying what we've said. Total anarchy."

Silence filled the room, but it seemed to Levi that everyone liked that idea. "Let's do that. So how else could we get confirmation that Omar arrived safely?"

"Ask them to verify the next night by sending a light signal," Jordan said.

That made sense. "But what if they don't like our plan? Or what if they don't want to do it? And maybe they have a good reason for us not to do it yet but have no way of telling us. We need to be able to communicate consistently."

"Did you try your SimTalk really close to the Lowlands-Midlands wall?" Zane asked Omar.

"No," Omar said, "but I think Lonn said they have lead inside the walls to keep them from working."

"Okay," Zane said, "so when you get there, have them send someone back with their answer in Mason's balloon."

"The balloon is gone," Omar said. "Blew outside the walls."

"Have him build another one," Jordan said.

"It took him months to build the first," Omar said, "and besides, they have those new neck SimTags."

"I could send a lead collar with our first message," Zane said. "We keep the ghoulie tags in lead boxes. A lead collar might be enough to keep him from being seen. I'd just have to make one."

"You can't surround the tag though," Nash said. "Not like you do with a ghoulie tag box. You'd only be going around the neck. The signal would still have access through his head and feet."

"Okay, so we'll think on this some more," Levi said. "Hopefully we'll come up with a decent solution."

Most of the men left then, and Levi and the smaller team went over the plan to rescue Jemma. The day had almost arrived, and Levi didn't want to make any errors.

When Levi felt confident that everything was set, he looked down at his agenda and saw the last remaining item: Shaylinn. "We have a problem with Shaylinn. Ciddah is worried that the babies are going to come any day and she doesn't have an incubator to put them in. She says without one, they probably won't survive. Zane? Incubators?"

"Shouldn't be too hard to find. They're big, though. On wheels, most of them, from what I've seen on the cameras. But we could take it to the dumpsters and bring it down that way."

"I'd like to help," Nash said.

"No, I've got this," Omar said.

"*I've* got this," Jordan said.

"Great," Levi said. "If you three are going to argue over Shaylinn, then you three get the job."

"Can I make a suggestion?" Zane asked.

"Always," Levi said.

"Send Nash and Beshup to get the incubator at the same time you and Jordan go after Jemma. While Omar the Owl distracts enforcers in another part of the city."

"I don't know," Levi said. "I don't want to complicate the Jemma rescue."

"It won't," Zane said. "Dusten can drive for you instead of Nash. It's a simple switch. And the Owl's distraction should keep the enforcers away from you."

Maybe it was a good idea. Anything to help Jemma's rescue go smoother. "Okay," Levi said. "Do it."

The new Prestige building sat halfway down Anthracite Drive. From the Highlands, the harem car would pass through the wall to the Midlands at the Gothic Gate. Levi and Zane both figured the harem driver would take Gothic down to Winterset, then circle back to Anthracite. But there was a chance they'd weave their way through the old town area, taking Gothic to Belleview to Cinnamon Mountain and then come up Anthracite from the other direction.

There was no way of knowing which way they'd go. But that didn't really matter. Zane said there was no way for him to control the door locks on the car, so they had to wait for Jemma to get out before grabbing her.

So Levi was waiting in the parking lot of the Prestige. Once he heard from Zane that the car was almost there, he and Jordan would get out and walk into the lobby so they could exit just before Jemma entered. And the moment Dusten saw them, he'd drive past and pick them up on his way out of the parking lot. Two blocks away, he'd drop them in an alley and continue on.

"Her car just passed through the gate," Zane said. "It's staying on Gothic."

"They're coming from Gothic," Levi said.

"Won't be long now." Dusten tapped his fingers on the dash.

Levi was nervous. The last two months had been agony, waiting for this day, ignoring the new threats that Renzor's people kept leaving in theater nine. Levi had wanted to trade Ciddah so badly. It was foolish, he knew. He couldn't trust that Renzor would give him Jemma. It would be a trap. Better to do things their way than kowtow to any demands from City Hall.

"How far along is Jemma?" Jordan asked. "Pregnancy wise?"

"I don't know." Levi didn't even want to think about the fact that these people had made his wife pregnant.

"I'm just wondering if she'll have trouble in the tunnels," Jordan said.

Levi would help her. "You helped Naomi through the tunnels when she was almost due. Jemma's not that far."

"Right," Jordan said. "That's right."

"They're on Winterset now," Zane said in Levi's ear.

Agony. Levi just wanted it over and Jemma back in his arms. "Where's Omar?" Levi asked Zane.

"Wreaking havoc on Villa Bonita. Enforcer 10 just got their first complaint from a resident. Shouldn't be long before they send someone to check it out. The car is on Anthracite now. Better head inside."

Levi and Jordan got out and walked across the lot. The night was chilly, the asphalt icy underfoot. Levi's breath clouded out through his lips. His gaze flickered between the lobby doors and the driveway to the theater, watching each set of headlights, wondering if they belonged to the harem car.

They reached the building and went inside, where warm air greeted them. The lobby was packed with people in fancy clothes, eager to celebrate the opening of yet another place to party. Levi hated them all. These people valued nothing that he did: family, hard work, honesty, sacrifice. These people did what they wanted for their own sakes, to please themselves, and their greed and selfishness showed with every flake of their skin. No amount of paint or fancy fabric could hide the truth. These people were reaping what they'd sown, and Levi wanted no part of it for him or his people.

"The car is stopping," Zane said. "Doors opening. I see Luella Flynn and Finley Gray. They're coming inside. I don't see Jemma."

Levi's stomach flipped. "What do you mean?"

"The car is driving off to park," Zane said. "No Jemma."

No! She had to be there. "Why not?"

"Levi, how should I know?" Zane said. "I'm sorry, peer."

Sorry? Levi started toward the entrance. The automatic doors opened just as Luella and her partner started inside.

Levi stopped directly in her path. "Where is she?"

"Where is who?" Luella had green glitter on her eyelids and cheeks. She blinked, looked him up and down. "Do I know you, trig?"

"Jemma was supposed to be with you," he said.

"Queen Jemma, yes. I'm sorry, valentine. She was going to come, but she isn't feeling well today. Maybe next time." She patted his arm as she walked around him, waving to the crowd that had formed.

Next time? What next time?

Jordan tugged on his arm. "Levi, we need to go."

Levi let Jordan drag him out to the lot where Dusten picked them up. As they rode back to Zane's house in frustrated silence, all Levi could think was *What if there isn't a next time?*

CHAPTER
26

Omar loved everything about his costume: the fit, the texture, the stretch, his paint job, the mask, the way the spray cans and stunner in his holster belt jangled as he ran, and especially the way the cape soared behind him like wings.

He'd missed being the Owl.

He darted from alley to alley, careful to stay in the darkness as much as possible. He and Zane had already worked out this route ahead of time, and he recited it in his head to keep it fresh.

Villa Bonita was tonight's target. For the Midlands, it was about as upscale as one could get for apartments. Some complained that only people in Renzor's favor were permitted to live there. It seemed like a place that most Midlanders would appreciate seeing the mark of the Owl.

Omar made his way out of an alley and onto 7th, lurking along the wall, hoping not to be seen just yet. Villa Bonita was on the corner of 7th and Winterset, just the right distance from the Prestige. Enforcers should get tied up chasing both parties.

He came to Winterset and waited until there were no cars, then ran across the street without bothering to wait for the light, pretending to be a real owl, trying to make his steps smooth. He held out his arms and admired the shape his shadow took on the street. He even skidded gracefully over an icy patch on the street.

He set to work immediately. He threw up his stencil, sprayed the words "Hoo is the Owl?", filled in the stencil, and ripped it away quickly. Over the sign to Villa Bonita, he used white to spray over the word "bonita." Then he stenciled an owl over the Wyndo that flashed images of happy people in their apartments. He went back and sprayed "Owl" over the white so that the sign now read "Villa Owl." Nice.

Around the corner he painted another owl, then wrote, "The Owl sees all." Nash had better be able to get the incubator for Shay. And Omar also hoped that Levi would succeed in rescuing Jemma. This night of missions felt like the practice before the real thing. Operation Lynchpin was really going to happen, and Omar couldn't wait. But he had to. First, tonight. Two small victories before the big one.

"What are you doing out there? Hay-o!"

Omar glanced up. Someone was leaning out their window, looking down on him. Good. Hopefully they'd call Enforcer 10.

"Zane? What's the status?"

"Levi and Jordan are in the lot. The harem car is just now turning on Winterset."

Omar looked down the road, as if he might actually see the car in the dark three blocks away, turning the opposite direction from him.

Levi's waiting for you, Jemma.

A siren pinged. Omar's heart jolted. He turned around, looking for the red and blue lights.

Nothing.

Something moved out on the street. A car with all its headlights off. It had stopped a few yards behind him. What was that all about? Did they think they'd sneak up on him this time? Interesting.

Omar had two options for escape. The nearest crossway gates were either a half block down to 8th or two blocks up to Prospector Drive.

"Zane? Any calls for Enforcer 10?"

"A call went out, but I've yet to see a response from Enforcer 10. It's like they didn't get the call, even though I saw it go through."

"That's weird." Time to go.

Eighth was closer and Omar knew that crossway better. He took off, straight across the street, right in front of the mystery car. The vehicle started up and came after him, lights sending his silhouette long and massive on the street before him.

The Owl.

Awesome.

He darted into the alley that would lead to another alley that would cut back out to 8th a few yards before the alley that led to the crossway. It was a maze of nameless streets, and Omar loved it.

He wondered again why no enforcers had come. They'd come every other time.

He slipped around the corner where his alley met the next and …

Whack! Something struck him in the chest.

He fell flat on his back, the wind knocked out of him. Breathe, he told himself. He needed to get up. Keep moving.

Three shadows loomed over him, reached down. Omar moved without thinking, but it was too late. There was a pop, some sparks, and a stunner ended his chances altogether.

They picked him up and carried him along. He tried to take note of where they took him. Back out the alley the way he'd come. They cuffed his hands behind him. Shoved him into the backseat of a car. A nice one. Not enforcer issued, though. A detective's car, perhaps?

They pulled a fabric sack over his head and he couldn't see anything else. The way he was almost sitting on his hands made the metal cuffs dig into his wrist. Omar had no idea where he was being taken. To the RC, probably, back to a cell, then before the Guild, who would liberate him again.

Lonn and his mother would be pretty disappointed. Shaylinn too.

Forgive me!

It felt like the car drove long enough to cross the Midlands and Highlands both. They stopped several times, though Omar had no way of knowing if they'd gone through one of the gates to the Highlands. Finally the vehicle stopped and shut off.

Omar was led inside a warm building. Over soft carpet. Across hard floors. A staircase down. The temperature dropped. The floor was still hard, but no longer as smooth as upstairs. They walked about twenty paces. Door hinges squeaked.

"Sit." A man's voice.

Omar squatted carefully until his hands behind him felt a hard surface. He sat on what felt like a metal chair.

A door closed.

"Hello?" Omar said.

No answer.

"Hey? What's the deal? You're just going to leave me here?"

Nothing.

He stood up and thought about trying to leave, but that would be stupid when he couldn't see where he was going. He shook his head and tried to get the sack to slide off. He leaned forward and tucked his head between his knees. Shook his head again. Felt the bag slide a little. He shook harder until his head filled with pressure.

The bag slid off and plopped to the floor.

Excellent.

He sat back up and looked around him, his face tingling with gravity's effect on his blood flow. It was a plain room. Sheet-rocked and taped but not painted. Omar had spent a few weeks tasking on a paint crew that painted rooms like these every day. He wondered why no one had bothered to paint this one.

He got up and walked to the door. Turned around and tried the knob with his hands still cuffed behind him. Locked. If he wasn't cuffed he could probably get out of here, break through the wall. Sheetrock was pretty brittle and thin.

Maybe he could do it anyway.

He locked his hands with his wrists behind him, braced forearm to forearm, then tried to elbow the wall. That didn't work, though, and he ended up hitting his funny bone.

He stepped back and gave the wall a good side kick. His foot dented the sheet rock. Nice. He kicked it again. Again. Now that was making a good start. Again. Turned and kicked with the other leg. Good. He walked up to the hole and peeked through.

The room on the other side was dark. Powdered chalk misted the air around the hole and made it harder to see. He sneezed. Then backed away and breathed in some clean air.

A noise outside sent him scrambling. Should he sit? Get behind the door?

The door opened and Omar lashed out with a kick to the man's chest. The man stumbled back into another man, who was right behind him. The second man pulled a stunner from his buddy's belt.

The next thing Omar knew he was back on the chair, hooded again, and unable to move as the stun wore off. He could feel them tying his ankles together with some kind of rope.

So much for getting away.

Hours passed. No one came. Omar's eyes started to sting from lack of sleep.

He'd almost given up when he heard footsteps outside the door. He straightened in the chair. Whoever this was, the Owl had to give his best.

The door hinges squeaked. Footsteps. Some scuffy ones, some that clicked.

"You really did it." A woman's voice. "Take that off."

Fingers tugged at the hood over Omar's head. Pulled it off. Before him stood the two men in black suits he'd seen before and a woman in a formal gown.

Omar couldn't believe it. "Luella Flynn?"

Her lips stretched into a beaming smile. "Caught you."

CHAPTER
27

"Shay? You up?" Jordan peeked through the cracked open doorway. Shaylinn was up. She'd barely slept since the men had left the previous night. And now her heart sank heavily. "You didn't get Jemma."

"What makes you say that?" Jordan asked.

"If you'd gotten her back, she'd be here right now instead of you."

Jordan pursed his lips. "Can't fool you, can I?"

Tears filled Shaylinn's eyes at the knowledge that Jemma was still lost. "What went wrong?"

"She wasn't in the car. Just Luella Flynn. I guess we misread the calendar or they changed it or she really wasn't feeling well. That's what Luella Flynn told Levi — that Jemma wasn't feeling well tonight."

Shaylinn wasn't feeling well either. She'd been in bed for nearly three months. She wanted the pregnancy to be over. She wanted to be able to walk around.

"Nash brought back the incubox," Jordan said. "Ciddah's got it in my kitchen right now, washing it. Said it needs to be clean. He only found one, so your kids are going to have to sleep head to toe or something."

"I'm sure they'll manage. I'm glad Ciddah is here."

"Yeah, she's not half bad," Jordan said, coming to stand at the head of her bed.

"Did something else happen? You're hovering."

"How am I hovering?" he asked.

"You're standing over me. If you were relaxed, you'd have sat down by now."

He sat on the edge of her bed.

"Too late. Out with it, Jordan."

He sighed and rubbed his face. "Omar didn't come back, kid. He got caught, actually. Zane saw it on the cameras."

"Oh." Shaylinn shuddered and folded her arms. Omar caught? Again?

"The little maggot was finally starting to grow on me too, the way he got out of the Lowlands like that — though I guess that was really more Mason's brain than Omar's brawn."

"It was enforcers?" Shaylinn's voice cracked, watery. She heaved in a breath.

"Zane thinks so."

"What does that mean? Will he go back to the Lowlands?"

"We don't know." He took hold of Shaylinn's hand and squeezed. "You'll be okay?"

She shook her head and tears blurred her sight. She blinked to wash them out of her eyes, but they were instantly replaced by more. So many tears for the girl who didn't cry.

Jordan scooted closer and pulled Shaylinn into his arms. He held her close and rocked her. "It's going to be all right. Know how I know?"

Shaylinn shook her head.

"Because you deserve every good thing. And I'm going to see that you get it."

Shaylinn wanted to argue with him, remind him that very few good things had happened to any of them in the past few months, but her tears overwhelmed her and all she could do was cry.

Jordan must've stayed with her until she fell asleep, because when she awoke, he was gone and the room was dark. She couldn't see the clock without the lights on, and she didn't feel like getting out of the warm bed just to know that it wasn't time to wake up yet — not that she *could* get out of bed. So she cried herself back to sleep.

She awoke the next morning to a knock at her door. Ciddah came in, pulling something behind her. The incubator bed.

"The boys got our incubator."

Shaylinn forced a smile. "I heard."

Ciddah rolled the clear plastic box around the foot of Shaylinn's bed and up against the wall on Shaylinn's left. She crouched and plugged it in.

"I think we should keep it ready just in case. How do you feel?"

"Angry."

"I know, femme. I'm so sorry. And I know it's hard for you to hear this, but you have to let it go for now. Find a way to relax. Severe emotional stress can trigger preterm labor. So try not to think too much about it. I guess that's impossible, though, huh?"

"Have you stopped thinking about Mason?"

Ciddah sighed and fell into a slouch. "I see your point."

"I'll think I'll go back to sleep for a while," Shaylinn said. "Then I don't have to think about anything."

"Okay. Send one of the boys if you need me."

"I will."

And Ciddah left.

But sleep would not come to Shaylinn that day. She got up to use the bathroom and found her bed sheets spotted with blood.

Panicked, she pulled the bedcovers over the stains to hide them and walked to the door. She opened it. Could see two heads on the couch. "Hello? Is Ciddah still here?"

The heads moved, and the faces of Joey and Weiss peeked at her over the back of the couch.

"She left," Joey said.

"I need her," Shaylinn said. "Can you fetch her for me?"

"We can do it. Let's go, Weiss."

The boys ran to the front door and were soon gone. They'd left the front door wide open, though. Shay crept out from her room, inching over the old rug. She closed the door, then started back to her room. Halfway around the couch she felt the familiar, slow spasm of a contraction.

Oh no.

There was very little pain. No more than a minor headache, and it was soon gone. Still, Shaylinn hobbled back to her room and climbed onto the bed, arranging herself in the position Tova had taught her. "Not yet, babies. Ciddah said thirty-two weeks. So you go back to sleep."

But the contractions did not stop. Another came just as Ciddah arrived with Naomi and Aunt Mary.

"Oh, honey," Naomi said, taking in Shaylinn's position.

"It helped last time," Shaylinn said.

But thirty minutes later, the contractions were still coming and Shaylinn gave up trying to stop them. They were stronger now too, like the pulsing throb of a major headache. Ciddah helped her roll to her back and tucked her in.

"We should check you," she said. "And, Naomi, please help me keep track of the contractions."

"Shay, where do you keep your paper and pencils?"

"In the drawer."

Naomi whisked out writing utensils and Ciddah set about "checking" Shaylinn to see whether babies were on their way or not.

"Well?" Naomi asked, pencil and paper ready as if she needed to write something down.

Ciddah looked pale. "Not yet."

"What do you mean?" Shaylinn asked. "What's wrong?"

"Oh, nothing, Shaylinn, don't worry. It's just ... With Kendall, the baby was already coming. To be honest, I'm not sure what I'm looking for. They don't teach this in medic school, since labor in the Safe Lands is a simple surgical procedure."

Ciddah didn't know what she was looking for?

The door opened then and in came Penny and Nell, squealing

about babies to hold. Shaylinn stopped worrying for a while, and soon her room was a flurry of noise. More had come: Chipeta, Eliza, and Aunt Mary. Which made it five women looming over her bed, arguing over who should "deliver" the babies, while Penny and Nell played with the incubator.

"I'm delivering them," Ciddah said. "I am her medic and have been from the start."

"But you've never done this before, right?" Aunt Mary asked. "And you admit you don't even know what to look for."

"I've not done it on my own, no," Ciddah said. "I've assisted. With Elyot."

"You should have seen Harvey and Elyot today," Naomi said to Chipeta. "We had them on the floor and they were cooing to each other."

"I think Chipeta should do it," Aunt Mary said.

"Well, I've never done it either," Chipeta said. "Eliza, why don't you run and see if any of the Jack's Peak women have experience birthing babies."

Shaylinn heard the clump of the door, which must have been Eliza leaving. But all she could see from her position was a wall of women circling her bed. "We already decided." Shaylinn panted, surprised that uttering only three words would leave her winded. "Ciddah is going to."

"But that was when we thought Jemma would be back," Aunt Mary said. "Jemma and Ciddah as a team is perfect, but alone ..."

"I *am* capable," Ciddah said. "Once they start coming, I know exactly what to do."

Shaylinn didn't like this at all. They'd made a plan, but without Jemma, everything was messed up.

The door opened and closed again. "I'm here, Shayleen. Let me see you." Tova. She pushed through the crowd and up to Shaylinn's beside. She smiled down at Shaylinn, and brushed her hair back from her cheek. "Oh, yes. They are coming today, aren't they? Now you will see, Shayleen, with all of your letters. Pfft. Now you will learn the real hard work of a woman."

Shaylinn wanted to spit back an angry retort, but another contraction came, this one surprisingly strong. It felt like a giant had picked her up in his hand and squeezed.

Tova took her hand. "You must breathe. In and out. That's right." She brushed her hair back again. "Medic. How far along is she?"

"We don't know," Ciddah said.

"What do you mean?"

"I don't know what to look for." Ciddah winced. "I missed that part of Elyot's birth."

"Okay, listen up!" Tova yelled. "Everyone leaves but the medic and one other." She looked to Shaylinn. "Who do you want to stay?"

"Naomi," Shaylinn said.

"Okay, Naomi, fetch two large bowls of warm water and towels. Ladies, help her. Medic, you have some materials? Show me."

The room cleared out, and Ciddah pulled a box up on the foot of the bed. Tova looked through it, selected a few things.

Naomi returned with one bowl of water and a pile of towels draped over her arm. Chipeta held the door for her as she carried them in and set the bowl and towels on the desk. Naomi left and shut the door behind her.

"Medic, we wash our hands first." Tova waved Ciddah to the bowl and washed and dried her hands. Ciddah did the same.

The door opened again. Naomi back with more water.

"Put that one here on the floor." Tova showed Naomi where. "And please empty that one and bring a new one." She waved at the hand washing bowl.

Naomi obeyed and was soon gone again.

"Okay, now we check," Tova said. "Medic, come learn."

Shaylinn couldn't see the clock. She didn't know how long she'd been doing this. But it seemed like days. Her whole body ached to the point that she really wasn't sure where the pain was coming from anymore.

Well, she knew, of course, but that didn't keep the thought from coming to her each time a contraction took control of her body.

Naomi had been sent for more bowls and towels. Shaylinn didn't know why. She didn't care. She just wanted the pain to stop.

"Here comes another, Shayleen," Tova said. "Soon. It will be soon."

Shaylinn gritted her teeth as the pain swarmed, burning and deep. She hated the Safe Lands for doing this to her. She hated Ciddah! And Omar too. Omar, who had abandoned her again and again.

And then the contraction was gone. But not like before. Not completely gone. Now when the contractions left, she was left feeling bruised and beaten, like she was trying to recover but couldn't. Another would come. It would never end! She would probably die.

What if she died?

"Shay." Naomi took hold of her hand. "How are you? You want some water?"

Shaylinn shook her head.

"You're doing good, sweetie. I'm so proud of you."

"I don't want to die."

"Oh, no, Shay. That's not going to happen. You're doing great. Almost there, Tova says. Aren't you glad she's here?"

Shaylinn was.

The contractions came faster, seeming to possess her body. The agony was so intense she could barely breathe.

"Time to push, Shayleen!" Tova said. "Push, girl. Now! Push, push!"

Push? Shaylinn tried, swallowed with the effort. A faint moan slipped past her lips.

Naomi's face remained calm. "Good, Shay. You're doing great." Her voice was soft and soothing, her eyes focused on Shaylinn.

As the pain grew more intense, so did the voices. Louder, excited. A chorus of demands.

"Push! Push!"

Squeals of joy.

A light cry. An infant's cry.

"Okay, medic. You watch for the second baby." Tova stood, holding a grayish pinkish squirming thing.

Shaylinn saw blood. "It's bleeding? Is it okay?"

"Oh, yes, Shayleen. This is a strong boy." Tova picked up a pair of scissors and cut the gnarly cord, then brought the baby to Shaylinn. "See your precious boy, yes? See how much you love this one. Just one look and see if you don't."

A boy? It looked inhuman. An ugly doll covered in too much pinkish-gray skin that was slimy with blood and something white. Floppy arms and legs. Slimy black hair. Wrinkled slashes for eyes. A frowning mouth. His whole body fit in Tova's hands, head in one, rear end in the other.

He scared her.

"Is he okay?" she asked.

"Yes, love. He's just fine. A fine boy."

He didn't look fine. He looked weird.

Tova handed the boy off to Naomi, who oohed and ahhed as if he looked just like a sweet little puppy. And then it was time to push again. And soon a girl arrived! But she looked as strange as her brother, though she was redder, it seemed, and louder too.

But it still wasn't over. And Shaylinn had to push again to expel the things that her babies had been living in all this time. Then Tova called Aunt Mary and Chipeta to hold the babies while she, Naomi, and Ciddah cleaned Shaylinn up. Once Shaylinn was settled in a new nightgown and a bed of fresh blankets, Aunt Mary gave her the boy to hold.

He looked much better now that he was dried off. He had a tiny little head the size of her fist that looked to be all eyes. Deep brown eyes the size and shape of almonds. Those wide eyes locked onto hers, and Shaylinn smiled and touched her thumb to his cheek. His skin was so soft. Tears filled her eyes. She'd brought life into the world. This little person had come from her.

So strange.

The women started to argue then. Tova wanted Shaylinn to try and breastfeed the boy, but Chipeta said it was too early and Ciddah wanted to give him formula. And Chipeta said that breast milk was not merely food, but medicine for the babies' little bodies. And Ciddah said that she was fed the formula and turned out fine.

"Can I see the girl?" Shaylinn asked.

Naomi was holding her now, and she sat on the edge of Shaylinn's bed and helped Shaylinn take the girl in her other arm so that Shaylinn was holding both. The girl was even smaller than the boy. She looked better too now that she was dry, but her skin was still very pink. She had even more hair than her brother, but her face seemed perfectly proportioned. Little brown eyes, a tiny nose, small lips. Shaylinn looked from one to the other.

"I like them." And she did. Her heart felt full yet totally vulnerable.

Naomi laughed. "I'm sure they're glad to hear it."

"Do they have the thin plague?" Shaylinn asked.

Ciddah broke off from her argument with Tova. "I don't think so, Shaylinn. But I have no method of testing them down here. You should only hold them a little while, then put them in the incubator to sleep. They'll need to spend a lot of time in the incubator. Several more weeks. You can take them out to feed and hold them, but they need to go right back in. They both look perfectly healthy, but there's no fat on them. The incubator will help keep them warm until they bulk up a bit."

And so Shaylinn kissed her babies and then allowed them to be put in the incubator. She submitted herself to Tova's lessons on how to hand pump breast milk so that the babies could be tube fed until they were old enough to learn to latch on.

So much work still.

Shaylinn realized then that her childhood was over. She was a mother now, and her only concern was for her babies. And she knew it would be her concern for the rest of her life, and that was okay because these two were part of her and she must do what was necessary to see that they were healthy and safe.

And she would need to name them.

And she wondered if they would ever see their father.

CHAPTER
28

Lonn returned to bunk 2C the next morning, to Mason's great relief. He had a blackened bruise under one eye, but other than that, he looked remarkably well. His attackers had come back too, and everyone was pretending that nothing had happened.

"You okay?" Mason asked.

"Me? Are *you* okay?"

Mason nodded. "Tell you at breakfast."

Mason and Lonn went to the strikers' cafeteria and sat by themselves at a table near the doors. Mason had gotten toast and orange juice. Lonn was eating a pile of scrambled eggs and bacon that looked to have more fat than meat. Mason filled Lonn in on Scorpion's mercy.

"Fortune saved you," Lonn said.

Mason had no desire to debate religious theories this morning. "I told Cadell about you."

Lonn frowned, his cheeks full with a bite of eggs. "Told him what?"

"That you were here. He knows who you are, of course, though I had to fill him in on some of the more recent stuff. The Lowlands ColorCast doesn't show any current events." Not that you could trust the ColorCast reports, anyway. "I told him he should ask for you to be reassigned as a medic."

"It won't happen," Lonn said.

"He's been helping me. He let me build a lab, and I'm testing the meds. Cadell's meds didn't contain Xiaodrine but Inergia."

Lonn chewed thoughtfully. "That's another amphetamine. For insomnia."

"That's what Cadell said. He asked about compounding his own meds and was told no."

"Not surprising," Lonn said. "But, Mason, you're far too trusting. What do you really know about this man?"

"That he fought to get me moved from the feedlot to the MC. That he's still fighting to get my housing changed."

"So he says."

"Sometimes we have to trust people," Mason said.

"But are you certain you must trust him? Absolutely certain?"

"I am. He helped get Omar ready for the balloon. He's a good man, Lonn."

Lonn sighed and nodded in resignation. "Then I will trust him too, if given the chance."

Mason read the name of the stimulant from the blood meter. "This one has Focastat XR."

"That's a new one," Cadell said.

"Another amphetamine?"

"Yes, actually. That one is usually prescribed for patients who can't focus. Try this one." Cadell handed Mason a vial. "I'll be back." He left exam room two and shut the door behind him.

Mason's lab had grown. He'd taken the mattress off the bed and spread his experiment out over the metal surface and all along the counter. Cadell had sent him here the moment he'd arrived this morning with instructions to test another seven vials he'd gotten from patients. And since then he'd brought Mason the meds of every patient he'd seen that morning. Mason had tested a total of fifteen meds so far.

He'd made a chart of his results. He'd put the patient's ID on the far left, then the stimulant that was found in that person's meds. He also made two more columns: one for the reason the patient had come to the MC and another for the patient's overall health. Cadell had been filling those in as he came in and out between patients.

Mason studied the results. Of the fifteen, three had the same Xiaodrine that had been found in Ciddah's original meds, and three had Centralin, three had Excitare, four had Inergia, one had Validum, and one had Focastat XR. Mason could not yet see any patterns in the patients' health, needs, or stimulant. They'd need to test many more meds to get such results.

Tedious. But at least he was doing something.

The door opened. Cadell set a vial on the counter. "Come out. Quickly. Two enforcers just arrived."

Mason left the room with Cadell and walked to bed three. "How are you feeling, Mrs. Silver? Is the pain still there?"

The elderly woman looked up at him. "Oh, it feels much better, medic. Thank you. I just hate that my hands don't want to work for me anymore. It's the most frustrating thing. But the pain makes it so much worse."

Mason nodded, but glanced toward the lobby as the woman told him again how the pain made her drop things. Sure enough, two enforcers were walking around the counter now. Coming toward Medic Cadell.

Mason's heart thudded. They knew! How? There were no cameras in the private exam rooms. Had Cadell set him up?

"I demand more information than that!" Cadell yelled. "Besides, you can't just take my assistant and give me no replacement."

They'd come for Mason? Why? There was nowhere to run, so Mason walked toward them. "Is there a problem, Medic Cadell?"

"These men have orders to take you into custody."

"On what charges?" Mason asked.

"No charges," the enforcer said. "The liberator wants to speak with you."

"Why?"

"You think the liberator tells us his business? How'd you get to be a medic?"

"Very well," Mason said. "Before we leave, would you give me a moment to inform Medic Cadell about my patient's needs?" He gestured to Mrs. Silver's bed. "In private, please. Only a moment."

"Yeah, fine." The enforcer jerked his head toward the lobby, and the two walked back that way.

"Richark Lonn," Mason said to Cadell. "He's in the Strikers' Bunkhouse in sector five. Room 2C. If I don't come back, see if you can get him to be my replacement. He knows way more than me, anyway."

"What makes you think you aren't coming back?"

Mason grimaced and glanced at the enforcers. "Omar."

"This has never happened. Not as long as I've been liberator, and that's been" — the man frowned and looked off to the side — "close to thirteen years now. I don't know whether to shake your hand or write you off as dead."

"What exactly is happening that's so rare?" Mason asked.

"The task director wants a word with you."

"Write me off as dead." Mason should have expected it sooner. Omar's disappearance from the MC could not have gone unnoticed forever, and now that Mason was tasking there, they'd assume he had something to do with it.

Fine. He only hoped they'd leave Medic Cadell alone so he could continue the experiments.

Mason sat with the liberator until two enforcers arrived. It was the same two he'd met when he'd first entered the Lowlands.

"Take him to the turnstile," the liberator said.

"Yes, sir."

Both men looked terrified, as though Mason were an explosive device. Or maybe they simply knew that where Mason was going could not possibly be pleasant.

Mason entered the turnstile like before, and when the door opened on the other side, two younger enforcers were waiting with Colonel Stimel.

"Step forward," one of the enforcers said. "Hands above your head."

Mason complied. The enforcers cuffed his hands behind his back and led him out the long hallway. They passed the room where he'd been scanned.

"No scan this time?" he asked.

"You're not returning to the SC to task, Mr. Elias," Stimel said. "Nothing you might have brought out from where you've been could cause any trouble. Not where you're going."

"Knowledge is a powerful thing," Mason said. "Do these guards know what's through those doors?"

"If he speaks again, stun him," Stimel said.

"Yes, General."

General? Mason's eyebrows rose as he regarded the patches on Stimel's uniform.

"Someone had to replace General Otley," Stimel said.

The enforcers loaded Mason in the back of a transport vehicle similar to the one he and Omar had arrived in. This time, he had no ankle cuffs though, so he merely sat on the bench on the side of the vehicle.

Eventually the truck started moving. It traveled a very long way, stopping and going again and again — at stoplights, perhaps? Mason could only guess that they were taking him to the Highlands Rehabilitation Center.

But when the transport finally stopped and the back doors were opened, they were inside a building again, so Mason had no way of knowing if his guess had been correct.

The enforcers led him to a small room and locked him inside. The room was a cement cube. Gray floors, walls, and ceiling. No bed, chair, toilet. This wasn't a cell. Just a room in a place that no one could see.

That thought sent his gaze searching for the yellow camera. He found it behind him, in the corner above the door.

So, someone could see after all.

His hands were still cuffed behind him, so he crossed his ankles and sank into a cross-legged position on the floor in the near middle of the room right beside a drain. That's when he noticed that the floor wasn't level but sloped toward the drain.

The realization made his stomach tighten. This was the kind of room that could be hosed clean. How much blood had been washed down that drain? Would any of his follow?

He supposed they'd left him here to worry, so he tried to use the time more wisely and prepare himself for the interrogation and torture that was likely to follow. He needed to give as much truth as he could. Creative lies would be difficult to remember if pain became a factor. They'd undoubtedly ask about Omar. As far as any cameras had recorded, Mason had last seen his brother in the MC when he was comatose. Perhaps if he kept that qualification in his mind, it would make the statement true for the lie detector. But if they asked about —

The door opened. The rubber sweep on the bottom brushed dully over the concrete. General Stimel entered, the same two enforcers behind him. One carried a lie detector box. The other a molded plastic chair with metal legs. He set the chair beside Mason, then the enforcers each grabbed one of Mason's arms and pulled him up. Dropped him on the chair.

The enforcer with the lie detector crouched at Mason's side and reached for his bound hands.

"It's not there," Stimel said. "It's in the back of his neck now."

The enforcer stood and moved behind Mason. Cold plastic pressed against the back of his neck. A beep.

"All set," the enforcer said.

"Thank you."

Such manners from the man about to interrogate him. So different from Otley. In looks too. Stimel was Otley shrunk by 5 percent, which might not sound like much, but it made a big difference. The man just wasn't as scary.

"Mr. Elias, where is your brother?"

"Which one?"

"Omar Strong?"

"I don't know."

A glance to the enforcer holding the lie detector. A nod.

"When was the last time you saw him?"

On camera, Mason added, "In the MC."

Another nod.

Excellent. Maybe Mason was smart enough to beat the box.

"Was your brother awake the last time you saw him?"

Awake? "Uh, no. He was in a coma." But the hesitation had been enough. The enforcer shook his head.

"Try again," Stimel said.

This man was smarter than Otley had been.

"I don't have to answer your questions," Mason said, annoyed he was flustered so soon.

Stimel cocked an eyebrow. "Are you sure?"

What a way to word things. Mason eyed the second enforcer, who was leaning casually against the door, then looked back to General Stimel. "I'm sure." Sure that he was about to experience a great deal of pain.

"I don't suppose you'll tell us where Ciddah Rourke is, either?"

"I don't know where she is," Mason said.

A nod.

"And the location of the survivors from your village?"

"I can't be sure where they are either. I've been gone for months."

"Will you tell us where they once were?"

"No."

Stimel nodded. "So much for my asking nicely, then." He stepped back and motioned to the enforcer by the door. "Hadley, it seems he'd like to try things your way."

Mason's gaze locked with the enforcer's. Hadley pushed off the door and walked toward him. Stopped in front of his chair. Mason glanced down at the man's hands. No gloves.

The man lifted one hand to Mason's face. Mason winced. The man scratched his cheek. Grinned. "You scared?" Hadley kicked the side of Mason's foot.

"There's certainly no joy in my anticipation," Mason said.

Hadley swung his fist at Mason's face.

Mason squeezed his eyes shut.

Nothing.

He looked up to see Hadley's fist inches from his cheek. The man chuckled. Tapped Mason's jaw.

"Enough," Stimel said. "I have other things to do. In fact, there's no reason for me to remain. You've been briefed on the questions. If he starts talking, tap me." The man walked to the door, each step a thump that brought Mason closer to extreme pain.

The door swung open and closed. Stimel was gone, leaving a fading gust of chilled air behind him.

"Time to cry," Hadley said. And this time, he landed his punch.

CHAPTER
29

W hen did you get this?" Levi asked.

"Saw enforcers put it in there this afternoon," Zane said. "Sent Dusten to fetch it."

"Could this have been doctored?" Levi asked.

"I'm sure it *could* have," Zane said. "I don't see why they'd need to bother, though."

Sure. Why bother pretending to beat someone up when you could just do it?

"Need me to play it again?" Zane asked.

"No." Seeing his brother beaten to unconsciousness once was enough for him. "What do you think?" Because at this point, Levi didn't know what to do.

"That Renzor really wants the girl," Zane said.

"But you agree that he wouldn't really trade Jemma for her," Levi asked.

"No way. Jemma and that baby are too important to the Safe Lands. Mason, on the other hand ..."

"We still have the same problem," Levi said. "We can't trust her. Though she hasn't done anything untrustworthy since she's been here."

"True," Zane said.

"It's too big a risk. We can't risk all these people on our hunch that she might actually be trustworthy."

"Maybe you should show her this. See how she reacts."

"How would that help?"

"Well, she claims to love Mason, right? Let's see what she does when she sees this."

"Kind of cruel, isn't it?" Levi asked.

"Kind of cruel to leave your brother to die."

That was for sure. "Okay. You want me to bring her here?"

"Upstairs. I'll put this on the Wyndo up there," Zane said.

"All right. I'll go get her."

Levi went into the basements and got Jordan and Ciddah, and brought them both back up to Zane's house.

"You're not going to trade me for Jemma, are you?" Ciddah asked. "I'm willing, but I don't believe for a second that Lawten means to give her to you."

Now she was echoing what they've known all along. "This isn't about Jemma," Levi said. "There's been a new development." He nodded to the Wyndo wall screen. "Zane?"

"Wyndo: power. Play."

The video came on then. Mason on the chair being pummeled by some General Otley minion.

Ciddah cried out and stood up, reached for the screen.

Every three or four punches the enforcer stopped hitting Mason long enough to ask a question. "Where is Omar Strong?" More punching. "Where are the rebels hiding?" More punching. "Where is Ciddah Rourke?"

Levi hadn't wanted to watch it again, though this time he couldn't help feel a surge of pride for how well Mason was holding up under such force. He'd have bet Mason would have given in long ago. He felt badly to have misjudged his brother's strength.

"Turn it off," Ciddah said. "I can't watch it anymore."

"It's almost over, and you need to see the end," Levi said.

One particularly loud punch knocked Mason off the chair. The camera zoomed in on his unconscious face, froze for a moment, then switched to Lawten Renzor, sitting at a fancy desk.

"Had it not been for the need to protect my unborn child, we would have taken this approach with Ms. Jemma Levi long before now. Since Mr. Elias does not suffer the complication of pregnancy, he's a logical candidate for torture. But I assure you that what you have seen today is not torture. Mr. Elias will tell us what we want to know. Unless" — he smiled, which looked wrong somehow on his face — "you bring me Ciddah Rourke and Baby Promise. I will trade Mr. Elias for Ms. Rourke and the baby, no strings attached. You have twenty-four hours to reply."

And the screen went black.

Ciddah whirled around to face Levi. Her flaking face was streaked with tears. "Trade me," she said. "There's nothing to think about."

"There is, actually," Levi said. "It's the same problem we've had all along in deciding not to trade you for Jemma."

"It's not the same at all," Ciddah said.

"How do you figure?" Levi asked.

"Don't you see? He's not hurting Jemma, and he won't hurt her. But he'll kill Mason if only to hurt me. You have to try to get Mason back. It's the only chance he has. You'll have more chances to free Jemma, for as long as she's pregnant — but Mason is out of chances because Lawten is out of chances. He's desperate. And if he sees he's going to lose, he'll kill Mason just to feel better."

Levi had no reason not to believe her. And she certainly looked like she cared deeply for Mason.

"What do you mean that Renzor thinks he might lose?" Zane asked. "What do you know about his plans? What does he want so badly?"

"Me. He wants me." She sighed then, wiped her eyes. "I don't fully understand what he's up against, but I have a theory. He's nearing the liberation date. He turns forty on March twelve. He knows what liberation means, and he doesn't want that for himself. Plus there are no openings on the Safe Lands Guild, and they haven't given him another alternative.

I think he plans to leave the Safe Lands. He's traveled to Wyoming before on various political matters. He once said that Wyoming has strict immigration policies, that they only accept family units. I think he's trying to create a family so that Wyoming will give him residence."

"Don't they have a policy against infectious diseases coming across their borders?" Zane asked.

"I don't know," Ciddah said. "It's only a guess on my part."

"If we return Elyot, he doesn't need Jemma to leave," Levi said.

"He'll keep her close until he's certain he has me back," Ciddah said. "My guess is that she's his backup ticket into Wyoming. That must be why he insisted on being the donor for her child."

A comment that put fire in Levi's veins.

"Trade them," Ruston said. "If Ciddah is willing. I hate to subject little Elyot to such an environment again, but the child is Lawten's flesh and blood. Of all the children we rescued, Elyot is the one that we truly don't have a say over."

"You would give a child to that man?" Levi asked.

"I wouldn't," Ruston said. "But the child is his."

"He's better off here," Levi said.

"My point, son, is that a child belongs to his parents. Kendall is dead. Lawten is alive."

"But what about what she knows?" Jordan asked, looking at Ciddah.

"What does she know?" Ruston asked. "She was brought here blindfolded. She knows we're underground. They all know that much. She knows the entrance is through a house. There are a lot of houses in the Safe Lands. I'm not worried that they'd find us. But I'm even less worried that Ciddah will tell them anything."

"You're the boss," Levi said. "If you're certain."

A knock at the front door.

A hush fell over those in the living room.

The knob shook. Another knock.

Zane got up and walked to the door, looked through the peephole. "Unbelievable!" He jerked open the door. "Maybe Fortune does exist. You seem to have nine lives."

Omar slipped inside the room, pulling a second person with him, a person wearing a hood. "Maybe I'm just a cat."

"Brother!" Levi had thought he'd lost Omar for good this time.

"Have you caught a mouse?" Zane asked. .

Omar grinned. "Sort of."

"Why do you insist on bringing people here without asking first?" Ruston asked.

"This is a special situation," Omar said. "Anyone who doesn't want to be seen should leave."

"What does *that* mean?" Jordan asked.

Omar gestured to his hooded guest. "Just what I said."

"I saw you captured," Zane said. "I saw enforcers cuff you."

"Not enforcers." Omar looked around the room. "Everyone is staying? All right then." He pulled off the hood.

Levi's jaw dropped. "Luella Flynn? Are you mad?"

"We weren't followed." Luella's gaze fell on Ciddah, and her eyes widened. "Oh, Ciddah Rourke. Hay-o, femmy. You *are* a rebel."

"Luella," Ciddah said in greeting.

"Who needs to follow you when they can just track her?" Zane said.

"I checked her for trackers, and I cut out her SimTag," Omar said. "She's clean."

"Being a rebel is all very exciting," Luella said.

Levi folded his arms. "*You're* a rebel?"

"I'm a reporter. I bring truth to the people of this nation. And there are certain stories that have eluded me for far too long. Liberation, for example. And the Guild Intelligence League."

"The what?" Levi asked.

"She caught me," Omar said. "And when she told me her plan, I thought you all needed to hear it. She can help us. She is the lynchpin."

"How can she be the lynchpin?" Levi asked. "We can't trust her."

"You're wrong. She's the lynchpin because everyone *does* trust her. The people, anyway. And she wants to show the people the truth."

"I can help you," Luella said. "And you don't even have to tell me all of your plans. Just let me broadcast it."

"How?" Zane asked.

"Think about our plans," Omar said. "Zane can hack the ColorCast for thirty seconds tops. But Luella can show it for hours. She controls the ColorCast. So she'd show Operation Lynchpin to everyone, live. And everyone will know the truth *as it happens*."

"I'm tired of the lies the Guild tells its people," Luella said. "I've been a tool in Lawten Renzor's drawer long enough. I want answers. I saw this man liberated." She nodded to Omar. "I thought that meant death. But here he is. Back from … where? The people have a right to know."

"We agree," Omar said. "But this information is valuable. Lives are at stake. So I suggested that Luella hook me up with some of those special video recording contact lenses, then she can broadcast my trip back."

He didn't say where, but Levi knew he meant to the Lowlands.

"We won't be able to show our attack on the dam," Jordan said.

"*Jordan!*" Levi gestured at Luella. How was this keeping their plans secret?

Jordan looked at him. "What?"

"Don't blow the dam," Luella said. "That's the only clean water source we have. And yes, clean water is still an issue for our nation. Wyoming hasn't been willing to trade the secret of their purifier. They'll sell us water, but at a very steep price. We want freedom for Safe Landers. Without the dam, we'll only put ourselves in a position to be exploited."

"But we need to take control away from the Guild," Ruston said. "He who controls the resources controls the people."

"In theory, yes," Luella said. "But I control the majority of the people. Whether or not they should trust me, they *do* trust me. Forget the dam. Instead, we interrupt the Guild meeting. We demand the truth from the Guild. Then we call for new leadership."

"Why would that work?" Levi asked.

"Because minutes before we interrupt the meeting, the Owl will reveal the truth about liberation on the air. Then we'll enter the meeting demanding answers. Yes, there will be enforcers on hand, but most will be too shocked to follow orders. Omar said the truth about liberation is *that* shocking."

"It is that," Zane said.

"Won't you tell me now?" Luella asked. "I promise I won't ruin your plans."

"No," Omar said. "You've got to wait. Then you won't have to *pretend* to be shocked when I show you the truth."

Luella heaved a sigh, but her eyes were sparkling. "It's going to be wonderful to do this through the eyes of the Owl. You'll be the true hero of the Safe Lands. You'll have made good on your promise. I think we should reveal your identity at the end of all this."

"That's not important," Omar said. "At the end of Operation Lynchpin, I want three things to happen: I want the harem disbanded, I want the doors to the Lowlands and outside opened so that people can come and go as they please, and I want the task oath lifted so that doctors and scientists can start working together on a cure."

"I think we have found a new leader, boys." And Luella winked at Omar. "Don't his words just send a shiver up your spine?"

Omar pointed at Luella. "We should also demand a new election for the Guild. Let the people elect the members."

"The Guild *is* elected," Luella said.

"It's always a yes or no ballot," Ruston said. "This time, run elections for what names go on the ballot, and don't make it yes or no. Majority wins."

Luella beamed. "Yes! Let the people choose. The same way they've been voting for the details of Lawten and Jemma's Vow Exchange."

"If that helps you," Omar said.

"Okay, but let's sit down and plan out exactly how we're going to do this," Levi said. "And trading Ciddah for Mason too. We need to make sure everything is just right."

Because they wouldn't get a second chance, Levi felt. This was it. Operation Lynchpin was about to commence.

CHAPTER 30

Shaylinn stood in the kitchen washing out baby diapers. Her twins ate nothing but milk, so she was surprised at how messy their diapers could be. They were still too little to breastfeed, which meant Shaylinn's life now consisted of trying to extract enough milk so the babies could drink it through their feeding tubes. It didn't sound like much, but it was exhausting.

"You really should let me do that for you," Nell said.

"Thanks, but I'm tired of lying around all the time. I needed to get up and do something." Even if it was washing out dirty diapers.

"Maybe we could walk to the park later?" Nell suggested. "Or you could go visit Nash."

"I have no need to visit Nash, but a walk to the park sounds nice."

"But he likes you. And I think ..."

The sound of the door opening cut off Nell's words. Shaylinn couldn't see the door from the kitchen, so she didn't know who'd arrived. Nell was staring, though, and looked embarrassed for some reason. Shaylinn hoped it wasn't Nash and that he hadn't overheard what Nell had said.

"Is Shaylinn in her room?"

The blood drained from Shaylinn's face at the sound of Omar's voice.

"She's there." Nell pointed at Shaylinn in the kitchen. "We thought you were dead for sure this time."

"Turns out I'm not so easy to kill," Omar said.

"I should go somewhere else." Nell stood up, turned, shot Shaylinn an overly dramatic surprised face, then turned back and vanished around the other side of the kitchen/entryway wall. "I'm glad you're okay, Omar."

"Yeah, me too. Bye, Nell."

The door clumped shut.

Something wet dripped on Shaylinn's foot. She was clutching a baby diaper in her hands, and it was dripping water all over the floor. She tossed it back in the sink, dried her hands on a towel, all while watching the edge of the wall for his appearance.

Omar stepped into the kitchen. He looked okay. Really good, actually. He was wearing jeans and a green shirt. Emerald green, he'd probably call it.

"Hay-o, Shay." His bluer-than-blue eyes locked onto hers.

"Hi."

"I heard you had the babies." He glanced at her belly and she blushed.

"It takes time to lose the weight."

He took a step toward her. "I'm sorry I wasn't here."

"I thought they'd caught you."

"Luella Flynn caught me. She didn't turn me over to the enforcers. She was determined to learn the identity of the Owl."

Oh no! "And she let you go?"

"Yeah." Omar grinned and Shaylinn melted just a bit. "She's going to help us get out of here. She's the lynchpin."

Shaylinn wasn't sure what he meant by that. "So it's not over?"

"No. Soon though. Tomorrow, actually."

"You're going back out?"

He winced and held up his hands. "I have to. This is our chance — to get our mothers back, to be free again. I've got to do my part."

"Of course. I'm proud of you."

"Thanks." He shoved his hands into his pockets. "Shay, could I see them?"

She stared at him a moment, wondering what he was talking about, then she gasped in a breath when it hit her. "The babies. Of course." *Duh, Shaylinn.*

She walked slowly across the kitchen and living room to her bedroom door and opened it. The lights were off and she left them that way, but she flicked on the bedside lamp, then sat on the edge of the bed and motioned for Omar to sit beside her.

The lamp illuminated the incubator and the babies inside. They were dressed in little sack-like outfits that Shaylinn and Naomi had sewed out of some of the fabrics Omar had brought. The boy wore the red-and-brown stripes with white dog-bone shapes. He lay on his back, arms stretched above his head. The girl was dressed in the purple-and-yellow plaid with smiling duckies. She lay beside her brother on her belly and knees, her little rump up in the air.

Shaylinn glanced at Omar.

He was staring at them, eyes liquid with tears that had yet to fall. "They're so small."

"They came early."

He glanced at her. "They're okay?"

"Seem to be. They can't eat on their own yet, so that's been a challenge, but they've already grown some since they were born."

"They have?"

"Yeah."

"Did you name them?"

"I accidentally named the girl Rosie because of how pink she is. I know that's kind of close to Rosalie, so ..." She shrugged. "I'm not set on it. And I hadn't named the boy yet because I was trying to think what you might name him."

He smiled at her and took hold of her hand. "What had you thought of?"

"Well, I thought maybe Eli after Papa Eli, but I know Papa Eli didn't like anyone naming their kids after him."

Omar nodded. "He thought everyone deserved a fresh start in the world with no expectations to live up to."

"So then I thought maybe Nicolas, after the Owl from the comic book you like so much."

He laughed, a low and surprised chuckle. "After Detective Nick Terry?"

"Yeah."

"How do you even know who Nick Terry is?"

"You left your comic in the meeting hall once. I read it."

"Wow. Okay. Yeah. Let's name him Nicolas, then. It's a good name."

Yay. Shaylinn felt happy that they had agreed on that. "And Rosie?" She wrinkled her nose.

"I like Rosie, but it's really close to Rosalie, like you said. What if that's her middle name?"

"Okay. Does Nicolas need a middle name too?"

"Elias, whether Papa Eli likes it or not." He winked.

Shaylinn squeezed his hand. "Then what will be her first name?"

"What about Coraline or Cerise or Carmine? Those are shades of pinkish red. Or we could call her Ruby."

"Ruby Rose?" Shaylinn shook her head at that one. "I like Cerise. That really means pink?"

"More red than pink. It's French for cherry."

"It is? Oh, I like that. She is a little cherry. Just look at her nose." Shaylinn leaned close to the incubator.

Omar leaned with her. "She's beautiful. Just like her mama."

Shaylinn turned her head fully to face Omar. "I'm fat again."

"Hey, don't say those things." He gripped Shaylinn's shoulder, closed his eyes, leaned toward her, and kissed her ... forehead?

He pulled back, staring into her eyes, then leaned in and softly kissed her lips.

Shaylinn felt like her insides had caught on fire. "Omar."

"I know. I don't have the right. I should have asked first."

"It's not that. But I'm afraid you'll disappear again. I don't think my heart can take it. And I don't want you to feel like you have to be with me. Like you're obligated or something."

"That's not how I feel."

"Then how do you feel?"

He sighed and looked at the babies. "I'm uncertain. About every-thing." He glanced at her. "I want to be a good father. But I'm afraid I'll mess it up. And I want to take care of you, but I'm ... well, afraid I'll mess it up. Tomorrow I'm going to be the Owl one last time, because someone has to go back to the Lowlands to expose liberation for what it really is. And that's going to be dangerous. But if everything works out, well, I don't know if you'll like my plans, but I'm going to stay inside the Safe Lands."

Oh no. The words seemed to make everything fall. "You are?"

"If I can. Shay, I didn't tell you, but ... I tried to kill myself when I was in the Lowlands. Not that long ago, actually. It was dumb, but I was tired of hurting. And, well, I didn't die. So I figure God gave me another chance to do something important."

Kill himself? Shaylinn's eyes flooded with tears. "What are you going to do?"

He blushed then, from his cheeks and down his neck. "Don't laugh, but I was thinking of starting a church."

In a million guesses, Shaylinn would never have guessed that. "Like, in a building? With bells?"

He squirmed a little. "I don't know. Maybe. I don't think I can do it by myself, though. I'd like your help."

"My help? Why?"

"Because you see people, Shay. And I want our church to be a place where people can come and be seen. To feel accepted the way they are. And to get help and support if they need it."

"So I'd ... talk to people?"

"Maybe. I haven't really thought it through. Only that I wanted your help. If you wanted to, of course."

She looked at her babies. "I think I'd like that."

He smiled, leaned in to kiss her again.

But Shaylinn pulled back. "Omar. Don't you want to ask how I feel about you?"

His hair fell in his eyes and he pushed it back over his head. "How do you feel about me, Shay-Shay?"

She pursed her lips, trying to look tough. "I'm completely infatuated with you. But I'm a mother now, and I have to be smart and look after my children first. And I've seen so many good things from you. But I've also seen a lot of poor decisions. Like trying to kill yourself! Really? I just ... need to know who you really are before I make any commitments."

"I understand."

Really? "You do?"

"Yeah. And I will win you, Shay. Just see if I won't."

She smiled and glanced back at the babies. "We'll see."

CHAPTER
31

A kick to Mason's solar plexus woke him.

An enforcer loomed over him. "Get up."

Mason's body ached. His hands were still cuffed behind him, so he used his elbows to push himself up off the concrete. His shirt made a ripping noise as the fabric peeled away from where it had stuck to the floor with dried blood. Sitting upright made fluid drain down his throat. He coughed to clear his airways.

The enforcer kicked his thigh. "Up, I said. We're moving you."

Mason's head ached as he stood. He followed the enforcer out into the hallway, where a second enforcer was waiting. The three of them walked to the elevator, which they rode to the eighth floor. Mason recognized the interior. This was the elevator in City Hall, where he used to task. Lawten Renzor's office was on eight.

Sure enough, the enforcers led him from the elevator to the fancy penthouse office. Lawten was sitting behind his desk. As always, Kruse stood beside him.

When Kruse saw Mason, his eyes lit up and he smiled. "The handsome medic is back! Hay-o, Mr. Mason."

"Hey," Mason said.

"That will be all." Lawten pierced the enforcers with a stare that sent them scurrying from the office, leaving Mason standing alone in front of Lawten's desk.

Lawten turned those beady eyes on Mason. "Did you enjoy your time in the strikers' bunkhouse?"

"Not really, no," Mason said.

Lawten grunted a wheezy chuckle. "I know what they do to each other down there. As chairman of the Safe Lands Guild, I've seen many unpleasant things, especially in the bunkhouses."

"There are plenty of unpleasant things down there," Mason said, "though I managed to avoid most of them. If you had a conscience, you'd do something about it."

"Where is your brother?" Lawten asked.

"I don't know where either of my brothers are. And if I did, I wouldn't tell you."

"I see. You've put me in an unpleasant situation, Mr. Elias."

Mason almost laughed at that. Yes, Lawten was the one in an unpleasant situation.

"Fortune must be smiling on you," Lawten said. "But don't think you'll get everything you want. You're about to find out what you lost." He nodded to Kruse. "Do it."

Kruse called back the enforcers, who took Mason out of the office and back to the elevator. This time, Kruse came along.

"So you're going to beat me again?" Mason asked.

"Mr. Mason," Kruse said, "much to my dismay, you're leaving us. We can track you, of course, so do keep that in mind when you run off to your rebel friends."

Mason twisted around to look at Kruse. Was the man warning him?

One of the enforcers picked up on it as well. He shot Kruse a glare. "Why'd you say that? He might have forgotten and we could have tracked him to the rebels."

Kruse sighed, as if the enforcer had a very small brain and often exasperated him with stupid questions. "Mr. Mason is a genius. He doesn't need me to remind him of how SimTags work."

The enforcer's eyebrows sank low over his eyes. "But — "

"Please don't hurt yourself," Kruse said.

The elevator stopped on the ground floor, and the enforcers took Mason outside the front entrance to City Hall. A sleek black car was waiting. They loaded Mason into the backseat.

The car didn't go far. Three blocks later they stopped at Champion Park. The enforcers got out and dragged Mason with them. Kruse led the way across the dark, wet grass to where two other enforcers were waiting in the middle of the park.

"Where are we going?" Mason asked.

No one answered.

They stopped when they reached the enforcers.

"Have they given the signal?" Kruse asked the new enforcers.

"Yeah, they're waiting."

"Then let's get this over with." Kruse raised his eyebrows at Mason, who had no idea what to make of any of this. What had Lawten said again? Fortune must be smiling on him?

One of the new enforcers tapped the Wyndo watch on his arm. His voice amplified through the watch speaker. "Levi Elias, we're ready when you are."

Levi? Mason's heart rate spiked. What was this?

And then, about fifty feet away, Ciddah appeared, holding a baby. Her name came from Mason's lips involuntarily. "Ciddah."

An enforcer pushed Mason's back. "Go on. Walk toward the girl."

Walk? Mason started to run, which was awkward with his hands cuffed behind him. They met halfway across the expanse. The baby started to cry, and she bounced him.

"Ciddah," Mason said. She looked different without any Roller Paint. Her skin was flaking badly, but Mason still thought she was beautiful. "What's going on?"

"Are you hurt badly?" She reached up and lightly touched his cheek.

His adrenaline was all over the place. He wanted to hug her, but his arms ... "I'll live."

"Mason, I love you. I've never really loved anyone before."

"I love you too," he said.

She beamed. "You do?"

"Yeah."

"I'm sorry." She raised up onto her toes and quickly kissed him.

"I don't understand."

"Keep moving!" the enforcer yelled through his simplified Wyndo watch.

Ciddah stepped past him. Mason turned with her. The baby was still crying.

"Shh." She bounced him. A tear rolled down her cheek. "He's trading you for me and Elyot."

"No! Ciddah, please. I never asked to be rescued. I got caught in the first place because I wanted you to be free."

"I know. But I want you to be alive. And he'll kill you, I know he will. He won't kill me." She continued on, so Mason turned and walked alongside her.

Two enforcers approached them, and the amplified voice said, "Mr. Elias, turn around or you will be shot."

Mason stopped, and his right foot slid on the wet grass. "It was Xiaodrine," he called after her. "In your meds. We tested some others too. A dozen before I was taken. Some had Centralin, some had Focastat XR. Uh ..." He struggled to remember the others. "There was also Validum, Inergia ... uh ... Excitare!"

She turned around and stopped, bouncing Elyot in her arms. "Amphetamines?"

He nodded. "Lonn thinks they might be experimenting on the population, to see what works best."

"Only nothing seems to be."

"Exactly."

"This is your last warning. We will shoot."

"I'll never forget you," she said.

"I'll get you back."

"Mason, please don't risk your life for me. He's obsessed. He'll have you killed."

"I'm not afraid of him."

"Well, you should be."

Two enforcers reached Ciddah and took hold of her arms, dragged her away.

"This isn't over," Mason yelled, not wanting to stop talking to her. Someone grabbed his arm and he pulled away.

"Mase, it's me." Jordan. "We've got to move quickly because we know they're going to follow us."

Mason felt like someone had ripped his heart out of his chest. He stumbled alongside Jordan for ten feet before he stopped cold. "I can't go with you. My SimTag."

"Don't worry about it."

"It's in my neck. You can't cut it out. They'll track me."

"We know, okay. Calm down. Omar told us. We're taking you someplace special. They can track you all they want. It won't matter."

"The Technology Research Organization building?"

Jordan snorted. "You think too much. No, this place is even better than a building with lead walls. You're going to Luella Flynn's apartment."

Jordan used a pair of bolt cutters to remove Mason's handcuffs. As he drove Mason across the Highlands, he filled him in on what had been happening with the remnant from Glenrock.

Shaylinn had given birth to her twins early, a boy and a girl. And Ciddah's wisdom in locating an incubator was likely the reason they were alive and growing. Jemma was in the harem, pregnant with Lawten Renzor's child, which Mason could not fathom a logical reason for, though Lawten had never been a very logical man. Levi had taken over Omar's Owl patrols, another surprise. Omar had returned. And finally, Luella Flynn was going to help the rebels.

"Are you certain we can trust her?" Mason asked.

"It doesn't matter. We're not telling her anything until it goes live.

That means you have to watch what you say. Don't tell her the truth about liberation. You get me? That's very important. We can't have her going live with it until we're ready."

If it worked as they were hoping, the idea of using Luella to broadcast the truth was brilliant. "I won't tell her. But tell Levi that once we go live with the truth, I'll need his help to get Ciddah back."

Jordan hummed as if he just remembered something important. "Ciddah thinks he's going to take her to Wyoming. She said he mentioned that once before—that Wyoming accepts family units as immigrants or something. He's going to be liberated in a few months, and Ciddah worries he's going to run, using her and Elyot as his family in order to get past the immigration law."

"Then we've got to stop him!"

"Calm down. We'll figure it out, okay? But first, Operation Lynchpin."

Mason took a deep breath. He was tired of waiting. He wanted to help Ciddah now. What if Operation Lynchpin made Lawten run? What if he was leaving for Wyoming with Ciddah right now?

Then Mason would find a way to get to Wyoming and get her back.

Luella Flynn's home was located in the same neighborhood as Champion House. Though the home wasn't nearly as large, it was still massive.

Luella herself answered the front door. "Hay-o, trig! Come on in." She waved Mason inside.

Mason looked back to Jordan, who was already walking to the truck. "How is this a good idea?"

Jordan turned and walked backward for a few steps. "It's the only idea. Zane gave her an off-grid Wyndo. We'll tap you later and let you know where you can help tomorrow."

Mason nodded and turned back to face Luella. The woman was wearing a glossy black dress that looked like a trash bag.

"Come in! You're letting out all the heat. Don't you know it's the middle of winter?"

Mason stepped inside the house and kicked off his shoes. The floor was gray stone. The walls a light peachy color. As he followed Luella into a fancy sitting room, he took in the rusty brown drapes, dark wood furniture with pearl gray upholstery. The home was tastefully decorated, despite what its owner was wearing.

Luella leapt into a recliner, feet first, and sat on her knees. "Have a seat, trig. You look terrible. Did Lawten's people do that to you?"

Mason lowered himself gently into a wing chair. "Yes."

"Not very chatty, are you?"

"Just shaken. Being here. It's not where I expected to end up today."

A wide smile broke out on her face. "I suppose not." She clapped once. "So, what shall we talk about? Not liberation, of course. Though I have to say, in the history of the Safe Lands, no one has ever returned from being liberated. And now you and Mr. Strong have both returned in the same week. It's quite extraordinary."

"Yes, well, how did this arrangement come to be?" Mason couldn't imagine that Ruston or Levi would have thought to ask Luella Flynn for assistance.

"I caught the Owl. Mr. Strong. Had him in my basement here for several hours." She said all this as if it were the juiciest secret of the year. "He wouldn't tell me the truth about liberation, but he promised me a video exclusive."

"Meaning?"

"He's going back to ... wherever it is you go when you're liberated. And when he does, I'll be recording through his eyes."

Mason wondered how Omar was going to get back. Maybe he still had the hot air balloon. "Tomorrow?"

"That's right. And I'm going to accompany Mr. Elias and Mr. Neil to the monthly Safe Lands Guild meeting. We'll show the Ancients and Lawten our footage of the Owl exposing liberation, then we will issue our demands. We'll be a voice for the people." Her eyes went wide with excitement. "It's going to be astonishing."

Mason didn't doubt it. "I have something to add. The monthly blood draws all nationals must get ... It's only a theory at this point, but Rich — " Should he tell her that Lonn was alive? Why not? "Richark Lonn and I believe that the bio — "

"You spoke to Richark Lonn?" Her eyes were round, amazed.

"I'll give you a hint, Miss Flynn: Liberation is not death. Yes, I came to know Mr. Lonn quite well. He and I are looking for answers in hopes of finding a cure."

"There is no cure."

"Are you so sure? We feel there has been no cure yet because of the task oaths everyone is required to take. The task oaths, we feel, were set in place to keep people from learning about all the lies the government was hiding. If the doctors can work with the biochemists, instead of being so separated, we think we will make progress toward finding a cure. But as is, our theory is that the biochemists have — without patient consent — turned every Safe Lands national into a test subject as they search for a cure."

"That's preposterous." But she fidgeted, like she was wondering over his words.

"Is it? I've been in the Safe Lands for less than six months, and I've seen people in terrible health. Surely in your profession, you have too."

"Of course we're in terrible health. We have a terminal disease."

"Yes, but Lonn and I, we think the biochemists are doing more harm than good. One of your demands on the air should be that doctors and biochemists work together toward finding a cure. And that they stay accountable to the public with their findings."

"You're saying that my meds are hurting me more than helping me?" Her voice was high-pitched, borderline hysterical. "That they're *doing this* to me?"

"I don't know that for certain, but I do know that something in them is harmful. And that should be disclosed. You should have the choice whether or not to further harm your health."

"Well, we agree on that much, trig."

CHAPTER
32

The car stopped outside the front entrance to the ColorCast building. Jemma broke out of a daydream about Levi and looked at Kruse, waiting for him to get out and open the door for her as he usually did, but he remained seated. When she looked at him, she found him holding out a slip of paper, a finger held up to his lips.

She took the paper and read it.

Rebels are about to make their move against the Safe Lands. Today, in your interview, Luella will ask you to tell the truth about your situation in the harem. This will not be edited, and I'm sure that Levi Elias will see it at some point. Use it wisely. This is your one chance to let Safe Landers and Mr. Elias hear your true story.

Jemma looked at Kruse, and he winked. "We've arrived, Ms. Levi. Shall we?"

Was Kruse a rebel? Had he been helping her all along? "Yes, I'm ready."

Kruse opened the door and helped Jemma out. She couldn't believe how big she felt already, and she was only twenty-eight weeks along. She wondered how Shaylinn was feeling with two babies in her belly.

Kruse led her inside the building. As usual, the couches were already arranged on the stage. But there was no one in the audience today. In fact, the entire building appeared to be deserted.

"Isn't anyone here?" Jemma asked.

"Only the necessary staff today," Luella said, coming at them from the back booth. She was wearing a slinky black dress that looked to be made out of rubber. "I hope Kruse briefed you on today's twist."

She glanced at Kruse. "He did."

"Excellent. Then let's get started, shall we? I've been waiting years for a day like today. So much excitement. I can hardly wait."

A day like today. What had Luella meant by that? Jemma followed the woman up onto the stage, wondering if she could really say that her baby was Levi's. If she did, wouldn't Luella Flynn edit that out?

"Why don't you go ahead and get comfortable on the sofa, femmy?" Luella said. "It's a new one. Just replaced. I'll join you in a minute."

"I don't have to walk out from the side?"

"Oh, not today. This is a special interview! New things are happening." Luella took Kruse by the arm and dragged him to the side of the theater.

So Jemma walked up onto the stage, settled herself in the middle of the little white loveseat, and waited. Luella and Kruse looked to be discussing something important, then Luella turned around and ran backstage on her high-heeled shoes. How could she move so fast in those things? Jemma could see her behind the curtain, just offstage, checking her own makeup.

My, this *was* a special day!

A few minutes later, Luella joined her onstage. She sat on the sofa beside her and Alb started recording. Jemma relaxed a little. Luella was an easy person to talk to when you weren't worried that she was twisting every word you said.

"Jemma, our lovely queen, welcome. We have a very serious topic to discuss today, and I'm so thankful that you've been brave enough to come forward. My guess is that you aren't the first who has had to deal with this, but it is my fervent hope that you will be the very last. Tell us the truth, Ms. Levi: Are you and Lawten Renzor really lifers?"

Jemma couldn't speak. Tears flooded her eyes, and she cursed the hormones the medic at the SC kept giving her.

"This must be very traumatic for you. Take your time."

Jemma met Kruse's gaze where he was sitting in the front row. He nodded for her to speak. "No, we're not lifers." She paused for another breath, having worked up her emotions too high. "The people who edit the interviews made it look that way. But I never said those things to him."

"So your baby . . . ?" Luella leaned close. "I thought Lawten was the donor."

"No! He wasn't," Jemma said.

"This is all very shocking," Luella said. "How did you come to be in the harem, Ms. Levi?"

"The first time or this time?"

Luella leaned back on her couch. "Both, if you're willing to share."

"Well, the first time, Safe Lands enforcers came to my village and killed many people. They captured the survivors and brought all of the women to live in the harem and told us we had to be surrogates."

"Our Guild killed your people and kidnapped them? Outsiders? I'm so sorry. That must have been a terrible shock."

"It was. We found out that the people in the Safe Lands are dying because of the thin plague, and plague is the reason it's been five years since a baby was born here. Your government was worried about that, so they went looking elsewhere for uninfected people."

"Yes, but Kendall Collin," Luella said. "Don't forget Baby Promise."

"Baby Promise," Jemma said, "as dear as he is, was a failure to your Guild. Kendall Collin was uninfected when she came here, but her donor was an infected Safe Lander, which means Baby Promise is also infected."

"That's terrible news. We had thought Baby Promise was our hope for the future."

"He's a sweet baby, but he's infected with the thin plague."

"How did you come to leave the harem?" Luella asked.

"I was rescued by men from my village. We lived underground with Black Army rebels until we came back to free more captive women from the harem. It was then that I got caught and put back into the harem the second time. That was when the task director general told everyone that he and I were lifers and that this baby was his own."

"And that's not true?"

"No. I'm not going to exchange vows with the task director general because I'm already married to Levi Elias. I'd like everyone to know that I was pregnant before I was captured this second time. The medic confirmed this on my first appointment in the SC. Lawten Renzor wanted you to think the child was his, but that's a lie, like so much of what he says. The child belongs to me and my husband, Levi."

"So even now, you're a captive in this place. What do you truly want?"

"I want enforcers to open the gates and let me and my people go home. I want to be with my husband and family."

Luella looked at the camera. "There you have it, Safe Landers. The truth. The first of many you will hear. It's hard to believe that this has been going on in our fair city. But as promised, today we will discover many ways we've been lied to by our task director general and the Safe Lands Guild. Next up, what liberation truly is!"

"We're clear," Alb yelled.

"Wonderful." Luella set her hand on Jemma's knee. "We pre-recorded this, but I promise you it will air unedited. We just don't want to be here when it does."

Jemma wanted to believe her. "When will it air?"

"Today. Early afternoon. The Safe Lands Guild meeting starts at two. I plan to show this right before. And if I'm not mistaken, your Levi will be coming for you around then, so be ready."

CHAPTER
33

Everything was set. Luella Flynn had given Omar two sets of contact lenses that could record. Omar wondered if she knew Lhogan in the Technology Research Organization. Ruston had also made a crossbow that would shoot a grappling hook and rope up to the top of the Safe Lands wall. This was how Omar would get back ... at least that's what they all hoped.

In the middle of the night, Omar rode the Midlands train all the way through the manufacturing district and got off at the very last stop. It was an extremely cold night, and Omar was thankful for the layer of clothing he was wearing over his Owl costume. Hopefully that layer and the climb would keep him warm. The night was silent but for the swish of his pant legs, the crunch of each step over the snowy sidewalk, and the occasional clink of the items in his backpack.

Snodgrass Road ran parallel to the Midlands/Lowlands wall. Omar followed the road until he stood about halfway between the first and second turnstile towers to the north of the Midlands/Lowlands gate. He walked between two buildings, toward the wall, until he could see the metal fence that ran along the wall about ten feet out. Behind it loomed the Midlands/Lowlands wall. It was merely a black shadow obstructing the view but for the red lights that ran along the top. Omar looked behind him, up the space he'd walked between the buildings. He looked to his left, his right.

No one.

"SimTalk: tap: Zane."

"Where are you?" Zane asked through Omar's SimTalk implant.

"Between the first and second turnstile towers. Standing right in front of the fence."

"Hold on and let me find you."

Omar slipped off his backpack and pulled out the wire cutters.

"Found you," Zane said. "Just let me figure out where to shut off the fence and you'll be on your way." Omar could hear Zane's fingers tapping dully over his GlassTop. "Okay. The fence should be off. You're going to have to go fast. Are you ready?"

"Yeah, I'm going."

Omar ran up to the fence and started cutting. He only needed to cut a space big enough to squeeze through, but this was chain link, and that meant a lot of cuts. He snipped the links up in a straight line and stopped about three feet up from the ground. Then he took a big side step and did the same thing two feet down the fence. When he finished, he pushed his back up against the middle section. Like the flap of a pet door, he was able to back through the chain link. Once he was on the other side, the fence snapped back in place, jangling. Hopefully that would make it difficult to notice any holes if anyone came looking.

"I'm through," he told Zane.

"Okay, then I'm going to turn the fence back on."

"Do it." Omar turned and looked up at the wall. It had been fairly easy coming down, but going up ... He shook off his fear and traded the bolt cutters for the crossbow in his backpack. The moment his hand closed around the crossbow's grip, Levi's words came back to him.

You can't afford to miss.

And he couldn't. He had one shot to get this right.

"Fence is back on," Zane said. "You ready?"

"Yeah, I'm ready."

"The motion detectors in the section in front of you should be off. There's a truck passing by on the wall above. So hold up for a minute before you shoot."

Omar looked back to the wall. The little red lights were out now in a six-yard strip at the top of the wall above him. He took a deep breath. His father's words came to him this time, the day he'd missed the buck and scoped himself between the eyes.

"How could you miss that? He was four yards away!"

Omar touched the bridge of his nose. His fingertips came away bloody. But it didn't hurt nearly as bad as his pride did. "Maybe I should try the crossbow."

"Crossbow?" Father snorted his exasperation. "If you can't shoot a rifle, you can't shoot a crossbow. Go home and have your mom look at that. Levi! We're going to see if we can chase down that buck Omar scared off."

Omar rubbed his scar.

Enough stalling.

He removed a pillowcase from his pack, then carefully withdrew the coil of rope. He set it out in front of his feet where he wouldn't accidentally step on it. All the little knots made it look tangled, and Omar checked it to make sure it was still perfectly wound. It was. The hook should carry it right up into the sky with no difficulty.

"The truck is gone now, Omar," Zane said. "You can go ahead."

"Okay." Omar raised the crossbow and forced himself not to think about Levi or his father. He aimed, exhaled, aimed again, and fired.

The hook soared into the dark sky, the rope lassoing out in coils in its wake. He stepped back, lowered the crossbow to his side, and watched the pile of rope continually shrink as the hook carried it higher and higher.

He bit his lip as he watched. *Please, please, please . . .*

And then the rope stopped ascending. It fell, lax, against the wall. Yes! Omar ran to it, lifted it carefully, and pulled slowly, hand over hand, hoping for the tug that would secure the hook so he could climb.

"I see your hook," Zane said. "You're pulling it across the road. Good thing it didn't fly much higher or you might have caught it on the rail across the road. That would've been bad."

Ooh. Yes, it would've. "Can you still see it?"

"Nope, I just lost it. My angle is no good from this camera. You should have no problem catching it on that rail."

"That's the hope." Omar pulled slower now, hand over hand, staring up at the black wall.

"I see it!" Zane said. "A little more."

Omar pulled another hand's width.

"It's caught. You got it!"

Omar pulled again. And again. "It doesn't feel like I —" And the rope went taut. "I do. I've got it." He sighed his relief and smiled to himself.

"Now get going," Zane said.

"Yeah, yeah. I'm going."

Omar put the crossbow back in his pack, put on the pack, then started to climb. His time in the Lowlands GMC had likely wasted away what little muscles he had built up lifting weights, but he hoped he had strength enough to climb to get up the wall. Because it was a very tall wall.

That's why they'd tied the knots. To give him a rest every few yards. When his hands passed the first knot, he tried to watch it as he climbed, to see when his feet reached it. He didn't spot it again until it was past his feet though, so he gripped the rope between his feet and slid down a little until he felt the shape of the knot press into the arch of his foot. He held himself there, testing it. He let go with one arm. Shook it out. Grabbed the rope again and shook out his other arm.

Good. This might actually work.

Up he went, hand over hand, taking rests when he needed to. Zane kept him company in his ear, and the rest of the journey went without a hitch. Omar reached the top and climbed over the rail. The road was deserted at the moment, and Zane still had control of the camera. Omar gathered the rope carefully, then removed the grappling hook, and carried it across the road and hooked it to the rail on the other side.

From where he stood, he looked down on the Lowlands. He couldn't tell one sector from another in the darkness. But he did see the grid of glowing greenhouses. And it looked like two of them had been set on fire.

"Nice," Zane said. "I see the fires through your eyes."

"Yeah, but only two." And they were relatively small. Two of the four dozen greenhouses. "Think I should wait?"

"No, the patrol is headed back your way. You've probably got five minutes, but don't linger. He'll likely have more going by the time you get down."

Hopefully the fires would be distraction enough to keep the watcher busy even if he accidentally set off the wall's motion detectors. Zane seemed to think the motion detectors only ran around the bottom thirty feet of the walls, but there was only one way to prove that, and Omar had no intention of finding out.

He climbed over the rail until his feet were hanging off, then slipped over, hands clutching the rope. He squeezed the rope tightly, slipping down inches at a time, trying not to touch the wall. It curved out about six inches along the top, creating a very small overhang for Omar to try to stay under. Once he had descended ten feet or so, he went hand over hand, but his arms were already very tired and soon he was sliding down. The friction made his hands warm beneath his thick leather gloves.

Another thing he didn't know: whether the motion detectors monitored the surface of the wall or the area in front of it.

It didn't matter. The Owl was going down, motion detectors or not.

By the time he'd reached the halfway point, at least a dozen greenhouses in sector one had caught fire. Flashing red and blue lights of the fire enforcer vehicles lit up the night below his feet.

"They're getting a bunch of them," Zane said.

Yes, they were. "I've got to get down there while there's still a distraction going on."

"Jump," Zane said. "I think you can make it the rest of the way."

"Ha, ha." But Omar let his hands slide a little faster, letting three knots pass through his grip before squeezing again. He was only about three levels up now.

Keep going.

He stopped himself just above the top of the fence. Time to see just how well the supposed motion detectors worked. He took a deep breath and resituated himself with his feet facing the wall. The smell of marijuana made him pause. Not grass in juice form. Fresh marijuana. Like someone was smoking it.

The greenhouses must have been growing it. And now they were burning.

"What are you doing?" Zane asked.

No time to think about the smell. He glanced behind him at the fence. This was probably going to hurt.

He stretched his legs until they touched the wall. Pushed off with his toes. No alarms went off — that he could hear, anyway. The push got him swinging. The next time his feet touched the wall, he gave a good jump. He came back to the wall hard and jumped again.

One more time.

On the last jump, he kicked out with all his strength and eased up on his grip on the rope. As he sailed out, he slid down. At the apex of his swing, he let go of the rope. His body flew over the top of the barbed wire fence and toward the ground. He bent his knees and tried to land in a crouch, but his momentum was too high and he fell onto his backside and rolled right along his back. He tried to stay in a ball. His backpack got in the way and the tools inside beat against his spine. But it also helped slow him down, and on his second turnover, he stopped rolling.

He hurt. His back and his head throbbed. He lay there, panting, trying to decide just how bad he was hurt.

"Omar, you okay?" Zane asked. "I can't see anything. Open your eyes."

He did. The sky above was dark. He shifted, straightened his legs, then managed to sit up.

"There you are," Zane said. "Speak to me, peer. You hurt?"

"I think I'm okay."

"Then get up and run! Someone might have seen you."

Omar groaned and tried to stand.

Someone grabbed him from behind. Omar elbowed the person, pulled away.

"Hey! Calm down. It's me. Lonn. I got you."

Omar relaxed and leaned on Lonn for a moment. "Is everything on track?"

"Yes, you maniac. We're right on track. How are you? That fall looked rough."

"I'm okay. Is there someplace I can sit a minute?"

"Yeah, sure. It's not like every enforcer in the Lowlands isn't out tonight. But we'll get you to a nice place to sit. Would you like some lemonade too?"

Zane chuckled. "Oh, I've missed Lonn."

"Shut up," Omar told them both.

"That's the spirit," Lonn said. "You've got my contacts?"

"In my pack."

Lonn pulled the pack off Omar's back and held it up. "Where?"

Omar unzipped the little side pocket and pulled out the contacts case. He handed it to Lonn. "There's fluid in the container, so be careful they don't slip out when you open it."

Lonn put the contacts in his eyes like he wore them every day. "These really recording?"

"Tell him yes," Zane said. "I've got you both, and your audio is still good too. The cube is working."

"We're good," Omar said. "How much time do you have?"

Lonn glanced at his watch. "Fifteen minutes."

Omar took a long breath — a marijuana-filled breath. Panic gripped him, and his breathing became short and shallow. He shouldn't inhale the smell, right? He'd get hooked again.

He pinched his nose and took several deep breaths, trying to calm his nerves. But when he let go, he could still smell the marijuana.

"You okay?" Lonn asked.

"The smell. What if it gets me hooked again?"

"What smell?" Lonn looked to the greenhouses. "The plants?"

"That's marijuana," Omar said.

"Yes, but you can't get high from smelling the plants like this. The chemicals have to reach your brain, and you're leaving right now."

"Okay." Omar let himself inhale. "So, I'll see you tomorrow morning."

"Be careful, kid." Lonn handed Omar his backpack and jogged away.

With all the fuss over the fires in sector one, Omar easily made it to his mother's apartment.

She embraced him, then helped him take off his coat. "Mason is gone. I don't know where. We haven't seen him for days."

"Yes, he's okay. Renzor beat him up trying to get answers about where I went. But Levi traded him for Ciddah and Kendall's kid. So he's fine but probably not happy about it. I didn't get a chance to talk to him."

"What does that mean, traded?" Mother asked.

"Renzor wanted the medic. Bad. So bad that he gave Mason back to Levi."

"The medic is the one Mason likes?"

Omar barked a laugh. "You could say that. Mason told Levi he wanted to marry her."

Mother frowned at this. "Does she feel the same about him?"

"Who knows? She might."

"And how about you? Did you see Shaylinn?"

Omar grinned. "She had the babies, Mom. A girl and a boy. They're so little. We named them Nicolas and Cerise."

Mother mirrored Omar's smile with her own. "But are they all right? Isn't it too early?"

"I think they're going to be fine. Shay seemed to think so."

"Congratulations, son. I'm glad you got to see them."

He stood a little taller then. "Me too."

"Get some sleep. Tomorrow will …" Mother blew out a deep breath. "Tomorrow is everything."

"It seems so far away right now," Omar said, "but I know that it's not. Soon it will all be over."

Mother put her arm around Omar's waist and squeezed. "Yes. Well, fear not tomorrow, for God is already there."

That very well may be. The question was, what would God do?

CHAPTER
34

I'd like everyone to know that I was pregnant before I was caught this second time," Jemma said. "The medic confirmed this on my first appointment in the SC. Lawten Renzor wanted you to think the child was his, but that's a lie, like so much of what he says. The child belongs to me and my husband, Levi."

"*Mine?*" Levi jumped up from his chair, where he'd been sitting on one side of Zane, watching Luella Flynn's interview with Jemma. His chair clattered to the floor behind him, knocked over in his excitement.

"You okay, brother?" Jordan stood up and righted Levi's chair.

"Mine!" Levi said again. He embraced Jordan, who thumped him on the back a few times.

"Best news I've heard since you told me Harvey had been born," Jordan said.

Jemma was still on the screen, so Levi released Jordan and stared at his wife. His amazing, beautiful, precious wife.

He was going to be a father!

But that was the end. Luella said something about revealing what liberation really was, then the screen went to a commercial.

Really? A commercial today?

"Congratulations, peer," Zane said. "No wonder they were able to make her a queen so fast."

"Yeah," Levi said. "Yeah! Why didn't I think of that?" He glanced at the time on the Wyndo wall screen. Twenty minutes before they were supposed to leave to get Jemma.

He wanted to go now.

He managed to sit back down on his chair and watch Luella Flynn introduce the Owl's "Liberation Exposé." It started with the Owl in some apartment building. He even had his creepy Owl voice working.

"This is not an error. The Messenger Owl has truth to deliver to the people of the Safe Lands. Truth brings freedom. Listen well. Today the ColorCast is safe. I am working together with Luella Flynn to deliver my promise. I promised to expose liberation for what it really is. You deserve to know. People deserve freedom."

Then he introduced Richark Lonn, who Omar pointed out was very much not dead. Lonn told viewers that he had been working on a cure for the thin plague when he was fired from his task in the MC years ago. He said he was now working with the Owl to bring truth to the people.

Then Richark and the Owl ran all over the Lowlands, capturing footage that Luella narrated. She was able to speak to the Owl through Omar's SimTalk device and urged Safe Landers to try to tap friends who had been liberated.

Then the Owl and Lonn went to the strikers' bunkhouse, where Lonn lived. After that, they went through something called the Car Wash, explaining how the people in Lonn's bunkhouse were required to do this once a week.

It was all fascinating and shocking, but Levi was distracted and kept a close eye on the time. The moment the clock switched to the appointed time, he stood. "Time to go."

And so Zane tested Levi's earpiece one more time and they were off to free Jemma, once and for all.

He hoped.

With Luella distracting the entire nation, Levi felt confident that their plan would work, but his head kept saying that such an attitude was foolish. How many times had they gone through this before? Could the ColorCast truly be *that* powerful? Could it keep enforcers from doing their jobs?

He and Jordan went through the storm drains into the Highlands, picked up a truck that Dayle had left for them, and drove right up to the drop-off zone in front of the harem. No one came out to meet them.

"That's a good sign, right?" Jordan asked.

"Let's hope so." Levi got out, left the truck in the drop-off zone, and walked inside, Jordan right beside him.

People stood in clusters around Wyndo screens, staring. No one even so much as looked at them as they walked to the elevators.

"I guess they're all pretty shocked," Levi said.

"Can you blame them? It's mad. Their whole lives have been a bad joke."

Levi was thankful that his great-great grandpa Seth had sacrificed himself all those years ago so that Papa Eli and his friends could escape. He'd always been thankful, but he was more thankful today. And he hoped that the truth would truly set these people free.

The elevator quickly took them to the sixth floor. They stepped out into a gaudy hallway with vaulted ceilings.

"This place is fancier than Renzor's office," Levi said.

"I think it's hideous," Jordan said.

"This carpet sure is." Levi paused and looked both ways.

"To the right, peers," Zane said through the earpiece.

They walked up to a garish door with some kind of hybrid creature sculpted on the surface. Levi tapped his glove against the SimPad beside the door. It didn't open.

"Zane? Can you open this door?"

"Not that one," Zane said. "The SimPad is actually a doorbell. Just wait there. Someone should come and open it."

Great. The question was, who?

Sure enough, some ten seconds later the door opened. A maid.

"We've come to make a pick-up," Levi said, pushing past her.

"You can't come in here," the woman said from behind him.

But she didn't try to stop him, so he and Jordan walked inside a fancy living room. A handful of women were sitting in front of a massive Wyndo screen that covered the two-story windows that overlooked the harem gardens. Levi had stared at those windows so many times, pining for his wife. Now he was finally here.

And they were watching the ColorCast. Good.

"Yeah, I'm looking for a Jemma Levi. Is she down here?" he called out.

"Levi?"

On the far side of the room, Jemma stood up. He could hardly see her in the darkness, but her voice was unmistakable. She hurried to him. He ran to her. They met behind a couch. He swept her up in his arms and twirled her in circles, breathing her in. She felt wrong in his arms though. It was her belly. Large and firm, it separated them in a wonderful way.

He kissed his wife.

"Matron! Intruders!" some woman yelled. Not the maid, though. She was still standing over by the door.

"Shhh!" This from someone watching the ColorCast.

"Let's get out of here," Jordan said from somewhere beside him.

Levi released Jemma and took her hand, pulling her toward the front door.

Jemma pulled back. "Not without Alawa." She let go of him and he followed her like a shadow, behind the couch to a group of chairs. "Alawa, come."

"Shut up!" someone yelled. On screen Lonn and the Owl were touring a poultry slaughterhouse.

A pregnant girl stood up and walked to Jemma. "You think we can really go?" she whispered.

Another pregnant girl rose from her seat on the couch. "You can't leave!" She walked around the couch until she was standing between Levi, Jemma, and Alawa, and Jordan and the exit.

"Mia!" someone yelled. "Stop talking!"

Mia. Levi gritted his teeth at the sight of so many problems.

"You're welcome to come with us," Jemma said in a low voice. "Your mother too."

"Oh, Mia, let's go with them." Another pregnant woman came to stand beside Mia. Levi barely recognized Jennifer in the darkness.

Time to go. Levi took hold of Jemma's hand and pulled her toward the exit. The pregnant girl walked alongside Jemma. Jordan pushed open the front door and held it.

And they walked into the gaudy hallway. Free.

Almost.

"You can't just leave," Mia said from behind them. She looked to be as pregnant as Jemma and followed them to the elevator. Her mother was right behind her.

Jordan pushed the elevator button and it opened right away. He stepped inside and held the door.

"Come with us," Jemma said. "There is no life here."

"That stuff on TV?" Mia scoffed. "That will blow over."

"Their government has been lying to them, and now they know the truth," Levi said. "Life here is going to change. And we're going home." Levi maneuvered Jemma to his other side, urging her to go into the elevator.

Mia stepped up to the door, but she was looking at him. "You lied to Jemma. You're no better than they are."

Levi flexed his jaw. "I never lied to her." He turned Jemma to face him. "But I didn't tell you everything either. Mostly because I was afraid."

"I don't care what you did two years ago," Jemma said. "I just want to get out of here."

"Right this way." He walked with her into the elevator.

Jordan let go of the door, but Mia caught it. "How can you not even care?"

"Mia, why do *you* care so much?" Jemma asked.

"Because I'm the prettiest. Everyone always said so. My whole life.

Yet no one chose me." The haughty tone of her voice had changed to anger.

"The fairest of them all, is that what you think?" Levi asked.

"I know it."

"There is more to beauty than appearance, Mia," Levi said. "I've always thought Jemma was beautiful, but what made me choose her above every other girl was who she is. How she can make everyone she speaks to feel better about themselves."

"Mia, come with us," Jemma said. "You're my friend."

"I don't want your friendship." She huffed and crossed her arms. "Mother and I will stay here."

Levi nodded at Mia. "Fine. Let go of the door, then." He wanted to push her hand off it. But Jemma was crying, and he wanted to please her as best he could. So he told Jennifer, "We don't know what will happen with the Guild, but you're both always welcome in our home. Please come and visit someday."

"Thank you, Levi." Jennifer pulled Mia away from the door and it slid closed.

They met no trouble at all leaving the harem. Their truck was still parked outside. Levi was tempted to try to drive back to Zane's house in the Midlands, but Zane told him to stick with the plan.

It took a while to walk through the icy storm drains with two pregnant women, but they eventually made it back to Zane's basement and into the next. Naomi and Tova were there with blankets to help the girls get warm. They all sat around the Wyndo wall screen in the nest to watch the rest of Operation Lynchpin unfold on the ColorCast.

The ColorCast was still on the Liberation Exposé. The Owl was in a medical facility, and Richark Lonn and another medic were conducting some sort of test.

"The Safe Lands Guild has lied to you about the thin plague," Richark Lonn said to Omar's contact lens cameras. "Your meds are not given to help you, but to experiment on you. The next time you see your medic, demand meds that are stimulant free. Demand clean meds!"

After that, the cameras changed to Lonn's view of the Owl standing on a table in a cafeteria of some kind. The tables were filled with men wearing orange jumpsuits.

"Liberation is not death but it is prison," Omar yelled, and the prisoners yelled their agreement. "It's slavery." Another yell. "For decades, the liberated have worked so that you the people in the Highlands and Midlands can play and take your ease." The men yelled again. "That's no Bliss." Again. "And there's little 'pleasure in life' when most of your choices are taken away." Another yell. "Safe Landers, do not let this go on!" A cheer this time. "We must elect a new Task Director General." Another cheer. "We must elect a new Safe Lands Guild." Another. "And we must insist that the doors to this place be open for good, so that all can come and go as they please." The prisoners jumped to their feet, applauding, cheering, some with arms thrust in the air.

Levi got chills.

It looked like Operation Lynchpin was going to be a success.

The camera switched to Luella Flynn, sitting on the couch on the stage in the ColorCast theater. "Safe Landers, I'm appalled. To see my fellow nationals in prison? To discover that Bliss is a lie? That we don't have multiple lives but only one? The Owl is right: We must not let this go on another moment. Today is the monthly meeting of the Safe Lands Guild, and I think it's time we asked the Ancients and Lawten Renzor a few questions, don't you agree?"

The footage shifted away from the stage to show Luella Flynn's back as she walked down the hallway outside Champion Theater. Mason walked beside her on her left, Ruston on her right. They reached the double doors that led to the Champion Auditorium. Ruston grabbed one door handle, Mason the other. They pulled them open at the same time, and Luella Flynn walked inside.

CHAPTER
35

Mason and Ruston entered Champion Auditorium side by side behind Alb, who followed Luella Flynn with a camera on his shoulder. The audience seats were empty, but the hooded Ancients of the Safe Lands Guild sat up on the dais, as did Lawten Renzor and General Stimel.

Mason saw Lawten stand up at his place in the center of the front table. He was wearing a black suit. "What is the meaning of this interruption, Ms. Flynn? You can't bring a camera into this meeting." His voice was amplified somehow, and it rang out from all sides of the room.

"Have you not been watching the ColorCast, Lawten? It's been quite a day." Luella's voice sounded soft in comparison to Lawten's, but she was speaking into her handheld microphone, so viewers likely didn't notice the difference.

"We are occupied with important matters, Ms. Flynn," Lawten said. "And while I know how entertaining your program is, we have serious work to do."

Luella reached the witness box. She climbed the steps to the top. Alb stayed on the floor and walked to a place in the front of the room where he could get both Luella and Lawten Renzor in his shot. Mason and Ruston followed Luella into the witness box but stayed behind her.

"If you haven't seen the ColorCast today, you don't really know what kind of 'work' you have to do." Luella pointed to the Wyndo wall screen behind Lawten. "Can someone get that wall screen on channel two?"

"Ms. Flynn, I will not ask again," Lawten said. "Please vacate this auditorium at once."

"Mr. Task Director General, I don't think you understand me," Luella yelled. "The Owl has taken over the ColorCast. He is showing the people what liberation really is. He has been showing them for the past hour and a half. You are finished."

"Preposterous." Lawten sat back in his chair. "That vigilante is nothing but a liar."

"If he is a liar, he is a very good one," Luella said. "He's in the Lowlands, Lawten. He and Richark Lonn have shown us all the truth. We've seen the strikers' bunkhouses, the fields, the feedlots, and the slaughterhouses. We've seen our liberated friends slaving away in Bliss. Though the Lowlands really aren't Bliss, are they?"

"What is the meaning of this, Lawten?" a hooded Ancient asked.

Lawten tapped his fist against the table. "I need some enforcers in Champion Auditorium. Now." He tapped his fist again. "Hay-o? Get me enforcer 10."

The Ancient beside Lawten stood, his black robe billowing around him. "Wyndo: power. Channel: two."

"Don't give in to her," Lawten said.

But the theater went silent as everyone stared at the wall screen. It came slowly into focus. The Owl was standing in the middle of a crowd, but he could hardly be heard.

"Volume: sixteen," the ancient said, and Omar's voice broke the silence.

"Do you have SimTags down here?"

"Yes," a man said. "But they just started implanting them in our necks to keep people from cutting them out. If anyone tries that now ... well, I don't think it's safe to stab yourself in the neck."

"But these SimTags work differently than those in the Highlands or Midlands, isn't that true?" the Owl asked.

A woman pushed up on Omar's right. "One thing that's different is if you miss your curfew, they're programmed to stun you, wherever you are. You'll go down."

"Stunned?" the Owl asked.

"Yes, sir. It's a curfew warning. Just a little tweak to remind you it's ten minutes 'til."

"'Til what?"

"'Til you'd better be in your bunk."

"And what happens if you miss curfew and are stunned?" the Owl asked.

"Enforcers come get you and take you to the RC," the first man said. "Unless you get a bad bunch, then they might steal all your credits and beat you up. It's not supposed to happen, but it's happened to more people that you'd think."

"I'm sorry, Mr. Task Director General," Luella said from her place in the witness box. "That's channel two. We've seen that footage already this morning. Channel one is live. Perhaps we should see what the Safe Lands people are watching right now?"

The Ancient who had turned on the Wyndo said, "Wyndo: channel one."

And the channel changed to show the feed from Alb's camera: Champion Theater and the members of the Guild staring at the wall screen of themselves.

Lawten jumped up, hands on the table, leaning toward Luella in the witness box. "This is *not* acceptable. Turn that camera off this instant! I need some enforcers in here!"

"You have no more servants, Mr. Task Director General. Your enforcers want answers like everyone else," Luella said. "The people are watching. They know that you've been lying. And they'd like to know why."

"You'll get no answers from us," Lawten said, "not like this. Not under threat. Give me a private interview, Luella, once I've had time to prepare."

"I'm a reporter," Luella said. "It's my job to uncover the truth. And I won't give you time to prepare any more lies."

"What are your demands?" a grizzled voice on the left wall asked.

"Excellent. I'm very glad you asked." Luella waved Ruston to the front of the box. He moved up to stand beside her. "Safe Landers, this is Seth McShane II, also known under the rebel name of Ruston Neil. He's the leader of the Kindred, who are known to us only as Naturals."

Gasps and whispers from the Ancients.

Luella turned around. "Mason, step up here, please."

Mason moved to Luella's other side. It felt strange to have the attention of the Safe Lands Guild again. It hadn't been all that long since he'd stood here with Omar. Since this same group of people had liberated him.

"This is Mason Elias," Luella said. "Mr. Elias is from Glenrock, an outsider village that our enforcers destroyed this past June. The Guild liberated Mr. Elias a few months ago, but he's back. Mr. Elias is named after his tribe's founder, Elias McShane. These two men have a connection in their past. A similar donor, if you will. Ruston, can you tell us why Mason and our Task Director General both bear the number nine?" She held her microphone out to Ruston.

"I can," Ruston said into the mic. "It's the same reason that if I was to be assigned a number, it would be a nine as well. It's because we have similar DNA or genetic code. That's because, for Mr. Elias and myself, generations back, we had a donor in common. Mr. Renzor, however, he and I have the same donors on both sides. He is, after all, my little brother."

Mason leaned out of the box, trying to see Ruston around Luella. "What?"

"We don't have to listen to this talk," Lawten said.

"I'd like to hear it," the Ancient beside him said.

"As would I," said the grizzled voice.

"Lawten is a Natural," Ruston said. "Our mother went into labor early with him. We didn't have the ability to help her. My father was worried that she or the baby would die. So he took her to the Midlands MC where she delivered Lawten. The medics took him away, of course. And that was the year the Guild offered stipends for delivering a child, and so my mother was paid in credits for giving up her child."

"Did you know this, Mr. Task Director General?" Luella asked.

When Lawten didn't answer, Ruston did. "He knew. After he graduated from the boarding school, I found him and told him. He didn't want to believe me, but I could tell he knew I was telling the truth. He wanted nothing to do with me, of course. Promised he'd turn me in if I ever came to see him again." Ruston looked to Lawten now. "And so I've not bothered you, my brother. But times change, and this city is changing. The people will demand trust from its leaders from now on. And the people will only trust those they elect themselves."

Mason stepped around Luella and leaned between her and Ruston so that he could reach the mic. "And if your meetings are shown on the ColorCast where the people can watch."

"That's an outrageous demand," an Ancient in the back corner said.

"That is our offer," Ruston said. "We'll open nominations today, and you, distinguished members of the Guild, are welcome to make nominations and even nominate yourselves. However, the nominating committee will accept no more than six incumbent nominations, so decide amongst yourselves whom you will nominate. And also keep in mind that just because you make a nomination, it doesn't mean the Safe Lands people will vote for you."

"Ruston," Luella said, "could you explain what you mean by the people voting? Safe Landers have voted for our task director general for years. How will this be different?"

"This will be very different, Ms. Flynn. First of all, a nomination page has been set up on the grid. You can find it by looking up the page for *The Finley and Flynn Morning Show*. You can nominate people from now until next Saturday evening at six o'clock. At that time, we'll post the results of the nominations and Ms. Flynn will begin interviewing the candidates."

"Finley will help me, of course," Luella said.

"The interviews will run as long as necessary," Ruston said, "and they'll be recorded here so that you can come and listen in person if you don't trust ColorCast recordings. Once every nominee has had their chance to speak to the people, the people will vote. The top nineteen candidates will be our new Safe Lands Guild. And they will nominate the new Task Director General of the Safe Lands."

"I would like to speak." An Ancient stood from his seat in the middle of the row on the left-hand side of the auditorium. He pulled off his hood.

And there stood Bender.

"You?" Ruston looked as shocked as Mason felt.

"May I have the floor?" Bender asked.

No one said a word.

"Twenty years ago, this Guild discussed a terrible bit of news. Biochemists told us that the thin plague had mutated. That is was progressing. Aging people faster than normal. They claimed not to know why. So I started an investigation. What I learned … it was not pleasant. In their search for a cure, the biochemists inadvertently made things worse. It was accidental. And there was nothing to be done but to try and fix it."

"By making every Safe Lands national a test subject without their consent?" Mason asked.

"Yes," Bender said, "I'm afraid that's true."

"So the stimulants in the meds slow the aging process?" Mason asked. It was all that made sense in his mind.

"That's right," Bender said. "It's a no-win situation right now. We've been trapped for years. Caught in our own lies. And we each have them, for our various departments. There's been so much corruption, to try and change things would mean revealing the truth to the public. None of us were brave enough."

"You were." Three places down from Bender, another Ancient removed his hood. He looked to be in his mid-seventies, but with the thin plague, who could make a fair guess? "The Guild Intelligence League kept most of us in line."

"I merely tried to keep us from making things worse," Bender said.

"What is the Guild Intelligence League?" Luella asked in an excited voice.

"It's a secret organization I started to gather intelligence on the Safe Lands government," Bender said.

"Then who gathered intelligence on you?" Luella asked.

"The taskers in my office monitored me as much as any other member of this Guild," Bender said.

"But you pretended to be a rebel," Mason said.

"Sometimes the rebels knew more about goings on in the Safe Lands than my own staff. I'm sorry, Ruston."

"I never once suspected who you really were," Ruston said.

"Yes, well, Mr. Task Director General, I'd like to make some recommendations, if I may," Bender said. "Where are you going?"

While everyone had been focused on Bender on the side of the room, Lawten had left his seat. He was walking down steps in the front corner of the amphitheater that were hidden by the tables on the dais.

"He can't go far," Luella said. "I'd like to hear your recommendations."

But Mason knew he could go far. That he wanted to leave the Safe Lands and might already have a plan to do so. "I'm going after Lawten," Mason whispered to Ruston.

"With what?"

A door opened in the front corner of the amphitheater, one that was painted green to match the walls. Lawten was gone.

"He has Ciddah!" Mason descended the platform steps as Bender answered Luella's question.

"I recommend that we abolish liberation and abolish the law that states that anyone over the age of forty must conceal their face. And I'd also like to surrender myself to the new Guild for questioning."

"I second the motion," someone said. "And I too would like to surrender."

Mason ran up to the dais. He lifted the tablecloth and crawled up underneath the table onto the platform floor.

"What is the matter with you?" someone yelled. "Ancients of the Safe Lands don't surrender. We are the law."

"That's over now."

"And who will rule in our stead? Luella Flynn?"

"Why not?" Bender said. "She has as much right as any of you. In fact, I nominate Luella Flynn and Seth McShane as temporary co-task directors until a new one might be elected."

Mason crawled to the other side of the table and slid down the stairs to the mystery door.

"We still have a motion on the floor that hasn't been voted on."

And that was all Mason heard as he ran out the door and it slammed behind him. There was only one way to go. A hallway that led him to an exit on the side of the building. Mason ran through it and just caught sight of Lawten entering the next building over. City Hall.

Mason ran into City Hall and pressed the elevator button. One elevator was on five, going up. The other was on two going up. He couldn't afford to wait. Mason ran for the stairwell. Where Lawten Renzor went, Ciddah would be.

Mason had just reached the fifth floor when someone entered the stairwell above him.

"Up, quickly." Lawten's voice. And a crying baby.

"Why? Where are we going?" Ciddah!

Mason kept climbing, trying to make his steps soundless.

"Don't ask stupid questions," Lawten said. "They're going to arrest us. Do you want to spend the rest of your days in the RC?"

"I've done nothing wrong," Ciddah said. "You're scaring the baby. Please, give him to me."

"He's my child. I'll carry him."

Hinges squeaked and light flooded into the stairwell from above, as did the sound of a motor of some kind, which muted whatever Lawten said next.

Mason could see their ankles now. Ciddah's and Lawten's as they walked out the door and onto the roof. The door clumped shut behind them, making the stairwell seem dark and quiet again.

Mason ran up the last flight, wishing he'd thought to find a weapon of some sort. Maybe Lawten didn't have a weapon either.

He pushed open the door and peeked onto the roof. A helicopter! That's what was making all that noise. The blades on top were already a spinning blur. An enforcer was helping Ciddah inside. Lawten passed her the baby and climbed in.

"No!" Mason ran toward the helicopter. No one seemed to have heard him. The enforcer reached for the door and pulled it closed. Mason reached it just in time. Grabbed the door. Pried it back open. "Stop! Ciddah, get out!"

"Mason!"

"Shoot him!" Lawten yelled. "Pilot, take off."

The enforcer drew a stunner, and Mason ducked. The door opened farther and the enforcer leaned out and aimed for Mason again. Ciddah screamed.

Mason dove under the helicopter. A stunner cartridge hit the roof and slid past Mason's feet. He lunged back out and yanked the enforcer's leg. The man fell out the door, landed in a crouch on the roof, then tumbled forward into a somersault.

The helicopter lifted off the roof just a few inches. Mason threw himself down on the right landing skid. The helicopter continued to rise, and gravity made Mason's body twist around the skid until his back faced down. Oh, dumb! What was he thinking? He wrapped his arms and legs around the skid, holding on with the joints of his elbows and knees.

He looked down on the roof as the helicopter rose into the air. The enforcer was sitting on there, holding his ankle, watching.

The helicopter banked sharply to the left, steering right off the roof and out over the city.

"Oh, God!" Mason squeezed the skid, which pushed his head to the side. He watched the ground underneath them with squinted eyes.

They flew over the tall buildings of downtown, past the wooded area where the mansion homes were. Mason caught a glimpse of Champion House.

They must not be going there.

The air was so cold that Mason could feel ice crusting his eyelashes together. His fingers were already going numb. He couldn't hold on like this much longer. The helicopter flew right over the Safe Lands walls and the foothills of Mount Crested Butte. The snow-covered slopes and trees would give him a quick death if he were to fall. He'd be frozen before he could decide if he'd broken his back.

He caught sight of a large white flag hanging off the branch of a barren willow tree. No, not a flag. His balloon. Apparently Omar had cut it loose.

The helicopter banked hard left again, and Mason clung to the skid with all his strength. They passed over more frozen terrain. Then a frozen lake. And then he saw the runway, a charcoal slash through the white, snow-covered land. On the south side of the mountain. It was the old Crested Butte Airport. Mason had heard Papa Eli and his father talking about the planes that had come and gone from here, wondering where they'd been flying to.

Wyoming. Lawten was trying to leave with Ciddah and Elyot.

Mason had to stop him.

The helicopter flew to the far end of the runway and made to set down in the cul-de-sac there. Mason needed a plan. He could see a plane waiting about fifty yards from the cul-de-sac, facing away from the helicopter, pointed up the runway like it was ready to take off. The side door was down, making a set of steps up into the airplane. And the helicopter was about to land facing away from the plane. If Mason were quick, he might be able to make it to the plane without being seen.

He didn't wait for the helicopter to land fully. The moment the ground was within six feet, Mason let his legs drop. His feet hit the icy asphalt and he let go of the landing skid and skated out of the way. His first few steps were pretty wobbly, but soon he was running.

He reached the plane and grabbed the rail on the steps. His momentum sent him skidding past the steps, over ice and tiny pebbles, but he held on until he stopped, then ran up the steps. He glanced back at the helicopter as he entered the cabin, just as the helicopter door opened.

Mason knew little about airplanes. This one was like stepping into an apartment. Against one wall, four beige leather seats sat two on each side of a dark wood table. Across from them were two more seats, one behind the other. Farther down the aisle were six more seats facing the back of the plane and a Wyndo wall screen on one side of a narrow doorway. Mason ran to it. He passed through an area with a kitchen counter on one side and a bathroom on the other.

A curtain covered the end of the aisle. Mason slipped behind it. His shins struck a full-sized bed that filled in the tail end of the plane. It was covered with a white blanket and cinched across the middle with a long seatbelt. On the wall behind the bed, another Wyndo wall screen hung on a wood panel wall that closed off the rest of the tail.

He heard voices outside. A crying baby. Hide! Where to hide?

He squeezed in between the curtain and the partial wall that held the bed in place and pulled some of the excess folds of the curtain around his body.

The baby's cry grew louder. It was inside the plane now.

"Put her in the back seat," Lawten said, his voice somewhat muted. He was up near the front of the plane. "And make sure you buckle her in."

"Yes, sir." This voice was male, soft and young.

The plane trembled as people walked around. Mason held his breath. He could hear movement just past the kitchen/bathroom area. Was the "her" Ciddah? If so, why didn't she speak?

"The woman is secured, sir," the young man said.

"Good," Lawten said. "Now go ask the captain what I should do with the baby." Elyot was still crying. "And you, get me some coffee."

"But I don't know how to make coffee, sir." This voice was deeper and somewhat offended.

"Then get me some wine, water, whatever you can find, okay?"

"Yes, sir."

Footsteps brought someone back toward the bed. Mason could hear him opening cupboards and drawers.

"The captain said someone needs to hold him or we could strap him down on the bed." The young voice again. "At least until we're in the air."

"Then put him on the bed. Maybe he'll go to sleep. Be sure and strap him in, though."

"Yes, sir." Silence followed but for Elyot's screaming until, "What are you doing?"

"He wants coffee. Do you know how to make it?"

"I don't even drink it. Let me past with this kid, will you?"

Something pushed against the bed curtain. Mason pinched the fabric around himself so that no one could see him.

The curtain shifted again, and an enforcer leaned into view and laid baby Elyot on the end of the bed. He reached up and fumbled with the seatbelt. Once he got it apart, he moved the baby to the center of the bed and buckled the belt over Elyot's middle. The baby continued to scream. Hadn't they brought any milk for the kid? Ciddah would know what to do, but where was she?

The enforcer walked back to the kitchen area. "I don't understand why he's traveling without his assistant. He always takes his assistant."

"He said it was a vacation for him and his lifer."

"That woman didn't sound like she was his lifer," the younger one said. "And who orders an enforcer to stun their lifer?"

"She was going to make us crash, trying to get the door open like that."

"I'm just saying she wasn't acting like Mr. Renzor's lifer. I think he's taken her against her will."

"That ain't our business, so you just be quiet about it."

"Yeah, but what about that tap from Pep? He said — "

"What's taking so long to find me a drink?" Lawten bellowed.

"Be right there, sir!" Then he lowered his voice. "Pep was messing with you. How could liberation be in the Lowlands? People would know. Now, let's get out of here."

The enforcers' footsteps faded as they approached the front of the plane. Mason stayed put. Elyot was still crying, fussing, and kicking his legs with great force for one so small.

They'd stunned Ciddah. She'd been trying to get to Mason. So she must be in the back seat. He wanted to lean out and see, but he didn't dare. Lawten's raised voice in the front of the plane caught his attention.

"Well, one of you is coming with me. I need help on this flight. Decide now."

"I'm off at eight," the deeper voice said. "I have plans with some of my peers. We're going night skiing."

"I have a shift in the City Hall lobby tonight from six to ten," the younger enforcer said.

"You're both coming," Lawten said. "Grab a seat and buckle up."

"But sir — ?"

"I don't want to hear another word out of either of you. Buckle up!"

Silence gripped the plane. Even Elyot's crying had softened to whimpers.

"I'll shut the door and we'll be on our way." This from a new voice.

Mason wanted to look, but he stayed put. The fact that Ciddah had been stunned was a problem. He didn't think he could incapacitate both guards and Lawten without her assistance. But if he waited until they were airborne, the odds of escaping would shrink drastically.

The plane rolled forward, ending Mason's debate on the subject. He held onto the top of the half wall, but as the plane increased speed, he fell back and landed, sitting, on the bed just below Elyot's feet. He carefully pulled the curtain across the doorway so that it completely hid the bed from view.

His body slid back on the bed toward the tail. He lay down beside Elyot and grabbed hold of the seatbelt. The boy had started to cry again. Mason stuck his finger in the baby's mouth, and the little guy clamped on and began to suck.

The plane lifted off the ground. It wasn't like the helicopter. The sensation was similar to the feeling of riding to the top of City Hall in the elevator without stopping.

He had no doubt that they were headed to Wyoming. But how long did it take to get there? From the Old maps he'd seen, Wyoming had been directly north of Colorado. Planes flew at high speeds. Anywhere from sixty to six hundred miles an hour, depending on the type of aircraft. He had a feeling that the flight wouldn't last long. An hour, maybe?

Plenty of time for him to be discovered. And what if he was? Would they kill him? Not likely on an airplane. Planes traveled much higher than helicopters and had pressurized cabins. A gunshot might only create a small leak in the hull, but there was also the danger of breaking a window, which could depressurize the cabin in seconds. Or the bullet could hit wiring on the instrument panel in the cockpit, or hit the pilot.

Or it could hit the fuel tank.

Surely enforcers knew better than to fire a gun on an airplane. They might not even be carrying those dual action pistols. If he were caught in flight, they'd most likely stun him and deal with him later.

Maybe he should stay put, wait until they landed in Wyoming, and steal Ciddah away when Lawten let down his guard?

Elyot had fallen asleep, so Mason got down on the floor and peeked out from the curtain. Ciddah was sitting in the chair closest to him. At first glance, she looked to be unconscious, but her eyes shifted, looking up at the ceiling. Her fingers tapped against her legs. Stunned, but quickly recovering.

In the front of the plane, the enforcers were sitting across from each other at the table, the younger one facing the back of the plane but deep in conversation with his partner. Lawten was in the front seat across the aisle from the table. Mason could barely see the top of his head over the seat.

What to do?

There was nothing to do but wait for Ciddah to recover. Right? He looked back to her and met her eyes. She stared at him, no expression on her face at all, which was weird since he was almost positive she must be glad to see him.

He smiled at her, then slipped back behind the curtain. Better not press his luck. He would wait for her right here. She wasn't restrained. Once she could move again, she'd let him know. He felt fairly confident that no one would bother him as long as Elyot was sleeping. As it was, the other men had been letting him cry. Clearly they weren't all that concerned with his care.

While Mason waited for Ciddah, he thought through as many scenarios as possible to subdue the men. It would be best to divide them. If he and Ciddah tried to face them all at once, they'd be overpowered. But if they could immobilize them one at a time, they might stand a good chance.

"Hey, little peer. Mr. Renzor says there are blankets in a drawer under the bed back here. You hogging all the blankets?" The curtain shifted and the younger enforcer appeared. Mason was already moving before their gazes met. He swiped the enforcer's SimScanner, leaned back on the bed, and fired.

The enforcer grunted and collapsed on the bed. Mason dropped the SimScanner and pulled the enforcer all the way up, fixing the curtain so that it hid the man's feet. The movement jostled Elyot awake, who shared his displeasure with a wailing cry.

Mason stuck his finger in Elyot's mouth and whispered to the enforcer. "I'm sorry I stunned you. Listen, your friend was right. When people are liberated, they're sent to the Lowlands to task hard labor. But the people down there fought back, got word to Luella Flynn, and she confronted the Safe Lands Guild this afternoon.

"That's why Renzor is running. They want to arrest him, so he's trying to move to Wyoming. And he kidnapped Ms. Rourke and Baby Promise because Wyoming only accepts family units, like Old families. Bringing a lifer and child is the only way he can be allowed to live there. But I'm here to stop him. He needs to answer for his crimes against the Safe Lands. And he can't take Ms. Rourke against her will. That's not right."

The young enforcer merely stared at Mason. Hopefully that had been information enough to conflict the guy. Mason took his finger out of Elyot's mouth and brought out the enforcer's handcuffs. He secured the man's right hand to a metal ring on the wall that could be used to pull back the curtain, but he couldn't find anything to gag him with. He hoped the stun lasted long enough for him to finish his task.

He examined all the weapons on the enforcer's belt. There was a stunner, the SimScanner, a dual-action pistol, and an expandable baton. Mason removed them all. He checked the dual-action pistol for ammunition, left the sleeper slugs in the gun, but removed the bullets and flipped the action to sleeper mode.

First, do no harm. No one was dying, if he could help it.

Mason tucked the SimScanner into the back of his pants and shoved the bullets and the baton into his pocket. He took the stunner in his right hand and the pistol in his left. That way, he could stun the enforcer, but put Lawten to sleep. He wanted Lawten to be out the longest.

A deep breath and he was ready.

He peeked out the curtain. Ciddah was still sitting there, staring out the window. Lawten and the other enforcer were in their seats, facing the front of the plane.

Might as well move as quickly as possible and get this over with.

He stepped through the curtain. Two more steps and he pressed up against the counter. He made eye contact with Ciddah, whose eyes widened. But she didn't move her limbs, so she might still be incapacitated.

Mason stepped out into the main cabin, walking slowly past the seats.

"Check on the baby while you're back there, will you?" Lawten yelled.

Mason froze, gripped the guns tightly, slid his fingers over each trigger. Heat washed over him. Adrenaline. Mason had never been a very good shot, and pistols were harder to shoot. But the entire cabin couldn't be more than forty feet in length. He just needed to get a good shot at each of them, which meant he'd need to walk right up to them or they needed to be standing.

"Go see what's his problem," Lawten said.

"Yes, sir." And the enforcer stood.

Mason fired the stunner at the enforcer's back, but the enforcer had been moving, slipping out into the aisle. The cartridge shot past the man's side and struck the wall.

"Hey!" The enforcer reached for his own gun, so Mason aimed the pistol and fired. A hit! The enforcer kept coming, though his eyes went wide with shock. He drew his own pistol and Mason knocked it out of his hand. It dropped beside Mason's foot, so he kicked it back behind him. The enforcer fell to his knees. Mason glanced over his head at Lawten, who was watching the scene over the top of his chair with an expression of hate.

The feeling was mutual.

Once the enforcer had passed out, Mason grabbed each weapon from his belt and tossed them back behind him. Then he stepped over the man, heading toward Lawten.

"No!" Ciddah screamed.

Mason glanced behind him. Ciddah was holding the enforcer's pistol and walking toward him. She was taking slow steps, but he couldn't tell if that was because she was weak or being cautious.

Mason also had no way of knowing if she had the gun set on sleeper or kill. "Ciddah, put that down."

"No, Mason. This is my fight, not yours. I'm going to do this."

He walked toward her. "Ciddah," he whispered. "You can't fire a gun in an—"

She raised the gun at his face. "Mason, look out!"

He spun around and ducked. Lawten had been coming his way, but the airy pop of the pistol stopped him. Lawten cried out in pain. Then a second shot. A third. Fourth. Fifth. Sixth. Ciddah was screaming, firing every bullet in the gun. Lawten moaned now. And a strange whistling sound had filled the cabin.

Mason had to stop her. He saw the enforcer's stunner under the nearest chair. He reached for it, rolled onto his back, and shot Ciddah.

The cartridge struck her against her neck. Mason winced and

jumped to his knees to catch her. The sound of cracking plastic made him push Ciddah into a chair by the wall and buckle her in. He sat in the chair beside her and buckled himself.

Then he looked for the damage.

He could still hear the whistling sound. He and Ciddah were sitting in the chairs at the very back of the plane, the ones facing the back, so it wasn't easy to see from his position. He looked over his shoulder and up the aisle. The enforcer lay on the floor one seat away. Up by the table, Lawten lay on the floor. Mason could see no blood. Mason spotted a hole in the wall above the first window beside the door. And another one above the second window. That might be the cause of the whistling. He scanned the rest of that wall. Everything looked okay. Then what had made that cracking s — ?

Craaaack.

He twisted around and looked between his and Ciddah's seats at the other wall. A window above the table was splintered like a spider's web. The fuselage was breaking open. Mason unbuckled himself and lunged for the sleeping enforcer. He dragged the guy down the aisle, pulled the handcuffs off the man's belt, and cuffed him to the leg of Mason's chair. Then he ran for Elyot.

He was halfway back to his seat carrying the baby when the window shattered.

Mason leapt into his seat, settled Elyot on his lap and buckled them both, cinching the belt as tightly as he could. Elyot was screaming, but Mason ignored him and reached over to tighten Ciddah's belt.

Besides the shrieking of the wind and Elyot's anguished cry, at first nothing seemed wrong. Then a beeping alarm started from above and oxygen masks fell from the ceiling. Only two were within his reach, right above their seats. Mason pulled down Ciddah's and put it over her head, fixing the mask over her mouth and nose. Then he put on his own. He breathed deeply for two breaths, then put the mask over Elyot's face and held his breath.

The plane went into a dive, sending Mason hard against the back of his seat. The guns slid across the floor. Then things started to fly past him. Napkins from the kitchen area, fluttering by like a flock of doves. Cans of soda pitched right over his head.

Mason tried to remain calm. He continued to share his oxygen mask with the baby, but there was nothing more he could do for the enforcers or Lawten.

When the plane came to a stop on the runway, Mason left the oxygen mask over Elyot's face and tried the air. It seemed fine. He let go of his mask and checked on Ciddah. She glared at him, which meant she was fine, so he unbuckled himself and stood up, cradling Elyot in the crook of his arm.

The enforcer on the floor was unconscious, so Mason handed Elyot to Ciddah and pulled his oxygen mask down and put it over the man's face. He ran into the bedroom and was surprised to see the enforcer there wearing an oxygen mask and fumbling with a key and his handcuffs.

Maybe Mason should have thought to find the key from his enforcer belt.

Mason backed out of the bedroom and scanned the floor for a stunner. There were none. Everything had been sucked out the window when the cabin had depressurized. He walked toward the front of the plane and the cockpit door opened.

The two pilots stepped out. The first man took a step toward the cabin.

"What *happened* back here? Why did we lose pressure?" the second pilot asked. "Is anyone hurt?"

That's when Mason realized that Lawten Renzor was not on the plane. He crouched and glanced under the table, but no. His gaze went to the window. He walked toward it. Looked out.

"I think Lawten Renzor is dead."

CHAPTER
36

On Monday, January 10, 2089, all the gates in the Safe Lands were opened. Levi, Jemma, and Jordan were in one of the first few vehicles to leave. Beshup and Mukwiv were in a truck behind them. The remnant from Glenrock and Jack's Peak were going to keep living in the basements until Levi and Beshup could check the villages to see if they were habitable. It was the middle of winter, after all.

Right after that first attack on Glenrock months ago, Levi had used up all the firewood he'd been able to find to create the funeral pyre. It would take time to cut more wood for heat and cooking. No doubt Jack's Peak would face a similar problem. As much as they all wanted to leave, they needed to be smart about it.

There were about two dozen vehicles leaving the Safe Lands that morning, way fewer than Levi would have expected. The people seemed to be afraid to leave. Maybe more would go out when summer came. Levi would have to encourage it somehow.

He wondered at that thought. Why should he care about helping any Safe Landers? But he did care. He had skills that Safe Landers did not. And if people wanted to find another way of life, Levi would show them.

The roads were not plowed so they were difficult to even see. Levi was thankful that Dayle had loaned him the bigger truck. He went slowly, though, having no desire to get stuck in the icy cold forest with his pregnant wife. The closer they got to Glenrock, the stranger Levi felt. It was like coming back to both life and death. Memories of his childhood mixed with what he'd experienced the last time he'd been in Glenrock. So many dead bodies. His father, his uncles, little Sophie. Papa Eli dying in his arms. Digging the graves. Moving the other bodies to the funeral pyre. Lighting it.

"The forest always looks so pretty in winter," Jemma said. "I've missed it."

His wife's words cleared his mind of such solemn thoughts as he took in the beauty around him. They would just have to make new memories to replace the bad ones.

"There's a buck!" Jordan said. "Aww, man. I wish I had a rifle."

"He'll be there later," Levi said, glad to see a sign of wildlife. There was no reason to think there wouldn't be any, but the buck affirmed his decision to come back to Glenrock.

They *could* live here again. Life *would* get back to normal someday. He knew it. Though "normal" would be a little different from now on.

He drove the truck into the village square. He could barely see the remains of the funeral pyre, jagged pieces of snow-covered wood in the middle of the roundabout. He was careful to steer clear of it, hoping he was staying on the actual road. He parked on the far side of the square, closest to his and Jordan's homes.

Jordan jumped out before Levi had completely stopped the truck. Levi shut off the truck and watched his friend bound through the snow to the Zachary tribe's home.

"The place looks okay," Jemma said.

"It's only been six months," Levi said. "As long as the doors and windows stayed shut, all the houses should be fine." Should be. They were all well-built cabins, that much he knew.

Levi got out, went around to help Jemma. Once he was convinced she was steady on her feet, he shut the door of the truck. Zane had loaned him gloves with a ghoulie tag so he could drive the vehicle. Levi wondered if he'd always need a ghoulie tag on hand.

Jemma took a long breath and sighed, a smile claiming her face. "It smells so good out here. The pine and the fresh air."

Levi took her hand, and they followed Jordan's footsteps so that Jemma could see her family's home. They found Jordan in the living room, sweeping up a snowdrift on the floor under a window in the front room.

"The place is in pretty good shape," Jordan said. "All but this window. A bullet must have broken it during the raid."

"Good thing no squirrels thought to come inside," Levi said.

Jordan shrugged. "No trees outside that window, maybe?"

Levi and Jemma inspected Jemma's room, and she exclaimed joyfully over the presence of several childhood dolls that she showed to Levi. He faked happiness at the recovery of the dolls, but it wasn't much of a fake, because he was truly glad to see her so joyful. When they finished at her house, they went to Papa Eli's, the house Levi had grown up in. The original house of the Elias tribe.

It wasn't in as good shape as the Zachary home. The front door had been left open, and the place looked to have been ransacked by several hungry animals. There were jars all over the floor, but only a few were broken. Hungry as the animals might have been, it didn't look like they'd found all that much to eat. No broken windows, at least.

After that, he and Jemma started up the hill to the little cabin he'd built for them to live in once they were married.

Jemma waddled beside him, looking like a brown bear on its hind legs the way she took tiny steps and how her layers of coats wrapped over her huge belly and made her look twice her size. She probably shouldn't have come in her condition, but she had wanted to. And so long as Levi could help it, he had no intention of being apart from her ever again.

He helped her up onto the porch. The mounds of snow on each step kept them from slipping. It came up to Levi's knees. He kicked it away from the door as best he could.

"I never got to see the inside," Jemma said, bouncing on her toes beside the front door.

"Of course you didn't," he said. "Only my wife is allowed in here."

"Then open the door," she said. "Your wife wants to go in."

He grinned and knocked the snow off the latch. "Looks shut up tight. That's a good sign." He hit the latch with his fist until it slid out of the notch. The door popped open a few inches. Levi grabbed it with two hands and pulled it against the snow on the porch inches at a time until the door cleared an arch that they could walk past.

Jemma stepped toward the entrance.

"Wait!" Levi put his arm in front of her. "I'm supposed to carry you inside."

She grinned and sniffled, her cheeks rosy with cold. "Well, hurry up and carry me then. I want to see my house!"

Levi swept her into his arms and walked sideways through the door. It was fairly dark inside as the windows — besides being covered with the curtains his mother had made — were covered in frost and snow. Levi set Jemma on her feet in the middle of the rug her mother had made for them. Shanna had given it to Levi for the living room floor, and he'd put it exactly where she'd told him to.

It took a moment for his eyes to adjust. The place didn't look any different from how he'd left it. Just cold. He walked to a window and tried to push the curtains aside, but they were frozen to the glass.

"They're stuck?" she asked.

"Frost," he said.

"Levi, I love it."

He looked at her, standing where he'd left her in the middle of the rug. Her breath clouded in front of her. "Do you?"

"Yes." Their gazes met and held until she smiled. He always won their staring wars. She wandered toward the rooms on the back half of the house and peeked in the first one. "What's this room?"

He walked up behind her and set his chin on the top of her hat, then wrapped his arms around what passed for her waist these days.

"Your mom was going to give you one of her sewing machines. I was going to put it in here. But maybe this should be the baby's room."

"Naomi says Harvey is too little for his own room," Jemma said.

"Well, he won't be forever."

"But for a while we'll have to keep the baby with us."

"Okay." He took hold of her shoulders and turned her around. "So maybe this will be our room for when the baby is sleeping." He kissed her. Their noses were cold, and their breath made their faces moist.

She broke away first and looked up at him, her brown eyes searching his. "Will we live happily ever after now?"

He searched his memory for one of the stories she loved. "If we promise to outlive each other," he said, "which I promise this very moment."

She put her arms around his neck, grinned, then delivered her line. "Oh, my sweet Westley, so do I."

He tried to remember the alternate ending from the book and added his own twist. "But that was before Mason's gunshot wound reopened, and Omar fell back to vaping, and Shaylinn's children turned into owls and flew away, and Zane lost his other ear to frostbite. And the forest around us was filled with the sound of Lawten's pursuit ..."

"Peace! I will stop your mouth." And she kissed him again. He thought about telling her that she was mixing up her stories, but the kiss was more pleasant than teasing her would be.

They didn't stay long in Glenrock. Just long enough to look around and for Levi and Jordan to assess the amount of work it would take to get everyone in their homes again.

Two or three weeks, tops, they figured.

They piled into the DPT truck and started back. Levi really didn't want to go back to the Safe Lands, but until he could get out here and cut some firewood, they'd have to spend their nights in the city.

"It's weird that so few tried to leave today," Jordan said.

"Not really," Jemma said. "Where would they go? To someone who's never left the walls, the land would look like a frozen wasteland. I don't blame them for staying where it's warm."

"I guess," Jordan said. "I'd just think they'd want to get out, you know? Now that they know they've been prisoners."

"I think they will in the spring," Levi said. "It will have to happen gradually. It's the price of paradise. People who live in such a place go soft. They have no reason to learn to survive on their own. And a little bit of work completely overwhelms them."

"They're lazy," Jordan said.

"They've never had to be anything else," Jemma said.

"Now they'll have the opportunity," Levi said. "It will be interesting to see how much things change."

And as much as Levi didn't want to care how things in the Safe Lands would change, he did care. And he'd go back and help the people who wanted to leave. And he'd also go back to visit his brothers, who, he knew, were not planning to move back to Glenrock.

CHAPTER
37

"W"atch the steps. The middle one has a crack. I'll have to fix that." Omar grabbed Shaylinn's elbow as she climbed the steps to the cabin, Cerise in her arms.

"I'm fine, Omar," Shaylinn said, casting him an exasperated smile.

Shanna followed, holding Nicolas. Omar ran ahead of them all and opened the door. The cabin still smelled musty inside, despite his having aired the place out all week. Ruston had told Omar that he could have it, and so he'd offered it to Shaylinn since it felt similar to home but was still in the Safe Lands.

He'd already brought over two cribs that Zane had helped him get from the nursery in the MC. He'd put them in the room that used to be Naomi and Jordan's and set up Shanna in the room that used to be Shay's.

Omar walked inside first, straight back to the bedrooms, and opened the door to Shay's new room. "The cribs are already here," he said. "And I got fresh bedding for your bed too."

Shaylinn stepped inside and gasped. "Omar! It's lovely."

Shaylinn's bed had lavender blankets. Cerise's crib was pink. And Nicolas's was green. Omar had also painted the room's walls yellow and covered them in his own paintings, save one. *The Starry Night* by Vincent Van Gogh was hanging on the wall opposite Shaylinn's bed so she could see it when she drifted off to sleep and when she woke each day.

She stopped to look at it now. "Omar, wasn't this painting hanging in Champion House?"

"You saw it?" He was surprised she'd remember such a thing. "It's a present from Luella Flynn. I asked her if I could have it. She said she thought it looked like a kid painted it." He laughed at that. "I didn't bother to tell her that it was priceless."

"I think it's beautiful."

"Thank you," Omar said, as if it was his own painting.

Shaylinn walked to the pink crib and laid Cerise inside. "Are you staying for lunch?"

"I'm staying all day, if you don't mind," Omar said.

"Really? I thought you'd be at the Yellow House."

"I changed the name to Hope House. And it's being painted today," Omar said.

"Painted yellow?" she asked.

"The inside is being painted. White, actually."

"I like Hope House better than the Yellow House, but shouldn't you call it a church? Or at least put a cross on it?"

"No." Omar said. "The word 'church' is obsolete. As is the cross symbol, for now anyway. But the open door logo speaks to people. They're free to come and go from the Safe Lands now. And Hope House will always have an open door."

"That sounds lovely, Omar. And you don't have to pay to use the building?"

"Luella said it's mine. For as long as she's task director, anyway."

Shaylinn shot him a wide-eyed smirk. "Luella Flynn, the Task Director General. I still think that sounds a little scary."

"The rest of the Guild will keep her in line. And she might find that politics isn't for her."

"I'm glad Lonn got elected. And Ruston."

He walked over to her until they were standing side by side, looking down on Cerise. "I'm glad you decided to stay here with me."

"Not with you exactly," she reminded him. Again.

"Not yet, anyway."

She looked up at him with only her eyes, so it looked like she'd rolled them and they'd gotten stuck. "*Omar ...*"

He grinned and bumped his side against hers. "I know. But I swore I'd win you, and I'm not giving up until I do. Where is *Nash*, anyway?"

"I haven't seen him since the day Levi moved everyone else back to Glenrock."

"Good. Maybe he moved out there with them."

"*Omar!*"

"I just like to know where my competition is, that's all."

She took hold of his hand and squeezed. "You don't have any competition, and you know it. We're your family."

He smiled at her. "Then I'm a lucky man."

CHAPTER
38

"How is he?" Ciddah asked.

Mason sat in the chair in front of Ciddah's desk in her office in the SC. He studied the results on the CompuChart. "Better. His red blood cell counts are up. The white too."

"But it's not a cure."

"No." Mason had shared some ideas with Lonn, Medic Cadell, and the biochemists in the compounding lab. Taking the stimulants from the meds could only be done if a suitable replacement could be found. Because the stimulants had been what was keeping metabolic rates somewhat normal. They'd been doing other damage, of course, which was why they weren't an ingredient in the new meds.

Mason's knowledge consisted primarily of natural remedies. Lemon oil stimulated white and red blood cell formation. And grapefruit oil was said to increase metabolism. And there were herbs that could help promote blood cell production too: echinacea, dandelion extract, licorice root, and even deer antlers. And certain herbs to increase metabolism as well.

Mason clicked off Omar's page on his CompuChart and set it

down on a stack of folders on her desk. He made sure the stack was steady before he let go.

Ciddah leaned on her elbows on her desk. "What's wrong?"

He shrugged. "I enjoy being a part of the team that's researching a cure, but sometimes I feel totally inadequate."

"You're not inadequate."

"Maybe. But it pains me to remember how arrogant I was when I first came here. Thinking I could find a cure for this plague that's been here almost since the Great Pandemic. Me, not even a fully trained doctor. And even now, what do I know?"

"Mason, you know lots of things our doctors and scientists don't know. You're invaluable. Plus you believe in the possibility of success. And you care about people. The others had no concern for the individual patients. They were focused on trying to cover up their mistakes. But you're honest and eager and willing to try anything. We will succeed because your faith and enthusiasm is contagious."

Mason swallowed, slightly embarrassed by her high praise. "I still think it has to do with the water," he said. "The water in this mountain was never tainted with the original strain. If they could find the progression, then they'd be able to reverse it."

"I agree that the water is an excellent place to start, and they're working on it. But it's going to take time."

Time. Mason sighed deeply and studied Ciddah's face. He'd moved back to his apartment in the Westwall. Ciddah had moved back to her apartment in the Westwall too. And they'd both come back to task in the SC, working hard to make sure their patients were getting safe meds, and helping the Cure Committee in their spare time. But there was still no cure, though Lonn and Cadell were confident that one would be found now that they were free to search without restraint.

Mason was being impatient. That was the problem. Time wasn't passing by *that* quickly. He just hadn't decided what to do about Ciddah yet. He wanted to marry her, but he thought it would be wise to wait until a cure was found.

"You never said whether you were going to come to dinner," Mason said.

She straightened her posture and started looking through papers on her desk. "No, I didn't."

"Well?"

She pierced him with a steady gaze. "I still haven't forgiven you for shooting me."

He laughed at that. "Ciddah, you were shooting a gun on an airplane. We all could have died. I was trying to save us."

She rolled her eyes. "You're always right, aren't you?"

"You shot out a window! The plane had a hole in it." He didn't add that her actions had killed Lawten Renzor. She had to appear before the Safe Lands Guild in a week to answer for it. And Mason had his own hearing. Luella Flynn assured them that the fact that Lawten's having kidnapped Ciddah would help her case, but Mason was still worried.

She folded her arms and leaned back in her chair. "I think I should get to shoot you with a stunner. Fair is fair."

Oh, really? "You're absolutely right, Ciddah. Fair is fair. But you forget I already got shot with a stunner when I rescued you from Champion House. *And* I got shot in the leg. If anything, I should get to shoot you in the leg."

She faked a shocked gasp. "Mason!"

"But how about we call it even and you come to dinner with me?"

"Where are we going?"

"To the cabin. Shaylinn invited us over. Omar too. And Shanna."

"Do you think it's fair that I asked her to watch Elyot while I'm at work?"

"Shanna loves it. My brothers and I are all grown now. And she wants to help Shaylinn with the twins. One more for her doesn't make a lot of difference, I don't think."

"And you know that because you've raised so many babies yourself."

Mason stood up and walked toward the office door.

"Wait! Where are you going?"

He opened her office door and turned back to face her. "To dinner. Are you coming or not?"

"You're not going to shoot me, are you?" she asked.

"You're in luck. I've quit using guns. They're very dangerous."

"Oh, well, in that case, let me get my coat."

And Mason and Ciddah took a taxi to the cabin in the Midlands, where Omar and Shaylinn and her mother had dinner waiting in a home filled with the sounds of new life and love.

J.3.3 (CHAPTER ONE)

Martyr stared at the equation on the whiteboard and set his pencil down. He didn't feel like practicing math today. What did math matter when his expiration date was so near?

His wrist still throbbed from Fido's teeth. Martyr touched the strip of fabric he'd ripped from his bedsheet and tied around his wrist to stop the bleeding. He hoped the wound would heal before a doctor noticed it. A trip upstairs to mend it would be unpleasant, as the doctor would likely use the opportunity to perform tests. Martyr shuddered.

To distract himself, he glanced at the other boys. Every Jason in the classroom except Speedy and Hummer scribbled down the numbers from the whiteboard. Speedy sketched Dr. Max's profile, staring at the doctor with intense concentration. His hand darted over the paper, shading the dark face with a short, black beard.

Hummer—as always—hummed and rocked back and forth, hugging himself. Martyr never understood why the doctors made Hummer take classes instead of putting him in with the brokens. Perhaps it had to do with Hummer's being so much older than the other brokens, or the fact that he could walk and didn't need special medications.

Movement at the back of the room caught Martyr's attention, and he twisted around to get a better look. Dr. Kane stood outside the locked door, looking in through the square window. A stranger wearing glasses stood beside him, much shorter and a little rounder than Dr. Kane. The man's head was also shaven like Martyr's, but the way he carried himself next to Dr. Kane showed he was nothing like a clone. Martyr's pulse increased. There hadn't been a new doctor on the Farm in a long time.

Dr. Kane opened the door, and both men stepped inside. Martyr gasped. The new doctor wore color! A narrow strip of fabric ran from his neck to his waist. Martyr jumped up from his desk and headed for the stranger.

"J:3:3!" Dr. Max's tone slowed Martyr's steps. "One mark. Take your seat immediately."

Yes, but one mark was not so bad. Martyr quickened his pace. *If I could just touch the strip once ...*

Dr. Kane shooed the new doctor back into the hallway, pulling the door closed behind him. Desperate, and knowing the door would lock once it closed all the way, Martyr stepped into the shrinking exit. The door slammed against his bare foot, and a sharp pain shot through his ankle. He winced and wedged his torso into the crack.

He was met by Dr. Kane's hand pressing against his chest. "J:3:3, return to your seat this instant. Two marks."

But the color on the new doctor was too tempting.

Something indescribable stirred inside Martyr. "He has color, Dr. Kane." He tried to remember the word—like carrots, like the caps on the doctors' needles, like the slide. "It's orange!"

Martyr pushed the rest of his body through the doorway, and Dr. Kane moved with him, keeping his imposing form between Martyr and the new doctor—the same way Martyr did when a Jason picked on Baby or another broken.

Chair legs scraped against the floor, and the Section Five math class rushed from their seats. With a quick glance that seemed to hint more marks were coming, Dr. Kane reached around Martyr and yanked the door shut before any other Jason could escape, leaving Martyr in the hall with the doctors.

Identical faces filled the square window, but Martyr could barely hear the Jasons inside. The silence in the hallway seemed to heighten the severity of Martyr's actions. He glanced from Dr. Kane's stern expression to the new doctor, to the strip of orange color.

The man stepped back, face pale, eyes wide and slightly magnified through his thick glasses. He clutched the orange fabric with both hands as if trying to hide it. "Wh-What does he want?"

Dr. Kane rubbed the back of his neck and sighed. "It's my fault, Dr. Goyer. It's been so long since I hired someone. Years ago we stopped allowing any adornments below level one. They were a danger to the doctor wearing them. Plus, the boys don't encounter much color down here. It causes problems, as you can see." Dr. Kane turned to Martyr with a tight smile. "J:3:3 is harmless, though."

Dr. Kane's casual tone emboldened Martyr to carry out his plan. He reached out for the orange color, exhaling a shaky breath when the doctor allowed him to touch the fabric. It was smooth, softer than his clothes or his sheets or the towels in the shower room. A napkin, perhaps? Maybe it hung there so the doctor could wipe his mouth after eating. "What's it for?"

The new doctor tugged the orange fabric from Martyr's grip. "It's a tie."

"Enough questions, J:3:3," Dr. Kane said.

Martyr cocked his head to the side. "A napkin tie?"

"Three marks, J:3:3. Back against the wall, or it'll be four," Dr. Kane's deep voice warned.

Martyr inched back and glanced down the hallway. Rolo jogged toward them, clutching his stick at his side, his large body bouncing with every step. Johnson, the other day guard, loped along behind.

Martyr fell to the ground and immediately wrapped himself into a ball, covering his head with his arms. His curiosity had gotten him in trouble again. Three marks meant three hours of lab time. All to touch the orange napkin tie.

It had been worth it.

"What's he doing?" the man named Dr. Goyer asked.

Rolo and Johnson's footsteps on the concrete floor drowned out Dr. Kane's answer.

Rolo jabbed the stick between Martyr's ribs. "What's up, Martyr?" Another jab. Rolo liked when the Jasons fought back. "Getting into mischief again?"

Johnson's familiar crushing grip pried Martyr's arm away from his face, despite Martyr's efforts to keep it there.

Rolo stopped poking long enough to whack Martyr on the head, sending a throbbing ache through his skull. "Get up, boy."

Martyr complied as best he could with the stick still poking his side. He hoped the stinger wouldn't engage.

Rolo grabbed Martyr's other arm, and Martyr bit back a groan as the guards dragged him up and pushed him against the wall.

Rolo slid his stick under Martyr's chin and pressed up, forcing Martyr to look at him. "See, now? We're not so awful, are we?" Rolo's eyes were clear and cold. Martyr knew it was best to nod.

Johnson smirked at Martyr over Rolo's shoulder. Johnson had thick brown hair, a bushy brown beard, and a mustache. The boys were not allowed beards or mustaches or hair. They visited the groomers once a week to be shaved—to keep from looking like Johnson.

"These are our day guards," Dr. Kane said. "Robert Lohan, known as Rolo to the boys, and Dale Johnson. Men, this is Dr. Goyer. He'll be starting next week."

"Was it necessary to strike him?" Dr. Goyer asked Rolo. "He wasn't being violent."

Martyr looked from Dr. Kane to Rolo, then to Rolo's stick. Rolo always used his stick. Most of the time it wasn't necessary.

Rolo snorted, like Dr. Max sometimes did when one of the boys asked an ignorant question. He tightened his grip on Martyr's wrists.

"The guards know how to keep the boys in order," Dr. Kane said. "I don't question their methods."

"But why sticks?" Dr. Goyer asked. "Why not something more effective? A taser?"

"We use tasers if things get too far." Johnson bent down and snagged up Martyr's pant leg, revealing the stinger ring on his ankle. "They're remote controlled, and each has its own code. Lee, up in surveillance can turn each one on manually or in a group. If the boys gang up on us and manage to swipe our weapons, the tasers knock 'em flat in a hurry."

Dr. Kane put his hand on Martyr's shoulder and squeezed. "But J:3:3 doesn't cause those kinds of problems. He sometimes gets a little excited, that's all. Take him up to Dr. Goyer's office, Robert." He turned to Dr. Goyer. "This will give you a chance to try our marks procedure and get to know one of our subjects."

Martyr eyed Dr. Goyer. Would the new doctor be angry that he had touched the orange napkin tie? Would the marks be miserably painful?

"What do I do with him?" Dr. Goyer asked.

The guards pushed Martyr toward the elevator, and he struggled to look over his shoulder at the new doctor.

Dr. Kane's answer made Martyr shiver. "Whatever you want."

Martyr lay strapped to the exam table in Dr. Goyer's office, which he'd discovered was the third door on the right. He twisted his head to the side and squinted. The lab-like office rooms were always so bright. The lights buzzed overhead and the smell of clean made him sick to his stomach, reminding him of the hundreds of times he had lain on a table in such a room while a doctor poked and prodded. All the labs looked the same: a desk for the doctor, an exam table, and a long counter stretching along one wall with cupboards above and below. It had been five years since Martyr had been in this particular lab, though. He would never forget the last time.

The third door on the right had belonged to *her*. To Dr. Woman.

Many years had passed since the incident. Martyr was certain Dr. Kane would never allow another woman to enter the Farm because of what had happened, and the thought made him feel lonely. Dr. Woman had been kinder than any other doctor.

But it had gone bad.

Martyr blamed himself.

The door opened and Dr. Goyer entered. The light glinted off the man's head as he looked down at a chart, and Martyr wondered why this doctor had to see the groomers when the other doctors were allowed to grow hair.

Dr. Goyer jumped back a step when he saw Martyr on the table and put a hand to his chest, but then moved about the lab as if he hadn't seen Martyr at all. Martyr waited and watched Dr. Goyer file some papers, wipe down his counter, and sit at his desk. He was no longer wearing the orange napkin tie, only a white coat over a white shirt and black pants. Martyr frowned. Dr. Goyer would probably never wear the orange napkin tie again.

He hoped Dr. Goyer wouldn't use pain today. Occasionally he got lucky with his marks and only needed to answer questions or try new foods. Dr. Goyer hadn't carried in a steamy sack full of food, though.

Dr. Goyer suddenly spoke. "What am I supposed to do with you?"

Martyr met the doctor's eyes. They were brown, like the eyes of every Jason on the Farm. Martyr knew the color brown well. "What do you *want* to do?"

The doctor rubbed a hand over his head. "I don't know … I don't know. They gave me a list of starter questions, but you've probably had all those by now."

Martyr had answered them often. "What's your number? Do you have a nickname? What's your purpose?"

Dr. Goyer smiled. "That's right. Can we just … talk?"

Martyr relaxed. Talking would likely be painless. "Yes, we can."

"Do you like living here?"

The question confused Martyr. Where else would he live? "What do you mean?"

"Do you enjoy it? Do you find it fun?"

"Some days."

"What makes a good day?"

"No marks. No fights. Food with color. Being with Baby. Especially a day where no one is trying to hurt Baby."

"Is Baby your friend?"

Martyr nodded. "He needs me."

"Why?"

"Baby is a Broken, so a lot of Jasons pick on him."

"Broken."

"Yeah, you know. Something went wrong when he was made. He's small and doesn't speak. The doctors think he's ignorant and can't learn, but they just don't know his language. He talks with his hands, so I'm the only one who understands him."

"Why did the guard call you Martyr?"

"It's my nickname. I got it because I help Baby and the other brokens."

Dr. Goyer paused for a second. "Tell me about a time you helped one of them."

Dealing with bullies wasn't Martyr's favorite thing to talk about, but it was better than being poked with needles. He didn't want the doctor to change his mind, so Martyr answered quickly. "A few days ago, Iron Man and Fido attacked Baby, and I called Johnson to stop them. Fido found me later and was angry."

"What happened?"

Martyr saw no harm in pointing out the wound since he was already in a lab. He jerked his head to the strip of bedsheet tied around his wrist. "Rolo was close by, so Fido only bit me."

Dr. Goyer stood and walked toward the exam table. "And that's why they call him Fido?"

"Fido is a dog's name." Martyr knew this because Rolo said it almost every time he spoke to Fido. "Rolo says that Fido acts like a dog."

"Have you ever seen a dog?" Dr. Goyer released the strap holding Martyr's wrist to the table, loosened the sheet, and inspected the bite marks. Then he went to his counter and opened a cupboard.

"Only pictures we're shown in class. Have you seen a real one?" Martyr had heard dogs were small and hairy and drooled a lot. Sometimes Hummer drooled, but no one called him a dog. Baby drooled a lot when he cried, but no one called him a dog either. Apparently Fido's dog-ness was due to something else, because he certainly wasn't small or hairy.

Dr. Goyer closed the cupboard. "I've seen lots of dogs."

Martyr's eyes flickered around the lab while he waited. A thick, black coat was draped over the back of Dr. Goyer's chair. "You can go outside?"

"Of course." Dr. Goyer stepped back to Martyr's side and rubbed cool alcohol on his wrist.

It stung and Martyr stiffened. "You take the antidote?"

Dr. Goyer paused and looked away. His throat bobbed. "I, um ... yes."

Martyr blew out a long breath. He couldn't even imagine what it must be like in the outside world. "I know I'll never see things like dogs, but someone has to stay underground so people and dogs can exist." Sometimes, the knowledge of his purpose was the only thing that made the Farm bearable. "You took off your napkin tie. Will you wear it again?"

"It's a necktie, not a napkin tie, and I'm not allowed to wear it. I'm sorry I broke the rules today. It was a mistake."

"I'm glad you did. Orange is very rare on the Farm. So is red. Red is my favorite. Where did you get the … necktie?"

Dr. Goyer peeled a bandage and stuck it to Martyr's wrist. "My daughter gave it to me for Christmas."

A tingle traveled down Martyr's arms. Daughter was woman. He lifted his head off the table. "You have a woman?"

Dr. Goyer's eyebrows crinkled over his eyes. "My daughter. She's seventeen."

"What does she look like?"

Dr. Goyer reached into his back pocket. He unfolded black fabric and showed Martyr a colored picture. The doctors sometimes showed them pictures, but never in color. Martyr had never seen so many colors in one place. He stared at the face and exhaled a long breath. The daughter had orange hair! And it was long, past her shoulders, and very curly, like spiral pasta. His eyes were the color of peas.

"He is very colorful." Martyr's eyes did not leave the picture when he asked, "What are the colors of peas?"

"Green."

Martyr stared at the daughter's eyes. "His eyes are green."

"Her eyes."

Martyr glanced at Dr. Goyer. "Her?"

"Women's belongings are *hers* instead of *his*. They're called *she* instead of *he*. Personal pronouns are gender specific."

Goose pimples broke out over Martyr's arms. This was why Dr. Woman had been called *Her*. Martyr wished he could remember more about Dr. Woman, but it had been so long ago, and he had been so young. "I would like to see a woman."

Dr. Goyer's eyebrows crinkled together again. He put the picture back into the black fabric and tucked it into his pocket.

"What's that you keep the picture in?"

"A wallet. It holds my money and credit cards, my driver's license."

Martyr shook his head slightly, confused by the strange terms.

None of the other doctors ever showed him things like this. He wished he could see the picture again—wished he had his *own* picture—but Dr. Goyer had seemed upset when he put his wallet back into his pocket. Martyr hoped Dr. Goyer wouldn't stop showing him fascinating things in the future.

As the silence stretched on, Martyr tried to think of something to say so Dr. Goyer wouldn't get bored and decide to use needles. "What is Christmas?"

Dr. Goyer leaned against the wall by the door and folded his arms. "It's a holiday. You don't celebrate Christmas here?"

"What's *celebrate*?"

"Celebrate is ... being happy together." Dr. Goyer straightened and looked into Martyr's eyes. "What do the other doctors do when you have marks?"

Martyr swallowed, torn over how to answer. If he didn't tell Dr. Goyer the truth, the other doctors would, and Dr. Goyer would know Martyr had lied. Lying always made things worse. "Mostly they use needles to test the contents of different vials. Medicines for outside, I think. Sometimes the vials cause pain, sometimes they make us sleep. Other times the doctors put sticky wires on our bodies that buzz our insides. And occasionally they just ask questions."

"What kind of questions do they ask?"

"Questions about pain. Questions about math and science. Questions about Iron Man and Fido, or Rolo and Johnson."

"Who is Iron Man?"

"The doctors call him J:3:1. He's the oldest who is still living, which makes him the leader. But many of us choose not to follow him. He's cruel. He's cruel to Baby."

Dr. Goyer walked to his chair and sat down, glancing over the papers on his desk. He picked one up and read from it. "What's the most important rule here?"

It was the standard list of questions. "Obey the doctors."

"What is your purpose?"

Martyr swallowed and closed his eyes. "My purpose is to expire.

To be a sacrifice for those who live outside." Martyr opened his eyes and met Dr. Goyer's. "Like you."

Dr. Goyer folded his arms and stared at his lap.

Did the doctor want a longer answer? "I expire in twenty-five days, when I turn eighteen. Then my purpose will be fulfilled."

Dr. Goyer looked up. "Does that scare you?"

No one had ever asked if he were scared. "I don't want to expire."

"Because you want to live?"

"Yes, but not for myself. I'm content to sacrifice my life to save thousands from the toxic air. But if I'm gone, who will take care of Baby? And if Baby doesn't live until he's eighteen, he'll fail to serve his purpose. That wouldn't be fair."

"It's important to you to serve your purpose?"

"It's why I'm alive."

Dr. Goyer rubbed his mouth with his hand. "Can I answer any questions for you, Martyr?"

Martyr thought about the orange necktie and the picture of the daughter. "How do you celebrate Christmas?"

"You give gifts to those you love."

Dr. Max had explained gifts once, when they talked about being nice to others. But the other word was new. "What is love?"

Dr. Goyer ran a hand over his head again. "Uh … it's when you have kind feelings for someone."

Dr. Goyer had been kind. He had given enjoyable marks and mended Martyr's wrist with no lecture. "Will you give me a gift?"

"Maybe someday."

"An orange necktie?"

Dr. Goyer pursed his lips as if fighting a smile. "Probably not."